THE SWIMMER

THE
SWIMMER

JOAKIM
ZANDER

TRANSLATED BY

ELIZABETH

CLARK

WESSEL

HARPER

An Imprint of *HarperCollins* Publishers

HarperCollins books may be purchased for educational, business, or sales pro-motional use. For information, please e-mail the Special Markets Department at SPsales@harpercollins.com.

Originally published as *Simmaren* in Sweden in 2013 by Wahlström & Widstrand.

Designed by William Ruoto

Library of Congress Cataloging-in-Publication Data has been applied for.

ISBN: 978-0-06-233724-5

15 16 17 18 19 ov/RRD 10 9 8 7 6 5 4 3 2 1

For Liisa, Milla, and Lukas

"Around us, the madness of empires continues."

—JANE HIRSHFIELD

THE SWIMMER

E VERY TIME I HOLD YOU is the last time I hold you. I've known that since the very first time. And when you came back, and I held our child in my sleepless arms, all I could think was, this is the last time.

You look at me, eyes as pure as the promise of rain, and I know you know. That you've known as long as I have. My betrayal. Tonight it's so close that we can both feel its stinking breath, the pounding, irregular rhythm of its heart.

The baby whimpers in the crib. You stand up, but I get there first and lift the child up. Hold her against my chest. Feel her breathing, feel her heart racing through the thin, light blue blanket your mother knitted. This heart is my heart, and there is no convincing way to explain abandoning your own heart. Just disguises to assume. Just varying levels of lies to tell. Both of which I, if anyone, can master.

The city is beyond hot. After two months of relentless dryness, it glows like lava. When evening finally comes, the city ceases being gray or beige and becomes transparent, quivering like jelly. No one thinks clearly here. Everything smells like trash. Trash, exhaust, garlic, and cumin. But I only smell my child. I close my eyes and breathe in deeply, my nose pressed against the top of her almost hairless head. And the baby is still hot. Way too hot. The fever refuses to break.

You tell me this is the third day. I can hear you rummaging through drawers looking for aspirin or whatever you can find. This heat. It drives us insane. We both know I don't have anything like that here, in my apartment, in my mirage. Why are we even here?

"Give me the car keys," you say.

You wave your hand, like a vendor in the bazaar asking for money. And when I hesitate:

"Give me your goddamn keys."

Your voice is an octave higher, a shade more desperate.

"No, wait . . . isn't it better if I . . ." I begin.

The baby is completely still against my shoulder. Breathing so weakly, it's almost imperceptible.

"And how the hell do you plan on getting into the embassy? Well? Surely you can see we need something to stop the fever?"

I reluctantly grab the keys in my pocket. Balancing the child against my chest, I lose hold of them, and they land with a dull clatter on the marble floor of the hallway. The heat even muffles sound, I think. Delays it, slows it down. We both bend down to pick up the keys. For a moment our fingers brush against one another, our eyes. Then you snatch the keys, stand up, and disappear into the echoing stairwell. You leave behind only the muffled sound of a slamming door.

I stand with the baby in the sliver of shade on the balcony facing the street. The memory of a breeze floats across my face. The heat makes it difficult to breathe. In the air: exhaust, cumin. What happened to the jasmine? Once this city smelled like jasmine.

The locket you gave me, before everything turned to heat, fever, and flight, burns against my chest. The one that once belonged to your grandmother, your mother. I'm thinking about leaving it here.

I'm thinking of leaving it on the sideboard in the hallway, the one with inlays of mother-of-pearl and rosewood that we bought together in the bazaar when this bond had been growing for less than a week. I don't feel like I have the right to take the locket with me. It doesn't belong to me anymore. If it ever did.

I know everything there is to know about surviving. I know every street in this city, every café. I know every mustachioed antique-store owner with shady business contacts, every gossipy carpet dealer, the boy who sells tea out of the huge samovar he carries on his back. I've sipped imported whiskey with the president in smoky rooms, together with the leaders of organizations he officially repudiates. The president knows my name. One of my names. I've been handling the money. Making sure it ends up in hands that benefit the interests I've been sent here to protect. If you meet me, I speak your language better than you do.

At the same time: move me somewhere else. Drop me in the jungle, on the steppes, in the lobby of the Savoy Hotel. Give me a minute. I'll become a lizard, a yellowed blade of grass, a pinstriped young banker with hair that's a little too long and a motley but privileged past. I know your friends from university, vaguely, through others. They never remember me.

You don't know it, but I am so much better than you. I change faster. Fit in better. I have hazier outlines and a harder core. I keep my bonds loose. If they tighten, I cut them. And now? I lost my concentration and let them grow beyond my control, let them harden, coagulate. Blood bonds.

━━━

The game is forever, but this round is over. I hold the child tighter against my chest and shuffle impatiently on the concrete. When images of death sweep through me, I squeeze my eyes shut and shake my head. Whisper to myself. "No, no, no . . ."

The swollen face in the open sewer out by the highway to the airport. Those staring eyes. The flies in the heat. The flies.

"No, no, no . . ."

Why didn't I just let him be? I already knew everything. Why did I persuade Firas to have another meeting when the trail was already red-hot, glowing? But it was too inconsistent, too hard to believe. I had to hear it again. Look into Firas's nervous eyes one more time to see if something was hiding there. See if a shadow passed over his face when he reluctantly repeated the details one last time. See if his nervous tics had escalated or disappeared completely. All of those signs. All those little nuances. All those things that make up the almost imperceptible line between truth and lies, life and death. I close my eyes and shake my head while anxiety and guilt wash over me. I should have known better.

And now there's no time to waste. One of my contacts has rented a car, and it's parked around the corner. A backpack with clothes, money, and a new passport is waiting in the trunk. The escape route is activated, tattooed across the inside of my eyelids. It's the only solution now. To become mist and then just air. To become part of cumin, garlic, garbage, exhaust. And perhaps on a good day, jasmine.

I hold the baby up in front of me. I'm relieved to see she has your eyes. It'll be easier that way. What kind of man leaves his own child? Even if it's to protect her. Betrayal after betrayal. Lie after lie. For how long can relativity save a person's soul?

The sounds from the street. Slower, more indolent in the heat. Traces of voices that barely reach me on the third floor. Cars crawling forward—dehydrated, racked—over the scalding concrete.

And then, a car gasping as its ignition refuses to bite. A key is being turned, but the sparkplugs don't respond. Once:

Aaaaannnnnananananananan.

I move out into the sun, up to the balcony rail, shielding the child. It feels like slipping into a bath that is much too hot. The sweat runs down my cheeks, my armpits; my back and my chest are already completely soaked. I bend over the railing, my gaze finds the rusty, old green Renault. Across the street. Thoughts run through my head. How happy I was to find that particular parking spot. How I thought it would end up being parked there for weeks, months. How maybe one day you'd finally find the keys and move it. But why would you care about the car?

The reflection of the sun flashes off the driver's-side window. But when I squint, I see you. Your beautiful, blond hair, flat and greasy from sleepless nights, water shortages. Bent forward, your face contorted with irritation, headaches, all your worry, your mind racing. I think you're the most beautiful thing I've ever seen, and this is the last time I'll see you.

You turn the key in the ignition once more:

Aaaaannnnnananananananan.

It's the sign. One of the signs. One of the thousands of signs I've learned to recognize for my own survival. And I know it's too late. The realization rushes through me. Fear of death, hopelessness, guilt, guilt, guilt. All in the amount of time it takes for a nerve to respond to pain.

By the time the explosion tears my eardrums to pieces, I'm already lying on the balcony floor. The explosion isn't muffled, not muted by the heat. It's awful, majestic. It's a whole battle compressed into one moment. I feel thousands of small, very light, very sharp particles cover me like ashes. Glass and what might be chunks of the concrete facade, bits of metal.

Afterward, it's completely silent. I seem to be lying under a blanket of glass, a blanket of cheap concrete, rusty steel. I think I must be bleeding. I think, if I'm thinking, I must be alive. I think, my arms must be here somewhere, I can feel them under the concrete. I think, what am I holding, what am I lying on top of? I manage to roll onto my side. Concrete and glass crunch and clatter around me. I start to sit up carefully, lean on an elbow that seems to be responding to my nervous system.

The child is lying under me, my hands pressed tightly against its ears. The child blinks at me, takes a thin, feverish breath. Not even one sliver of glass has reached her.

MAHMOUD SHAMMOSH WASN'T WHAT YOU'D call paranoid. On the contrary. If someone were to ask, he'd describe himself as the exact opposite. Rational. Academic. And above all else: stable.

Mahmoud had never believed in the claims of alienation or the conspiracies that had been so common in the Stockholm projects of his youth. That was for teenagers, jihadists, and foil-hats. He hadn't fought his way out of suburban concrete and hopelessness, through all that and more, making it all the way to a Ph.D. program at Uppsala University, by finding excuses. If there was anything he was sure of, it was that in nine cases out of ten the simplest explanation was the right one. Paranoia was for losers.

With a little jerk, he pulled his rusty Crescent bike free from the bike stand in front of the Carolina Rediviva library. It'd been bright blue long ago. But only freshmen had nice bikes in Uppsala. Old hands knew they'd be stolen in the first week. Mahmoud's bike balanced on that fine line between perfect camouflage and complete inoperability.

He stomped a few times on the pedals and then let the slope down to the city do the rest. After nearly seven years in Uppsala, he still loved racing down Drottninggatan with the wind in his face. The air was cold as ice against his knuckles. He threw an unwilling glance over his shoulder. The electric lights on the hill leading up to the library glowed, lonely and melancholy, in the early December darkness. No one was following him.

———

The reception desk at the Faculty of Law on Gamla Torget square sparkled with Christmas decorations. Even on a Sunday, they kept the Christmas tree and Advent candles lit, but the hallway on the third floor was dark and quiet. He unlocked the door to his small, cluttered office, walked in, turned on the desk lamp, and started his computer.

With his back to the window, he sat down in his chair, moving away two books on the privatization of state functions and human rights. Soon, if all went as planned, he too would be the proud author of a book on the same subject. *The Privatization of War*. That was the title of his dissertation. He'd written about half of it.

What he'd written so far was actually quite traditional. It probably contained more fieldwork than the usual doctoral thesis in law. But that was the idea: something modern, interdisciplinary. He'd interviewed fifty employees of various American and British companies in Iraq and Afghanistan. Companies who performed functions that used to be carried out by armies, everything from transport and supply to different types of guard duty and even actual combat.

Initially he'd hoped for a scoop, an Abu Ghraib or a My Lai. To be the academic who revealed the great, terrible crimes. And his background had been an advantage, he knew that. But he hadn't discovered anything spectacular. Just done a good enough job of surveying and cataloging the companies and the rules to publish an article in the *European Journal of International Law* and a summary in *Dagens Nyheter*, Sweden's largest daily. And after that there came an unexpected interview with CNN in Kabul, which led to invitations to international conferences and symposiums. It wasn't a scoop, but it was the sweet, sweet taste of imminent success.

Until the message came, that is.

———

Mahmoud lifted a fifty-page-thick stack of papers from his desk and sighed: his latest chapter. Already the first page was covered with comments scribbled in red. His army reserve officer turned academic adviser saw through any attempt at taking shortcuts with the material. Lysander, with his gray suits and French cigarettes, was a legend at the faculty and Mahmoud had feared him already when he was a student. No less so now, when he was essentially his boss. Mahmoud felt his heart sink and put down the stack. E-mails first.

The old computer grumbled when Mahmoud tried to open up his e-mail program, as if protesting against working on a Sunday. The department's hardware was far from new. But that was a status symbol. You didn't come to this department for its modern facilities. You came for the opposite: five hundred years of tradition.

Mahmoud glanced at the December darkness outside his window. His office might be small, but it had one of the best views in Uppsala. In the foreground was the Fyris river and the house Ingmar Bergman used in *Fanny and Alexander*. What was it called? The Academy Mill? Behind it, the way the cathedral and the castle were lit, they looked almost ghostly in all of their immaculate academic high bourgeoisie.

Finally the computer gave in and allowed Mahmoud to access his messages. Only one new e-mail, with no subject. Not surprising, since he'd checked his e-mail only fifteen minutes ago in the library. He was about to delete it as spam, when he saw the return address: Trooper00@hotmail.com.

He felt his heart begin to pound. This was the second message he'd received from that address. The first came just after his most recent trip to Afghanistan, and it was the reason for his last few weeks of reluctant paranoia.

The message had been brief, in Swedish, and obviously sent by someone who was on the ground in Afghanistan:

Shammosh,

I saw you on CNN a few days ago. Looks like you're real serious these days. Can we meet in Kabul? I have information that's of interest to us both. Be careful, you're being watched.

Determination, courage, and endurance.

That intimate tone. "Determination, courage, and endurance." Familiar words from another time. It was obviously someone who knew him.

And the ending, "You're being watched." Mahmoud had dismissed it. Laughed at it. It had to be from a friend. Someone was just joking around. Soon he'd get a new message: "LOL! Gotcha!" There were aspects of his background that were unique within his current social circles, and sometimes that was the source of jokes among his new friends. But nothing else arrived. He slowly became more aware of his surroundings. Just to be on the safe side. Old routines and processes reactivating, taking over his system. Methods once practiced until automatic. It surprised him that they were still there, latent, waiting.

And then that very evening, he'd seen it. An ordinary Volvo V70. Bureaucrat gray. Parked under an unlit streetlight in front of his small studio apartment in the Luthagen part of town. And later that week, he saw it again while coming out of the campus gym after his weekly basketball game. It had been enough for him to memorize the registration number without even actively thinking about it.

He turned toward the computer and opened the new message. Would the joke be revealed now? He'd never admit to the jokester that he'd been somewhat affected by it.

The message was in Swedish:

Shammosh,
    I'll contact you in Brussels. We have to meet.
    Determination, courage, and endurance.

———

Mahmoud felt his heart pound even harder. Surely only his adviser knew that he'd accepted an invitation to speak at a conference organized by the International Crisis Group a week from Thursday. Maybe it was still a joke after all? The Volvo was just in his imagination? Still . . . Somewhere inside he felt a familiar sense of excitement, a small, barely perceptible surge of adrenaline.

He shook his head. Perhaps he should just wait and see if someone approached him in Brussels. But he had one more thing to do before he left the office, a message he had to write. Someone who'd been waiting a long time to hear from him.

———

Klara Walldéen had appeared in his life suddenly and from a completely unexpected direction. One day she was just there with her arms around him, with her head on his shoulder, with her hands in his ever-longer hair. It had been such a tumultuous period in his life. He'd been empty and confused, exhausted and sleepless. Utterly, utterly alone. And then, one day, she was just there in the doorway of his bleak, unfurnished apartment.

"I've seen you at lectures," she had said. "You're the only one who looks even lonelier than I feel. So I followed you. Crazy, right?"

Then, without saying another word, she'd stepped over his threshold and laid her loneliness down next to his. And Mahmoud left his loneliness there, until they began to merge, until they grew together. Until they were not lonely anymore. It was a relief that they often didn't even need to talk. That they could just lie there on his Spartan mattress or in Klara's narrow, hard bed on Rackarberget listening to her worn-out portable record player play one of those crackling soul singles she bought at flea markets.

Not a day went by that he didn't think about it. About how they used to breathe as lightly as they could to avoid injuring the fragile membrane that enveloped them, how their heartbeats would harmonize to the rhythm of Prince Phillip Mitchell's "I'm So Happy."

Still, he'd known from the beginning it wasn't going to work out. That there was something inside him that wasn't enough, something inconsistent with what he and Klara were creating. Something he kept to himself, deep down in the most hidden corner of his heart. When Klara had been admitted to a master's program at the London School of Economics at the end of law school, they solemnly swore that they'd commute, that they'd make it work, that distance was irrelevant to a relationship as strong as theirs. But Mahmoud had already known it was the end. Inside of him the light he'd struggled so long to stamp out blazed with a new, resolute flame.

He would never forget Klara's eyes as they stood at the airport, as he stammered through his memorized speech. That he thought it might be good to take a break. They'd be a burden to one another. They shouldn't see this as an ending, but as an opportunity. All of which were good reasons, but not the truth. She said nothing. Not a single word. And she never looked away. When he was finished, or when words finally failed him, all love, all tenderness had left her eyes. She looked at him with a contempt so merciless that tears began to stream down his cheeks. Then she picked up her bags and walked to the check-in desk without turning around. That was three years ago. He hadn't spoken to her since.

━━━

Mahmoud bent over his computer and opened a new message. He drummed on the keyboard. It was the only thing he'd thought about since he'd been invited to that conference in Brussels: he should contact Klara. But he hadn't. He hadn't been able to bring himself to write to her.

"Come on, man!" he said out loud to himself. "Come on!"

It took him almost a half hour to write a message of only five lines. It took yet another fifteen minutes to delete whatever might be construed as ambiguity, desperation, or references to a history that he no longer had access to. Finally, he took a deep breath and hit "send."

———

The first thing he saw when he left the building twenty minutes later was the gray Volvo, sitting in a dimly lit parking lot down by the river. When he unlocked his bike, he heard the engine start, saw the headlights turn on, a ghostly cone of light lit up the old metal railing along the Fyris river. For the first time in a very long time, he actually felt afraid.

December 8, 2013

Sankt Anna's Outer Archipelago, Sweden

THE SILENCE THAT FOLLOWED WAS almost as deafening as the two ear-splitting explosions of the shotgun. The only sounds were ducks quacking on their way over the bay and the dog struggling against its leash, whimpering weakly. Anxiously. Everything was gray. Cliffs and sea. Bare trees and bushes. The wind rustled in the faded reeds at the water's edge.

"You missed," said the old man holding the binoculars.

"Not a chance," replied the young woman at his side. She was still resting the shotgun against her shoulder. The cherrywood of its butt felt cool against her cheek.

"Maybe the first round, but no way I missed on the second," she said. "Let Albert go, and then we'll see."

The old man bent forward and unhooked the leash from the spaniel's collar. The dog bolted with a shrill bark, out through the reeds and up toward the cliffs in the same direction as the gun was shot.

"You missed both times. Believe me. You've gone soft, Klara."

He shook his head in disappointment. The shadow of a smile flashed across the young woman's lips.

"When I come out here you always say that, Grandpa. You say I missed. That I've gone soft."

She mimicked the old man's worried expression.

"And every time Albert comes back with our Sunday dinner in his mouth."

The man shook his head.

"I just say what I see in the binoculars, that's all," he muttered.

He took a thermos and two cups out of the worn backpack leaning against a rock at his feet.

"A cup of coffee, and then we go home and wake up Grandma," he said.

They heard a short bark followed by wild splashing down by the shore. Klara smiled and patted her grandfather on the cheek.

"Gone soft, huh? Was that what you said?"

The man winked one of his ice blue eyes at her, poured a cup of coffee, and handed it to her. Fumbling with his other hand, he took a small flask out of a hidden pocket.

"Would you like a little bit of lightning to celebrate your triumph, big game hunter?" he said.

"What? You brought booze? Do you know what time it is? You know I'm going to have to tell Grandma about this."

Klara shook her head sternly but let her grandfather pour a little drop of moonshine into her cup. Before she could take a sip, her phone started ringing deep inside one of the pockets of her oilskin coat. She sighed and handed the cup to her grandfather.

"You can't hide from the devil," her grandfather said with a crooked smile.

Klara fished out her BlackBerry. She wasn't surprised to see the name Eva-Karin flash across the display. Her boss. Social Democratic dinosaur and member of the European Parliament: Eva-Karin Boman.

"Ugg," she moaned before answering.

"Hello, Eva-Karin," she said in a voice an octave higher and considerably faster than usual.

"Klara, darling, how lucky I am to catch you! Things are really getting tight, if you know what I mean. Glennys just called me and asked what our position was on the IT security report. And I haven't even had time to open it yet, as you know. There's just been so much going on with . . ."

Her voice disappeared for a moment. Klara threw a quick glance at her watch. Just before nine. Eva-Karin was probably on the express train to Arlanda airport. Klara's gaze swept over the gray, windblown cliffs. It felt absurd to talk to Eva-Karin out here in the archipelago. Eva-Karin's voice felt like an intruder into her only refuge.

". . . so if you could get a summary to me by—what time shall we say? By five o'clock today, okay? So I can look through it before the meeting tomorrow? You'll have plenty of time, right? You're an angel, darling. "

"Of course," Klara said. "Actually, Eva-Karin, maybe you don't remember, but I'm in Sweden right now and won't be flying back to Brussels until two this afternoon. I'm not sure I can have that to you by five o'clock—"

"Klara, of course I know you're in Sweden," Eva-Karin interrupted in a voice that brooked no further discussion. "But you can work while you're traveling, can't you? I mean, for goodness sake, you've already had the whole weekend free, right?"

Klara squatted down in the wet moss and closed her eyes. It was Sunday morning. She'd only had Saturday free. It was as if all zest for life was being sucked out of her.

"Klara? Klara? Are you still there?"

Eva-Karin's voice sounded in her ear.

Klara cleared her throat and opened her eyes. She took a deep breath and tensed her voice, forcing it to sound alert, forward, and willing to serve.

"Absolutely, Eva-Karin," she said. "No problem. I'll e-mail the summary before five o'clock tonight."

———

Half an hour later, Klara Walldéen was back in the room she grew up in, surrounded by the pink wallpaper with the floral trim that she'd begged for when she was ten years old. The smooth, worn floorboards beneath her bare feet. Outside her window the Baltic Sea glimmered through the bare trees. She could see the whitecaps on the sea. A storm would be blowing in before the day was over. They had to hurry up. Her childhood friend Bo Bengtsson, who lived farther out in the bay, was going to bring her in to Norrköping by boat and car. Then she'd take the train to the airport and a flight down to her regular life in Brussels.

She pulled the pilling Helly Hansen shirt over her shoulders, and replaced it with a light, tight top and an asymmetrical cardigan. She replaced the worn-out corduroy pants, which were actually her grandmother's, with jeans of Japanese denim. She stepped into a pair of limited edition Nikes, forgoing the insulated rubber boots she'd worn on the morning hunt. Applied a little bit of smoky makeup around her eyes. A few strokes of a brush through her jet-black hair. She looked like a different person in the mirror above the small white dressing table. The floorboards creaked as she moved.

Klara rose from her chair and opened the door to a crawl space. Carefully, with much practice, she leaned into the darkness and pulled out an old, worn shoe box from which she took out a pile of photographs. She spread them out on the floor and crouched down in front of them.

"Are you looking at those old photos again, Klara?"

Klara turned around. Her grandmother seemed almost translucent in the pale light streaming in through the small attic windows. Her body was so brittle and fragile. If you hadn't seen it for yourself, you'd never believe she could still hoist herself up to the top of the gnarled apple trees to beat the birds to the last of the fruit.

She had the same ice blue eyes as Grandpa. They could have been siblings—but that was no joking matter out here in the archipelago. Her face had a few lines but no wrinkles. No makeup, just sun, laughter, and salt water, she used to say. She didn't look a day over sixty, but she was turning seventy-five in a couple of months

"I just wanted to take a look, you know," replied Klara.

"Why don't you take them to Brussels with you? I've never understood why you don't. What good are they doing here?"

Grandma shook her head. Something sad and lonely flashed through the blue of her eyes. For a moment it looked as if she wanted to say something but changed her mind.

"I don't know," Klara said. "That's just the way it has to be. They belong here. So tell me, are there any saffron buns left?"

She collected the photographs and put them gently back into the shoe box, before following her grandmother down the creaking stairs.

———

"Oh, there she is! She's got her city slicker clothes on and everything!"

Bo Bengtsson was already waiting on the dock when Klara

walked down toward it. As she had so many times before. It was as if her feet found their own way. As if her brain or spine weren't needed to avoid the roots, rocks, puddles.

"Quit it, Bosse. You sound like Grandpa," Klara said.

They hugged each other awkwardly. Bosse was a few years older than she, and they'd pretty much grown up together out on the island. He was like a brother to her. Two siblings with opposite appearances and personalities.

They were an odd couple. Klara was small and slight, always top of her class, but so good at soccer that she'd played on Österviking's boys' team for a while. Bo liked fishing and—when he got a little older—hunting, drinking, and fighting. She was always on her way out of there. He would never even consider leaving the archipelago. But they had gone to school together day in and day out. During the warmer half of the year they took the school boat, and in the winter they traveled by hovercraft. Things like that create a bond stronger than most.

Klara jumped on board and lifted the battered fenders of Bosse's old workhorse of a boat while he maneuvered away from the dock. When she was done, she joined him in the small wheelhouse. The waves were rising outside the dirty portholes, their peaks white and purposeful.

"There'll be a storm tonight," Bosse said.

"That's what they say," Klara replied.

THE SMALL PARK LOOKED BARE, icy, and nasty from George Lööw's panoramic window on the seventh floor of the office building of Merchant & Taylor—the world's largest PR firm—situated next to the Square de Meeûs in Brussels. George Lööw hated December. Above all, he hated Christmas. He could see the Christmas decorations along the rue Luxembourg that led down to the European Parliament, and they filled him with irritation. And it wouldn't be over even when December finally came to an end, because the lazy goddamn municipal workers would leave that shit up until February.

Just a few more weeks until he'd be forced to go home to his family's huge apartment on Rådmansgatan and give the annual accounting of his life. The apartment would be decorated with candles and an Elsa Beskow tree. The tasteful Advent stars would be lit, his old man's desserts table would groan under all the marzipan, the toffee made by his new wife, Ellen, and the absurdly expensive chocolate George brought home from Brussels every year that they dutifully, and not without some embarrassment, added to the table.

His family, stuffed and bulging with Christmas food, would sit scattered around on classic Svenskt Tenn sofas with steaming cups of homemade mulled wine in their hands. Full of their pathos and their bloody hypocrisy, they'd exchange condescending glances while asking George about his job as a *lobbyist*, a word they pronounced as if it were *excrement* or *arriviste*.

"Assholes," hissed George to his empty office.

———

The little coffeemaker sputtered and filled his Nespresso cup halfway. It was his third espresso this morning, and it wasn't even ten o'clock yet. He was uncharacteristically nervous about his morning meeting with a new client calling themselves Digital Solutions. George's boss, the American CEO of the European division, Richard Appleby, said they had specifically asked for George. That was good in and of itself. Word about him had apparently started to spread. That he was a man who got things done in Brussels. That he could change which way the wind was blowing.

But it was uncomfortable as hell not to know anything about them. There were literally thousands of firms named Digital Solutions. Impossible to know what this one actually did. There was no way to prepare. He would just have to use his charm and drive. As long as they paid his generous fee there was nothing to worry about. Merchant & Taylor had no scruples. *You pay, you play* was the unofficial motto. Chemicals, weapons, tobacco. Go right ahead. Hadn't Appleby even represented North Korea for a while back in the early 1990s? Or was that just a rumor? Whatever. But George preferred to know something about the client he'd be sitting across from before a meeting began.

He was still sweating from an early squash game at the gym. The light blue Turnbull & Asser shirt stuck to his back. Hope it stops before the meeting, he thought. This coffee probably wouldn't help matters.

He knocked back the espresso with a grimace. George drank his coffee like an Italian. Just a quick espresso on the go. Sophisticated. Stylish. Even when he was alone in his office, he took his coffee standing up. It was important never to drop the attitude.

Nine fifty-five. He gathered a stack of papers, a pad, and a pen. The papers had nothing to do with Digital Solutions. But the client didn't need to know that. He didn't want to look like a goddamn intern, going into a meeting with just a pen.

———

George had loved the conference room on the corner of the seventh floor since joining Merchant & Taylor, and always booked it when it was available. The corner room's two glass walls faced the interior of the office floor, where George himself had begun his career. If you pressed a button next to the power switch behind the door, the glass walls instantly frosted over, becoming as opaque as thick ice. The first few weeks on the job, when George sat in front of his computer, working on uninteresting business analyses for customers in the sugar industry, auto industry, polymer industry, whatever, and writing brain-dead newsletters, he thought those glass walls were the coolest thing he'd ever seen. He loved to watch the more experienced consultants float across the wooden floor in their handmade Italian leather shoes and disappear into the ice cube. Epic.

Nowadays George was the one gliding across the floor on his way to the ice cube. He felt their eyes. Looks just like the ones he used to throw when he was sitting there on the floor. Many of the people he'd started working with were still there. Not all of them had had the same rocket career trajectory as George, and maybe not all of the eyes following him were entirely adoring. But everyone put on a good face. Waved. Smiled. Played the game.

It still felt like a fluke that he'd managed to land this job after resigning from Gottlieb, a Swedish law firm, three years ago. The fact that he was working at Gottlieb on something as crude as corporate law, and mergers and acquisitions, had been difficult for his old man to accept. In the Lööw family if you became a lawyer in private practice, you practiced criminal law. Big principles, right and wrong. Nothing as *dirty* as business transactions and money. That was for upstarts "without ancestry, habits, or wit," as the old man used to say. At least he wasn't aware of the actual circumstances surrounding George's resignation.

Though the old man had been somewhat appeased when George, after his sojourn at the law firm, had been accepted into a prestigious postgraduate program at the Collège d'Europe in Bruges. A bona fide elite school in the French mold with a fast-track into the EU crème de la crème in Brussels. They'd finally make something out of the kid. Maybe he'd end up at the Ministry for Foreign Affairs? Or the European Commission in Brussels? Something proper.

George knew that a career in Sweden was out of the question after his short stint at Gottlieb, so with his recent EU law degree in hand Brussels was the natural place to start looking for a job. He dismissed the idea of working at a law firm immediately. He was finished with boxes full of dry annual reports and endless nights of searching through hard drives for contracts and more or less fishy settlements.

PR firms proved to be something else entirely. Lavish offices. Hot chicks from all over the world in slim suits and high heels. Refrigerators stocked with free soda and beer. Espresso machines instead of filtered coffee.

To go from the gray, dirty sidewalks of Brussels into the cool and softly lit glass and wood office building of Merchant & Taylor, with its silent elevators and overall whisper noise-level, was heaven. Sure, the starting salary wasn't as good as at the American law firms, but there was the possibility of really big money. After a few years they gave you a company car. And not just any old crappy car, but an Audi, a BMW, maybe even a Jag.

The huge English and American PR firms were the mercenaries of Brussels. They sold veneer, information, and influence to the highest bidder, regardless of ideological or moral convictions. A lot of people looked down on lobbyists. George loved them unconditionally from the first second. He was in his element. These were his people. His old man and the rest of the family could think whatever the hell they wanted to.

———

George stepped into the cube and closed the door behind him. It bothered him that his client was already sitting in one of the bright leather seats. The secretaries were instructed to have visitors wait in the reception area if they were early. But George didn't let the client see his annoyance; he just casually frosted the glass with the twist of a button.

"Mr. Reiper! Welcome to Merchant and Taylor!" he said as he slapped on his widest, most self-assured smile, and held out a well-manicured hand to a man, around the age of sixty, who was sitting slumped in his chair, in a position that seemed unaware of, or in direct opposition to, everything that might be considered ergonomic.

Reiper looked like he lived a profoundly unhealthy life. He wasn't exactly fat, more half-inflated, with the loose outline of a neglected helium balloon. He was almost completely bald, and around the sides of his head ran an unruly wreath of slush gray hair. His face was sallow, as though he rarely went outdoors. A thick white scar ran from his left temple down to the corner of his mouth. He wore a shabby black polo shirt with a pair of dry-cleaned, pleated khakis, and had holsters for an iPhone and a flashlight in his belt. A dirty notebook and a blue Georgetown Hoyas cap were lying on the shiny glass surface of the conference table. His position in the chair, the slow movement of his finger on the screen of his phone, the way he didn't even look up when George entered the room, gave Mr. Reiper an aura of authority that seemed as obvious as it was ruthless. George felt the hairs on his forearms stand up: a purely primal response to the feelings of discomfort and disadvantage that his new client evoked. He knew instinctively that he never, ever wanted to hear the story behind Mr. Reiper's scar.

"Good morning, Mr. Lööw. Thank you for taking the time to meet with me," said Reiper, finally taking George's outstretched hand.

The pronunciation of his surname was almost perfect. Unusual for an American, George thought. His voice was throaty and a little sluggish. Maybe southern?

"Have you had coffee? I apologize, our receptionist is brand-new. I'm sure you know how it is."

Reiper gave a quick shake of his head and looked around the room.

"I like your office, Mr. Lööw. The detail of the frosted glass is, well, spectacular."

They sat down across from each other, and George carefully

arranged his completely irrelevant papers into a rough semicircle around his notebook.

"So, what can we help Digital Solutions with?" George said and switched on yet another smile that he considered worth every cent of the 350 euros he cost per hour.

Reiper leaned back and returned George's smile. There was something about that smile, something about how it faltered because of the scar, that made George want to look away. And there was something about Reiper's eyes. In the warm light of the conference room's meticulously positioned spotlights they sometimes looked green, sometimes brown. Cool and expectant, they seemed to change color at random. Combined with the fact that he never seemed to blink, it gave Reiper the lazily ironic, utterly lethal expression of a reptile.

"So this is the deal," Reiper said and slid a couple of stapled documents across the table at George.

"I know you're very proud of your discretion here at Merchant and Taylor, but then I also know you sing like canaries when the tide turns. Purely a formality, of course."

George picked up the document and flipped through it quickly. It was a classic nondisclosure agreement between him and Digital Solutions. He couldn't reveal anything of what they discussed in their meetings. He couldn't even mention to anyone that he worked for Digital Solutions or was aware of their existence. If he were to do so, he could be liable for an almost astronomical amount, depending on the severity of his slipup. Nothing out of the ordinary, really. Many clients were concerned about their anonymity and were not always willing to be associated with a public relations firm known for being as ruthless as Merchant & Taylor.

"It says that it was signed in Washington, DC," George said at last. "But we're in Brussels."

"Yes," replied Reiper, somewhat absently. He appeared to be reading something on his iPhone. "Our lawyers think that would make it easier to avoid what they call a forum dispute if that became necessary."

He shrugged and looked up from his phone.

"But I'm sure you know more about *nondisclosure agreements* than I do?"

There was a new sharpness in his voice. Something like interest flickered in his otherwise dead eyes. George felt ill at ease. Sure, he'd signed a series of similar contracts during his time at Merchant & Taylor. However, there was something about how Reiper had said it, something more complicated. George pushed the thought away. It was impossible. No one could know anything about that. Reiper's allusion must just be a coincidence.

George pulled his Montblanc out of his breast pocket, signed the contract with a quick flourish, and pushed it back across the table to Reiper.

"There you go," he said, anxious to get the meeting started. "Maybe now we can begin?"

"Excellent," Reiper replied absently. Without looking up from his iPhone, he folded the agreement carelessly and jammed it into the inside pocket of his worn jacket. Finally, he slid the phone into its holster with care and met George's eyes.

"We need help with a translation," he said. "To start with."

August 1980

Northern Virginia, United States

SOMETHING IS WORRYING HER. I know that before Susan even opens her mouth. There's nothing strange or supernatural about that. Over time I've learned to read the signs, the nuances, the shift of a glance, hands moving like frightened birds, as if by themselves, or not at all. I almost always know what people are going to say. It's one of the thousands of ways I survive. But when she speaks, I don't hear her. I can only see her gray suit, her dyed blond hair, and watery eyes. See the traces of her daily commute: the coffee stains on her shiny lapel.

She lives in Beltsville, Greenbelt, Silver Spring. One of the endless suburbs where we all live. She drives a Ford, and everything she reads is classified. Like many of us, she's stopped drinking. We either drink too much or not at all. Donuts and watery coffee in the Methodist Church on Sundays. Appreciative words about the choir, pointless conversations about preschools and vacations. Susan is so ordinary. An ordinary, ordinary all-American woman of thirty-five with a house and a mortgage and a new car every other year. She and her husband are trying to scrape together college money for the two children. But all of that is part of the framework. The game within the big game. We all feel that the everyday is too slow, too mundane. Not important enough. Too little is at stake.

The air-conditioning is turned up so high that I'm starting to get goose bumps. My ears are still ringing from the explosion, and every terrible night I dream of white light, shallow breathing, and your greasy hair. I wake up sweaty, wild, the sheets twisted around me, protecting my pillow with my body.

"They were both in the car?" she says and sits on the edge of the only other chair in my microscopic room.

I nod, forcing myself to look her in the eyes, to neither hesitate nor move.

"Terrible," she says. "Terrible. I'm so sorry. This job, this life. We pay a high price."

She doesn't look sad. She's as neutral as her car, her house, her ill-fitting suit. I swivel my chair and stare out toward the parking lot and the thin, green trees on the other side of it. You can hardly sense the highway. We sit in silence for a while and let the dust swirl in the late summer sunlight streaming through my window. But she's not here for condolences. Not only.

"Why did you show up in Paris?" she says at last. "Why didn't you go directly to the embassy in Damascus or Cairo?"

I shrug, turning my gaze back to her, looking straight into her eyes again.

"That was the original plan," I say. "Boat from Latakia to Larnaca. Flight to Athens. Night train to Paris. I had tickets from de Gaulle to Dulles, but I thought that under the circumstances, it was better to check in in Paris."

"After what happened . . . Wouldn't it have been appropriate to deviate from the plan? To check in in Damascus?" she says.

Her voice is soft and friendly. On the surface, she's still here to make sure I'm okay, express her sympathy. But we both know that's just on the surface. There's always a subtext, always an underlying reason. And another reason beneath that one as well.

"I explained everything in my debriefing," I say. "The bomb was meant for me. I followed protocol and stayed under the radar until I felt sure I wouldn't get shot in the embassy's parking lot."

She leans back. Drums her wedding ring gently against the steel frame of the chair.

Click click click click click.

Only that and the rustling of the air conditioner.

"You overestimate the Syrians and their allies," she says. "A car bomb in Damascus is all they're capable of."

"Maybe," I say. "But as I said, I wanted to be sure."

Susan nods, allows herself to be satisfied. There's nothing here that doesn't follow protocol. Not a trace. She locks her eyes with mine.

"We'll get them," she says slowly. "You know that. Damascus, Cairo, Beirut . . . All the Middle Eastern agencies are looking into this now. It'll take time, but we'll find the culprit, you know that."

I nod. The thought of revenge is still just a seed.

She leans forward. A different look, a different tone when she speaks.

"And the information you received from your contact?" she says. "The weapons delivered to the Syrians. You've only given that information in my report, right? Not in the debriefing? Nowhere else?"

I nod my head.

"Only in your report," I say.

"It's probably a dead end, of course. A plant. But we don't want to raise any alarms."

"I'm aware of the consequences. It stays in your report."

She leans back for a moment. Following my gaze out the window. Finally, she gets up.

"Are you okay?" she says.

Her tone is constant, no matter how much suffering she demands.

"I'm okay."

"Take the rest of the week off," she says. "Go for a swim. Get a drink."

I see how she pats the plastic doorframe with the palm of her hand before leaving my room. It rattles. Encouragement, perhaps. Sympathy. She knows I swim. There's nothing they don't know about me.

———

The water in the public pool is too warm, but I still prefer it to the pool at Langley. When I surface for air every fourth stroke, I hear the shrill voices of a school class bouncing like radar waves between the chlorine-scented tile walls. Lap after lap. There was a time when I could have been a really good swimmer. The Olympics were an actual possibility, a goal within reach. But my motivation extended only to the University of Michigan and no further than that. I don't regret it. I don't regret anything.

———

I know that so much of this is a lie. But reality is fragile; without the lie it threatens to crumble. The lie is what's holding up the bridge. It's what allows you to cross from one shore to the other. There is no truth.

Still I requested the report before I left the office. I knew it would be classified at a higher level than I had access to. We're never allowed to read about what concerns ourselves. And I knew that if I were allowed to see it, if I read it with my own eyes, it would certainly be a lie. But my request was refused. It was a relief. I don't want to know when they're lying to me.

So now I'm sitting in this sad, dirty locker room, my legs trembling after hours in the pool. Paralyzing guilt is jolting through me like electricity. Swimming holds it at bay. The repetition and the habit hold it at bay. In the water, I'm temporarily safe. As soon as I stop, I hear the sound of the car ignition, see the image of a very small child under shards of glass, pieces of concrete.

Later I drink Rusty Nails in front of the TV. My living room is bare. Some moving boxes are stacked in the corners. They contain nothing of value. I'm sitting on my new couch and watching a rerun of a baseball game I don't care about. The apartment—a modern box, one of many, with a garage, conveniently close to the reassuring hum of the highway—smells faintly of paint and air-conditioning. The muscles in my arms feel tight. I swam six miles. Twice as long as I usually do.

The baseball game is ending as I pour my third drink, and I switch over to Johnny Carson. I realize immediately that I don't have the energy to listen to Richard Pryor's Ronald Reagan jokes. They don't interest me. They're trite, they move too slowly.

―――――

Everything is moving too slowly since I came back here. I'm a man for the field. Strategies, analysis, the eternal politics of Langley, Pentagon, DC, move too slowly. Give me another passport, another language, another life. Drop me in Damascus, in Beirut, in Cairo. I know how to make contacts, how to maintain them over a glass of sweet tea, whiskey, and cigars. I can make a tabouleh that will remind my guest of his childhood in Aleppo. Even when borders are hostile, I'll have the best Lebanese wine on my balcony.

And there, on the balcony, in the melancholy sweetness of sunset, with jasmine in the air and the buzz of diplomats, gangsters, and politicians inside at the dinner table, I'll make a transaction that means someone other than me will die in the end. We are always playing for a draw. Our ideal is the status quo.

———

They want us to meet with a therapist when we come back in nowadays. As if debriefing weren't enough. Already on the first day, when our tans are still brilliant under the fluorescent lights in the midst of the phones, copiers, and telex machines. With bodies still aching from jet lag and a change of climate. With minds still full of Arabic, Russian, Portuguese. We have to sit through these mandatory sessions. Talking about our transition after months, years in another country, another culture, far away from taking the highway to work, Kentucky Fried Chicken on the way home, and the deadly boredom of a normal life.

But when it comes to what they want us to talk about, we remain silent. How could we talk about what we do? What should I say? That I lived as an Arab businessman in Damascus, buying weapons, banal secrets, and shadowy influence with the taxpayers' money, waiting for something that might be worth the infinite price we are willing to pay? That I, when I caught the scent, froze like a rabbit in headlights and lost everything?

Should I talk about that? What I can't even acknowledge to my-self? If I start to talk about it, I would never stop. If I start thinking, I'm dead.

So all I do is smile and look at the clock. When the obligatory hour is over, I stand up, put on my anonymous dark blue jacket, and get on the highway, return here, back to this anonymous box that is anything but a home. And I bide my time and hope my quarantine will finally come to an end. That a folder with a different identity, airline tickets, and an account number will drop onto my desk so that I'll be able to continue, to start over. The only thing I live for is the next move, the next round.

THE TRAIN STATION UNDER THE Zaventem airport seemed like it was perpetually under construction. Everything was a jumble of orange cones, barrier tape, and scaffolding.

Mahmoud did his best to squeeze through the static crowd so he could catch the next train to Brussels. There were lobbyists and other foot soldiers in the cause of European integration with copies of that morning's recently leafed through *Financial Times* protruding from their streamlined Samsonite luggage, their cell phones glued to their ears; Orthodox Jews, dressed in black, waiting for the train to Antwerp; families dressed for their vacations, dragging oversize suitcases to a charter flight to Phuket. The conductor whistled, and Mahmoud pushed forward to catch his train. At that moment he felt the backpack he had slung over one shoulder slip off and down onto the concrete floor of the platform. He stopped but couldn't see it. Annoyed, he bent down to get a closer look. The crowd pushed him sideways toward the train. Someone tapped him on the shoulder.

"Is this yours?" A blond girl around his own age with a ponytail, loose-fitting clothes, and cool, green eyes held his backpack up to him.

"Yes, it is. Thanks a lot!" Mahmoud answered.

He grabbed his bag and managed not only to squeeze himself onto the train, but also to find an empty window seat. He sank down onto the cracked vinyl of the orange seat with a sigh.

As the rusty old train, protesting loudly, pulled away from the airport, Mahmoud took out the program for the next day. The roster was impressive. Members of the European Parliament, NATO officers, an ambassador, reporters from major international newspapers. All of a sudden, he felt intensely nervous. Why hadn't he started preparing earlier? He closed his eyes in order to concentrate. Within thirty seconds, the previous day's late night took its toll, and he fell into the deep, immediate sleep that only traveling evokes.

———

"So it's not even a five-minute walk, Mr. Shammosh," the dapper porter at the Hôtel Bristol told him in a slightly stilted voice that sounded much older than his smooth, twenty-something face looked.

"Perfect," Mahmoud said. He folded the map and slipped it into his backpack, which was worn and camouflage-colored. It looked like its life had started in the army; the picture of a small parachute was sewn onto the flap.

Like its porter, the lobby of the Hôtel Bristol seemed to lay claim to a history it didn't actually possess. With its red carpets, mahogany and leather, and English gentility, it made a halfhearted attempt to mask being part of an international hotel chain.

"By the way, Mr. Shammosh, someone left a message for you," the porter said and slid a thick, carefully sealed envelope across the counter.

Mahmoud's room was predictably small and sandy-colored. The décor was flat, like in a soap opera. There were no halfhearted attempts at English eccentricity here. Only hotel chain monotony and familiarity. Mahmoud opened the curtains as far as he could. The window overlooked a small, dirty atrium. A few snowflakes swirled alone out there. They seemed confused, as if they had gotten lost on their way to a sledding hill or a skating rink.

Mahmoud dropped his backpack onto the bed and sat down in the well-worn armchair by the window with the padded envelope in his hands. On one side his name was written with black marker in block letters.

With trembling fingers he tore open the glued flap. He sat with the package open in his hands for a moment while watching a few snowflakes randomly swirl outside the window. He took a deep breath and poured out the contents.

A clumsy cell phone, a charger, and a carefully folded piece of paper fell onto his lap. Mahmoud picked up the phone. It was a cheap Samsung. The kind of prepaid phone you buy for forty euros at a gas station. He put in the battery, which had been lying separately in the package, and pressed the power button. It turned on with a buzz. The contact list was empty. No messages.

After taking another deep breath Mahmoud unfolded the piece of paper. Inside of it was another paper, which fluttered down and landed on the carpet. The paper Mahmoud held in his hands contained a short, typed message in Swedish:

Mahmoud,
    I have information, and I don't know what to do with it. I need your

help. I think it might have something to do with what you're researching. We need to meet after your meeting tomorrow. Keep your phone switched on between 13:00 and 13:30 tomorrow and be ready to move out. Otherwise keep it turned off and remove the battery. I will contact you.

Determination, courage, and endurance.

Mahmoud refolded the message and glanced at the phone. "Ready to move out." "Determination, courage, and endurance." Words from another time, what seemed like another life. Someone knew things about him that he himself had almost forgotten.

Slowly, absentmindedly, he leaned forward and picked up the page that had fallen onto the floor. He unfolded it and instinctively shrank back from what he saw.

It was a fuzzy, printed photograph. Grainy and pixilated. A digital image file printed out on a common, older printer. But the scene was all too clear.

The photograph appeared to have been taken with a pocket camera or with a fairly good cell phone and took up nearly the entire A4-size page. A man was lying in the foreground, tied down on a stretcher with straps. The clothes he'd once worn were so tattered, they barely covered his body anymore. Through the rips, Mahmoud could see skin that looked soiled and raw. Down his arms, neck, and chest ran a trail of small, round burns. Cigarettes. Someone had burned him with cigarettes over and over again. But that was far from the worst.

The worst thing was his eyes. It took Mahmoud a terrified second to realize that the man's eye sockets looked empty because they were empty. He forced himself to hold the paper closer in order to see more clearly. The hollows of those eyes were dark abysses.

Their edges were caked with coagulated blood and dirt. With queasiness, it dawned on Mahmoud that the eyes must have been torn or burned away from the man's face. It was impossible to see if he was dead or alive.

Mahmoud stared at the picture as if paralyzed until he couldn't stand to look at it any longer, and he turned it over on his lap. It was a vision of hell. The clinical room in the merciless light of the camera flash. The stretcher with its straps. The blood.

Mahmoud had seen his share of suffering, misery, imprisonment, and even torture. A total of three months in Iraq and Afghanistan over the past three years had exposed him to more misery than most. But this . . . This was worse than Abu Ghraib.

"Oh my God," Mahmoud whispered to himself, even if his own God was much more complicated than the exclamation might suggest.

S HE SMELLED HIS COLOGNE—RICH WITH tobacco and va-
nilla, as sweet and dense as ambition—before she felt him gently grab her right elbow. The morning meeting she was on her
way to, everything, fell away, and she willingly let him lead her out
of the wide hallway and into the narrow light wood–paneled pas-
sageway outside of a European Parliament committee room. Wall-
to-wall carpeting dampened the din from the hallway and the press
bar nearby.

"I missed you," Cyril Cuvelliez said in English and pressed his
lips against hers.

His American pronunciation didn't disguise his French diph-
thongs. His soft, insistent lips. The natural way he helped himself
to what he wanted.

"I didn't know you'd be here this week," murmured Klara with
her lips against his.

She felt how her body immediately, uncontrollably, came alive.

"I didn't think I would be."

He said something more, but it was drowned out by the buzz
in her ears. Blood was suddenly pumping through her. The pure
physical attraction. He pulled away from her and smiled.

"As if I needed an excuse to come back to you," he added.

"You could have texted me," Klara said. "But I'm glad you're here."

As she stretched up to his lips again, she closed her eyes, determined to ignore how simplistic and seductive what he said was. Meanwhile her fingers snapped open the only button on his charcoal gray suit jacket. She slipped her hands under it and felt his skin shiver through the thin, light blue shirt. He sighed with pleasure. How she loved that he sighed when she touched him.

"I was a bit tied up," murmured Cyril. "But I'm here now."

"How long? Can we meet?"

Klara inhaled his scent. As if she could keep him captive inside of her by breathing him in.

"Just until tomorrow. I have a dinner tonight until quite late, I'm afraid."

She felt his breath on her cheek, his stubble, and his warm, dry hands. She was defenseless against this. Against him, against the disappointment she felt that she wasn't able to see him more often. She nodded.

"Not even a lunch date?" she said, and nibbled his ear.

"You're terrible," he said. "In a wonderful way. How could I refuse? Today?"

Klara nodded, felt a surge of excitement.

"I have a meeting until one. One-thirty at my place?"

Cyril fished out his phone, checked his calendar.

"I'll push my staff meeting forward to four. The dinner doesn't start until eight."

Klara stretched up and kissed him before pushing him away.

"Now go away," she said. "I'll see you in a few hours."

He smiled.

"I miss you already," he said.

She nodded, exhilarated, but also deflated. Like always after one of their brief encounters.

"It's best if you leave first so we won't be seen coming out together."

He nodded and kissed her again as he buttoned his jacket. He straightened his tie.

"I'll see you later," he said.

And with that, he disappeared without turning around, back out into the everyday of the European Parliament.

———

Klara stood there, leaning against the wall, the taste of Cyril still on her lips. She opened her eyes slowly. Her ears were still ringing. Her heart wouldn't stop racing. She blinked a few times. Ran her hands through her hair. How had this happened?

How had Cyril managed to get through her defenses, her searchlights and alarms, her locks and her barbed wire, everything she'd put in place to protect herself from this very thing? Or not this. This, whatever it was, was wonderful, as long as she managed to ignore what would inevitably follow. The inexplicable. The emptiness. The unfathomable opposite of what had slowly started to take root inside her.

Why now? Why couldn't she distance herself now? She looked good, she knew that. She wasn't starved for attention, quite the opposite. The European Parliament was full of young, intelligent men, a majority of whom she suspected she'd be able to enchant without much trouble. At least for a while.

And it wasn't that she hadn't tried. During her first six months in the European Parliament, she'd slowly come back to life. After Mahmoud. After her year in London had turned out the opposite of how she'd imagined it. The city she'd dreamed of living in since traveling there by herself the summer after high school. Dancing to soul at the 100 Club on Oxford Street. Buying 1960s dresses in Camden and scratched seven-inch singles at Spitalfields Market. The cafés on Old Compton Street just before dawn, the night buses and the awkward hookups with floppy-haired, anorexic boys in small, damp flats in Brixton and Islington.

But instead London had been a rainy, lonely prison. She could hardly remember the first few months. No details, just the purely physical sensation of spending the autumn in a miserable dorm room a few blocks from the Strand. The chill coiled its way through the thin walls and poorly insulated windows, and there wasn't a hot water bottle in the world big enough to keep it out. She had a vague memory of the endless hours spent at the library on Portugal Street that she escaped to with her textbooks and her emptiness. It felt like an eternity of nothingness.

And worst of all was the guilt. The feeling that she had let herself down. She was exactly where she'd wanted to be, where she'd always strived to be. At a prestigious postgraduate program in a city she loved. But for the first time in her life, she had no idea where she was going.

But then Gabriella had finally come to visit her for a short weekend in December. Klara would never forget the sight of her through the frosty window of her completely empty room. How Gabriella jumped out of the cab onto the street, the early winter snow in her red hair. How she paid so nonchalantly, with the sophistication of someone who'd already started to work her way up the winding steps of a law office. How she'd looked up and through the snowflakes and caught sight of Klara in the lighted window on the third floor. How Klara, even at that distance, could see the obstinacy in her eyes, the warm and indomitable determination.

They'd circled around each other in law school. Although they were in the same year, Klara hadn't initially been receptive to making friends at all, really. She'd met Mahmoud during her second semester, and that felt like more than she'd ever hoped for. She'd called him Moody from the first day. Because he looked moody. Temperamental. A little confused, as if he was brooding about something, like he was hiding a hot temper under that controlled surface.

Klara couldn't remember ever having a best friend while growing up on Aspöja. When she'd finally ended up in the same group as Gabriella halfway through law school, it was a revelation almost as palpable as when she met Moody. She couldn't comprehend that another person felt the same way she did about northern soul and vintage dresses. It had been an infatuation that Moody had made fun of. But Klara had thought it'd be good for them, good that she was looking outside of their airtight sphere.

But then, much later, in the darkest days of that dreary autumn in London, Klara sometimes thought that all of the terrible things had happened because she'd let Gabriella into her life. If she'd just stuck to Moody, if she'd just sealed the walls around them, never allowing anyone else to get close to her, maybe it would have worked out.

But that night, in the snow, when Klara saw Gabriella on the street in London, full of vigor and determination, she knew just how crazy those thoughts were. Sometimes there is no explanation. Sometimes you just die. And that bitterly cold Friday in December, Gabriella had come to save her life.

And she'd succeeded. London never became exactly what Klara

dreamed about, but she got her strength back, though not her desire. She passed her exams, wrote her thesis, and sent out her job applications. When Eva-Karin Boman, a well-known, respected politician with international ambitions, said she wanted to meet Klara for an interview, even Klara's desire returned. The unimaginable thrill of being around high-stakes politics, the important decisions, the money, the power.

The first six months with Eva-Karin had been wonderful. Klara had indulged her boss's whims and demands. And the world seemed full of men with good shoulders, acceptable taste in music, and freshly cut hair. Guys that, just a few months ago, she wouldn't even have noticed. It was exciting, fun, sometimes even really hot.

But what was happening with Cyril was different. Although it too had started out as a game, now she could feel herself teetering on the edge of losing control. Maybe she'd already lost it. She smoothed down her skirt and sighed. She thought of Mahmoud involuntarily. Maybe it was the e-mail she'd received a few days ago and hadn't yet decided how to respond to. She shook her head.

"Moody, Moody," she whispered. "What is going on?"

December 19, 2013

Brussels, Belgium

M R. SHAMMOSH? DO YOU HAVE anything to add? I'm referring specifically to the last part of Professor Lefarque's argument; that is, to the effects of the continuing persecution and radicalization of resistance fighters in Iraq and Afghanistan."

The former ambassador, Sir Benjamin Batton, moderator extraordinaire for the International Crisis Group Conference on the role of private contractors in war zones, leaned over the table with his kind, vigilant gaze.

Mahmoud looked up from his notebook calmly. A smile played on his lips. He was in his element. He hardly remembered the almost paralyzing nervousness he had experienced earlier in the morning, when he took his seat in front of the audience of fifty or so policy makers, journalists, and assorted dignitaries.

"Absolutely," he nodded. "I think there's no doubt that gruesome acts like the ones we saw at Abu Ghraib, for example, lead to radicalization. To put it plainly . . ."

He didn't even have to think about what he was going say. The words formed themselves and floated out of his mouth, calmly and precisely, in an articulate stream. Just like on those rare occasions when he was lecturing in Uppsala on a subject that truly interested him.

He could see faces in the audience turn to him with newfound interest; the yawning ended and pens bounced over notebooks taking down his comments. And everything he saw, everything he heard from his own voice, filled him with energy and pride. He was almost moved by his own professionalism and ability to deliver. Mahmoud Shammosh: academic superstar.

When Sir Benjamin, with the leisurely elegance of a seasoned moderator, took advantage of one of Mahmoud's rhetorical pauses to suggest they continue this discussion over the lunch laid out for them in the foyer, Mahmoud felt offended. Sure, he'd seen something glassy creep into the previously admiring glances, but still. It was his moment. His time in the limelight. Well, he'd have the chance to continue talking during lunch. Research in all its glory: this was the real reward.

As he stood up he fished the cell phone and the battery out of his backpack. The moment he turned it on, it started vibrating in his hand. Two missed calls from a number he didn't recognize. Mahmoud felt himself tense up. The phone rang again, and his heart skipped a beat.

He excused himself as quickly as possible and moved toward one of the side doors that he suspected led to the toilets. As he pushed open the door, he answered the phone. He was on edge. The adrenaline from the lecture mixed with the suspense of the incoming call. The horrific photograph flickered before his eyes.

"This is Mahmoud Shammosh," he whispered into the phone.

"How were the letters you received signed?"

The voice in Mahmoud's ear was deep and muffled, as if it was filtered through some device that distorted the speaker's voice.

Mahmoud's mouth suddenly went dry.

"Determination, courage, and endurance," he said as he walked through the doors into the men's room.

A urinal and a stall. Empty.

"Where are you now?"

"The International Crisis Group on Avenue Louise," he said. "Who are you?"

"Leave as soon as you can. Take the metro from Louise to Arts-Loi. Change to the metro toward Gare Centrale. Walk around inside the station until you've shaken off your shadows. Take the train back a couple of stops and change trains at the Gare du Midi. Keep an eye out all the time, okay?"

Mahmoud froze.

"We know each other from Karlsborg, right? Is that why you've contacted me?"

"Put the battery back in when you reach Gare du Midi and call this number for more instructions. Okay?"

Mahmoud strained to identify the voice. But there was nothing there to grab onto.

"Okay," he said. "But what is this about? What do you want to tell me? Is this a joke or what?"

"This is not a joke. Follow my instructions. I need your help. What do you have to lose?"

"All right," Mahmoud said. "I can get out of here in an hour at the earliest."

"Okay. Remove the battery and don't tell anyone about this. I'm serious. You're probably being followed. This is not a joke."

With a click, the voice disappeared. Mahmoud saw himself in the mirror above the sink. What was that feeling he had in his chest? Doubt? Nervousness?

Anticipation, he decided. What did he have to lose?

T HE MAN WITH THE CREW cut waiting for him in the entrance of Merchant & Taylor's looked about five years older than George and was buff in a way that made George's squash matches and halfhearted workouts at the gym seem laughable. Despite his nondescript suit and the white shirt he wore without a tie, he looked like he was destined for water or high altitude rather than lobbies, hallways, and offices. He was sleek and smooth, Teflon-coated for maximum speed. Like Matt Damon in the Bourne films, George thought enviously. Damn, the bastard must really work out.

"Mr. Brown?" George said and extended his hand.

"That's correct. You can call me Josh," the man replied, baring his chalk white American teeth in a quick smile.

"And my name is George."

The handshake was firm. They held each other's hands for slightly too long, sizing each other up. George let go first and guided his guest toward the elevators.

"Reiper explained the situation," Josh stated more than asked.

"Yes." George pressed the elevator button. "You have documents that need to be translated. For some reason you're paying double the rate for me to forget about these documents immediately."

Josh's smile wasn't unlike Reiper's. Indulgent, as if he possessed knowledge that made him irreplaceable. He shook his head almost imperceptibly.

"I don't know anything about payment. That's Reiper's area. My job is to ensure that these papers don't leave the room. Nothing personal, but this is sensitive. Let's just put it that way."

They left the elevator. George's handmade shoes clattered against the hardwood floor, no doubt made from an endangered species of tree. Josh's rubber soles were almost soundless.

"I'll have to ask you to lock the door," Josh said when they entered the room.

"Oh, sure," George said, and obeyed somewhat hesitantly.

Josh took out what looked like an older model of a black iPod from the navy laptop bag slung over his shoulder. With his eyes fixed on the screen, he walked quickly around the room. The outcome seemed to be satisfactory, because he put the device away and sat down in one of the leather chairs.

George considered asking what the hell was going on but didn't want to appear even more at a loss than he already was. Instead, he sat down on his side of the desk and waited for Josh to take the initiative.

"Here," Josh said, and took a small black laptop and green paper folder from his bag.

"The documents in this folder need to be translated. You type it into this computer, nowhere else, okay? It doesn't need to be perfect. We're looking for the big picture. We'll get back to you if we have any questions. Is it okay if I make myself a coffee?"

He pointed toward the machine next to the small fridge.

George nodded, lifted the folder from the table, and opened it. The first thing that struck him was that all references to names had been crossed out in black marker. At the top right corner of the first page someone, Josh himself perhaps, had worked hard at crossing out a square area. George quickly flipped through the folder.

The first document had been created by the Swedish Security Service and consisted of a brief personnel report.

George stopped and looked straight into the air. Säpo, Sweden's secret police. The square that had been crossed out in the top right-hand corner was almost certainly a classified stamp. It was a dizzying feeling to have classified documents in front of him. This was espionage. Pure and simple.

There was no other way to look at it. Whoever had released these documents to Reiper and his cronies was guilty of espionage. Inconceivable. George didn't want to think about what kind of crime he was committing by even holding these papers. But at the same time, it was intoxicating.

The first document contained what seemed to be a startlingly detailed description of an Arab guy from one of those deeply depressing housing projects outside of Stockholm. A picture of the ten-story building was enclosed. George had never understood how people could live like that. It looked like a Soviet nightmare.

The person the document described was the oldest of three brothers. He was raised by a single father who'd fled to Sweden from Lebanon after his wife died in what was apparently an Israeli bombing raid in the early 1980s. It seemed that the writer of the report had interviewed this person's teachers and maybe even his friends, and then translated the results into gratingly bureaucratic Swedish. "Scores at the top of his class." "Conveys strong desire and drive to rise from his current living situation." "Unusually strong motivation." "Excellent language abilities. Speaks and writes fluently in Swedish, Arabic, and English." "Politically interested, but not active."

A longer segment dealt with the man's religion: "Secularized Muslim without a strong connection to radical elements or to the local mosque" was the conclusion.

Under the title "Recreation and Social Life" the writer had made an effort to show that the person mostly found his friends through sports. Running and basketball, it seemed.

But his teammates were designated "acquaintances," and the person was described as "introverted, though paradoxically exhibiting strong and developed leadership skills." The report ended with the section title "Overall Assessment," under which the person was considered to be "particularly suited" for "special service." George had no idea what that meant. But his job was to translate this shit into English, not to understand it.

The second document was longer, over thirty pages, and according to its date only a few days old. The first page of the report was entitled "Reasons for Special Supervision." The text was short:

"Credible information from foreign intelligence agencies claims that the subject is affiliated with subversive elements in Iraq and/or Afghanistan, see dossier SÄK/R/00058349."

The pages that followed summarized the subject's current situation in life. Law degree. Formerly the chairman of the Foreign Policy Association. Ph.D. student at the Faculty of Law. The courses he had taught. Pictures of a house with his apartment window circled in red. Basketball at the Student Health Center twice a week. A serious romantic relationship with a Klara Walldéen, which ended a few years ago. That name wasn't crossed out.

George stood up from his chair and walked over to the coffee machine. He inserted a black capsule and pressed the green button.

"Klara Walldéen," he said quietly to himself.

"Excuse me?"

Josh looked up from his cell phone. He was sitting in the leather chair by the window that faced the park. George watched the raindrops beat against the windowpane and run down toward the windowsill. Yesterday's chill had given way, and a powerful storm seemed to be moving in over Brussels. The room had suddenly become dim, as if the sun were setting.

"Klara Walldéen," George said again.

George knew who she was. He kept an eye on most of the Swedes in Brussels. And he'd kept an especially close eye on Klara. Not that she had an especially important position. Her member of parliament, Boman, was a classic leftie dragon of the old school, mostly focused on foreign affairs. Not something George was usually interested in. No, he'd kept an eye on Klara for purely personal reasons. She was on his top-five list of the hottest assistants in Parliament.

"She works in the European Parliament," he said.

"Exactly," Josh replied calmly. "Reiper wants you to keep an eye on her. There are indications that she's had dealings with the terrorist we're after."

Terrorist. The word seemed to echo in the room.

"Keep an eye on? What do you mean by that?"

George felt uncomfortable. Terrorist. Säpo. "Keep an eye on." The almost euphoric experience of having classified information in front of him started to give way to the feeling that he might be in over his head.

"No big deal. Just start by following her on social media. That sort of thing. We'd do it ourselves, but our Swedish isn't so good. As you may have noticed."

George sat down again and continued working. The rest of the documents consisted of "intelligence reports." Brief descriptions of what the person did during the day. Damn, thought George, some poor bastard had had the dreary job of hanging out in front of a building all day long.

A couple of things bothered him about the report. First of all, it contained precise descriptions and even photographs from inside the subject's apartment and office. There was something uncomfortable and intrusive about Säpo, or whoever they were, having been inside this person's room.

Moreover, there were excerpts from the person's e-mails. Two messages were from a Hotmail address of someone who wanted to meet this person in Iraq and Brussels. The man under surveillance had sent a short e-mail to Klara Walldéen. The latter was sent only a few days ago and had been flagged, presumably by Reiper or Josh. George, not normally a man of principle, now started to feel uneasy. But he was just a cog in the machine.

"I expect this will take me most of the afternoon," he told Josh, and opened up a new document in his word processor.

"You'd better get started then," replied Josh, and he leaned back in his chair with a small smile.

December 19, 2013

Brussels, Belgium

MAHMOUD SPENT AN HOUR ON the Brussels Métro. Changing directions and trains, just like the voice on the phone had told him to. When he reached the Gare du Midi, he took the escalator to an empty platform. A low cloud hung over southern Brussels, making it seem like dusk. Drizzle swept across the cracked concrete. Everything was gray. Dreary. The only color in sight was the rust on the tracks and the flaking graffiti in the small sheltered waiting area on the platform.

He half-hid behind a pillar and then put the battery into the phone. From here he'd be able to see if anyone came up the stairs. He felt his pulse quicken, his throat tighten. The platform, the rain, it all felt more tangible, more real. In a way it was exciting. A game.

Mahmoud scanned the platform once more, even though he knew it was empty, and clicked on the only number stored in the phone. Someone answered before the first ring had sounded.

"Take a taxi to the Gare du Nord," said the muffled voice. "Change taxis and drive to the Africa Museum in Tervuren. You should be there in an hour. Okay?"

"Okay," Mahmoud replied.

"Take your time when you arrive. Look at the exhibitions. There is an emergency exit at the far end of the room with the giraffe. At six-fifty go through that door and down to the park. The door will be open and the alarm off. Walk around the pond in front of the museum on the right-hand side. On the other side of the hedge, opposite the museum, there will be a statue. You'll see it. On the right side of it, at the edge of the forest, is a bench hidden by some bushes. I'll be sitting there at seven o'clock. Don't be late. "

January 1985

Stockholm, Sweden

THE SNOW EXTINGUISHES ALL SOUND. If I close my eyes,
I'm no longer in a city. The crunch under my rubber soles,
wind rushing across my face. I'm on ice. Alone on a frozen lake
where the sky and the snow flow into each other and become part of
the same mass. If I ever allowed myself to miss anything, I'd miss
the Michigan winters.

The streets here are wide, reminiscent of another time. A time of
armies and parades, battlefields, banners flapping in the wind. The
simplicity of it makes me sad. The city is as beautiful and solemn as
a funeral. The cars keep their lights on, even now during those few
confusing hours between dawn and dusk. I'm dressed too lightly,
despite the blue down coat that I've barely worn since college.

They're waiting for me at the U.S. embassy. My new papers are
ready. Nobody here knows who I am. Nobody knows where I'm
going. But they have their instructions, and they know better than
to ask. I lock my bag in a safe in the military attaché's office and
decline his friendly invitation to dinner. I can feel his interest, his
curiosity. Behind every secret is another one. Behind every lie, a
bigger lie.

It takes me a moment to make up my mind whether or not to ask.

There is a risk, but one that I'm willing to take. This might be my only chance.

"I need the assistance of one of your local staff," I say. "Someone who speaks Swedish and knows how the Swedish system works."

"Sure, absolutely," he says and seems genuinely happy to be able to help in some way.

He's a decent man. A man suited for Irish pubs and the telling of war stories.

"But, of course, we don't have anyone with sufficiently high security clearance."

"That doesn't matter," I say. "This is purely personal. I just need help finding a friend who I believe is back in Sweden now."

"I understand. I think the press department has a couple of local researchers on staff. I'll ask my secretary to make sure you get the help you need."

——

I follow the route that I drew on a map in my room and memorized. Through winding alleys next to the other tourists until I'm sure my shadows disappeared already down in the subway. They say it's easier here in Stockholm. That Helsinki is worse. Maybe that's so.

There's one hour left. I take a taxi from the castle and ask to be taken to Djurgården. The taxi driver doesn't understand what I mean, so I show him on the map. This worries me. He'll remember an American passenger. A trace. I don't leave traces. But now it's too late. I ask him to drop me off at the bridge. He speaks terrible English, so I have to show him again. He looks like an Arab, but I can't change languages. Then the trace would become fluorescent. It doesn't matter. My shadows have lost me anyway.

In the bathroom, behind the gates of the Skansen zoo, I change from my blue jacket into a beige coat. Remove my red hat. Carefully take the light yellow folder out of the briefcase and place it in a dark blue nylon backpack. I leave the briefcase, empty and without fingerprints, under a trash can in one of the stalls. Then I leave the zoo, walk down the road to the ferry. Darkness is already falling.

At three-fifteen I board the ferry. He's standing alone near the stern. As agreed. Tinted glasses and a tan winter coat. His mustache rivals his leader's. It's a face worthy of a long career in the government buildings of Baghdad. I stand next to him and look down at the foam spraying from the propellers. Forgotten Christmas decorations glitter wistfully above the amusement park that we are slowly leaving behind. We have about ten minutes.

"*Assalaamu alaikum,*" I say.

"*Wa alaikum assalaam,*" he responds reflexively, surprised. "Do you speak Arabic?"

"Yes," I say.

"What would you like to communicate? It must be important if the Americans are sending representatives all the way to Stockholm."

"Satellite images from the day before yesterday. The Iranian fleet is positioned to blockade your traffic in the Persian Gulf. An artillery unit is moving into position for an attack on Baghdad. "

I look around and then hand the folder to my Iraqi contact. He nods and puts it in his briefcase without looking at it. Although we stand in the lee behind the ferry's superstructure, the cold is clawing at our cheeks.

"Is that all?"

The disappointment is plain on his face. No news for him. I shake my head.

"There is one more thing. We've found five companies willing to sell what you want. They want to meet in Zurich in two weeks. The details are contained in the folder. I hope I don't need to explain to you how sensitive this is?"

There's another glint in his eyes now. This was what he'd been hoping for.

"Chemicals?" He restrains himself, but he's interested now.

"Think bigger."

He nods. The distant lights of the amusement park are reflected in his glasses. I feel the vibrations under my feet.

"We are indebted to you," he says at last.

I nod.

"Don't thank me. I'm just the messenger. And of course my political leaders will expect some form of compensation when this is all over. You can discuss that further in Zurich."

We stand in silence. Let the thumping of the engine fill in the gap. If he's freezing, his face—behind his glasses, his mustache, the heavy burgundy scarf tucked between the lapels of his camel hair coat—doesn't show it.

"As for the rest," he begins.

His eyes look out toward the south pier: the big red and white ferry, the city rising up behind it. Atoms of snow, compressed by the cold and as hard as grains of salt, swirl weightlessly between us. I don't say anything, giving him the time he needs. Electricity jolts through me now, makes me crackle, makes the snow melt at first contact. The roots of revenge are electric.

"Nobody knows anything," he continues. "Not us. Not the Syrians. Nothing."

He turns to me and takes off his glasses. His eyes are warm, surprisingly naked.

"Was it your family?" he says.

I don't say anything but I don't look away. He knows anyway. All questions are rhetorical. But I have to see his eyes. I have to see straight into his eyes.

"I'm sorry," he continues. "Really. Especially since you've been so helpful to us. I wish I could give a more complete answer."

I nod now. If he's lying, he's a master.

"You know it doesn't mean anything that I don't have any information? You know our systems are more organic than yours? Fewer documents, you know. We have shorter, how shall I put this, decision-making procedures. It's rare for this type of information to reach anyone outside of the innermost circles of intelligence."

I nod again. I know all about the organic. All about decision making.

"Someone sends out a signal, someone else passes it on to a third party. There are many stages."

"But there are always rumors," I say. "Always."

"Sure," he says.

A nod. A smile tinged with sadness.

"But you shouldn't listen to rumors, right?"

"Only if that's all you have," I say.

He says nothing. His gaze is intense, straight, seemingly honest. He stands like that for a moment. The small granules of snow are dry in his mustache, his eyebrows.

"Sometimes it's better to just move on," he says at last. "To leave it to God. *Inshallah*. God's will be done."

We separate before the ferry docks. I'm already on my way out, full of doubt. Behind me, I leave the promise of death.

I don't care about evasive maneuvers as I walk down Strandvägen toward the U.S. embassy. They are welcome to follow me now. A locally employed woman named Louise is waiting for me at her desk in the little office she shares with another local staff member. We seem to be the only ones left in the building.

"You're late," she says and brushes the long, blond hair out of her face.

She's around thirty years old, not beautiful, but there's something about her seriousness that's appealing. Her English is American, but with the singsong accent that I know all too well.

"I have to pick up my kids."

"I'm sorry," I say and mean it.

Obviously stressed, she puts a few documents down on the table in front of me.

"Here's the woman you were looking for," she says. "This is her death certificate. You were correct that she worked as a diplomat with the Ministry for Foreign Affairs and that she seems to have died in an explosion in Damascus in 1980."

I nod quietly and fiddle with the page, which is written in a language I don't understand.

"I found some articles about it in the Swedish newspapers. It seems to have been a pretty big deal here. I remember it myself, actually. It's not often that Swedish diplomats are killed abroad. I made copies of a couple of the articles. It seems to have been an accident, a car bomb intended for someone else. They got the wrong car."

I sit down on the pale wooden chair next to her desk. My legs suddenly feel unreliable.

"She had a daughter," I say, and I can hear how empty, how flat, my voice is.

Louise nods.

"That's right," she says. "She had a daughter who survived, she was a few months old. It's a strange story. Very, very strange. In all the media coverage, it states that the daughter died along with her mother in the car, but if you dig a little deeper . . ."

She pushes the hair away from her forehead and glances impatiently at the small watch on her slender wrist.

"If you dig a little deeper, you find her in the public records. Klara Walldéen. I have a friend at the Foreign Ministry, who did a quick check."

She flips impatiently through her papers.

"There's no record, oddly enough. But, according to rumor, if you believe in rumors, she was found wrapped in a blanket at the Swedish embassy in Damascus on the day the bomb exploded. The whole thing was hushed up, of course. After the bomb and everything. I guess they were afraid that something would happen to her."

Electricity jolts through me, through my bloodstream.

"What happened to her?" I say.

"She lives with her grandparents in the Östergötland archipelago on . . . Let me see . . . Yes, here it is. On a little island called Aspöja."

K LARA TOOK A DEEP BREATH and turned her face toward the blue floral wallpaper, fighting the temptation to bury her nose into the fold of Cyril's neck as he lay in her bed just a few inches away, naked and drowsy. Despite their nudity, despite having explored every inch of his body with her mouth and her hands over the last few weeks, such a gesture would be disconcertingly intimate, surprisingly tender.

Their relationship was not tender. Passionate, absolutely. She felt a spark when Cyril came within a certain radius of her, a world-shattering sexual charge that she had never felt before, but suspected, without wanting to explore any further, had something to do with his inaccessibility. How many times in the last few months had she woken at dawn to see Cyril half-dressed and halfway out the door of her bedroom? How many times had she woken up from the creaking of the stairs down to the living room? How many times had Cyril cancelled their meetings, which were already too few and far between, because he was stuck in an airport, a meeting, a dinner?

And how many nights had they even spent together? Twenty, maybe? Fifteen? Barely. Cyril, like most Members of the European

Parliament, was only in Brussels a few days a week. The rest of the time he was either traveling or at home, connecting with the voters of his Parisian constituency.

When they'd started seeing each other a couple of months ago that had suited Klara perfectly. She hadn't wanted more. Cyril was exciting. Intelligent. And the charge between them was transformative. It made her weak and unstable, alternately inferior and dominant. And she could tell it affected him too. His tight grip on her arms, her neck. His fingers in her hair as he pressed her down against the mattress and entered her from behind. She could still taste him on her lips, in her mouth. This was passion, wonderful, burning desire. But it wasn't tenderness, not real intimacy. And it had been unexpectedly liberating. No demands, no history, just brief, intoxicating moments outside of time.

So it surprised her when Cyril turned over and looked at her for a long time without saying anything. His gaze was dark, and slightly ironic. She met his eyes hesitantly, suddenly embarrassed, and shared the silence.

"Why don't you have any pictures of your family?" he said. "I've been here several times a week over the last few months, and I still don't know anything about you. Well, I know a few things about you."

He pulled the covers up over his hips, as if suddenly becoming aware of his own nakedness.

"We talk about the parliament, the world. Food. But I know almost nothing about *you*. Your family. Your home. And it struck me, you don't have any pictures of them either. Expats always have pictures of their family on display. But not you. Why not?"

His voice, the gentle French accent, the American vocabulary. Had he studied in the United States? She turned her eyes away from him and lay on her back, staring straight up at the sloping ceiling above her bed, concentrating on her breathing.

She didn't feel ready for this. Not ready to break their unspoken pact, their casual agreement. At the same time, she wanted nothing more than to reveal her background and history to Cyril piece by piece, while he did the same. But she needed time to get used to the idea. It couldn't happen like this, without warning, without time to adjust.

"I don't know. I haven't really thought about it. I guess I'm not that into pictures."

She swung her feet down onto the cool wooden floor and sat up, with her back to Cyril.

"That's bullshit!" he said. "Everybody needs pictures of their family."

Couldn't he just wait a little, let her get used to the idea? Let her catch her breath and catch up with him.

"Can't you tell me something about yourself? Do you have siblings? What do your parents do? Anything."

She turned toward him. Allowed her eyes to show a gleam of irritation.

"I don't have any siblings," she said as she awkwardly pulled on a maroon T-shirt with LONDON SCHOOL OF ECONOMICS printed across the chest. She put her barely shoulder-length dark hair up in a sloppy ponytail.

"Only child."

She picked up her phone from the nightstand. Checked the time.

"Come on! I have a meeting in half an hour. We need to get moving."

She smiled sheepishly and rather unconvincingly at Cyril and pointed toward the narrow staircase that led from her minimal bedroom down to the living room of her little attic apartment.

"It makes you uncomfortable!" he said.

He threw out his arms, as if he'd finally made her admit something she'd long denied. The satisfaction of the gesture only made her more unwilling to continue the discussion.

"What?" she said.

Was this really what he wanted?

"Do you mean that it makes me uncomfortable to talk about my family? Okay, sure, it makes me uncomfortable to talk about family. Is that enough? Are you satisfied with that answer?"

She pinned him with her bright blue eyes. Not yielding an inch, a wave of annoyance crashing over her.

Cyril raised his hands in mock surrender and sat up in bed.

"Okay, okay. If you don't want to talk about it," he muttered, putting on his boxer shorts. "I just wanted to show a little interest."

———

They were standing fully dressed down in the living room a few minutes later. A taxi had been ordered. Ready to reenter their normal lives.

"I'm sorry," Klara said. "I didn't mean to overreact."

She reached out her hand and brushed his. Cyril still looked hurt. Offended. Perhaps his mistresses were usually more accommodating.

"No problem," he said and ran his hand through his hair. "I understand."

"My family," she said.

Cyril turned to her, attentive, interested.

"My family is easy to describe. It consists of my grandparents, who mean everything in the world to me. Period. And Gabriella, my best friend. I've had boyfriends. Shorter relationships. And one that was longer, which, sometimes on dark nights when I can't sleep, I wish had lasted longer. Is that enough honesty for you?"

"Why didn't it last longer if you wanted it to? I can't imagine him leaving you."

"That," Klara began. "That we can save for another time. But it was not a happy period in my life. And I was running away. First to London, then here. Later on I guess there wasn't room for a relationship. And maybe that's just as well."

"Your parents?" Cyril said gently, as if not wanting to risk interrupting her story.

"I don't have any parents. I ran out of them. My mother died when I was two months old. I have photos of her in an attic closet on Aspöja, but no memories. Nothing at all."

She looked directly into his eyes. Her tragic background. Her loneliness and her vulnerability. There was nothing she liked discussing less. The tender looks, the teary eyes that inevitably followed the story of the orphan girl from the archipelago. All that damned *understanding* and *sympathy*. It put her at a disadvantage, turned her into someone that she wasn't, into the person they thought she was.

But Cyril simply nodded quietly and brushed a wisp of hair from her forehead.

"I'm sorry," he said. "I didn't know."

He took Klara's hand in his. She didn't pull away, but she didn't respond to his caress either.

"I never met my father. I don't know anything about him other than that he was American and that my mother met him when she was working in Damascus. She was a diplomat. Maybe he was a diplomat. Maybe he was a businessman. Who knows? My mother never discussed it with my grandmother. And then she died in a car bombing in Damascus."

December 19, 2013

Brussels, Belgium

THE WEATHER WENT FROM BAD to worse as Mahmoud's taxi drove away from the EU Quarter toward the Africa Museum in Tervuren, just east of central Brussels. Sheets of sleet whipped against the old Mercedes. It was only five-thirty and already dark—ominous in some way. Mahmoud peered through the window, trying to see the tops of the gray office buildings where European power was assembled. The buildings seemed to continue upward, into the darkness, without end. The taxi crawled forward. Rue Belliard, the European Quarter's east-west artery, was apparently always in the midst of a traffic jam. At least one of the lanes was closed, and the taxi driver muttered and swore in French. Something about whores and politicians and the relationship between the two, that is if Mahmoud's rudimentary French hadn't failed him completely.

He looked around, out through the taxi's aquariumlike rear window. Headlights flashed off of the glass facades. In the darkness and the rain, it was impossible to see if any cars were following him. He didn't think it was likely. His maneuvers in the subway had been so irrational that even a large team of pros would surely have lost him. And a change of taxi after that. He should be safe. Had it not been for the Volvo in Uppsala, he would have found it difficult to even imagine he was being followed. Now it was a real possibility.

Somewhere behind them on the rue Belliard sirens began to wail. Blue light bounced off of the shining concrete and glass windows, coloring the gloom inside the car. From the corner of his eye Mahmoud saw the police approaching on motorcycles at breakneck speed down the closed lane. They were followed by a police car and a fleet of black Mercedeses that were much newer models than the one Mahmoud was riding in. An EU flag and what might be an Afghan flag were fastened on the front. They fluttered dramatically in the storm. Maybe they were on their way to preparatory meetings for the large summit on Afghanistan this spring? The Marshall Plan was being prepared. The one that would bring peace to the mountains. Or maybe it was just some lonely ambassador being driven to the airport.

Just when he'd given up hope of ever leaving the European Quarter, they were out of Brussels, driving on a straight road through a sparse deciduous forest. He felt his heart start to beat faster, and his mouth went dry. He started to regret that he hadn't told anyone where he was going. Maybe he should have contacted Klara after all? But how the hell would that have sounded, after years of silence: "Hi, Klara, I think I'm being followed, and I'm headed to meet somebody in Tervuren who would like to hand over sensitive information to me. Paranoid schizophrenia? Well, now that you mention it." Way too crazy. And he'd given his word he wouldn't tell anybody. He was alone. Might as well realize that. Breathe calmly.

———

It took no more than five minutes for Mahmoud to get to the museum from the roundabout, where he'd asked the taxi driver to drop him off. It was almost six o'clock. The parking lot on the side of the museum had turned into a mud puddle, and Mahmoud tiptoed to avoid getting completely filthy. When he rounded the corner of the massive museum building, he glimpsed a large, well-planned park with gravel paths, manicured bushes, and gray lawns. It was poorly lit, but Mahmoud stopped to try to figure out where he was supposed to be an hour from now. It was easy enough to identify the large pond in front of the entrance stairs. But to the right of that he couldn't see much more in the dusk. When the time came, he would have to rely on his intuition.

———

Half an hour later, he could only conclude how odd it was that a country with such a controversial colonial history hadn't tried harder to establish a more interesting museum. The best part was actually the building. Other than that, it seemed to consist of flea-bitten giraffes, weary display cases of smaller animals, and some obligatory Central African spears and shields. Your typical natural history museum, long past its prime. But he wasn't here to learn more about Belgium's colonial history.

It was almost ten to seven, and Mahmoud slowly made his way back to the room where the door was supposed to be. He took a deep breath. The time had come. He pushed down on the handle with resolve.

The door swung open, and Mahmoud had to hold tight to keep the wind from ripping it out of his hands. It had stopped raining, and to judge by how his breath turned to smoke, the temperature must have dropped a few degrees while he was inside the museum. He shivered and climbed down some steel steps to the muddy gravel path. The pond in front of the museum was dimly lit but the park, which stretched out down a slight slope behind it, was impossible to make out in the dark. Mahmoud stayed in the shadows on the right side of the pond, just to be on the safe side. He cursed himself for bringing only his dress shoes to Brussels; his socks were already soaked by freezing rain. It was imperative to keep your feet dry. There wasn't a soldier in the world who didn't know that. But Mahmoud had thought his soldiering days were over.

The luminous numbers on his G-shock watch read 18:53. Seven minutes left. Still in the shadows, he made his way through a thin hedge on the other side of the pond. He stopped to listen: the park was completely silent. The only sound was the distant hum of traffic. It was probably rush hour for the EU officials and diplomats living in Tervuren. From this position he had the entire museum within sight. It was deserted.

When he turned around and gazed into the darkness, it didn't take long for him to identify the statue from his instructions. The bronze glistened faintly in the light from the pond. He turned right and crossed a small, wet lawn. In front of him, he could make out a forest, or at least something that looked like a forest. He went on. And there, almost hidden among evergreen bushes, he could just make out a park bench. He stopped. On the right side of the bench was the clear silhouette of a man.

GEORGE STEPPED THROUGH THE DOORS of Comme chez Soi at exactly seven o'clock on Thursday evening. It was part of his new life in Brussels; he was always on time. Previously, he had been so-so about punctuality. Not anymore. He tried unsuccessfully to hide a smile. After George had finished the translation, Appleby had come by his office and suggested they take George's annual evaluation over dinner in the restaurant, which boasted two Michelin stars. It was just too fucking amazing. This was what he loved about his life. He'd wrestle with unintelligible tasks and stupid translations, if it meant he could live like this.

A waiter met him as soon as he set foot inside the door.

"Monsieur Lööw? Monsieur Appleby is waiting for you upstairs," he said in French.

"*Merci*," replied George, and he followed the waiter through the nearly empty public section of the restaurant—the restaurant had just opened for the evening. Starched white tablecloths. Painted windows. Quiet, yet lively, noise level. Ties and money. Small footstools for a lady's handbag. George's mood kept getting better and better. This was his style. Add a glass of champagne and maybe a tiny, tiny line of cocaine in the bathroom, and George would be in top form.

When they reached the top of the narrow stairs, the waiter opened a high, mirrored door onto what seemed to be a private room.

Appleby was sitting alone at a table set for two. He was busy writing something on his BlackBerry, but impatiently beckoned George inside. The room was paneled with light-colored wood. Heavy curtains framed the windows and a large, dark oil painting, a still life of some sort, hung on the wall behind Appleby. Two leather armchairs were placed near the window. That was probably where you sat when you were enjoying your cognac. The restaurant wasn't George's style. Too dusty and old-fashioned. George liked white walls, glass, and steel. *Wallpaper** magazine style. But it was impossible to deny that this place had class.

"Come in, come in, sit down, for God's sake! How are you doing, old boy?" Appleby liked using expressions like *old boy*. Probably they made him feel English. It wasn't always easy to be American in Brussels.

"Thank you. Excellent, really excellent!" George said.

"Garçon! We'll take a bottle of the house champagne."

Appleby pushed the send button on his phone dramatically, then put it down on the table next to his plate.

"Garçon," George thought. Only a certain type of American addresses waiters like that nowadays.

"So, George, what do you think of Comme chez Soi? Have you been here before?"

"Yes, a few times, actually—"

"Brilliant!" Appleby interrupted.

He seemed to have lost interest in his own question and started to wave the menu around instead.

"You know what you want? I have my favorites ready here."

George opened the menu. Colchester oysters. Sole with lobster medallions. Appleby nodded approvingly.

"That's it. Now all we have to do is figure out who's paying for this little soirée," he said with a wide smile.

Appleby's white teeth glistened in the low lighting. The secretaries are right, George thought. He looks like a shark. Large, smooth, and agile. Small, cruel, jet-black eyes. George responded with a slightly nervous smile. Surely the man didn't think that George should pay for a dinner he'd been ordered to go to? Especially not when Appleby's salary was probably ten times higher than George's—which was already quite generous.

"Tobacco or cognac," Appleby said and pulled a euro coin from his pocket. "King Albert means Philip Morris, and the euro side means Hennessy."

Both were clients of Merchant & Taylor. Appleby tossed the coin into the air. King Albert landed heads up.

"Brilliant! Philip Morris foots the bill."

He stuffed the coin into his pocket with a satisfied expression on his face.

"I suppose we better charge them for our time too. This is going to take at least three hours. Be sure to put it on their account tomorrow. I'll verify it later this week."

It was a dizzying sensation. It wasn't that uncommon for a lunch to be charged to a client, even if it might not have been directly relevant to their account. But putting a 400-euro dinner for two on a client's account, George had never experienced anything like that before. Add three times 350 euros for George's time and maybe 500 euros an hour for Appleby, and Philip Morris would be getting a hefty bill for absolutely nothing. Almost 3,000 euros for an evening that had nothing at all to do with them. George smiled. That was how it worked in the major leagues.

The conversation progressed smoothly. Appleby wanted to hear about George's big clients and accounts. After a while the conversation drifted into office gossip and rumors. It was pleasant. Relaxed.

Still, George felt uncomfortable for some reason. Dinner at Comme chez Soi was too extravagant, even for Merchant & Taylor. It felt like something was hovering above them, a cloud, a fog. A premonition of something else, something murkier. Something George saw reflected in Appleby's eyes. A glimpse of darkness or a stormy sea. And his movements were impatient, a hint that the dinner so far was a warm-up, preliminary. George downed the last of his champagne and smiled confidently at Appleby. Bring it on, he thought. I'm ready.

December 19, 2013

Brussels, Belgium

THEY MUST HAVE CAUGHT SIGHT of each other at the same time, because the person on the park bench stood up and took a few steps forward. Fewer than twenty feet separated him from Mahmoud. The man held up his hand. Mahmoud stopped.

"Keep your hands at your sides and walk slowly toward me," the man next to the bench said calmly in Swedish.

It took a second for Mahmoud to recognize the voice. It was lower, rougher than he remembered. For a moment he froze mid-step, suddenly flooded with conflicting emotions.

"Lindman?" he said.

"Shammosh," the other man replied. "Damn nice of you to come."

They stood silently facing each other for a moment without saying anything. Despite the darkness, it was clear that the years had been hard on Lindman. He was older, of course, it had been ten years, but it wasn't just that. He was bigger. Bulkier. Steroid bulk. With a tattooed neck and harsh cheekbones. The blond hair that he still kept cropped and tight, military style, looked like it needed a wash. His face appeared furrowed and tired. The clothes—wide jeans and a camouflage M-60 jacket—were worn and wrinkled, as though he'd slept in them.

"It's been a long time," Mahmoud said.

His voice was quieter and shakier than he'd anticipated.

"How did you know I was in Brussels?"

Lindman shrugged.

"Googled your name and got a hit for your seminar. Called the Crisis Group, or whatever they're called, and found out where you'd be staying. Simple."

His eyes flickered over Mahmoud's shoulder, across the park in search of something, anything.

"You're sure you weren't followed?"

"I did everything you asked me to do and more," said Mahmoud with a sliver of a smile on his lips, which lingered a moment, then disappeared. Lindman's behavior made him nervous. The whole situation made him nervous.

Lindman didn't answer. He seemed to be listening intensely. The only sound was the wind in the trees, the traffic in the background.

"Things have been a bit fucked-up lately," he said at last.

"Okay?" Mahmoud said guardedly.

Lindman shook his head almost imperceptibly, fiddled with his hands.

"I don't know how much time we have."

Again his restless eyes danced across the park, into the darkness. A deep breath. As if he was preparing himself.

"You know, that thing that happened. It was a long time ago. We were young," began Lindman.

"Not that young," interrupted Mahmoud. "We weren't that fucking young."

A flame flared up inside him. A new heat swept through his body. A wave of ripe, unresolved rage. It took a conscious effort to keep it in check, not to let it spill over the edges.

"Why the hell did you lure me out here?" he said. "And what's up with all this secrecy?"

Finally Lindman's eyes stopped roving. He looked at Shammosh as if seeing him for the first time, as if he hadn't been fully aware of his presence until now. He licked his lips. There was something eager and greedy in his eyes. He continued to fiddle with his hands.

"Well, it's like this," he said.

He cleared his throat and stared straight at Mahmoud.

"I've seen stuff you can't fucking imagine. Been through stuff."

He paused, shook his head. Manically scratched his cheek.

"Sick fucking stuff, you know? And I have information, okay? Really sensitive stuff. Really fucking sensitive stuff! What I've seen. You just wouldn't fucking believe it. Seriously."

"Like the picture you gave me?"

"Yes, yes, the picture, right? The picture. You saw, right? Right? That kind of crazy shit. That kind."

Lindman was moving back and forth, shifting his weight from one foot to the other. His expression: first volatile, then intense and direct. He clenched and unclenched his jaw. He was on speed. High as a skyscraper, Mahmoud realized.

"So, like, I've been working there, right? In Afghanistan. After the military academy and that shit. With the Americans. You wouldn't fucking believe the shit I've seen! And I've got more proof."

Mahmoud felt the air rush out of him. His excitement floated away into the darkness and was replaced by disappointment. How stupid he'd been. Not to figure out that the whole thing wasn't for real. The messages had made him start imagining things. He couldn't believe he'd even been convinced that someone was following him. That Volvo in Uppsala must belong to a neighbor who worked at the university just like him. A coincidence. The simplest, most obvious solution. Of course.

At the same time, he felt something close to pity for Lindman. The King of Karlsborg back in the day. Ranked first in their year. Reduced to the amphetamine-fueled steroid wreck standing in front of him now.

"What kind of proof? What are you talking about?" Mahmoud said wearily.

"I went to Paris from Kabul, okay? After I lifted their fucking treasure trove of documentation. You understand me?"

Lindman looked away from Mahmoud, peering out into the darkness again.

"No," said Mahmoud, exhausted. "I don't understand a damn thing."

Lindman turned to him once more. His gaze becoming intense and direct again.

"Fuck that. I have a ton of pictures. Movies. Like the things you saw in the picture I sent you, okay? Torture, murder, call it whatever the hell you want. A whole fucking computer full. A crazy amount. And something else too. Something to connect the dots."

Lindman moved his index finger in a pattern, as if actually connecting imaginary dots in the air in front of him, a knowing, smug smile on his lips.

"Something to connect the dots?" Mahmoud said.

Lindman nodded. "You'll see."

"Where? Where do you have this information, Lindman?"

"In a real safe place. A real safe place in Paris."

Lindman took a wallet from his inside pocket, waved it in front of Mahmoud. "You bet your ass on it," he muttered. "It's in a real safe place."

"Okay," Mahmoud said. "Sure. Let's just say for a moment that you actually have some amazing scoop? Fine. What do you want with me?"

Lindman leaned toward him. His breath was rancid. The wind howled in the trees above them, carrying with it the sound of the highway.

"Cash," he said. "I won't let go of this shit without getting a fat stack. This is my pension. Do you understand? You help me get cash for the pictures. You know who to talk to, right? Who pays? You fix that. First the cash, then the pictures."

"Cash?" Mahmoud said. "Cash? You think I'm going to pay you? Are you crazy?"

Lindman shook his head.

"No, no!" he said.

His voice a little higher now. Impatient. Restless. He took a breath, got himself under control before he continued.

"Not you, goddamnit, but you can hook me up with someone. CNN or whatever. They'll take you seriously. You're a fucking professor or something now. They'll talk to you. I want a million U.S. dollars. And not a fucking penny less. Tell them that. And there's one more thing. A small problem."

He suddenly froze. His eyes roamed out over the park again. Mahmoud felt it simultaneously. A sixth sense he'd learned to use in the military kicked in. They were no longer alone in the park.

December 19, 2013

Brussels, Belgium

DINNER WAS OVER, AND GEORGE and Appleby had moved to the leather chairs by the window. Calvados glittered in their glasses. George was feeling pure elation. Maybe he'd just imagined that there was a cloud hanging over this meeting?

"I'll be honest with you, George. I think you have what it takes to get all the way to the top. How long have you been with Merchant and Taylor? Three years?"

"Yes, three years and a few months," George said. "It's gone so damn fast."

"That's for sure! You've risen quickly. I don't think I had a private office after only three years." Appleby smiled. "You have at least twenty percent more billable hours than anyone else in your generation at the Brussels office, which means you pull in twenty percent more money. The clients like you. I like you."

He paused and seemed to be thinking. George didn't want to interrupt. This was good. Appleby leaned back in his leather chair and held up his glass of calvados to the candles on the dinner table, as if to analyze its contents.

"In our industry, it's all about bringing in the money, George," he said. "Bringing in the money while avoiding the problems that come with it. That's how it is for everyone, I suppose, but our industry is special. Lobbying. People don't understand what we do. The importance of what we do. Ignorant bastards continually attack us. They call us mercenaries and think we're completely immoral. In every goddamn survey regular people say they don't like us. That they don't trust us!"

Appleby threw his hands wide in a gesture of helplessness. As if it was utterly impossible for him to understand why anyone wouldn't trust him.

"Politicians say they don't like us. That our influence needs to be limited in every possible way. But the truth is that not a single one of them could survive a week without us whispering into their ears. Where would they be today if we didn't procure contacts and mobilize their voters? We are the oil in this machine. We lubricate the gears. So they really shouldn't mind if, now and then, when no one's looking, we shift the gears in a direction that best suits our clients' interests. It's a small price to pay for what we contribute."

Appleby took a small sip from his glass. George was craving a smoke, but he couldn't just stand up and walk out now.

"But what we do can't always be done in the light. Some of our clients feel more comfortable in the shadows; some of our methods work better in the shadows. There's nothing strange about that. Just part of the game. But sometimes we need protection. Backup."

He paused and stared into the air in front of him. It occurred to George that Appleby might be drunk. He hadn't seemed like it until now.

"I'm not sure I understand," he said and lifted his glass to his lips. Appleby turned toward him.

"You don't? Well, I can't blame you. What we're talking about is above your pay grade. And I don't really want to go into details.

You'll understand one day. Rather, you'll be forced to understand if you stay in this business and continue down the path you've been on so far. In any case, what I'm trying to say is that we have what we like to call *protectors* at various stations in society. Or we protect each other, you might say. We scratch each other's backs. And sometimes these protectors call in our debts. Honestly, it's not always a pleasant business when it happens. But it's necessary."

Appleby turned to George and looked him straight in the eye. He was definitely not drunk. On the contrary. He seemed completely sober. George felt nervous. Damn it, this was what he'd suspected. You never eat for free. Never.

"But it always pays to pay off your debts. Didn't your prime minister write a book about that in the 1990s? That a person in debt isn't free, or something like that?" Appleby smiled gently.

"Uh, yes, that's right. I didn't think it was translated into English. And he wasn't *my* prime minister, if you know what I mean," George replied.

"Yes, exactly," Appleby said and smiled wider. "Unlike the rest of your countrymen, you're not a Social Democrat. Anyway, right now, Merchant and Taylor isn't free. Merchant and Taylor has a debt to pay. More than one, to be completely honest. We've reached our credit limit, and now it's time to pay back our debts. We've got quite good credit. The few things we're asked to do, we get paid back for tenfold. And that applies not only to Merchant and Taylor at large, but also to the people who perform these services. Do you understand what I'm saying?"

George felt himself getting goose bumps. It felt like he was on the verge of being initiated into something big. A secret society, a brotherhood.

"I don't know," he said carefully. "Are you referring to something specific?"

Appleby didn't answer, instead he glanced at his huge wristwatch.

"Not all of our customers are what they appear to be, George," he said at last. "Just remember that. Make it easy on yourself. Don't think too much. Keep doing what you're doing. Do what you're asked. Bill properly. That will make everything easier. Much easier for all of us. And remember, at Merchant and Taylor we don't forget those who help us pay off our debts. You've already come a long way. It's time to take the next step. And the next step is not just about being a skilled lobbyist. It's about dedication. To the firm. To our clients. It's about loyalty. Those who demonstrate it go far. Very far. But lack of loyalty—well, let's just say it's not appreciated. Not at all."

Appleby looked at George, and something glinted from within his shark eyes. Something ruthless that George hoped he'd never become better acquainted with. He didn't know what to say, so he took a sip of calvados. It tasted stale, yeasty. George hated calvados. Digital Solutions, he thought. I knew there was something shady about that damn Reiper.

"It's late. I think it's time for us to call it a night. Not even I can bill Philip Morris for a whole night."

Appleby stretched and laughed drily, before he stood up. George followed his example. They walked together down the stairs and out into the street. George stumbled on the sidewalk; the cold air made him realize that he might be a little bit drunk after all. The first taxi pulled up and Appleby jumped in the backseat. Before he closed the door, he turned to George.

"Don't worry, George," he said. "Think of it as an adventure.

Everyone who's someone in this company has been in your situation. Just bite the bullet. And don't overthink it, okay?"

"Okay, I guess," George said. "I'm still not really sure what this is about."

"Fuck that. That's the point. Don't think. Just do what you're told. And bill like usual. You have it in you, I know you do. See you tomorrow."

With that, Appleby slammed the door. The taxi drove slowly away under the colored Christmas lights hanging over the cobblestone street. George lit a cigarette and pulled his coat tighter around him. A few snowflakes landed on his shoulders.

"Fucking December," he muttered and felt relieved when he found a small bag of cocaine in his pocket. Maybe he'd swing by Place Lux? It wasn't that late yet.

December 19, 2013

Brussels, Belgium

THERE WAS SOMETHING IN THE air. Something about the
sound of the park. Something had changed, something wasn't
right. Mahmoud hunched over instinctively, making himself
smaller, and turned around to face the park. His eyes were useless
in the dark. A snowflake landed on Mahmoud's cheek. The wind
had subsided, and the temperature continued to fall. He strained
to hear something. Sharpen his senses. All he heard was the wind
rustling in the branches far above him, and the sound of traffic far
away. But still. Something wasn't right.

When Mahmoud turned to Lindman again, he saw a red dot
jump across his cheek, like a small insect, for only a fraction of a
second. That was enough. He knew immediately what it was.

"Duck!" he shouted. "Fire!"

Mahmoud flopped down onto his belly in the grass, still keeping his eyes on Lindman. He felt wetness against his fingers, cold
against his cheek. Directly in front of him Lindman's head was
thrown back as he lifted an inch off the ground and spun a half turn
in a clumsy imitation of a pirouette. A monster ballerina in a Pixar
movie. Just a fraction of a second, then he collapsed into a sitting
position on the park bench. A marionette with the strings cut.

Mahmoud's pulse was racing, but instinct and training took over. Without really knowing how, he'd assessed what angle the shot must have come from, where the shooter must be hiding. On his elbows and knees, he crawled around the shooter's field of sight up to Lindman's lifeless body. Now he could hear whispers in the distance, the rustling of feet over the grass in the park. Mahmoud's hand bumped against something soft and thin in the grass. Lindman's wallet. He must have dropped it as he collapsed on the bench. Without thinking, he slipped it in his pocket. His hands groped along Lindman's legs. Grabbed hold of his military jacket, continued up along his arm. Time stood still. He tugged on Lindman's arm, pulled him from the bench onto the ground. Struggled to get him to relative safety, even though he knew it was pointless.

Before he succeeded, he saw the little dot again, for a moment, hopping across Lindman's mangled face. And then Lindman's body jerked once more, his head was thrown to the side. Something warm and wet splashed across Mahmoud cheeks. He immediately released Lindman's arm and threw himself, in controlled panic, into the bushes that bordered the small grove.

Blood, was his only thought. I have his blood on my face.

But he never even heard the shot. Then he saw the little red dot again. For a moment it stopped on a tree just in front of him. As if in slow motion, the bark was silently pulverized, the ball drilling into the tree. They're shooting at me, he thought, surprised, confused. They're shooting at me with a silenced rifle. He crouched down and ran as fast as he could away from the park. The ground in the grove was soft and flat. Ahead of him he saw electric lights coming from a street that appeared to lead back to Tervuren. Lindman's blood was dripping from his face onto his dark gray coat.

Sitting in the taxi on the way back to Brussels, he could barely remember how he'd made it out of the park. He vaguely remembered hearing footsteps running behind him. Snapping branches and American voices. Steam from his mouth and dripping blood. He remembered reaching the road, crossing it, and continuing through backyards and small streets until he came to Tervuren's small historic center. He had no idea how he'd found the taxi. Everything he'd done so far, he'd done automatically.

Mahmoud leaned back in his seat and closed his eyes. A wave of fatigue crashed over him. With his eyes closed, he saw the red dot dancing across Lindman's unshaven cheek, then his face being torn to shreds again and again. How had they managed to follow him to the museum? He must not have been careful enough, somehow. He had led them to Lindman. He was responsible for Lindman's death.

Mahmoud hadn't even noticed that the taxi's radio was on until the screech of a pop song faded away and was replaced by a dark, solemn male voice. The news. Mahmoud turned his wrist to see what time it was. 20:51. His first thought was that two hours had passed since he met Lindman. Two hours since his life was turned upside down. Had he hid for that long in the backyards of Tervuren? His next thought was, what kind of newscast begins nine minutes before the hour? And then he began to listen closely. Snatches of words he recognized in the fast-flowing river of Belgian French. *Assassins. Tervuren. Extrêmement dangereux.*

Words that could only mean one thing: he was wanted for Lindman's murder. It was as if the taxi shrank around him, as if the roof started to sink. He saw the Arab taxi driver fiddle with the radio nobs in a panicked attempt to change the channel. He saw him throw terrified glances over his shoulder. He remembered every detail he had learned in Karlsborg and afterward. And the most important lesson of all: "Be creative, not reactive."

Before the driver knew what was happening, Mahmoud was sitting beside him in the front seat with a ballpoint pen pressed against his throbbing carotid artery. He felt strangely calm, disconnected.

"Not a fucking sound, okay?" Mahmoud said in hushed Arabic. "I swear I'll cut your throat, okay? I swear."

The driver's face was sweaty. His eyes were panicked. I got him, was Mahmoud's only thought. I got him where I want him.

"Drive toward Brussels," Mahmoud said. "Nice and easy. Don't get any fucking ideas."

The driver's eyes darted back and forth between the black asphalt in front of the car and Mahmoud's face. He nodded almost imperceptibly.

Mahmoud felt the rhythm of the traffic change just seconds before he saw police lights reflected in the windows of the car, in the rain-soaked asphalt. A roadblock. Of course. The taxi slowed down, behind the ever-slower traffic. Change of plans. Creative, not reactive.

"Listen to me," Mahmoud said calmly to the driver. "I have a bomb strapped to my body. A real, fucking bomb, okay? Jihad style. "

He grabbed the driver's face with his free hand and forced it up against his own, blowing his acrid, adrenaline-fueled breath against the driver's mouth and nose.

"I will not hesitate to blow myself up. *Allahu Akbar*. And I'll take those pigs up there with me. Do you understand?"

The driver was hardly breathing. His pulse pounding against the pen Mahmoud was pushing ever harder against his neck. A tear slipped down his cheek.

"You can save yourself," Mahmoud continued. "When I tell you to, you open the door and run as fast as you can away from here. As fast as you can. It doesn't matter if someone's chasing you. If you don't get three hundred yards from here, you'll be blasted to smithereens along with me and the rest of the heathens. Do you understand?"

The driver nodded, sobbing.

"Yes, yes," he said. "Please, I have a family. I am a Muslim!"

"It's going to be fine, just do as I say. Take off your seat belt."

The driver obeyed eagerly. One click, and then the sound of the belt as it retracted into its holder. Mahmoud leaned forward, peering toward the flashing lights. He could make out a number of police officers farther up the road. Flashlights and automatic weapons. Three cruisers, from what he could see. Maybe ten cars between his car and them. Not yet. The timing had to be perfect.

"Do you see that little street over there?" he said.

He pointed diagonally across the immobilized intersection, toward a narrow, poorly lit street running between small, gray row houses.

"You'll be safe over there. On the count of three, you open the door and run faster than you've ever run before, okay?"

The driver's eyes followed Mahmoud's finger. He nodded and turned back toward him. His eyes filled with gratitude. As though Mahmoud really were about to save his life. Only five cars between them and the roadblock now.

"Ready?" Mahmoud said.

His mouth tasted like steel and blood. The stress was suddenly real, palpable, almost overwhelming. He took a deep breath.

"Yes!" the driver almost shouted. "Yes! I'm ready!"

"Good. On three. One. Two. Three."

Mahmoud had barely uttered the last number before the driver flung the door wide open and threw himself out. He stumbled at first, and for a second Mahmoud thought he might fall, but he regained his balance, got to his feet, and ran with a frenzy that belongs only to those who are hunted by death. Across the street, in between the cars, straight toward the small residential street Mahmoud had pointed to.

It took less than a second for the police officers, twenty yards away, to understand what was happening. An Arab was running as fast as he could away from the roadblock. A moment of chaos and confusion, before someone shouted an order, flashlights were turned, rubber soles began to move across the pavement.

Mahmoud didn't wait any longer. As gently as he could, he slipped out of the passenger side door and disappeared in the opposite direction. Behind him he heard loud voices, the metallic rustle of weapons. Crouching, he disappeared behind a hedge, onto a smaller street behind the roadblock.

Going to the police no longer seemed like a particularly good idea.

FINALLY, THEY SENT ME HERE. To beautiful, unyielding, horrible Afghanistan. Here, where time stood still, where time is standing still.

"You know the region," my new bosses say.

They know nothing but hallways and conference rooms.

"You speak the language," they say, their thoughts already elsewhere, on to the next meeting, the next fawning conversation.

I don't have the energy to explain that I speak Arabic, not Farsi, not Pashtun. In my hands, I already have a plane ticket, a new identity, the promise of oblivion, the promise of a future.

We drive a rusty old Toyota truck across the border from Pakistan, wearing head scarves and Kalashnikovs, indistinguishable from any other gangsters in these mountains. Just roads, potholes, gravel, and sand. In a market outside Jalalabad, I ask my interpreter to buy an English bayonet with the year 1842 stamped onto the steel. These mountains are the tombstones of the kingdoms who thought they could possess them. The English. Now the Russians. They retreat, confused, bruised. What is it about these mountains? I send reports back to my superiors about the mujahideen—they are indomitable, intractable. But also impossible to coordinate or control. One day we'll have some inkling of what we have created. The layers are peeled back one by one. In Washington, they pay no attention to the fanaticism. Religion is not a factor in this crucible. But one day. After ideology comes religion. Those who were our friends will become our enemies.

———

At last my crime has been atoned for, or perhaps just forgotten. Five years in Langley before they even let me serve as a courier. Endless days of paperwork and the freeway. The pool and TV. The endless, insurmountable boredom of daily life. It is my punishment for allowing the bonds to grow. It is my punishment for losing focus for a moment. As if I hadn't been punished enough.

I thought I'd be free from it someday. The thought of what I had given up, not once but twice. I told myself that I was free from it when I met Annie, when we got married after a year of fumbling but ever more convincing dinner dates, movies, evenings at home, and at last weekend trips to see her parents in Connecticut. But it was all just a facade. Putty and plaster. Colored lights and mirrors.

At last there was Susan standing in the doorway. In her well-pressed, dark blue suit, with her tired eyes, and her barely manageable, badly dyed hair. As I knew she would be eventually. Oh, how my heart raced in that moment. How my hands started shaking when I opened the gray folder stamped with impressive secret seals. How the room disappeared around me, how reality shifted as I read page after page of circumstantial evidence and gossip, and agitated, misspelled field reports from Amman and Cairo, Beirut, Paris, London. How I closed my eyes before flipping to the photograph that my hand had already felt was there.

I turned it over slowly. And looked your murderer straight in the eyes.

———

Annie just stared at me when I told her about my new post, careful to hide both the details and my delight, my gaping hunger for escape and revenge. I knew she wouldn't cry, it's not how she works, it wasn't how our relationship worked. She said nothing at all, just stood up and cleared what was left of our pitiful dinner from McDonald's. Her footsteps were silent on the thick carpeting.

And me, I wanted nothing more than to feel the adrenaline pump as I approached Beirut in a low-flying Blackhawk. Nothing more than to wake up every morning to the violence, the snipers, the explosions, instead of continuing this endless journey further into emptiness, further into regret. I wanted nothing more than to bide my time, waiting for the final piece of information that would open the window, the little rip in time. Dollar upon dollar. Threat upon threat. Flattery upon flattery, promise upon promise, drink upon endless drink. The registration number of the car, where it's parked at night, when it'll be driven the next time, by whom, where.

And then the calculations and rough estimates. Risk minimization and assessments of explosive power. The patient, laborious work that results in a bomb for a bomb. An eye for an eye. A meaningless exchange of pawns.

———

Up over the mountains. All we see are more mountains. I dream of mountains and open, snow-covered fields. Ice in pale sunshine.

Winters that never end. I drink tea with the local warriors, who call themselves "students," the Taliban. The interpreter tells me that they've been studying at the Islamic schools in Pakistan and are deeply religious. Wahhabis, as in Saudi Arabia.

But here they're rebels, not intellectuals. Their religion is simple and filled with rules. There is no authority beyond Allah. No writing beyond the Koran. And above all: no religion beyond Islam. They tolerate me because I give them the arms and ammunition to destroy the Soviet occupation. The war seems to allow them to compromise. Their faces are masks of hardened leather, their kaftans haven't changed in a thousand years, and they're about to defeat the world's largest army with small arms and a few rocket launchers.

And then? When the Russians have left, when the images of Lenin have been burned and only the ruins and the dead remain? Will these timeless men build a country in the name of Allah? Will we allow them to forbid music, theater, literature, and even ancient monuments? As they say they want to do? Do we prefer that to the ungodliness of communism? Into whose hands are we placing the fate of this world?

―――

It's a powerful experience, to exact your revenge. Few are that privileged. So many wrongs for which no one is held accountable. There is so much we are forced to accept. And yet I only barely remember it. Just the feverish intensity of the day before. Just the instructions to the technician, an old, half-deaf veteran from some elite unit with lots of experience and a bag of tricks, flown in especially for this. Just his grumbling and fiddling with cables and gray plastic explosives in a bombed-out house in a deserted suburb. How we shook hands, and how, suddenly, I was lying on a roof, in stark sunlight with binoculars pressed so hard against my eye sockets that I had bruises for two weeks afterward.

I remember a face in the binoculars. A face like any other. Eyes like any others. Anonymous features I had memorized from the last page of Susan's report. I remember the resistance of the button on the remote switch. Remember how smooth it felt in my sweaty hands, in the scorching sun.

Of the explosion, I remember nothing. Nothing at all. All I remember is smoke and sirens, distant screams. Everything was so impersonal, so completely a part of Beirut's very essence. I remember that I closed my eyes. That I thought, it's over. I have done what I could do. I remember the emptiness. Stone was placed on stone. Guilt on guilt.

My next memory is clearer. Three sleepless nights later, I hear Annie's crackling, alien voice coming through the strictly encrypted satellite phone into our little fort of an embassy in Beirut.

"It's still too early, we shouldn't get our hopes up," she said.

But her voice was so full of hope that I had to sit down and bury my face in my hands.

"Are you still there?" she asked, her voice filtered through stardust, metallic, static.

"I'm here," I said.

"Can you believe we're going to be parents?"

In the background I heard the evening open with shell bursts, the sky illuminated by traces of fire and searchlights.

"The ground is shaking here," I said.

"Here too, honey. Here too."

And then, if only for a moment, it actually let up. For a second I stopped punishing myself for your death, for my betrayal, for my revenge. Not because I deserved it, but because the unborn child deserved two parents. It was impossible to understand the enormity of a second chance, a second child. Maybe it was possible. Perhaps there was some compromise in me after all. Just Beirut, then I would never leave Washington's Beltway again. We already had the house, loans, new cars every other year. All we needed was the baby and me.

I came home from Beirut two weeks later, one evening in late August when the smell of freshly cut grass from the local soccer fields filled the air, when the hacking of sprinklers mingled with the hypnotic growl of the highway. I saw Annie sitting alone on the stairs to our bungalow, our suburban dream, as the real estate agent with bleached teeth and tragically provincial Wall Street dreams had called it. I saw Annie's eyes in the twilight. And I knew. Like I always know.

"Don't say anything," I said as I held her in that terribly inadequate way that is all I know.

"The baby," Annie said. "I tried to reach you."

"Shh, don't talk. I know, I know."

I held her on the stairs until the darkness was solid and the sprinklers had gone to sleep. Until the highway had diminished to a whisper.

Later, at the kitchen table, with Annie finally asleep in our bed in the room facing the garden, I was back where I started. No sorrow. Nothing except the desire to move away, move out, move on. Nothing except the realization that a lie may be false, but truth is the real enemy.

They wake me up at dawn, and we're sitting in the Toyota again before I have time to wipe the sleep from my eyes, before my dreams of mountains have been replaced by real mountains. We drive in silence through the orange canyons, through gravel and sand; an early winter without snow. This war is over. Politics is the only thing delaying David's victory over Goliath. A small victory in the eternal quest for the status quo. My time here is coming to an end, and I've asked to be replaced by someone who speaks Farsi or Pashtun. But my wishes are whispers in the wind. No one remembers the languages spoken in Afghanistan once the Red Dragon is on the run. We've gotten what we wanted, our goal has been achieved.

Maybe I'll be rewarded in Washington for my invaluable work in the field. The future scares me as much as the past. A desk job while I wait for everything to start over. Lonely nights in the bungalow with the silent echo of Annie's footsteps against the thick carpeting. Polite phone calls that end in tears. Explanations that I don't have. Thoughts of how I lost two families, two children. Thoughts of smoke and sirens. Boredom and then fatigue. The monotonous waiting for my next opportunity to forget, to disappear into a present without context.

Outside the car window, mountains are replaced by mountains, gravel by gravel. We're moving forward, but we remain in the same place.

GEORGE WRESTLED HIS WAY TO the bar at Ralph's, waving his American Express card. He dove skillfully through a group of red-cheeked, blue-eyed interns, surfacing at the front of the bar next to a loud Irishman, his tie askew, who was trying to get the bartender's attention with very muddled French verbs.

Ralph's wasn't much larger than two normal-size living rooms, but for the last few years, because of its perfect blend of hot interns, younger people from the EU institutions, lobbyists, and lawyers, it was the only bar in the EU Quarter to be at if you wanted to be seen. The perfect place to mix networking, partying, and hitting on young Italians with admiring eyes and low-cut tops under their tailored jackets.

It took no more than a minute before George had two glasses of champagne in his hands, much to the irritated surprise of the Irishman. Paid and done. George shrugged his shoulders at the Irishman and his renewed campaign for the bartender's attention.

He stretched a little in order to find the tall table he'd just left. Good, she was still there. Mette? That was her name, right? Danish. Intern for the Danish EU commissioner. Perfect. A good contact and super-hot. Sometimes this job was just too amazing.

Business and pleasure. He already had her business card, so now there was just pleasure left.

The only annoying thing was that it was impossible to understand what she was saying. Her Danish blended with the background noise at Ralph's—a mess of at least six other languages with a score by Lady Gaga—was more than he could handle. Danish was hard enough as it was. But switching to English was entirely out of the question. You had to pretend you understood the other Nordic languages. And she seemed to understand his Swedish without any problem.

Well, soon enough, he'd be taking her out of here anyway. Suggest they pick up some sushi and bring it back to his place. Pop a bottle of bubbly. After that, language wouldn't matter anymore. That was the advantage of living just a few steps from Place du Luxembourg.

He'd made it halfway across the room, when he felt his phone vibrating in his inside pocket. Holding the two champagne glasses in his left hand, he used his right to fish out the phone. Who the hell would call this late on a Thursday? DIGITAL SOLUTIONS was flashing on the screen. Fucking hell. His good mood evaporated like mist out of the room. After his dinner with Appleby it made him nervous to even think about Digital Solutions. The phone stopped flashing before he could reply. For a moment he considered blowing it off. Pretending he hadn't heard the phone. But then he saw Appleby's shark eyes in front of him. He shuddered as he placed one of the glasses on the high table in front of Mette.

"I'm sorry," he said.

He held up the phone and pointed meaningfully toward the door. "Duty calls."

Mette smiled and said something completely incomprehensible

that George interpreted as understanding. He gestured to her that he'd be right back, took his champagne glass, and started forcing his way through the well-dressed wall of meat toward the only door that led out to the square.

———

It was dark when he got outside, bitterly cold, and for once almost deserted. The only life George could see was the taxi queue outside the sports bar Fat Boy's on the opposite side of the square and a few frozen souls hurrying between bars in their too thin coats. At the bottom of the square the European Parliament, now closed for the evening, was also completely silent and dark. Nevertheless, its presence seemed almost organic. George thought he could hear it breathing.

Freezing drizzle hung in the air. He unbuttoned his coat, lit a Marlboro Red, and inhaled deeply. Before he had time to call Reiper, the phone started vibrating again. George put the hands-free in his ear while noting the time, 7:55 P.M., in order to bill Digital Solutions for the time the conversation took.

"Mr. Reiper," he answered, "what can I do for you tonight?"

"Good evening, Mr. Lööw," Reiper said. "Sorry to bother you. I assume you're not at the office?"

"No, that's correct. I just left. But as I said on Monday, at Merchant and Taylor we're always on duty. What can I do for you?"

George took a sip of champagne as he bent down, trying to peek through the glass door into Ralph's. In the dim light, he couldn't see if Mette was still standing where he left her.

"Good, good. Well, Mr. Lööw, I'm sorry to intrude on your evening, but it would be great if we could meet. Now."

George pressed down on the gas pedal of his Audi, even though he'd have to slam the brakes at the next traffic light, just down the street. He usually found it soothing to sink into the leather racing seats with Avicii blasting on the stereo. But that wasn't working right now. Not at all.

He turned off the music. He couldn't handle the pounding of the bass line. The evening's champagne buzz was already giving way to a headache. He squeezed two aspirins from a package he kept in the right pocket of his pants and swallowed them without water.

Normally, he loved this stuff, being called in during the evening like a consigliere. Feeling like he was indispensable. Damn, he'd seen it in Mette's eyes, or whatever her name was, when he'd said that he was leaving to advise a client. Admiration. Excitement.

And if this had been a regular client, it'd be no problem. He'd have called Mette on his way home. Picked up another bottle of Bollinger from a late night kiosk. But with Digital Solutions it was different. There was something about Reiper. Something about that Josh who'd showed up at his office. Something that turned his stomach. And those classified documents on top of it. And Appleby's dinner tonight. For the first time in a very long time George felt like he might be out of his depth.

Fifteen minutes later, George turned off Avenue Brugman and onto Avenue Molière in the district of Ixelles. He wasn't out here that often. Sure, he'd eaten brunch at some point at the haute bourgeoisie Caudron or, hungover, had eaten lunch around the corner, at that

American diner on Place Brugman, but otherwise he mostly hung out around the European Quarter or downtown.

Nevertheless, it was pretty sweet around here. There were a bunch of embassies along the Avenue Molière, and the street was elegant, with its art nouveau *maisons de maître* and the tall trees lining the sidewalks. He'd read somewhere that properties here were the most expensive in Brussels.

The GPS beeped and informed George that he'd reached number 222, the address Reiper had given him. He parked his Audi in front of the entrance to a magnificent three-story house. Like so many art nouveau houses, it made George uncomfortable. There was something so Gothic about the plantlike facade, with its soft angles and circular windows. All that vaulting ornamentation and thin steel embellishments seemed to be creeping all over the building. The front of the house was dominated by an enormous bay window, which almost reached to the street. The steel-framed windows must have been almost eight feet tall. Heavy curtains were drawn and made it impossible to see inside.

George felt his courage slipping further. The house suited Reiper perfectly. It projected the same feeling of intense uneasiness as its resident did. He climbed out of the car, locked it automatically with a reassuring beep, and walked up the four steps to the gate. DIGITAL SOLUTIONS stood on an A4-size brass plate next to the door. It looked brand-new. As if it had been put up yesterday.

George rang the doorbell. He was surprised to hear a modern *riiinnng,* instead of a muffled *ding-dong.* A camera was mounted on the door's upper right corner. It seemed to be moving. As if someone inside was directing it with a joystick.

"George. Come in."

Josh opened the door, wearing what looked like a pair of black combat pants made from some type of advanced Gore-Tex. A sweatshirt with NAVY printed across the chest. There was something heated about him. Stressed. He was oozing endorphins, and his face was red, as if he'd just come back from a run.

"Uh, thanks," replied George.

"Come in, come in. Reiper is waiting for you in the office."

Josh glanced out the door toward George's car.

"Nice car. Leasing? They take good care of you at Merchant and Taylor."

He didn't wait for George to respond, just turned and slanted across the hall.

George nodded and slunk after him. He felt uncomfortable. He didn't feel in charge of the situation. Not at all.

Josh opened an enormous oak door that led into a room resembling the library in an English country estate. The floor was covered by a worn red carpet, and the walls were covered with wall-mounted, empty bookshelves or dark wood paneling. Large French windows looked onto what George assumed was a garden at the back of the house. It was too dark outside to see properly. The room was completely unfurnished, apart from a brand-new sofa group that looked like it was from IKEA, and a huge table in the middle of the room. An impressive collection of computers, monitors, and other electronic equipment was spread out on the table. Reiper rose from his place in front of a black laptop.

"Mr. Lööw! Welcome to Digital Solutions. You'll have to forgive us."

He threw open his arms in what was supposed to resemble an apologetic gesture. He was wearing Gore-Tex trousers similar to Josh's. A black T-shirt on top. He had a bad case of hat head; the slush gray wreath of hair was glued to his scalp.

"We haven't really settled in yet, and interior design isn't my specialty."

George nodded and looked around.

"How many people work at Digital Solutions, anyway?" he said.

"Well, it's a little hard to say exactly. Some of us work on a contract basis, more as freelancers."

"But how many of you are working in Brussels right now?"

George felt his irritation growing. His headache. All this fucking secrecy.

"Right now, I guess we have five or six people in Brussels. That said, there are others who're on the road, so to speak. Involved in other projects, and so on. Let's have a seat. I have a couple of things I'd like to discuss with you."

Josh quietly turned around and slipped out of the room, closing the door behind him. Reiper and George sat opposite each other on two hard, cream-colored sofas. Between them stood a worn, old coffee table. It had started raining again. Sleet pattered against the French doors. It was pitch-black outside.

"First and foremost: thanks for the translation," Reiper said. "Quick and competent work."

George shrugged, trying to smile through his headache. When would those damn pills kick in? Reiper straightened up, put his hands behind his head, and gazed into the darkness, deeply engrossed by the sleet outside the window.

"Unnecessary, of course. But surely you understood that?"

George involuntarily shook his head, blinked.

"Excuse me? What did you say was unnecessary?"

"It doesn't matter."

Reiper waved his hand dismissively.

"You're not stupid. On the contrary. No genius, perhaps, but definitely above average. You realized the papers were classified, that handling them constituted some type of crime. Still that didn't stop you. That's interesting."

"I . . ." George began again.

But he fell silent. His pulse begin to race. It felt like he was sliding down a slippery rock. As if his feet were struggling for a foothold but continuing to slide.

Reiper rose with unexpected grace, walked over to the computer table, and lifted a thin yellow folder, which he began to flip through absently. After a few seconds, he turned to George and stared at him with blank eyes. In the dimly lit room they looked green. Luminous. Like a cat's.

"But if we're going to continue working together, I have to be absolutely certain of your loyalty. One hundred percent sure. So, I've taken out what you might call an insurance policy on you."

He walked back to his couch and laid the yellow folder down gently in front of George.

December 19, 2013

Brussels, Belgium

THE VIBRATING PHONE DEEP IN Klara's coat pocket cut through her fatigue like a laser. The week—full of reports, team meetings, endless hours in airless meeting rooms, lunches on her feet, and late nights at the computer—fell to the side. The only bright spot this week had been the hours spent today with Cyril in her apartment. She was still tingling.

This wasn't the first time they'd stolen a couple of hours in the middle of the day and taken separate taxis to her place to have sex. No need to deny it. That's how it was. And in the beginning, that had been the whole point. The forbidden. Sneaking off from her high-performance life, getting him to sneak off from his. A little shabby somehow, a little dirty, but still harmless. A game where no one got hurt. And it paid off to be cautious. Gossip was devastating in the European Parliament. A Swedish adviser and a French parliamentarian would be gossip gold.

Her heart racing, she grabbed hold of the phone in her pocket. Maybe his dinner ended early? Maybe he was on his way over? But her hopes died as soon as she saw the screen. JÖRGEN APELBOM. Shit. She'd completely forgotten about him.

"Sorry, Jörgen!" she answered.

Her voice was as sweet and sincere as she could make it. She held the phone in place against her shoulder while rooting through her bag for the keys to the front door of her building.

"I'm so sorry. I had so much——"

"Yeah, yeah, yeah," interrupted Jörgen. "You had a lot to do. Blah blah blah. As usual. You canceled on Tuesday as well."

He babbled on, trying to sound ironically hurt. But it was a bad show. Behind the irony, Klara glimpsed his real disappointment.

Sure, she'd let Jörgen get her to promise to have a drink with him in the press bar after work to talk over some report on Internet anonymity that the Swedish Pirate Party was evidently over the moon about. She owed it to him for all the help he gave her every time a question about the Internet or computer security popped up in the European Parliament. He undoubtedly wanted to convince the Social Democrats to vote with the Pirate Party on this issue. That was how it worked. A favor for a favor. They helped each other out as much as possible.

But recently Jörgen had started maneuvering their monthly meetings so they took place weekly and later in the day in more and more informal settings. Klara suspected Jörgen's interest might not be purely professional. And now this whiny, feigned martyrdom.

"Well, what do you want me to say?" she interrupted him.

She was surprised by the irritation in her own voice as she pushed open the door to the narrow stairwell and took a deep breath.

"Seriously, Jörgen, I forgot. It sucks, but it happens. It's nine-thirty. Why didn't you call before now, if it was so important?"

The staircase was dark. She hit the light switch. But nothing happened. The bulb in the stairs must have burned out. A gust of wind pulled the door shut behind her. She suddenly got the feeling that something wasn't right.

"I was in a meeting," Jörgen said in her ear.

A meeting with World of Warcraft, Klara thought, but said nothing. The stairs creaked under her as she began to walk up the four flights in the dark.

"Here's what we're going to do," he continued. "Since you've canceled two times in a row, you have to buy me dinner next week."

Somewhere above she heard the creak of a door gently opening. A lock clicked as it was cautiously closed again. Creaking wood, like echoes of her own footsteps. She stopped on the landing between the second and third floor. The footsteps were coming from farther above. The creaking sounds. She was the only one who lived on the fourth floor. Her brain was so slow, so unprepared for something like this. The door that had been closed. It could only have been her own.

She turned around, heart pounding, threw herself down the stairs, stumbling over the next landing in the dark. Spinning a half turn, taking the stairs two at a time, not even listening for footsteps behind her. It took a few seconds. It took an eternity. She twisted her ankle when her foot landed on the cracked mosaic tiles of the ground floor. Ignored it. Staggered to the front gate, fiddled with the ancient lock. She heard only silence behind her now. Nothing. Somehow it scared her even more. She turned the lock and opened the door into the rain-soaked Brussels night.

And fell out into a completely ordinary world. The streetlights in front of the park, the young people dressed up and on their way to a bar or a late dinner, the light from the small Spanish tapas place next door. She ran over to the restaurant. The safety of the half-full wineglasses inside, the small plates of cured ham, tortillas, olives. The loosened ties and glittering earrings. She stopped in front of the window, let its yellow, warm light envelop her. She turned toward her door. Nothing.

"Hey, Klara? Are you still there? What are you doing?"

Jörgen's voice, coming distantly from the phone. She pressed it against her ear.

"Sorry," she said. "There . . ."

At the same time, she saw the door to her staircase being opened from inside.

"I'll call you later," she whispered breathlessly into the phone and turned it off.

She turned to face the bar's window, as if she were reading the menu. Pulled up her coat collar to cover her cheeks. Glanced toward the door.

A young woman, maybe a few years older than herself. Blond ponytail and dark, serious running clothes. The reflective stripes on her pants and top glittered in the headlights of the cars rolling by on the street. Straight, confident posture. A backpack strapped to her back. She stretched a few times, looked around, apparently without paying attention to Klara. Then she jogged calmly toward and past Klara without seeming to notice her at all.

Klara waited until the woman rounded the corner of the block, until her own breathing calmed down. Then she picked up the phone again. There was a moment's hesitation before she pressed Cyril's number.

He answered after six rings. Whispering, an ounce of annoyance in his voice.

"Klara, now is not a good time."

"Sorry," she said. "But something's happened. I just wanted to check . . ."

She could feel his impatience through her phone.

"Yes, what? What is it?"

"Can I sleep at your place tonight?"

"What?"

She could almost see him frowning, feel how tiresome he thought this was.

"What's happened?"

Klara took a deep breath. She felt stupid and childish. But also annoyed with Cyril. Did he have to ask? Couldn't he just say: "Yes, of course, come."

"I think I've had a break-in."

Cyril said something to someone else in French. Glasses clinked.

"You think you've had a break-in? What? Have you called the police?"

"Never mind," Klara said. "Forget I asked. I'll figure it out myself."

She heard him stifling a sigh.

"No, no, of course you can spend the night at my place. Can you take a taxi there? We're waiting for dessert. Give me an hour and a half, okay?"

Klara closed her eyes.

"I don't even know where you live."

G EORGE SWALLOWED AND LEANED OVER to open the yellow folder. Somehow he already knew what was hidden inside. It was impossible, but he knew it.

And as soon as he saw the Gottlieb law firm's logo on the first page, he knew it was game over. He slowly took the document out of the folder. It was as if the room were vibrating and crackling around him.

What he held in his hand was a copy of a confidentiality agreement between himself and Mikael Persson, partner in the law firm of Gottlieb. There were only two copies. George had locked one of them in a safe-deposit box in Stockholm, and he had watched Persson lock the second one into a safe in his corner office at Norrmalmstorg. He glanced at it briefly through squinting eyes. Actually, he didn't want to see it, didn't want read it, didn't want to take in the fact that he was sitting with that very same agreement in his hand, in a poorly furnished living room in Brussels with a man who looked like Gene Hackman's evil twin. But even if he had no doubts at this point, he still needed to check that it in fact was the right agreement.

It was, of course.

Everything was there. Every watertight paragraph. It was neither long nor detailed, just enough to specify that George and Persson would not disclose anything dealing with their possible relationship to the investment fund Oaktree Mutual. Even divulging the existence of the confidentiality agreement was a breach of contract. Which did seem to make it difficult to invoke it. But George had been in no position to suggest amendments on the day he signed it.

The agreement itself wasn't particularly damning. But it was dizzying, agonizing, that Reiper had had access to it and was even able to make a copy of it. That was, of course, why Reiper had put it at the front of the folder.

George didn't want to continue looking through the folder. He knew what he would find there.

Yet, he couldn't help it.

And just as he'd suspected, there were roughly thirty-five pages of e-mail correspondence and bank statements. Together they proved beyond all reasonable doubt that George had leaked information to Oaktree Mutual about a big merger he was assisting Persson with in exchange for payment.

Oaktree had been one of the investment firms funding the merger. But they'd also, using front organizations, traded shares in both companies. Using the information from George, it'd been impossible for their investments to fail. They were playing high-risk poker with marked cards. George didn't even want to think about how much money they must have made from his information. In comparison to that, they were only paying him a pittance, though it was big money for a freshly minted lawyer with expensive habits.

But George didn't even receive any of the money before Persson started getting suspicious. He was an old fox when it came to high finance and quickly realized Oaktree Mutual was batting for both teams. It wasn't his problem, as long as they weren't using information that came from him. George never did understand how Persson figured it out. There had been at least ten associates and three partners working on that deal at Gottlieb. Maybe Persson had scanned all the e-mail correspondence going to and from people working on the deal. Maybe he'd had a hunch that it was George.

Whatever it was, one day George had been called into Persson's office. Persson was sitting there with a puzzled look on his face. On the desk in front of him was basically the same folder that George was holding in his hands right now.

Persson had drily explained the fact that serious insider trading meant imprisonment for at least six months to four years. And fines on top of that. His legal career would go up in smoke. Not to mention his old man's reaction. He was ruined, and he was only twenty-seven years old.

He'd actually thanked Persson when he told George to resign effective immediately and never breathe a word about the whole incident. Persson claimed that he'd wanted to go to the police. He'd wanted to see George pilloried in the Stockholm District Court. But the damage to Gottlieb would be far too great if it came to light that they were somehow involved with insider trading. A law firm of Gottlieb's caliber couldn't afford to be associated with that sort of thing. Caesar's wife must be above suspicion, Persson had said.

George had signed the necessary papers, received his severance pay, and thanked his lucky stars. Until just a few minutes ago, he'd almost managed to repress the shame and the terrible fear of that day.

"I'm sorry, George, but as I said, I really need your help, and I can't afford to doubt your motivations."

George winced. He hadn't noticed Reiper creeping up behind the sofa he was sitting on.

He turned around.

Reiper didn't look particularly sympathetic. Rather, he seemed to enjoy the fact that the formalities were over.

"How?" George's voice was just a lonely croak.

He was suddenly having a hard time breathing, and he loosened his bright yellow Ralph Lauren tie.

"How the hell did you get a hold of all this information?"

Reiper waved his rough hands dismissively.

"That's not important. We have our methods, as you're probably becoming aware of. But now let's focus on your future role."

He looked at the clock.

"You'll have to excuse me, I've got a rough night ahead of me, so we'll need to hurry this up a bit."

George couldn't manage to do more than nod. His throat was sore, his heart pounding. It felt like his immune system was about to collapse.

"Here," Reiper said and tossed George a USB stick.

"There's a useful program on that little fella. It allows us to see exactly what's happening on any computer on which it's installed. What I want you to do is to take that to the European Parliament and install it on Klara Walldéen's computer and laptop. If possible, be sure to install it on the rest of Madame Boman's computers as well."

"But how?"

It was the only thing George could get out.

"I'm sure you'll figure something out. We have, as you've noticed, pretty impressive resources, but we're never better than our agents on the ground. Now you're our agent in the European Parliament. You have access there whenever you want in your capacity as a lobbyist. You glide through the halls like you own the place. "

This must be what Appleby was referring to during dinner, George thought. He couldn't imagine Merchant & Taylor's senior management sneaking around and breaking into stuff in their youth.

"And here," Reiper said and set a couple of round plastic cylinders down on the table.

They looked like caps from plastic bottles.

"Microphones. Under the desks in both Klara's and Boman's offices. And in their colleagues' rooms if you get the opportunity. It has to be done early tomorrow morning. We're pretty sure her computer is still at her office. And don't worry about the technology. It's a piece a cake."

George closed his eyes and leaned back in the couch.

"Sorry, George, no sleep for you just yet. Josh has a few technical things to show you to prep for tomorrow."

———

George didn't really know how he made it home. Just that he found himself sitting in his Audi outside of his apartment with the engine running sometime after half past twelve that night. He was completely exhausted. He could feel the USB stick in his pocket. Had it not been for the USB, he might have thought the night had all been a bad dream.

MAHMOUD WAS LYING IN THE hard hotel bed, wide awake. He was exhausted, so tired that he couldn't sleep. And his brain was giving him no opportunity to recuperate. He hadn't slept a wink since checking into a budget hotel just a stone's throw from Avenue Anspach in central Brussels, late the night before. He turned his wrist. The green, luminous numbers on his watch showed 4:35.

He'd just put his head back down on the pillow to make a new, futile attempt at falling asleep, when he heard it. The crunching sound of rubber against asphalt, a car rolling forward slowly with its engine off. The crunching stopped outside his window, followed by the sound of doors opening and closing gently, almost silently.

Far too gently. Nobody closes a car door without slamming it unless they have an explicit purpose, Mahmoud thought. He sat up, his full concentration on his hearing. The poorly insulated window let in almost all the sounds from the street, even though he was on the fourth floor. What he heard sounded like boots and whispering, disciplined voices. Gore-Tex and automatic weapons. Memories from another time. An operation was being prepared.

Mahmoud threw on his clothes and cautiously pulled aside

the curtain to peer out at the street, which was illuminated by streetlamps. He half expected to see police cars and roadblocks. But there stood just a single, black delivery van. He could just make out what seemed to be three men dressed in black, jogging around the corner toward the hotel's entrance.

A fourth man was standing by the front bumper of the van, preoccupied by something near the lamppost. He had his back toward the hotel, so Mahmoud couldn't see exactly what he was doing. But suddenly the lamp was extinguished, and the street went completely dark. Something green, like text on an ancient computer screen, gleamed for a second in the place where Mahmoud assumed the man's head must be.

Night vision, thought Mahmoud and drew back the curtains with lightning speed. The man must have killed the lamp in order to keep an eye on Mahmoud's window using night-vision equipment. This was definitely not the police.

When he pressed his ear against the thin door facing the hallway, he thought he heard steps coming up the stairs farther down in the building. Stealthy rubber soles on the stained carpet. But even these pros couldn't hide the fact that the stairs creaked. Mahmoud realized he didn't have much time. He was clenching his teeth so hard that his jaw ached. He'd probably be dead within five minutes. He couldn't sit here and wait for his killers.

He quickly shoved his things into his pack and swung it onto his back before carefully opening the door to the hallway. It was still empty, but he could hear those efficient, stealthy steps closing in. They sounded like they were on the floor beneath him.

The emergency exit was just across the hall from Mahmoud's room. The regular stairs were at the other end of the hallway. He decided to chance it. Ten quick steps on legs shaking with adrenaline. He pushed open the door to the emergency stairs. A puff of air, saturated with concrete and damp, washed over him.

The stairs were empty, quiet, and dark. He assumed whoever was coming after him would leave a guard at the front desk, or even at the door to the stairs, so he decided to climb up. As he began groping his way through the pitch darkness up the next flight of stairs, he sensed steps below him in the hallway. It sounded like several people. He heard them approaching, they couldn't be more than ten yards away.

He climbed up to the next two landings as smoothly as he could, two steps at a time. He swore quietly when he stumbled on the first landing and scraped his knees. It was pitch-black, and he didn't dare turn on the light.

Through the thin walls he could hear someone kicking in what he assumed was his door, somewhere behind and below him. Wood splintering. Muted voices hissing staccato orders. Despite the chill in the stairwell, he could feel sweat on the nape of his neck. He continued upward. Halfway up to the hotel's fifth and top floor, he heard a door open beneath him. A crack of light spread out a couple of floors down and a shadow fell on the stairs. Someone seemed to be standing in the doorway to the emergency stairs.

Mahmoud was at the top of the stairwell. Beneath him was a group of people who seemed determined to kill him. The only way forward was the door to the hallway on the fifth floor. If he opened it the killers would see the light and know that he was in the stairwell. He squatted down and tried not to breathe, not to move. Not to do anything that would reveal his presence.

Mahmoud groped along the wall in search of the door handle. His hands grazed a square, glossy box on the wall. He slowly turned toward it. Opened his eyes as wide as he could to see in the dark. A fire alarm. Inside his own head, he heard a voice from another time:

"If the odds are against you, chaos is your friend."

Chaos. Mahmoud fumbled in his pocket and snatched his hotel room key. Chaos. He stood up as quietly as he could. Took a deep breath. He raised his arm, key in hand, and slammed it as hard as he could against the glass of the fire alarm.

The stairwell exploded with a deafening, old-fashioned fire alarm. The volume shocked him, and he plugged his ears.

It took a few seconds. Then the figure beneath him started to move forward, upward. The lights came on, and the whole staircase was bathed in fluorescent light. Several pairs of feet rapidly started moving up the stairs. They're coming after me, thought Mahmoud. It's over now. It's really over now. The alarm sang around him, inside him. Threatening to drive him crazy.

He pressed down on the handle to the hallway door, pushed it open, and hurled himself onto the fifth floor.

"He's up there! Let's go!" he heard a deep voice say somewhere beneath him.

Mahmoud staggered out into the hallway. Looked around desperately. At the far end of the corridor he saw a stairway that continued up. He had no idea where it led, but he ran toward it. When he reached it, he saw that it consisted of just a couple of steps leading to a padlocked door. Beside the door hung a large fire extinguisher. Mahmoud picked up the fire extinguisher and threw it with all his might against the padlock. He missed badly and dropped the extinguisher on the floor. He lifted it up again with trembling hands.

On the second attempt, he hit the padlock, and it flew off in a gratifying arc. The padlock fell and bounced off the carpet. Mahmoud depressed the handle of the door as he heard his pursuers coming through the door to the hallway behind him. When the door swung open, the icy cold hit him so hard it almost took his breath away.

Ahead of him lay a poorly maintained roof, half the size of a tennis court. He was in the corner of the hotel building, seven stories above the street. The two sides of the terrace that overlooked the street were fenced in by broken and rusty chicken wire. Below him he heard the distant sound of sirens. The firefighters were already on their way. He was getting his chaos.

Behind him, next to the door he'd just exited, there were a couple pieces of rebar fastened to the building. Like a makeshift ladder. He didn't have much choice. All he could do was to continue going upward. Somehow he managed to climb and crawl up the hotel's sloping roof. The roof tiles seemed to move beneath him. There was no time to think about how high in the air he was.

He thanked God the roof didn't slope more than it did. With his arms on one side of the roof ridge, and his body on the other, he started sliding in one direction. He had no idea where he was going. But a few meters farther along the roof, he discerned a square, black metal hatch that seemed to be open by a small gap. Maybe it was the outlet of a ventilation shaft or the door to an attic. Mahmoud started moving toward it. On the terrace, just below him, he heard his pursuers step out onto the roof.

"So, what's the status? The fire department is here. What a fucking circus." Mahmoud heard one of the men say in English.

Another man seemed to be running to the other side of the terrace. It sounded like he was shaking and bending the chicken wire.

"There's no one here. Unless he jumped," the man informed his colleagues after a few seconds.

"He must have gone up."

Mahmoud heard someone starting to climb the rungs he'd just come up. At that very moment he reached the hatch.

If he could just get it open, maybe he'd be able to climb in and hide there. Gently, he bent down, swaying in the increasingly cold wind. His hands were stiff, and the enamel was slippery. Adrenaline. His heart was pounding a hole in his chest.

On his third attempt, he was able to reach around the edges and start rocking the hatch to see if it could be opened. Just as he felt it giving way, he heard someone swing over the same roof's edge.

"Locked on target!" a calm voice said.

K LARA WOKE UP TO HER phone beeping. She rubbed her eyes
and stretched out her hand to read the message. Eva-Karin.

8:30 OFFICE OK? Her customary brevity. The keyboard was
too small for Eva-Karin's fingers. Something she refused to acknowledge, of course.

Klara ran her hands over her face, trying to wipe away the sleep.
The phone showed it was just after seven. She vaguely remembered
that Cyril had already tried to wake her up. That she'd fended off
his attempts and fallen back asleep. He'd taken an early train back
to Paris. Something about meetings, his constituency, whatever.

Eva-Karin probably wanted to give instructions for the rest of
the week. Her plane back to Sweden was leaving before lunch. But,
of course, she wanted to stop by Parliament and check her name
off on the compensation list as well. Parliamentarians received per
diem for every day they worked in Brussels. Many of them took an
early flight on Friday, rather than the night before, to get an extra
day's compensation.

As if they weren't already being paid enough, thought Klara.
Greedy bastards.

OK she replied and sat up in bed.

She looked around. The bedroom was bright and clean. No clothes thrown on the floor. A translucent, rounded plastic chair from Kartell sat in one corner. A wall of closets. A signed and numbered abstract print in red and blue hung on the wall next to the door. Windows facing the street, covered by heavy, white curtains lent the room a comfortable darkness. Neutral, European upper-middle class. A tasteful, unexceptionable pied-à-terre.

Klara didn't know how long she'd stood outside the tapas restaurant last night. Long enough to feel confident that Ponytail wasn't coming back. Finally, she'd gathered her courage, and walked back to her front door with determination. Her senses on edge, she'd crept up the creaking stairs and stopped in front of her own, thin door on the top floor. She'd taken a deep breath, turned the key in the lock, and thrown the door wide open.

The apartment had been dark and quiet. Her heart pounded as she'd stepped over the threshold and turned on the light in the living room. She didn't know what she'd expected. That the apartment would have been ransacked? Ripped sofas and a battered TV? But everything was as usual. The pillows on the sofa arranged just like they usually were. The newest issue of the *New Yorker* lying open to a review of John le Carré's latest book, just as she'd left it that morning, before she and Cyril had come back here. She'd climbed the stairs to her attic room. The sheets were in disarray. Her pink Agent Provocateur panties tangled at the foot of the bed, just where they had landed when Cyril tore them off of her eight hours ago. Everything had been exactly as it usually was, just as it should be.

Maybe she'd just imagined the whole thing? Maybe she'd heard sounds coming from somewhere else? The girl who came out of the gate might have been a neighbor she didn't recognize?

Klara sat on the toilet in Cyril's clinically clean bathroom, rubbing her temples with her fingertips. A slight headache had set in as soon as she'd gotten out of bed. If she didn't take some type of pill soon, she'd have to deal with it when it arrived in full force. She got up and opened Cyril's mirrored bathroom cabinet.

On the top shelf stood a pack of Panodil. Klara took out a sheet of them, pushed out two tablets, and washed them down with tap water. She was about to shut the cabinet door when she saw something that made her flinch. Two toothbrushes.

One blue.

And one pink.

Against her will, she picked up the pink one and held it up to the light. It looked used. As she was putting it back, she discovered one more toothbrush. A smaller one, also pink, with Snow White on its handle.

Her anxiety increasing, Klara went out to the combined kitchen and living room. A white Miele kitchen behind the island. Floor-to-ceiling windows looking out over the bare trees of Square Ambiorix. A white, expensive divan sofa in the living room area, a TV mounted on the wall. A dining table in oak with six Kartell chairs identical to the one in the bedroom. A few prints, belonging to the same series as the one in the bedroom. Everything clinically clean and completely impersonal. A tasteful hotel room. Cyril's words from yesterday echoed in Klara's head. "Expats always have pictures of their family on display."

Klara went back into the bedroom. She stood in front of the bed. Two nightstands, one on either side. Two designer reading lamps with cylindrical screens in white enameled metal. She walked around to the table on the side where Cyril had slept. His pillow still bore the imprint of his head. His scent was still there when she leaned over it. She closed her eyes and slowly pulled out the nightstand's only drawer. She took a deep breath and opened her eyes.

There lay a single upside-down frame. She suddenly felt heavy. As if her legs no longer had the strength to hold her up. Carefully, she sat down on the bed and turned over the picture.

MAHMOUD TURNED IN THE DIRECTION where the voice was coming from. All he could see was the upper body of a man dressed in black wearing a ski mask with holes for the eyes and mouth. The man was holding a small, compact automatic weapon against his shoulder. He looked competent. As if sitting on a roof aiming his gun at people was what he was born to do.

It was over. It was almost a relief in a way. Mahmoud straightened up carefully. He was standing with his heels on the back of the hatch, leaning back unsteadily against the sloping brick roof. Above the rooftops, he could see the lights of the city glowing in the morning darkness. He closed his eyes.

"Hold your fire," said a deeper voice from down on the terrace. "The risk is too high. We need him alive."

Mahmoud heard the voices as if he was on the other side of a thick wall. Just a monotonous rumble. He didn't dare to open his eyes.

"Control says abort! Repeat: the orders are abort and return."

It was the deep voice down on the terrace again.

"We have to get out before the fire department comes up here. There should be a fire escape in room five-oh-four. We have to get out of here. It's more important than the objective right now. Let's go!"

Mahmoud glanced cautiously up at the man taking aim at him. He wasn't far away. Ten yards. The man slowly lowered his weapon without releasing Mahmoud from his gaze.

"You're a dead man walking," the man said.

Then he disappeared behind the gable again.

———

According to Mahmoud's watch it was almost eight when he heard, through the hatch on the roof, people moving on the same terrace he'd come from. The fire department and the police must still be searching the hotel. Somehow, he'd made it through the hatch into the attic of the hotel. And he'd been sitting there for hours on uncovered thermal insulation without moving. Waiting patiently for everyone to leave.

But now his stress was being replaced by restlessness. He had to get away. He had to take control of this situation in some way.

———

It took Mahmoud fifteen minutes of crawling over the attic's unfinished wooden floor before he found a hatch. With a quick, creaking pull he managed to open the hatch and jump down into the hallway he'd run through in terror several hours before. A fire escape in room 504, they'd said. The room was at the end of the hallway. He touched the door with a sweaty palm, and it swung open. It looked like the Americans had completely pulverized the lock. The room was empty and similar to the one he'd been staying in until this morning; the only difference was that the single window looked out over the building on the shorter side of the hotel. There couldn't be more than a few feet between the buildings. Mahmoud went over to the window and cautiously peered out through the curtain. There was indeed a rusty fire escape to the left.

Mahmoud gently opened the window overlooking the alley and peeked down toward the ground. To his horror, he saw a man dressed in black crouched and leaning against the building at one end of the alley. He was wearing a knit cap, and at his feet lay a black nylon bag. The Americans were still here.

Mahmoud closed the window again. The man hadn't seen him. He seemed to have been busy reading something on his phone.

Fuck.

Mahmoud left the room and crossed the hall to the emergency stairs. He held his breath and pushed open the door. But no one seemed to be guarding it.

Carefully and quickly he made his way down to the ground floor. There were two doors. One seemed to lead to the front desk. Mahmoud didn't dare touch it. The lobby was definitely under surveillance.

Instead he tried the other door, which also turned out to be unlocked. Bingo. A staircase leading down into damp darkness. Mahmoud flicked a light switch that flooded the concrete stairs and everything around them with fluorescent light. The stairs led to a corridor between two rows of doors. It appeared to be a basement lined with a bunch of storage rooms. Mahmoud tried the first door. Locked. The second was as well.

But then he looked up. At the far end of the corridor there was a dirty window that had to be at street level. Mahmoud ran down the hallway. He tried the latches next to the window. There was no lock and the window swung inward and upward. Mahmoud lifted it up and stood on tiptoe so he could see out.

An alley. Some trash cans. No black-clad Americans, at least as far as he could see. Maybe this was his only chance. He put one foot on the hinge of the door closest to the window, grabbed the windowsill, and pulled himself up. The window frame was just big enough for him to fit his head and shoulders through. First he pushed his backpack through, then he climbed up in order to squeeze through. It was easier than he expected, and he suddenly found himself lying flat in the alley.

He glanced in both directions. So far, no one seemed to have seen him. He got up and ran for the protection of the trash cans.

He squatted down, breathing heavily, and tried to get an overview of the situation. His escape didn't seem to have attracted any attention. He brushed off the dust from the attic and the dirt from the street, stood up, and started walking calmly toward the entrance to the alley. When he reached the street, he stopped. He cautiously peeked around the corner to the hotel entrance. The street was completely empty. The Americans were lying low. But if they were guarding the fire escape, they must certainly be guarding the entrance. Whether or not he could see them. He knew he wasn't more than a block from Avenue Anspach, and on the other side of that was the tourist district. If he managed to get there, he could disappear into the mass of shoppers and tourists. His survival depended on a five-minute race.

He tugged his backpack into place, fastened the buckles, and tried to calm down. All his senses were stretched to the breaking point. He took three deep breaths, and then he ran as fast as he could out into the street, to the right, and away from the entrance. After fifty meters he turned left toward Avenue Anspach.

He heard voices far behind him. Profanity in English. Running footsteps. Orders. Mahmoud ran faster than he had in his entire life. He reached Avenue Anspach without turning around. He sensed more than saw the cars slowing down around him as he crossed the street. Honking and curses filled the air. He didn't dare turn around, just ran, ran, ran. Away from the hotel, straight ahead, away from Avenue Anspach. After a few minutes of sprinting across cobblestones, he found himself on the short side of the glittering Grand Place, the Flemish heart of Brussels. He stopped, back pressed against one of the facades.

The Christmas market was about to open, and the rising wind carried the scent of mulled wine and Christmas cookies. A giant Christmas tree stood in front of the city hall. Its red and silver ornaments rattled faintly in the frosty breeze. Exhausted and with the adrenaline still pumping through his veins, Mahmoud looked over his shoulder. It seemed as though he had shaken his pursuers.

A few icy snowflakes hit his cheek, and he leaned his head back, closed his eyes, and breathed deeply. He'd survived. He opened his eyes and let his gaze wander over the Flemish facades with their almost comical extravagance of gold leaf ornamentation. For how much longer?

Spring 1991

Kurdistan

I T'S SO BEAUTIFUL. THE ROLLING hills have the dull luster of
raw silk in the afternoon sun. A haze hangs over their crests. A
sky so high and blue it's nearly white. I'm silently singing a song I
don't know the name of, by a band that might be called Dire Straits.
I don't know anything about music. I'm no more interested in music
than I am in fiction. But there's something about that line about the
mist-covered mountains. Something about the warm, comforting
tone of the electric guitar.

There are no smells here. This landscape is completely void of
scent. Just diesel from the Land Cruiser's leaky engine. Sweet,
black tea when we stop to eat. The food is simple: bread, yoghurt,
nuts, sometimes lamb. The food of peasants and soldiers. War
rations, even though we see tomatoes, figs, pomegranates at the
stands along the road. So far the war's been easy on them. Maybe
they're preparing themselves for what's to come?

My body aches, acutely aware of every hollow, rut, rock that the
car's shocks can't handle. How many miles have we been traveling
in this car? How many miles have I been traveling in these kinds
of vehicles, on these kinds of roads, donkey trails, tractor tracks?

It's a different time. We make increasingly shortsighted alliances out here now. In the field. The real field, not the metaphorical one. We build confidences one cup of tea at a time, only to forsake our promises before the taste of tea even leaves our mouths. We don't live in disguises anymore. Not in the same way. The parameters have changed. This is no longer a zero sum game. The goal is no longer not to lose. Who even thought it was possible to win until the incomprehensible day they climbed over the wall? At the same time, nothing has changed for me. It's still all about survival.

"I'm so fucking sick of this shitty ass car," says my colleague to no one in particular, but I'm the only one besides the interpreter who speaks English.

It's his way of setting the tone. His way of creating a surface that he can stand steadily on. It's not new to me. I know his type.

"What did you say?" I say.

Although I heard what he said. I glance in his direction. He's sitting next to me in the backseat, slumped over the cracked seat in a position that, if he doesn't change it, will guarantee him back problems by tonight. The bare crown of his head, his incipient balding. The thick, poorly healed scar running like barbed wire from his hairline down his yellowish left cheek. The scar pulls his face tight, making his rare smiles asymmetrical and impossible to interpret.

Actually I don't know anything about him, other than that he drank Jim Beam until the bottle he'd brought with him ran out yesterday and then moved on to something resembling turpentine, which he expertly procured on the outskirts of a market in Mosul. He misses college football, he says.

I no longer drink anything stronger than black tea. I miss the monotony of swimming. Miss laps in the pool, the smell of chlorine, the sound of the tiles. Miss muscles tight and aching from exertion.

"I said I'm fucking sick of this shitty ass car. We're pouring a hell of a lot of money into this war, but we can't get any real cars on the ground. Typical fucking Pentagon bullshit. Right?"

I shrug. I'm not interested in the whining and bullshitting typical of his kind. We haven't discussed it, but it's obvious he's ex-military. He lacks the deadly, quicksilver intelligence of a Navy SEAL, so he's probably Special Forces. His intelligence is blunt, focused, ruthless. He doesn't know anything about the Middle East, about the importance of drinking tea, about anything other than the shortest distance between two points. A man made for squares and straight lines, not for the inconsistency, frustration, and patience of the twilight zone.

In the old world—the one that ended less than a year ago, that we already barely remember—his type came in after me, acted on the information I gathered. In the old world, we worked in different shifts. Now we're working side by side.

"The interpreter says it'll take another half hour," I say.

I lean back, close my eyes. Let the monotonous sounds, the uneven road, the almost imperceptible irritation rock me into hollow sleep.

═══

It's nearly dark when we roll into the village. All the villages look the same. Gray, full of stones, gravel, laundry, goats. In the dusk it could have been the one we came from, the one we're going to tomorrow. Some children running alongside the car shout something that I can't hear or understand. We are the traveling salesmen of promises and weapons, and we're greeted like heroes in every corner of this temporary country. Hopes are high, and we're doing nothing to dampen them. Our job is to enthuse.

"Is this the place?" I ask the driver in Arabic.

He nods and slows down at what might generously be described as a dusty little square. Dirty men in ankle-length kaftans and head scarves, carrying a motley mix of weapons, stand in a small group outside one of the little stone houses. They shoo away the children.

My colleague is asleep, so I give his shoulder a hard shake. He wakes up immediately, as if he never slumbered.

"We're here," I say.

"What a fucking dump," he says.

We jump out of the car and are greeted by the men. We exchange pleasantries. My colleague smiles ironically when he bows but pronounces the greeting phrases perfectly. He has an ear for languages, but not the patience to learn anything other than English. The shadows would have devoured him in a second. He's uninterested in nuance.

Inside the house, which isn't much more than a shack with a dirt floor and an open flame, we drink our thousandth cup of tea, and I lie about my country's intentions. My colleague is uninterested in all this; he wants to move on to the next part. He asks for something stronger than tea, and our hosts pull out a bottle of a brand of whiskey I've never seen before. They are intoxicated by victory. Their eyes radiate immortality. Right now, at this very moment, they've achieved what they've been fighting a thousand years for. They control the borders of their own fictional country. They took Mosul a few days ago and can't stop talking about heroism, historical relevance. I congratulate them again and again and explain how impressed we are by their courage. I promise weapons. Air support.

"Air support?" they say as they always do, the Kurdish word apparently isn't clear enough.

"We'll bomb the shit out of Saddam if he comes up here," says my colleague, tired of me always saying the same thing. "Translate that," he says, nodding to the interpreter, who obeys.

Our hosts laugh, pound each other on the back, pour another glass of that dubious whiskey.

By the end they're happy with my promises. They want to touch American power for themselves, so we take them to the Land Cruiser.

My colleague unloads the three boxes and opens the first in the headlights.

"Mortar," he says. "Three of them. These brutes will blow away any tank you want."

The farmers who are now partisans, soldiers, freedom fighters, legends bend forward reverently and pick up the weapons. Pass them around.

"We'll teach you how to use them later," he says.

"Not necessary," say the freedom fighters, the legends. "We can handle weapons."

My colleague firmly takes back the mortar and puts it in the box with the others.

"We'll teach you how to use them later," he says.

"Can we see the ammunition?" say the soldiers.

My colleague opens the second box and shows them the shells. Twenty shells, barely enough for tomorrow's training.

"Is that all?" say the partisans.

"That's all we have today," I say. "But as I said, we will deliver more within the week."

They mutter.

"But if the Iraqis get here before you do?"

"Then we'll bomb the shit out of them," says my colleague and turns to the interpreter. "Translate that."

The farmers laugh, shake their heads.

There's more ammunition for their Russian weapons in the last box. They're disappointed. They were hoping for more. The glow in their eyes burns less intensely. But it burns.

———

The farmers, partisans whisper among themselves. Weapons training is settled. The late dinner is eaten. The tea is replaced by bottles like my colleague's. They're excited and eager. I see my colleague's movements slowing down, his face relaxing. He's been drinking constantly, consistently since we arrived.

The interpreter shrugs.

"They want to show you something, it seems. But I don't know what. "

In the end they all agree, they take us by the hand. Intoxicated. Their disappointment over the mortars was apparently temporary. They've become soldiers, freedom fighters, temporary legends again. They lead us out through the village. Over moonlit gravel and stone, through darkness and silver. To yet another collection of small, low houses, stinking of goats. Maybe the buildings are storage or barns. In front of one of them stands a bearded legend, a partisan. A Russian machine gun hangs from his shoulder. A barely burning cigarette sits in the corner of his mouth.

He drops the cigarette on the gravel, stomps it out, and opens the warped wooden door to let us in. The lights from the men's flashlights hop and shake in the darkness, making it hard to focus. The stench is unbearable. Animals and something else, something more acrid. Finally the flashlights focus on a pair of sacks in the far back corner, as far away from the door as you can get. Three of the men go over to the bags and kick at them, scream at them, tear at them.

The sacks move, moan, shrink. The men lift them up. Two boys, barely eighteen, with smashed-in faces, wearing torn, baggy uniforms. Two terrified Iraqi boys.

The legends laugh and spit on the boys. Swear at them in Arabic. The interpreter turns to us, shrugs.

"They say that the prisoners are refusing to talk. That they claim they're just infantry soldiers."

I shake my head.

"That's because they're just infantry soldiers. What do they want them to say?"

From the corner of my eye I see my colleague disappear out the door.

I catch up with him at the Toyota. He's fiddling with something. The hood is up. There are jumper cables hanging around his neck.

"What the hell are you doing?" I say.

He doesn't answer. Reaches into the engine with both hands, grabs hold of the battery, and lifts it straight up and out. Sets it down in the gravel.

"Help me out here," he slurs.

"Why?"

Even though I know.

"Don't be an idiot," he says.

He looks me in the eye. A new radiance. A flash of naked sadism. The metallic sound of the jumper cables when he smacks them together.

"Some of this straight to the cock will loosen our Iraqi friends' tongues."

"How fucking drunk are you?" I say. "They're just a couple of infantry boys who got left behind in the retreat from Mosul."

"If you don't wanna help me you can wait in the car," he says and bends down to grab the battery.

My control seeps out of me like leaking oil. I see his eyes dance. There's nothing to say. No argument that will work.

I loosen the Glock in my belt. Feel its weight in my hand. Wailing coming from the stables. Loud voices. Blows. Where the hell is the interpreter? The driver?

"I'll give you one last chance to put that goddamn battery back in the car," I say.

He turns his head in my direction. Shakes it. Spits on the ground in front of me.

"Well, well you're quite the little, fucking cunt, aren't you," he says. "Just like your little whore in Damascus."

I hit him in the nose with the barrel of the gun. Hear the crunch of bone and cartilage. See the blood pour out onto the gravel. I'm straddling his chest before he even has time to put his hands over his face.

"What the hell did you say?" I say. "What the fuck do you know about Damascus?"

My mouth tastes like metal and endorphins. There's no turning back from this. I press the barrel of the Glock to his eye, forcing the back of his head into the silvery, bloody earth.

"You got your little whore killed," he hisses. "Got her blown to smithereens . . ."

"Shut up!" I bellow, pressing the gun even harder against his eye. Then someone lifts me straight up and back. Hands grab hold of mine. The Glock is ripped out of my hands. I see the farmers bending over my colleague, see them lift him up. Keep him upright, away from me. He spits blood into the gravel, sniffling and shaking his head. Hisses.

"It should have been you. You know that don't you, faggot. "

—————

We leave the village early the next morning. It's raining. Drizzling. Behind us we're leaving three mortars, twenty grenades that won't crack armor, a few rounds for their Kalashnikovs, and two abused Iraqis. We're leaving our memories behind too. The blood on the gravel. What was said and what wasn't said. There is never any alternative except to keep going forward.

I turn around. My colleague is already asleep in the backseat. An improvised bandage and the stench of a hangover are the only reminders of yesterday. My thoughts are still racing. I think about the rumors and gossip. What the Iraqi on the ferry in Stockholm didn't want to tell me. What I didn't want him to tell me.

I think about the wide eyes of the baby, about how I abandoned her. About how nothing will ever fix that. I think about the rooftops in Beirut. The heat and the resistance of the trigger. I think of all the things we have to trust in when trying to keep the world from ending. The shifting alliances. I think about the plans for destruction that I gave the Iraqi that frigid evening, the Christmas decorations reflecting in the water, in his glasses. All part of an arrangement that has now been inverted.

I think of the farmers we just left behind who will be executed as soon as Saddam turns north. I think we never do what we say. We never keep our promises. We always end up sacrificing the ones we set out to rescue.

HOW THE HELL HAD THEY found him again? That was the question that kept running through Mahmoud's mind since, still shaky, he'd fled into the subway after the chaos of the morning. How the hell was it possible? Were they following him yesterday? To the African Museum and then to the hotel. If they had been following him, they must have been invisible. He'd chosen the hotel completely at random. His picture was not in the Belgian media as far as he knew. He'd stayed away from the Internet, hadn't used his phone. It didn't make sense.

Mahmoud bought a Coke and a pan pizza from a hole-in-the-wall at the Gare Centrale. The pizza was hard as a brick and seemingly stuffed with glue and gravel. He continued down onto one of the platforms. It was constantly present: the stress and paranoia. As if he were on a stage. As if everyone were looking at him, inspecting him, waiting for the right moment to strike.

He couldn't go on like this anymore. He had no direction, no goal except to hide. He was completely passive, reactive rather than active.

As things stood now, it was hard to imagine how he could take less initiative. Something had to change. He sat down on a bench and waited for the next train, jiggling his legs nervously. Beside him, he heard a man in a suit swearing in English about having no cell coverage.

Mahmoud froze. He couldn't believe he hadn't thought of it before.

Filled with new energy, he shoved the remains of his sad meal into the nearest trash can and hurried up the stairs and back through the urine-stinking tunnel he'd just come through. He followed the rusty signs to the toilets in the basement of the central station.

He paid thirty cents to the forbidding woman at the door. The two coins clinked against the worn porcelain dish on her picnic table. The stalls were empty and surprisingly clean. He chose the first one, locked the door behind him, and lowered the toilet lid. Wriggled his backpack off. He emptied out its contents onto the toilet lid. Passport, wallet, mobile phones and batteries, The PowerPoint presentation and the program from the lecture. Underwear and socks. A shirt and a T-shirt. A Pocket Edition of *Torture Team* by Philippe Sands that he'd been reading when he fell asleep on the plane. And also Lindman's wallet. He went through it quickly. An American Express, one VISA. Not even a gold card. Two hundred euros in bills of twenty. A driver's license and a receipt for a storage locker in Paris. Mahmoud stopped. Picked up the receipt again, turned it around. Lindman mentioned that he'd hidden something in Paris. Was there any better place than a storage locker? Maybe it was worth a try. He slipped the receipt into his own wallet and continued rummaging through the contents of his backpack without knowing exactly what he was looking for. Whatever it was, it didn't seem to be among his things. He felt the pockets of his backpack and the pockets of his clothes. Nothing. Finally he turned the nylon backpack inside out.

And there, at the bottom left corner, something was held in place by black tape. He tore off the tape excitedly and held the object up in the cold fluorescent light. It looked like a high-tech matchbox, completely encased in hard plastic. A GPS transmitter. That was how they'd managed to follow him, how they'd found him at the hotel.

And even worse: that was how they'd found Lindman. He sat on the floor of the bathroom, the transmitter still in his hand. He'd led the Americans, or whoever they were, right to Lindman. It didn't matter how many evasive maneuvers he'd made. The thought made him sick. Lindman's death was his mistake, his fault. How could he have been so naive? But he hadn't been taking it completely seriously. Even though he'd seen indications that he was being followed, he hadn't totally believed it. But he couldn't allow himself to be overcome by remorse and anxiety now. Maybe the time would come for that. But that time was certainly not now.

With effort he got up and gathered his things. He threw both of the phones and batteries into the small bin next to the toilet. For a moment he considered throwing the transmitter in there too, but he changed his mind and put it into his pocket. The rest of the things—the book and underwear, passports and wallets—he shoved back into the knapsack.

On his way through the train station, he wondered how they'd managed to get the transmitter into his bag. He hadn't checked it on the plane, and he'd never let it out of his sight. Except when he'd dropped it at the station at the airport. The hot girl with the blond ponytail and blue eyes. Could it be possible? Why not? Why would a good-looking girl be a more unlikely culprit than anyone else? He shook his head. What a careless idiot he'd been.

Mahmoud followed the signs to a bus stop and jumped quickly

through the doors of the first one to come by. He sat down on an empty seat next to the rear doors. Using his left hand, he stuck the GPS transmitter under the seat. The tape still held. When he was sure it was secure, he jumped off the bus before the doors could close. He had no idea where the bus was going, but at least it would keep his pursuers occupied for a while. And as for him, it was time he started taking the initiative.

N O ONE COULD ENTER THE European Parliament without a specific invitation or without a special card, a *badge* in Brussels lingo. All EU officials had badges, as did some lobbyists who had special, permanent cards. George's lobbyist badge allowed him access to Parliament on weekdays between 8:00 A.M. and 6:00 P.M.

At two minutes to eight, George was standing in line for a mandatory security screening, waiting for his briefcase to be x-rayed. He was pale. Covered in a cold sweat. He had dark circles under his eyes that made him look like he'd been on the losing side of a boxing match. Which was how he felt too. He hadn't slept a wink since coming home from Reiper's last night. He lay in bed, wide-awake, turning the situation over and over again in his mind, without finding a way out. Refusing to do what Reiper wanted would mean his life was over. Prison. Definitely fired from Merchant & Taylor.

That wasn't an option.

On the other hand, if he did what Reiper asked he'd be an accomplice to more crimes. Reiper would have even more of a hold on him. That certainly wasn't an appealing thought. Where would this end? He had to face the facts: Digital Solutions, whoever they really were, owned him.

At five-thirty he finally gave up, got out of bed, showered, and dressed. It seemed like the only chance he'd get to execute this assignment would be if he broke into Klara's office before she arrived. Josh had given him some kind of electrical universal lock pick that would apparently open the office doors of the Parliament swiftly without destroying the lock.

"You can't go wrong, buddy. It's a piece of cake," he said, forcing a high five and flashing that chalk white jock's smile of his, which was as encouraging as it was derisive.

Of course, like all boys, George had fantasized about being a spy when he was little. He'd daydreamed about breaking into locked offices, gaining access to secret information, all while charming gorgeous girls. Secret handovers in dark parks. Shadowing and being shadowed. But this just seemed sickening. He felt like a common thief. Besides, he was completely terrified. What would he do if Klara were there? If she caught him inside her office? Or worse, what would Reiper do if he found out George had failed to carry out the mission?

It was rare for an assistant to be at work before eight-thirty. Meetings and phone calls at the Parliament usually didn't get going until after nine. If he could be out of Klara's office before 8:20, he should be safe. He hoped. The armpits of his shirt were stained with semicircles of sweat. Gross.

Before leaving home, he'd carefully studied the map on the European Parliament Web site to find the exact location of Klara's and Boman's offices. He knew from experience that each office had an entrance from the outside hallway, and a door that connected it to the adjacent office.

He grabbed his thin briefcase off the conveyor belt and started walking toward the elevators that led up to the Swedish Social

Democratic delegation's small domain, at the end of a corridor on the sixteenth floor.

The corridor was deserted, just as George had hoped it would be. His muffled footsteps on the light blue carpet were the only sound. Klara's and Boman's offices were located at the very end of the corridor. Anxiously looking around, he put his hand into his pocket and took out the electrical device Josh had given him. It looked like a small electric razor. He attached a long, thin piece of metal to one end of the device and quickly pushed the power button. It started buzzing, just as Josh had shown him last night. He released the button and the device went silent.

His hands were shaking. His shirt was stuck to his back. He cast another glance over his shoulder and took a small plastic bag of cocaine out of his pocket. Just one tiny line. Just to keep it together.

Sure, it was pretty disgusting to get high in the morning, but this was an emergency. Not exactly part of the plan. If it weren't for Reiper and this shitstorm, he'd never do a line in the morning. Never. Not a chance. But under these circumstances? No doubt about it, this was an exception. He shook a small pile of pure white powder onto his platinum American Express card. He didn't bother shaping it into a line, just plugged his left nostril and sucked up the whole mound in one go. He felt his synapses respond immediately. His body came to life. He could see more clearly. Became focused, controlled. He closed his eyes and shook his head before wiping his nostril clean with his thumb and forefinger. Maybe there was a way to fix this after all.

George checked his watch. 8:07 A.M. According to his calculations, he had thirteen minutes left. Better hurry up. He removed an oblong piece of metal with a small hook on one end from his briefcase. Without hesitating, he put it into the lock on Klara's door to hold part of the bolt in place and then inserted the thin blade of the electrical picklock beside it. He pressed the power button again and started moving the picklock over the pins in the lock.

It didn't take even twenty seconds for him to pick his first lock. His heart was pounding in his chest. Holding his breath, he pushed down on the handle and opened the door to Klara's office. He stepped in and locked the door behind him. If someone showed up, he'd have time to sneak into Boman's office through the connecting door. Klara's office looked just like any other assistant's office in Parliament. George had seen his fair share during his years in Brussels. This one was somewhat better because it was situated high up and in the corner. The view was amazing. But he really didn't have time to admire it right now.

Klara's thin, aluminum-colored laptop was sitting on the desk. Bingo. It was in standby mode. He lifted the screen to wake it up. Ten minutes left. As soon as the computer woke up, George inserted the USB stick into the port and clicked on the icon that popped up on the screen. He dragged the application onto the desktop. The program took care of the rest on its own. Josh had shown him what to do probably ten times last night. It would take about a minute. While he was waiting, he attached a small plastic capsule on the far underside of Klara's desk. It had some type of adhesive on top and stuck easily. He repeated the maneuver in Boman's office and went back into Klara's to see if the program had finished loading.

Just as he was sitting down in front of Klara's computer to remove the thumb drive, he heard a key being put into the lock. How the hell was that possible? Assistants never came in this early. He tore the stick out of the dock. Slammed the screen shut to put it into standby mode again. In one long stride he was back inside Boman's office. As he was closing the door, he saw the door to Klara's office open and smelled a faint odor of perfume. Why hadn't he heard her coming down the hall? Wall-to-wall carpets, of course. His legs were shaking. He could hear Klara moving around in the other room through the thin wall. Her cell phone rang.

"Hello, Eva-Karin," he heard her say. "Yes, I'm here now. Sure, I can print them out. Okay, I'll see you in a few minutes."

Fuck, Boman was on her way. George knew he should sneak silently over to the door to the hallway, but he couldn't bring himself to do it. He stood rooted to the wall, trying to regain control over his body. Finally he mustered the courage and glided slowly across the floor to the door. Gently, gently, he turned the lock. It clicked when it opened. George thought it sounded like a gunshot. But he had no time to lose. Thank God everything here was new, and none of the doors creaked. He pushed the door open just enough to slip out. There was no way to lock it behind him. Hopefully they'd think that the cleaners forgot it last night. He jogged to the end of the corridor, expecting the whole time to hear Klara's door opening behind him. But nothing happened. Finally he reached the elevators and pushed the button frantically. The elevator on the end dinged and the doors opened. In his eagerness to get in, he ran straight into Eva-Karin Boman.

"Sorry, I'm so sorry," he muttered, averting his face. Eva-Karin didn't seem to notice him at all.

Three minutes later George was sitting on the steps outside the main entrance with his head between his knees, trying to breathe normally again. What am I doing? he thought. What the hell am I doing? His left hand dug into his pocket for the bag of cocaine. If he didn't deserve a line after this morning, what did he have to do to deserve one?

December 20, 2013

Stockholm, Sweden

GABRIELLA SEICHELMAN HURRIED ACROSS THE reception hall of the Stockholm Administrative Law building on Tegel-suddgatan. Her eyes sought the screens indicating what room her hearing would be in. There was still twenty-five minutes left until it began, and she'd been prepping her client, Joseph Mbila, until six o'clock yesterday evening. It should be fine.

But this wasn't how things usually went before she appeared in court. She always made sure she had at least a half hour by herself in an available meeting room with a cup of tea and her papers. That was her routine, her lucky charm. She usually knew the case more or less by heart by the time of the actual hearing. But that half hour was her way of focusing. Her way of tuning everything else out, of staying sharp. Not having that whole half hour . . . that wasn't how it was supposed to be.

Gabriella was a master at tuning out the world. She knew that of all the workaholics at the prestigious law firm of Lind-blad and Wiman, she was the one who worked the hardest. No one was more devoted to her clients. No one stayed up later. No one got up earlier. There had been a lot of envious looks when she became a member of the Swedish Bar Association before any of her older colleagues. She was on the fast track leading straight up.

And she had begun to hate it. Slowly, at first almost imperceptibly, she'd started to become the kind of girl she and Klara used to despise in law school. A careerist. A climber with no interests beyond her job. How long ago had it been since she'd taken a vacation? How long since she stayed out all night partying? How long since she'd made out with someone? How long since she'd felt anything except the nagging anxiety that she wasn't reading enough, not arguing clearly enough, not putting enough hours into rescuing her client? How long since she'd listened to one of the albums that used to mean everything to her, but were now accumulating dust in the back of her closet, under the piles of papers that just kept growing?

She had been feeling it more and more lately. The walls were closing in around her. The emptiness, the thoughts hidden behind thick walls of work. The unfathomable futility of it all.

She was scared witless by it, which sent her diving headlong into the next goal, the next client, the next eighty-hour workweek. She persuaded herself that it was necessary. That her clients needed her. That once she became a partner in the firm, everything would calm down.

———

A red poinsettia and a white electric candlestick were placed inside the receptionist's glass cage. Tuesday was Christmas Eve. My God, the only memories Gabriella had from this fall were from courtrooms, police stations, and government agencies. And from her office. Most of all from her office. Just before she reached the reception desk, she heard a voice call out behind her.

"Gabriella Seichelman?"

She stopped, turned around a bit too quickly, and slipped on the gray stone slabs of the lobby. A hand reached out and steadied her.

"Wow, you move quickly, I'll give you that," said the voice attached to the hand.

Gabriella twisted her head up and gave a strained smile. Blushing, despite herself. The voice belonged to a man in his fifties. Short gray hair under a black cap, scruffy jeans worn a little too high, a cheap-looking dress shirt and a broken-in, short leather jacket. A plainclothes police officer. No doubt about it. If there was anything Gabriella could spot, it was a plainclothes police officer.

Before she could say anything, he flashed her his badge.

"My name is Anton Bronzelius," he said. "I work with the Security Service."

"Okay?" Gabriella said, starting to feel nervous.

She didn't have time for this. Not at all.

"Do you have a second?" Bronzelius said. "Or rather, I know you have . . ."

He turned his wrist to look at his plastic watch.

"I know you've got twenty-one minutes before your hearing begins. And I've taken the liberty of booking us a conference room."

———

Gabriella played with her cell phone. Checked the time. Nineteen minutes until the hearing began. Sure, Joseph was prepared. He didn't expect her for another fifteen minutes. Her legs twitched under the table. She played with her phone. Damnit, this was not the way it was supposed be.

At least Bronzelius didn't waste any time. They'd barely entered the room before he threw two tabloids onto the white table between them. All of these rooms were white. Gabriella felt as if she spent more time in this kind of room than in her own white-walled apartment.

The headlines were almost identical. Different versions of SWEDE WANTED FOR MURDER IN BRUSSELS. *Expressen* chose to add the word *TERRORIST*. *Aftonbladet* went for *ELITE SOLDIER*. What a bunch of idiots at *Expressen*, thought Gabriella. *ELITE SOLDIER* would sell much better than yet another terrorist story.

"Have you heard about this?" began Bronzelius.

"Well, I read the papers," Gabriella said. "So yes, I've heard about it. But I've only seen the headlines online this morning. Nothing more."

Bronzelius nodded calmly. There was something about this man. Something honest and sincere. Something safe and policelike. Gabriella felt calmer.

"What I'm about to say needs to stay between us. It needs to be kept in complete secrecy. You're a lawyer. You know what that means."

"Yes, I understand the concept of confidentiality."

She smiled a little warily. Bronzelius looked serious.

"The terrorist—or elite soldier, depending on which newspaper you read—is Mahmoud Shammosh," he said.

December 20, 2013

Brussels, Belgium

KLARA LEANED BACK IN HER chair and spun around from her desk to look out at the stunning view of Brussels from the window of her sixteenth-floor office. Away from her buzzing computer. Away from her notes from the meeting with Eva-Karin. The morning was ice-cold with clear blue skies. Smoke hovered, quiet and white, over the chimneys of houses, as if it had frozen on its way up toward all that blue. The sunshine was so intense, Klara had to turn her eyes back to her office.

She couldn't stand looking at it. Couldn't stand the reflections flashing off the European Union buildings; their contours were suddenly so sharp they made her eyes hurt. Today was one of those days when it felt like everything was happening for the first time. As if the earth had rotated a few degrees on its axis, as if the universe had expanded or contracted. As if she had woken up in a different body, filled with experiences she had no memories of. Her teenage years had been filled with days like that. Maybe everyone's teens were filled with days like that. She closed her eyes and wiped what might have been a tear from the corner of her eye.

After she'd turned the frame over, she'd sat staring into Cyril's stark white wall for a long time. Taking deep breaths. Thinking about what Grandpa used to say: "Rock and salt. That's what we're made of out here in the archipelago."

Rock and salt.

Slowly, she'd lowered her gaze to look at the black-and-white photo.

They were beautiful. All three of them were beautiful. The little girl was probably three years old. She looked so happy on Cyril's shoulders. Her long, thick hair mixed with his wavy, vacation-ruffled curls as she bent over him. Her large, dark eyes looked straight into the camera. Cyril was shirtless and leaning outward and upward to kiss her on the cheek. Beside him, with her long, smooth arm draped naturally around Cyril's waist was a woman who looked so perfectly healthy and relaxed that Klara almost couldn't breathe. With her tiny freckles, her pretty little nose, her salt-splashed hair, her casual shirtdress and her obviously tanned legs, she could have been a model. Maybe she was. A beach stretched out behind them, and beyond that waves and sea. It was the quintessential picture of a happy French family.

How long had she sat there with that picture, wrestling with the urge to throw it against the wall so hard the simple frame would crack and the glass would spread out across the parquet floor like mercury? Finally she calmly put it back into the drawer where she'd found it. Stood up and got dressed. Put her phone in her bag and went to work.

Rock and salt.

When the phone on her desk rang, she first considered not picking it up. She didn't want to talk, couldn't stand the thought of sucking up to Eva-Karin. But on the sixth ring, she decided that anything was better than what she was feeling right now.

"Yes?" she said into the phone.

"A Mr. Moody for you, Mademoiselle Walldéen," a receptionist said in French on the other end of the line.

Klara gasped. It was as if the composition of the air itself had suddenly changed, as if she had to work harder to get oxygen to her blood.

"Klara," said a voice on the phone. "Are you there?"

His voice was shriller than she remembered it. Pinched—the words somehow compressed. She tried to breathe normally, but it was impossible.

"Moody," she whispered.

Then nothing. It took several seconds for Klara to finally break the silence.

"It's been a long time."

She could hear him breathing on the other end. It had been so long. Still, she knew something wasn't right.

"I have to see you," Mahmoud said.

His voice was tense, as if buzzing with electricity. Klara started to feel guilty. She hadn't responded to his e-mail. Not because she didn't want to, but because she didn't know what to say.

"Now?" she said. "Do you want to meet now? Are you in Brussels?"

"Can you leave the office?"

"What is it, Moody? Has something happened?"

"I can't tell you now. Not like this. Can I see you?"

Klara thought it over for a moment. She got the distinct feeling that she was at an important crossroads.

"Yes," she said at last. "No problem. Where should we meet?"

W E'RE ALL SUSPECTS; MORE THAN that. Guilty until proven innocent. We move like shadows through the hallways. Shadows that are the shadows of shadows. The daring ones exchange knowing glances over mounds of shredded documents, whirring computers. Talks at the watercooler are quiet, intense, full of disbelief and carefully calibrated. Those already under formal investigation wear their stress like a bell around their necks, like a yellow Star of David. In the canteen, they sit alone with their trays and their thoughts of retirement, their children's college funds evaporating with each new interrogation, with each more or less explicit suspicion. Nobody is talking about it. Everybody is talking about it.

It's only been a few weeks since they took Aldrich Ames. Vertefeuille and her stubborn task force of old ladies and retirees on the second floor. A mole in Langley. Our very own Philby. Is it worse to betray your country for money than for ideology? The prevailing view at the watercooler is yes.

And now the building is full of FBI. Uncomplicated policemen in dark suits. They might as well be uniformed here, where khakis and dress shirts are the rule. They know nothing about us, nothing about our work. It's a joke. Lie detectors don't work on someone who can't tell the difference between truth and lies. They're irrelevant to those of us who don't even care which is which.

I'm not surprised when I hear the footsteps on the carpet outside my office, and I barely look up when they open my door without knocking. Their tactics are obvious, old-fashioned, as familiar as a pair of well-worn boots. A tired man around my age enters. He needs a haircut and to lose twenty-five pounds if he's going to avoid the heart attack he probably already feels panting in his chest. A rookie with high cheekbones wearing a new suit, struggling to keep the testosterone inside his shirt collar, follows him in.

"If you just tell us right away it'll make it easier for everyone," says the rookie, fastening his just-out-of-the-academy eyes at me. "We already know most of it, so you just need to fill in the gaps for us."

The older man sits down in one of the threadbare steel chairs in front of my desk and turns his eyes up toward the soundproof tiles in the ceiling. It's the oldest trick in the book. Fire off an accusation, throw your object off balance, see how he reacts. It might work on a junkie in the Bronx, in a Wall Street office on some sweaty stockbroker already starting to get cold feet about that insider deal.

But that's not going to work here. Not in Langley. Not on the people who invented that method, who are infinitely better at lying than at telling the truth. Not on those who, for once, have nothing to hide.

———

Fourteen hours later I'm sitting with electrodes attached to my body in front of a tired, old technician who seems all too aware of the futility of this task. It's a charade. We play our roles the best we can.

We go through the formalities, the control questions. Where I live, where I was stationed, my divorce, how much I drink.

"Is this the first time you've been under investigation?" he says at last, and glances at the controls in front of him.

"No," I reply. "I was under investigation between 1980 and 1981. Suspended one month, then released, but they kept me here at Langley until 1985."

"Do you know why you were under investigation?"

"Yes, there were circumstances in my private life that compromised an operation when I was deep undercover abroad."

"What circumstances?"

He looks up and meets my gaze with his gray, hangdog eyes.

"I don't know if you have high enough clearance for me to tell you that," I say.

"You can assume that I have clearance," he says.

"Sorry, I don't want to screw things up for either of us, but I can't just assume anything. My superiors would have to declassify it, and until you have a document to that effect, I can't say any more than that."

I make an effort to sound friendly. He's just an instrument, a speaker for the questions someone else has written.

"What was the outcome of that investigation?"

"I went back into service. I guess the reasons are in my dossier somewhere. I've never seen them."

He's satisfied by that and continues asking for names and dates. Friends and colleagues. I answer as best I can.

"January fifteenth, 1985," he says at last. "Stockholm."

"Okay," I reply. "If you say so."

"You stayed at the Lord Nelson hotel and your plane flew back to Dulles via London in the afternoon"—he looks at his papers—"at sixteen-fifteen.\At eight-thirty you rented a Volvo under an alias and returned it to the airport at fourteen-thirty. Do you remember?"

"I remember Stockholm. It was cold," I say.

"You had six hours with the car," he says. "Approximately. Where did you go?"

I look at my watch.

"That was almost ten years ago," I say. "I had some free time, so I rented a car. Where did I drive? I drove north along the coast, if I remember correctly. I'd had a mission and wanted some time to myself."

"You shook off your shadows," says the man, casting a glance at his controls.

"That's old habit. I shake off my shadows when I go to buy a box of McNuggets."

A brief smile dances across his lips. A dozen routine questions later we're done. We shake hands, and we both know that this investigation is closed.

Later, I sit in my room. The pale spring sun shines through the thin leafless trees. The highway roars in the distance.

I close my eyes and remember Stockholm. I remember the stern of the ferry from the amusement park. I remember promises and death. I remember the hollowness and what we fill the hollowness with. I remember every word that the helpful, stressed-out woman at the embassy said. I remember the Volvo, how I shook off my shadows, how I rented the car in a third or fourth name, how I drove south not north, how I thought the sun would never rise. I remember weak coffee and dry buns at a deserted gas station. I remember that it was snowing, and the Volvo moved soundlessly through the snow, as if in a dream. I remember that I finally stopped in a little coastal village called Arkösund.

I remember that I left the car, walked past a boarded-up country store, past snowed-in, yellow, late-nineteenth-century villas. I remember the silence that was only broken by the crunch of my feet on the snow. I remember standing on the bridge, peering out over the ice, protecting my eyes from the falling snow. I remember that I said my daughter's name. I remember that the tears froze on my cheek. I remember that I was as close as I could get. I remember that I whispered to the ice, to the sea, to the wind:

"I'll return."

I remember that I didn't mean it.

I remember that when I turned to go back to the Volvo the snow had already erased my footsteps, as if I'd been placed on that dock from above, as if my presence had no continuity, no context, no causality.

Later that evening. On my way home, I stop at the pool. I've forgotten my bathing suit, but I go inside anyway. It's empty except for two elderly men crawling purposefully through the chlorine green water. I sit down on the cold tiles, my back against the wall. Outside heavy raindrops begin to fall onto the damp ground. When I close my eyes, I walk over an icy blanket of deep snow, so white it's blinding. The wind stings my cheeks. Behind me my footsteps have left deep trenches, and no matter how hard I try, I can't cover them.

December 20, 2013

Brussels, Belgium

GOOD JOB, SOLDIER," REIPER SAID. "You've accomplished your mission with flying colors!"

With one arm around George's shoulders, Reiper pushed him toward the English living room that George had left less than twelve hours ago.

Soldier. That degrading tone. George wasn't a soldier. He was a general, or at least an aide-de-camp, an adviser to generals. The effects of this morning's cocaine had already worn off. If that hadn't been the case, he would've told Reiper exactly how he felt about him, told him to take his fucking Digital Solutions and go straight to hell. A place they probably already knew quite well. But instead George just felt depressed and exhausted from missing a night of sleep and from this morning's adrenaline rush. Terrified of Reiper and his gang, and the contacts and resources they obviously had access to, he said nothing, just nodded.

"Sit down, for God's sake, George," Reiper said. "You've had a productive morning. Coffee?"

George wanted to stretch out. Rub his eyes. Take off his shoes and jacket, curl up on the couch, and go to sleep. That's what he really wanted. Or better yet: stand up, shake Reiper's hand, and thank him. Then get into his Audi with Avicii turned up to a comfortable volume, drive home to his white, clean, tidy, and tasteful apartment. Take a shower and wash off the last vestiges and memories of Digital Solutions, then crawl between the ironed sheets in his Hästens bed.

"Coffee? Sure," he said instead.

"So," Reiper said. "Debriefing. It seems like the technology is working, as far as we can tell. Excellent. Now tell me how you did it."

"I guess it all went according to plan in the beginning. I did exactly what Josh told me to do. But Klara came in earlier than I'd expected, so things got tight in the end."

He shuddered inwardly at the memory of how he'd snuck into Boman's office.

"Okay," Reiper said.

He frowned. The scar was blazing on his cheek. His green reptilian eyes stared blindly at George.

"Did she see you?"

"No," George said. "Not a chance. I snuck into her boss's office. There's no way she saw me. She started talking on the phone, and I slipped out without her noticing. I'm sure of that."

It felt important, vital, to explain to Reiper that he'd escaped detection, that he'd performed the task flawlessly. He didn't even want to think about what the penalty for failure might entail. Reiper said nothing but seemed to be weighing what George had said. George sipped his instant coffee. It tasted awful. As he was setting his mug down on the small coffee table, the door to the living room opened. An attractive woman of around George's age, her blond hair in a high ponytail, peeked into the room. Reiper turned to her.

"Kirsten," he said. "News?"

"I think we have contact," replied the girl.

"E-mail?" Reiper said.

"Phone. We think it's Shammosh, but we can only hear Klara. She's talking to him right now."

Reiper turned to George.

"Hurry up, we need you to translate again."

Reiper started walking toward the door, motioning impatiently for George to come with him. They walked out into the hall and into a small room next door, which appeared to be a kitchen. Maybe this had been a maid's quarters, because the kitchen wasn't bigger than a large closet. At the far end of the room, under a small window overlooking the garden, stood a desk with two computer screens and a laptop. Josh was sitting there, wearing headphones. He motioned to George to sit down and put on another pair of headphones. A sound file was open on one of the screens.

"Forget the details. Just focus on where Shammosh is, and whether or not they're going to meet, okay? We'll figure out the rest later," Josh said.

George nodded.

Thirty seconds later he heard a click as Klara hung up. George lifted off one side of the headphones, turned back toward Reiper.

"Well, I can only hear her, not the other one. But it's definitely that Shammosh guy. And she's on her way to meet him," he said.

A few minutes later, George again removed the headphones and scratched his head. This was the third time he'd listened to the conversation between Klara and Mahmoud.

"No, there's nothing there. She asks where they should meet and he responds. She doesn't repeat the location. And I can only hear what she's saying. Not him."

Josh nodded. The two of them were alone in the room. Reiper

and the girl had disappeared as soon as George had given them his first rough translation of the conversation.

"You can sleep for a while if you want," Josh said. "Reiper will let you know when you're needed."

"You mean I can go home?" George said.

He felt his hopes start to rise. If he could just go back to his apartment. Take a shower. Sleep. Maybe all of this insanity would be over by the time he woke up.

"Wake up, buddy, you're not going anywhere. You can stretch out on the couch in the living room."

Josh turned back toward the computers and gently shook his head.

December 20, 2013

Brussels, Belgium

S HE DIDN'T KNOW HOW LONG she'd been standing in front of the Royal Palace—ten minutes? twenty?—before she finally saw Mahmoud on the other side of the uneven cobblestones. Barely discernible next to a tall gatepost at the entrance to the park, he wasn't moving. Klara felt her heart jump. When he understood that she'd spotted him, he held up his right hand and motioned for her to approach. Then he turned around calmly and disappeared into the park.

Klara had remained still for a moment after she ended the phone call earlier. Boman had already gone home for the weekend. There was nothing keeping her at the office. Nothing that couldn't be done later. She felt numb, still confused and shaky from what she'd discovered that morning at Cyril's apartment. Suddenly, it felt completely natural to meet Mahmoud.

He'd asked her to take a back way out of the Parliament. The only way she knew was through the parking garage, so she'd taken that. Then she rode the subway to the Gare du Nord and took a taxi to the palace. She'd done exactly what he'd asked. Without question, without thinking. She needed to get out and away in any case. And his voice had been so naked, so lonely and tense. Klara looked around one last time before she ran after Mahmoud into the park.

She'd felt very vulnerable standing between the gray, run-down palace and the wide, cobblestone avenue separating it from the park. But at least she'd been able to establish that she was alone. Mahmoud's paranoia was unwarranted. Maybe that's why he'd wanted to meet her here? To be able to make sure of that.

She saw him again when she entered the park. He was sitting on a park bench by the gravel path, waiting for her. He looked tired, older. His hair was shorter than she remembered it. Not as short as when they'd met, when he was a newly graduated paratrooper with a military buzz cut. But still definitely shorter than the tousled curls she remembered from their last time together in Uppsala.

She had trouble meeting his eyes, when he stood up. She'd put so much effort into leaving those eyes behind, into forgetting them. And now here they were again, right in front of her. Despite the large, dark rings around them, his eyes were the same as she remembered. Deep and with that irrepressible gleam of independence that made him seem arrogant to some. But at the same time they held a deep and melancholy warmth that she still, after all these years, realized she had a hard time resisting.

He was unshaven. His dark coat had dry specks of something red and sticky on the lapel and all the way down one side. He looked terrible. He was just as beautiful as she remembered him.

"Moody!" she said, and stopped in front of him. "Oh my God. What happened?"

He held up his hand, hushing her.

"Sorry," he began, whispering. "But you have to give me your purse, okay?"

Klara looked at him questioningly.

"What? Why?"

"Please," Mahmoud said. "I wouldn't ask if I didn't have a good reason. I promise."

Hesitantly she handed over her dark blue Marc Jacobs bag.

"Sorry," he said again.

Then he turned it upside down over the peeling park bench and emptied all of its contents.

"What the hell, Moody," Klara said in a high-pitched voice.

He didn't seem to hear her.

"You turned off your cell phone like I asked you, right?" he said instead as he quickly and methodically combed through all of the compartments in the bag: her makeup, her purse, her tampons. Nothing was left untouched.

"Yes, but are you going to tell me what you're doing?"

He looked up at her and started putting her belongings back in the bag.

"I know it seems crazy," he said. "But the last few hours have been very intense. Stretch your arms up in the air. "

Klara looked at him hesitantly. There was something pleading, something desperate in his eyes. A gleam of something she'd never seen there before. He stood up and came over to her, very close. She caught a whiff of his scent. Either he still used the same cologne or it was just his natural scent. Musk and jasmine. But weaker than she remembered it, hidden beneath the smell of dirt and sweat and blood. He put his hands into the pockets of her duffel coat. Quick and efficient. Then inside her coat, into the pockets of her pants, running quickly along her waist. Finally he felt along the seams of her clothing. Up and down her body. When he was finished, he took a step back and looked away.

"Sorry," he said. "Believe me, this wasn't how I had imagined what it would be like when we finally met again."

He sat on the park bench and rubbed his hands over his face. Klara cautiously sat down beside him. She put a hesitant arm around his shoulder. It felt so strange. So completely natural.

"Since you've already frisked me, maybe I can give you a hug?" she said.

He turned his face toward her, answered her crooked smile.

"You must think I've completely lost my mind?" he said.

Klara shrugged.

"Seriously, Moody, I don't know what to think. I saw your e-mail about coming to Brussels."

She cleared her throat. Looked out over the park.

"And honestly, I didn't know how to answer. It was hard for me. You know, what we had. When it ended. It took a long time for me to accept that I was never going to get an explanation. That you just stopped loving me. It's really hard to accept something like that, do you understand that? I didn't even know if I wanted to see you again. "

She turned back toward Mahmoud. He was looking down at the ground. His leg shaking, jumping. From nervousness or stress.

"And now this. What's going on, Moody?"

Mahmoud suddenly stood up.

"We can't stay here," he said. "Come on, we have to keep moving."

———

They walked deeper into the park, under the bare trees, over frozen gravel paths covered in dry winter leaves. The sun was pale and cold, as if it were even farther away than usual.

Klara said nothing while Mahmoud cleared his throat, took a deep breath. Prepared himself. And finally he told her. About his research, his trips to Afghanistan and Iraq. About the messages from someone who seemed to be a fellow ranger from the old days. About the conference and the phone call. About the meeting at the African Museum and Lindman's murder. And finally about the surreal attack at the hotel that very morning and the transmitter he'd found in his bag. He told her everything, holding nothing back. A mighty river flowed out of him, calm on the surface but with terrible force underneath.

"My God," Klara said, when they reached the other end of the park. "What have you gotten yourself into?"

"I don't know," he said. "Lindman seems to have—or have had, I mean—some information that somebody else is willing to kill both of us to get hold of."

"The Americans he worked for?" Klara asked.

"I don't know."

Mahmoud dug into his wallet and took out a little piece of paper.

"All I know is that Lindman said something about a train station in Paris, and he seems to have had luggage in a locker at the Gare du Nord. That's all I have to go on."

Mahmoud hailed a taxi that stopped at the curb. He held open the back door and looked questioningly at Klara.

"I'm not saying I want you to come to Paris with me, but do you have a little more time?"

He took a deep breath. It looked like he was blushing.

"I owe you a huge explanation. And oddly enough, or however you want to put it, the explanation involves Lindman."

June 2002

Karlsborg, Sweden

EUPHORIA AND ENDORPHINS. IT'S UNTHINKABLE, and yet so obvious, they can smell the freedom through the shoe polish and gun grease, the felt and the cleaning solution. So sudden and so real, they can taste the freedom through the vodka. They mix it with Fanta and drink it in their green plastic cups, the same cups they've had with them since the first day. With them through two-week marches, through endless survival drills in -25°C in Norrland, with them up Kebnekaise mountain and down again, and with them in the airplane from the first jump to the last. They laugh and laugh and laugh. Call each other nicknames. Tell stories about the draft, the jumps, frostbitten fingers, ranger marches. Stories memorized and refined, spun to perfection while they were cleaning their weapons and standing guard duty, through sleepless nights and early mornings.

It's like this is the first time. Like they just met, like they're in love. Like they've never been apart. Everything is bathed in a new light this evening. An initial, reflexive flash of nostalgia or sentimentality. They wrestle. They can't stop touching the warmth, the strength of one another. Fifteen months of a purely physical closeness the likes of which they will never experience again, though they don't realize it now. Not with girlfriends, not with wives or children. Not like this, not in the same way. They rub each other's buzz cuts. They're so relieved it's over; they can't believe it's over.

━━━

Mahmoud leans back on his bunk. For a moment he tunes out all of the testosterone and energy. He closes his eyes, feeling the vodka and the tight maroon beret around his temples. He wishes he could cry. He wishes his mother could see him now. It doesn't matter, she wouldn't understand. No one could understand what he went through. What he accomplished.

The tremendous discipline it required—the concentration to get his beret and his wings. To emerge from the hopeless concrete projects to this. He, if anyone, has shown determination, courage, and endurance. He rose above the suspicion and the insults. Commanders who called him Bin Laden for the first two months. Graffiti in black, thick marker. AL QAEDA. RAGHEAD. ALLAHU AKBAR. Every morning for those first few weeks. Sometimes a swastika. In the beginning he forced himself to get up an hour before anyone else, so he could rub the shame off of his locker. He'd ignored the voices behind his back and the sudden silences when he entered a room. He never yielded. Just grew up and out. Just got better than they were. Stronger. Harder. Until he couldn't be excluded anymore. Until, almost imperceptibly, he became a part of them. He went from being Bin Laden to Shammosh. Felt their trust, their respect. Felt like they no longer treated him differently.

Right now, here on this hard bunk, surrounded by the voices of young men that are more familiar to him than anything else, with the booze lifting him up and away, he feels like he just won an

Olympic gold medal. Right here and now, it is an accomplishment of unfathomable magnitude.

"Shammosh! Fucking heeeelll! Let's go!"

Someone's arms reach in under the top bunk, grab him, and pull him out on the floor. He spills his drink all over his Levi's. He doesn't even notice. Everyone is dancing and grinding against one another. Small, still controlled explosions of pent-up, male energy. Valves that might blow under the pressure, if they don't get out of here, away from here, right now. Away from the barracks and the regiment. Anywhere else. They'd really like to keep their stiff berets on. They'd really like everyone to see who they are, what they've accomplished. But discipline wins out, and they leave their berets in their lockers before dancing out into a small-town evening, their voices triumphant fanfares in the silence.

———

The bar is full of high school students and cashiers from the local supermarket. A big group of adoring privates, just enlisted, considerably lower in rank than theirs. They realize that they don't need their berets. Everyone can see who they are. Their eyes. Their stance. Their obvious, physical confidence. They find a table on the terrace, near the water, and some leftover conference attendee treats them to a round of licorice shots. It's that kind of night. The kind of summer night where dusk perpetually shimmers around them, makes them glitter like silver and water, makes them expand and lift off of the ground.

Later, Mahmoud is standing at the bar. He feels like he can drink forever. Not a drop for fifteen months and not much before that either, but now there's no end to how much he can drink. He stumbles and steadies himself against the bar. Tries to control his tongue. Shakes his head. He is Mahmoud Shammosh from the projects. He is Mahmoud Shammosh, paratrooper, soon-to-be law student in Uppsala. He is Mahmoud Shammosh, invincible.

"You're one of those rangers, right?"

A voice detaches itself from the din of voices and music. Very close, right next to Mahmoud's ear. He twists his head, replies before seeing who's asked.

"I'm invincible."

It's a man. Maybe ten years older than Mahmoud. He's wearing a dark, slim suit. A skinny tie that he hasn't loosened, even though he's in a bar, even though it's late. A smooth, well-ironed, white shirt. His face is also slim. Oval and attentive. A dimple appears in one cheek, when he laughs at Mahmoud's reply. Short, blond hair. Blue eyes that are more than just curious.

"Oh," he says. "Invincible. Not bad."

His gaze seems amused, seems to be looking straight inside Mahmoud. It's shameless, that look. It says to Mahmoud, it's your choice. But if you are still here, you've already chosen.

"Yup," says Mahmoud. "Invincible. I'm a paratrooper. Do you know how hard-core we are?"

He's struggling to pronounce his consonants. He thinks, he should get out of here, this can't end well.

"Wow," says the man, holding a hand up to his mouth, blinking. "How hard-core, soldier?"

"Very fucking hard-core."

It's trying to sneak out of him now. Out of hibernation and denial. Out of its hiding place. And he lets it. Let's the alcohol release him. Lets freedom flow through him. Invincibility. It pops and dances like carbonation through his frontal lobe. The erection pushes against his jeans.

"Are you staying here at the hotel?"

It's so easy now. As if he's never done anything else. If anyone deserves this, it's him. It's all over now. All of the games and the need to prove something. He has the beret. He is who he is.

"You're very straightforward, soldier," says the man, grinning. "I like that."

They don't waste time. They sneak out of the bar, out past the front desk, float up two floors of laminated stairs. The taste of beer in his mouth, the fresh new smell of wood and paint that barely conceals the mold. Mahmoud doesn't understand these stairs. They spiral and seem to lean at impossible angles in some sort of alien geometry. In and out, past doors and floors. It's an inconceivable labyrinth, it's an enchanted castle. Finally they stumble through a door, which closes behind them with a sound like a vacuum, the sound of hermetic sealing.

There's no time to get his footing, take his bearings. The wave trembles and strokes him. Threatens to engulf him. It pushes him forward, onto the bed. Eager fingers fumble with belts and buttons. Mouths, lips, and teeth kiss and suck and bite. Hands caress thighs and chests and their throbbing, pounding sex. Bare skin rubbing, pressing, pumping against bare skin. And Mahmoud lets it happen. He finally allows himself to let go and lose himself completely. Finally allows the wave to crash in and out. Allows it to sweep him away.

Afterward, he's sober. The bright summer night is no longer magical or supernatural, extraterrestrial, but cold and white and much too clear. The man next to him moves in the cheap sheets, rolls over on his side, and looks at him. A few gray hairs glitter in the sparse hair on his chest. That dimple. Those eyes won't leave him alone.

"I have to go," says Mahmoud. "I have to get back to the barracks."

He falls silent. It's over. It's too late. He has no times to keep anymore.

"I just have to go."

He gets up, pulls on his shorts and jeans in one fell swoop. Tugs the white T-shirt over his head. Buttons the snaps on his shirt. Not even bothering to tie his Nikes. Stumbling, tottering to the door.

"Can I call you?" says the man.

The voice comes from the bed, just as Mahmoud is pressing down the handle, the door already opened a gap, so anxious and pathetic that Mahmoud doesn't know what to say. So he rattles off his number without thinking. Half hoping the man won't remember it. Half hoping he'll call right away, all the time, always.

Evening or night or morning. It's a state outside of time. A triumphant, shameful, liberating, enslaving moment, which lacks markers or references. He is weightless and so heavy that he can hardly walk upright. Karlsborg seems only vaguely familiar. A memory without depth. Like déjà vu. It amazes him that he can find his way through streets and alleys back to the barracks. It amazes him that he has an ID card in his pocket, that the guard accepts it, it amazes him that he's the same person as the boy on that ID card, trying hard to look tough.

He knows it's over as soon as he opens the door to the barracks. He knows it when he sees the fluorescent lights are still glowing, the newly commissioned rangers aren't asleep. He knows it from the silence and the smiles and the averted eyes. The familiar feeling of alienation increases with every breath, with each endless moment he doesn't say anything, just stands there, like a thief, caught with his shirt in disarray on the doorstep. Between what he is, and what he also is. In the middle of the realization that there's no way back. The endless faces of discrimination.

It's Lindman who breaks the silence. Who rises from a lower bunk. It's Lindman who expands from nothing to six foot five, two hundred fifty pounds, like a helium balloon suddenly inflated. It's Lindman who sways across the floor, until he's very close. Standing in front of Mahmoud, his breath smelling like licorice and beer and adrenaline.

"So," he begins. "We knew you fucked camels, Bin Laden. But we had no idea you liked fucking people in the ass too?"

Laughter and giggles. A halfhearted "Lay off, man" from both Glans and Petrov. But it means nothing. Two sentences. That's all it takes to wipe out fifteen months of assimilation.

Mahmoud says nothing at first. He's overcome by an immense fatigue. He should have stayed out. What stupidity drove him back here?

"What the hell are you talking about, Lindman?" he says.

Staring back into Lindman's blue, native Swedish eyes. A couple of the others have stood up by now. He can make out Malm and Svensson. Landskog and Torsson. They move in on him from the walls like mist.

"What I'm talking about?"

Lindman turns back to smile at his Greek chorus, his extras.

"I'm talking about the fact that you're a fucking faggot, Bin Laden. That's what I'm talking about."

"Come on, Shammosh. We saw you with that homo at the bar, okay. Saw you sneak off."

It's Glans. His eyes are staring up at the bottom of the top bunk. Glans. Whom he's shared guard duty and stress with. Whom he's helped with his blisters and his terrible map reading skills. Nothing is left.

Two beeps sound through the barracks. Two muffled beeps from the pocket of Mahmoud's jeans. Before he can react someone locks his arms behind him. As if by secret command, an agreement. Lindman is on him, his fingers reaching into the tight pocket. Fishing, pulling, and grabbing. Holding up the Nokia in triumph. A few quick clicks. He clears his throat. It sounds like victory.

" 'Thanks for tonight, soldier,' " he reads off the phone. " 'You weren't kidding, you really were "hard-core." Take care . . .' "

He pauses for effect.

" 'Take care, Jonas'!"

The whole room explodes in laughter and disgusted triumph. Mahmoud feels them pushing him down onto the speckled linoleum. He doesn't even resist. Their bodies press down on him. Their breath.

"Fucking hell, Bin Laden," Lindman hisses in his ear. "Fucking hell, you're disgusting. Did Jonas fuck you good in the ass? Did he?"

They grab and pull him in opposite directions, apparently unsure what to do, what punishment should be meted out. Finally, they end up in the showers. Finally, Mahmoud's shirt and his undershirt are torn to pieces. His jeans are pulled down over his hips, over his thighs and his knees. He feels the shower turn on, feels kicks and punches. He lies naked, his jeans around the knees, under the icy water of the barracks' shower. Voices all around him; shrill, agitated voices bounce off of the shining tiles. Those voices he thought he had convinced. That he'd deluded himself into thinking he'd convinced. Now they are all saying the same thing in a thousand different ways: for someone like you, there is no mercy, no respite, nothing.

FIRST CLASS?" MAHMOUD SAID. "WEREN'T there any other tickets left?"

He set the backpack down on the floor next to him and peered out the window. The gray, efficient platform was full of travelers. Klara sat down in the aisle seat and pushed a strand of hair from her forehead.

"I don't know. I just thought there'd be fewer people in first class. It seems like you're, well . . . wanted by the police."

"You will be too, pretty soon," muttered Mahmoud.

He'd been objecting to Klara coming with him, ever since she'd suggested it, insisted upon it, in the taxi after he'd finally told her everything. Everything that he should have told her three years ago, five years ago. Everything he should have told her the first time he saw her, not now, in Brussels, after everything that had happened. He felt like an idiot. And incredibly selfish. The last thing he wanted was to expose her to danger on top of everything else.

Finally she'd given up, held up her hand and said, "Okay, fine. Whatever you want."

But when she came back from the ticket booth, she'd bought

tickets for both of them. She hadn't changed at all. She did whatever she wanted. At the same time, he couldn't help feeling relieved. He was so alone, so hunted. The last twenty-four hours had been a complete nightmare. Sitting next to Klara in this comfortable first-class seat on the TGV train to Paris allowed him to breathe again. He owed her more than he could ever repay.

"What did you say?" Klara said.

"I said that if you continue hanging around with me, you'll be wanted too."

"Whatever," she said and took a sip of water from a bottle she'd bought at the station.

"Or worse. It doesn't seem like they're pulling any punches."

Mahmoud let his eyes rest on the railway yard outside the train window. Rusty tracks and wilted weeds, graffiti and gray, abandoned buildings. Spinning above it all was the huge, grinning face of Tintin.

———

When Mahmoud finally turned away from the window, he could feel Klara looking at him. He steeled himself and met her eyes. At one time he'd been defenseless against them; their blue depths had overwhelmed him. The train accelerated through the station. The gray light was fractured by the train window, transforming it into a speckled canvas.

"You look different," Klara said. "Completely different."

Mahmoud stroked his unshaved cheek, dragged a hand through his sweaty, matted hair.

"Not that," Klara said. "I don't mean your hair. Or not just that. All of you is different. Your whole demeanor. Your eyes. You're older."

"It's been a long day," he said.

She nodded.

"I saw you on CNN a few weeks ago. Gabriella e-mailed me the clip. Things are going well for you."

"That feels like a hundred years ago," Mahmoud said.

"You looked good on-screen. The camera loves you," she said, winking at him. "That's a good thing, since you might be getting more media attention than you hoped for."

"Ha-ha," Mahmoud said.

But he couldn't help smiling.

"Ah, I knew I could get a smile out of you," Klara said.

She patted him gently, tenderly on the cheek, and then let her fingers slide down his arm until eventually she took his hand in hers. Mahmoud felt all the pressure he was under release, if just for a moment. He squeezed her hand back. A little too hard, but she didn't protest.

"So," she began. "It might not really be the time for this now. I mean . . ."

She was blinking quickly, suddenly looking so small.

"Oh my God, it feels so banal now. But still. Oh, whatever."

She went silent.

"Yes, Klara," Mahmoud said.

He took a deep breath and put his free hand on her face, turning it gently toward him, pulling her closer. Her cheek was very smooth, very soft. "Of course I loved you. More than I've ever loved anyone. Ever. It wasn't that. And I found you sexually attractive, if you're wondering."

"You better have," Klara muttered.

"It's just that it wasn't enough. I don't know. It's not easy to explain. I've known I like guys since I was in my teens. I mean, that

I like guys too. Or, whatever you say. But you know, on the streets where I grew up . . . that wasn't exactly something you bragged about. And in Karlsborg. Well, you heard what happened there. When we met, I thought that maybe it would all work out, that I might be normal after all. Or, whatever you want to call it. That's what it felt like. But still, there was something that just wouldn't leave me alone."

He fell silent. They looked at each other. The train was approaching its maximum speed. Paris was just an hour away.

"It's going to work out, Moody," Klara said at last. "We'll get through this, okay?"

He nodded and closed his eyes to hide the tears welling up inside him. Klara leaned against his shoulder. He could smell her, her shampoo, her perfume.

May 2003

Afghanistan

WHEN THE CAMERA ZOOMS IN on the red and white banner stretched across the bridge of the aircraft carrier, I leave the cheering, testosterone-fueled crowd and walk out onto the tarmac for some air. Out here the evening is mild and cool, no more than a whisper of heat in the gentle breeze. The roar of the generators mingles with the sound of the national anthem, the clatter of beer bottles, gullibility. I feel a nausea that refuses to subside. Maybe it's something I ate. Maybe I'm tired. Maybe my body is physically reacting to what we've become.

I can no longer watch the president on television without anxiety, and this latest spectacle upsets me. *Mission accomplished*. Both here and in Iraq, according to the secretary of defense. It's only been two and a half months since I held a young, overly patriotic colleague in my arms as he died out here in the dirt, in these desolate, terrible mountains. His blood in the dust, on my hands, my shirt. He liked German beer and America. Harvard Law School and soccer. His eyes burned, not with restlessness or rootlessness, but with idealism. What is it they say? Innocence is the first casualty of war? How long had he been here? A month? I don't keep track anymore. Not of months. Not of the dead.

I hear them cheering in the mess hall. They're celebrating the illusion of victory, a flickering, shaky hologram, a lie so poorly constructed that it's downright insulting that we're expected to take it seriously. But tonight, they just can't take it anymore. After months of heightened tension this childishly simple symbolism is exactly what they need. How long until they die out here in the dirt, their unarmored jeeps blown to bits, their body parts scattered over a mile radius? What do they know about the graveyard of empires?

I sit on my haunches with my back against the corrugated metal and I take a gulp of my Corona. I'm drinking again. It's been fifteen years since I sat with those students, the Taliban, in mountains not far from here. Fifteen years since I armed them, gave them satellite images, taught them about asymmetric warfare, promised them our friendship. Fifteen years. A whisper. A parenthesis. It's been eighteen years since I made a promise of total destruction to a man on a ferry in a bitterly cold Stockholm. If you're wondering why we're so convinced they have weapons of mass destruction, it's because they got them from us. We reap what we sow. Gravel, blood, lie after lie. We sow chaos and reap the status quo.

I see him just before he stops next to me. His white scar glowing in the evening sun. He's pale. Porous. His gray hair cut short around his balding head. Like me, he's dressed in a mismatched field uniform without insignia. A spy in wartime. He takes a sip of his beer and belches into his fist. He looks happy. This is his milieu, his war.

"That's some pretty impressive bullshit," he says and stretches.

A smile lurks on his lips. I don't say anything.

"Bush on that goddamn boat? That was some wonderful, fucking bullshit."

He throws his empty beer bottle in a wide arc toward a Dumpster thirty feet away. It lands with a ring without shattering.

I nod, signaling vaguely that I agree.

We stand in silence for a minute before he turns toward the door of the mess hall.

"You want another beer?" he says over his shoulder.

I shake my head.

"It won't hold up," I say instead.

He stops and turns around. He raises his eyebrows in exaggerated or feigned surprise.

"What? What won't hold up?"

I don't look at him. I just squint out the sun flashing off the windows of the dusty jeeps.

"You know what I mean. The interrogation policy. Our methods in the interrogation rooms. It won't hold up."

He turns back from the door, comes over to me again. That little smile in the corner of his mouth.

"Even if it did pay off," I say, "the methods are too brutal. People will say anything, admit to anything. Just to stop it. You can't trust the results."

"Bullshit," he says, looking me straight in the eye. "Bullshit. Do not give me that bullshit. You've seen the results. Intel rates have quadrupled since we started the enhanced interrogation program. We take more weapons. We know more about the leadership. More about what they're planning."

He steps back, eyeing me.

"What the hell . . . you're not losing your grip, are you?"

"Losing my grip? All I'm saying is that the methods are inhumane. And don't lead to reliable results. That's all. We break them down, and we don't get reliable results in exchange. All the research points to that."

"Research," he sputters. "What fucking research? Do you have a Ph.D. in interrogation techniques or something? We're in the middle of a goddamn war, if you haven't noticed. No matter what the president says on TV. War, okay? Eat or be eaten. If you can't handle it, get on a plane and go back to Langley where you can be discussing the latest *New York Times* editorial around the watercooler by tomorrow morning. But out here, it's what works that matters. And what we do works. It's as simple as that."

"But it doesn't fucking work!"

I don't mean to raise my voice, but his reptilian eyes, his thirst for blood, it triggers my fury. His kind have the upper hand now. Car batteries and electrodes. Everything has changed since Kurdistan.

My colleague says nothing. He just eyes me closely. So I continue. Kicking the sand, the empathy draining from my eyes. We stare at each other. The sound of the TV and the voices from inside the mess hall. The smell of fried food and a dry spring. He turns away first.

"It's time for you to rotate home," he says. "Your time in the field is past its due date, when you're not able to make the hard decisions anymore. Best you pack your bags."

I say nothing, just continue looking at him calmly.

"You know that, right?"

He takes a step closer. He's up in my face. His breath smells like beer and dust and tobacco.

"You always were a little cunt," he hisses. "I knew that back in

Iraq. I knew you were a little, fucking cunt. You better make sure you get a spot on the next rotation home from Kabul. You're done here."

He spits in the dirt, turns around, and goes back into the mess hall without turning around. Is this how it ends?

December 20, 2013

Stockholm, Sweden

GABRIELLA CLIMBED OUT OF THE taxi in front of Albert & Jack's Bakery and Deli on Skeppsbron, right next door to the law firm Lindblad and Wiman. Halfway up the three steps to the café, she changed her mind. It was past three, she still hadn't had lunch, but she wasn't hungry anymore. Her nagging unease overrode all other bodily functions.

Mahmoud, she thought. What's going on?

Bronzelius had asked her to contact him if Mahmoud reached out to her. It might make things easier, he said. Säpo, the Swedish Security Service, was convinced it was all a misunderstanding. Mahmoud would probably just need to turn himself in and explain what happened. The whole thing could probably be resolved informally.

Gabriella sighed. She didn't know what to believe. But it was definitely a relief that Säpo thought he was innocent.

Wet December snow fell into her thick, red hair as she walked the few steps to Lindblad and Wiman's entrance. Dark clouds hung over Djurgården and the Stockholm harbor. It had been a merciless December so far.

She sat down with a sigh in front of her computer and started answering the e-mails she hadn't had time to look through in detail on her BlackBerry in the taxi on her way back from court. But she couldn't focus, so she leaned back in her chair instead. Her tall windows looked out onto a red eighteenth-century house on the other side of Ferkens Gränd, a narrow side street.

She picked up her phone and tried calling Mahmoud, as she'd tried a dozen times already. When she couldn't reach him, she called Klara again, but her phone was also turned off.

Shit. What was going on?

"Why did I end up on the phone with a Cardigan from Säpo on my already nonexistent lunch break today?"

Gabriella winced and looked up from her computer. Hans Wiman was standing in the doorway. His intelligent, gray eyes, famous from countless televised press conferences and Swedish TV morning shows, were fastened on Gabriella. "Cardigan" was his infamous nickname for anyone belonging to a profession where a suit was not required work attire.

Wiman always wore a suit. Zegna or Armani. Even on Saturdays, as Gabriella had observed during the many weekends she'd spent in the office working on a case.

The first sign that your career at Lindblad and Wiman was nearing its end was if Wiman was heard describing you as a Cardigan. After that it was just a matter of weeks or months until you were told you weren't "partner material." You weren't fired, they had more tact than that, but it meant it was time to start thinking about Plan B.

"Säpo?" Gabriella said.

She wasn't prepared for this. She made a quick calculation. If the Security Service had talked to Wiman, he probably already knew she was acquainted with the wanted "terrorist" or "elite soldier"—depending on which tabloid you read—Mahmoud Shammosh. Might as well put her cards on the table.

"Regarding Mahmoud Shammosh?" she said.

"Regarding you, Gabriella," Wiman said. He continued to hold her gaze, his red tie glaring in the gloom.

"Me?"

She swallowed. If there was anything that could jeopardize a career, surely becoming the focus of a Säpo investigation must be it?

Wiman nodded. He seemed to enjoy watching her squirm. Was this a test?

"A Mr. Bronzelius, if I remember correctly. He mentioned he'd been looking for you at court?"

Gabriella cleared her throat. Why did she feel guilty? She hadn't done anything wrong.

"That's correct. He found me at the courthouse this morning and interviewed me about a friend of mine. Mahmoud Shammosh. He's wanted for a murder in Belgium, apparently. "

"Doctor Death," Wiman said.

He smiled a thin, barely perceptible smile. Apparently the evening papers had updated their description to include Mahmoud's status as a Ph.D. student. "Sometimes the tabloids really do nail it."

Gabriella said nothing, just nodded.

"Interesting friends you surround yourself with, Gabriella," Wiman said. "A terrorist, huh?"

He seemed to be savoring it.

"What else should we expect from your past? Bank robbers, perhaps? Simple thieves, rapists?"

Gabriella blushed. The insensitivity of Wiman's banter was unbelievable. She struggled with herself not to interrupt him.

"I mean, the more interesting your history is, the better it will be for business, right? A suspected terrorist could be a gold mine for a young lawyer. Especially in this sort of case. Lawyer and terrorist, friends since university. They moved in different directions but were finally reunited in a protracted lawsuit with international overtones. The media will hit the roof. Regardless of how it ends, you'll have made a name for yourself. And a name is the most important thing in this business."

"Okay," Gabriella said. "I'm not sure I understand. What are you trying to get at?"

She was confused. Where was Wiman going with this?

"I believe it's in our—your—interest to make contact with your friend the terrorist. When you do, make sure he hires you as his lawyer immediately, so Säpo can't ask you any tricky questions. Lawyer confidentiality won't protect you until he's your client, as you probably remember from your bar exam."

Gabriella was growing annoyed. She hardly needed reminding of one of the most basic rules of the legal profession. But at the same time, she felt relieved. Not only that Säpo's interest in her might turn out not to be detrimental to her personally, but that she also might even be able to help Mahmoud with her boss's blessing.

"Once contact is established," continued Wiman, "and I have no doubt that will happen in the very near future, make sure Shammosh comes to Sweden. It's absolutely essential, unless you happen to be a member of the Brussels Chapter of the Belgian Law Society, that is? Once he's here, we'll make sure to keep him hidden for a while, in order to maximize exposure. Eventually he'll have to be extradited to Belgium, of course. And then we'll have to cooperate with a Brussels firm—"

"Maximize exposure," interrupted Gabriella at last. She couldn't hold back any longer. "You mean this is a PR opportunity for the company, nothing else? This is my friend we're talking about. And besides, he's innocent. For God sakes, shouldn't that be our focus here?"

Wiman shook his head and smiled his razor thin smile again.

"Gabriella, I appreciate your . . . how shall I put this . . . ideal-ism? Loyalty?"

He articulated the words like questions, as if their meanings were genuinely unfamiliar to him.

"There are different kinds of cases, Gabriella. There are cases where we have to win to get noticed, to get a name. And then there are cases where it's enough to just be a key player. Where, in fact, it might ulti-mately be better not to win. Cases in which a draw is preferable, you might say. You call them PR opportunities. Well, maybe so. The law profession is a business. If *justice* is what you're concerned with, you'd probably feel more at home with the Cardigans in the DA's office."

Gabriella took a deep breath. She was close to being associated with the Cardigans. That was never good.

"Moreover, this isn't just a PR opportunity for the company, it's a PR opportunity for you. This could prove to be a decisive case for your career. This is how stars are made. Plus you'll have the chance to help your friend. It's win-win, Gabriella. Nobody loses. "

What was there to object to anyway? What Wiman was saying meant she'd have an officially sanctioned opportunity to help Mah-moud. If that was because Wiman wanted more media coverage for the company, well it didn't really make much difference. *Win-win*. Gabriella swallowed the sour taste in her mouth.

"Sounds good," she said. "Assuming he gets in touch."

"He will. Keep me updated on this. I want to follow it closely. If we need someplace for him to lie low, I can take care of that. And when the storm hits, we'll hand off your day-to-day stuff to your colleagues. A few more billable hours would do them good. "

Gabriella nodded, thinking that soon her colleagues would have even more reason to dislike her than they already had.

THE HIGH-SPEED TRAIN FROM BRUSSELS slowed, almost silently, under the art nouveau ceiling of Europe's busiest train station, the Gare du Nord in Paris. Klara turned to Mahmoud, who was still sleeping deeply. She untangled her hand from his. The intimacy of an hour ago still hung like a shadow, unfamiliar and foreign.

Mahmoud woke up with a start and looked around.

"Are we there?" he said, gazing out the window onto the crowded platform.

He looked more rested. An hour of sleep seemed to have done him good.

"Yes," replied Klara. "Now we'll see if we guessed right."

"There are police officers out there," Mahmoud said. "I thought you said they don't usually check passports here at the station?"

"I don't think so," Klara replied. "Only if they suspect something fishy. Aren't routine checks prohibited by the Schengen Agreement?"

"You're the hotshot EU expert," Mahmoud said and shrugged. "But I hope you're right. Otherwise things might get a little complicated."

"Because you're wanted for murder?" whispered Klara. She looked at Mahmoud wide-eyed, feigning innocence.

"Can you stop saying 'wanted for murder,'" hissed Mahmoud. "Seriously, it's not a joke."

Klara couldn't help giggling, nervously. The whole situation was too absurd not to joke about it. They stood up and joined the flow of passengers walking through the center aisle.

Klara felt the adrenaline starting to pump through her veins. So far so good. It was unusual to have your passport checked in Paris; she'd been here probably ten times and never been checked. The EU's goal of a Europe without borders seemed to be working so far. Many people commuted between Paris and Brussels every day. But she'd never traveled together with a person wanted for a crime. She could see on Mahmoud's face that he was stressed: his muscles were tense, and he was grinding his teeth almost imperceptibly, as if he was chewing a tiny piece of gum.

They stepped down from the train and moved with the other passengers through the turnstiles at the far end of the platform. Klara struggled to keep from looking at the two policemen who stood watching the new arrivals. They didn't seem very engaged; they mostly seemed to be gazing aimlessly out over the sea of people.

She and Mahmoud had almost reached the turnstiles, when Klara heard someone yelling behind her. The sound of running steps approaching the platform.

"*Monsieur Monsieur! Arrêtez!* Stop!" she heard a man shout behind them.

She felt as if her heart had stopped, as if it had suddenly dislodged from her chest and fallen down on the platform in front of her. Panicked, she glanced sideways at Mahmoud. He met her gaze.

Resolute. Hard. His eyes had a determination that frightened her. He slowly turned around.

But the person wasn't shouting at Mahmoud. Instead, one of the train conductors caught up with another passenger and handed him a bag that he'd apparently left at his seat. If she'd been able to breathe, she would have let out a sigh of relief.

Mahmoud didn't seem relieved. Instead he took firm hold of her arm and led her brusquely through the turnstiles and into the station.

"Just do exactly as I say," he said. "Do not turn around. We're being followed."

S THIS REALLY HOW IT ends? Not with a bang, but a whimper. A ten-hour flight, a week of mandatory vacation, a pat on the back and an empty, gray desk under the unforgiving fluorescent lights of a cheerless office?

"We'll get you an office soon," Susan tells me without meeting my eyes.

But the days go by and the room remains as elusive as my new tasks. Sympathetic glances, whispers around the coffeemaker. They don't know who I am—everyone here is younger than me—but the rumors have preceded me.

I'm the old field agent sent home because he wasn't able to make the tough calls required by war, who didn't have the stomach for Afghanistan. It doesn't surprise me. We're all spies. What do we have if not our rumors, our half-truths, our fragments taken out of context?

The only ones I know are my colleagues who rose through the ranks. Who accepted the proprieties and mastered the shifting alliances. Who have always done better in their town houses than in the shadows. Whose goals from the very beginning were breakfast meetings with presidential advisers and dinner parties with ambassadors. They didn't interest me back then, and they don't interest me now. Nevertheless, they stop by dutifully, glance at my tidy desk while they avoid meeting my eyes, their fingers drumming on the red plastic of my empty inbox.

"Your expertise will be invaluable here," they say, making a quick calculation of how many years are left until they can finally put me out to pasture. Someone recommends a contact at some private company in Iraq.

Everything is privatized now. *Contractors*. Fieldwork and big money. "Your expertise would be invaluable there."

But I can't bring myself to apply. Just sitting up and putting my feet on the floor after another twelve hours of whiskey- and pill-induced sleep is all I can manage. And barely even that. I don't so much as glance at the pool when I drive to work. Perhaps I've forgotten how to swim? God knows I've willed myself to forget everything else.

And I don't dream every night anymore. Not even the recurring nightmares, from which I used to wake up feverish, the sheets kicked off the bed, manically groping my chest, searching for imaginary bullet holes, broken bones, grief. I miss them. When I do dream it's about the mountains. An endless panning shot of gravel and grass in fractured Technicolor, Yves Klein–blue skies, snowcapped peaks, and roads that lead nowhere but farther away. I wake up wanting nothing more than to travel along them.

So go the days, the nights. The endless moments turn into weeks and then years. The monotonous drone of the highway follows me around like tinnitus. When Abu Ghraib has been in the headlines nonstop for a month, I finally get my office. Not a word, nothing. But it is a vindication. A barely audible whisper. A gesture of reconciliation or a bribe. That's how I want to read it. As if they can't really be sure of me. But they know exactly how sure they are of me. They've always known. Who but the most unswervingly loyal would still be here?

We change presidents and as a natural consequence the organization is shaken until everything falls into the exact same place it was from the beginning. No, that's not true. Things change. The madness finally lifts like a cloud of steam and leaves us as we once were. Rational and street-smart rather than evangelical. And we sit back and read about what we've created in the *Washington Post*. An alternative, private, for-profit war machine. Those endless subcontractors. The scope is shocking, even to those of us on the inside, who should know.

———

Slowly I force myself back into the pool, slowly I learn to swim again. Lap after lap, until I no longer keep track, until my arms are so tired I can hardly lift the remote control of the plasma TV in my apartment, which is furnished like an affordable hotel room down to the smallest detail.

Slowly, barely even noticeably, I exchange whiskey for tea, sleeping pills for five times twenty push-ups on the soft carpet of my bedroom floor, twelve hours of dreamless sleep for seven hours of choppy nightmares, sadness, and a shaky, skipping version of life. Until I'm not drinking at all anymore. Not even coffee.

Langley and the swimming pool and AA meetings in depressingly fluorescent-lit classrooms in Palisades or Bethesda. I don't have much more. Evenings watching cable television and eating takeout. One day at a time. That's what became of my life. It's not much. It's almost nothing.

I carry Damascus with me in the locket you gave me, which hangs around my neck. It never leaves me for a second. Everything I'm running from. Everything I've abandoned and sacrificed. It fills me with emptiness. Every Friday I search our records for my daughter's name. Let her name whirl through our endless database while I close my hand around the locket. I pray the only prayer I have, the only thing that matters to me now: Good God almighty, let there be zero results.

It's a week before Christmas. I've bought some twinkling electric lights to put out on my balcony in an awkward approximation of normality. The cardboard box of lights is big but so light I can carry it in one hand as I grope in my pocket for the keys to my Mazda in the gray, perpetual twilight of the mall's parking garage. My footsteps echo on the concrete.

There's a man standing next to my car. A hundred ingrained reflexes are transmitted and multiplied through my spine, my nerves. A hundred opposing impulses of violence and escape. The man straightens up, turns to me, stretches like someone who's been in the same position for a long time. It's an inviting movement, the slow gesture of someone from whom you have nothing to fear. I hear my steps slow in the echo. Finally, I stop. Twenty yards from the car. Just the rustling of a giant fan somewhere. Just the traffic three floors below us. Just a trembling moment, threatening to capsize.

The man stands still and raises his open hands with infinite slowness, in a timeless gesture of peace, good intentions. But it's only when he takes a few, short, slow steps toward me that I see who he is. Twenty-five years of shifting alliances. But I still know who he is.

The mustache is shorter. His face is lined and older. It's not his appearance that unmasks him. It's what seeing him does to my memory of a previous moment. How his gestures, his movements, bring me back, brings the past back. It's connection through pattern recognition, memory through context.

"*Salaam alaikum*," he says.

I clear my throat and take out the key to the car. Unlock it with a click, a beep.

"*Alaikum salaam.*"

We sit in the car. Two shelved spies in a Japanese car, in an American shopping mall, in a world that wriggled away from us, in this unpredictable present that we don't know how to relate to. At first, we say nothing. We just sit there. Not even looking at each other. Ultimately, it's up to me to begin.

"How'd you find me?" I say in Arabic.

He glances at me, obliquely from above. A flash of disappointment in his eyes.

"How did I find you? I've been in the U.S. for quite some time. I have contacts. You know how it works with our background. If you want to find someone, you do. "

I feel stupid. I should never have asked. I've insulted him, his skills, what's left of a life he might no longer lead.

"So," I say. "You live here now?"

He nods, sighs, raises his arms.

"I saw which way the wind was blowing. Already after 9/11. It

was only a matter of time. And your colleagues were accommodating."

"And now?" I say. "What are you doing now?"

He smiles wryly and leans back in the seat.

"Now I teach Arabic at a community college in St. George's
County. My wife is a nurse again."

He stops, shakes his head, clearly uncomfortable with that particular part of his new life. Finally, he shrugs.

"She's American now and seems to like it. It went quickly for
her. It's the American dream, right? Hard work, two cars, and a
small house in Millersville?"

He smiles again. A smile that's ironic but not resigned or bitter.
It's the smile of someone who's long understood the importance of
not fighting against the current, of not asking why or complaining
about how life has changed. It's the smile of a refugee.

"It turned out differently than we imagined," I say. "Everything
turned out differently."

He nods. "It's been a long time since Stockholm."

The diving bell has hit bottom. The reason he sought me out,
which must have been harder than he lets on. I nod.

"Twenty-five years ago," I say. "It feels like yesterday."

"Do you remember that you asked me about something before
our meeting? That you asked me to look into something? As a favor. Between spies."

"Of course."

My heart rate has now doubled in speed. I try to swallow, but my
mouth has stopped producing saliva.

"It was brave. You took a risk. Contacting someone you didn't
know. Adding a personal inquiry onto an official meeting. It's rare.
Right?"

He turns in his seat and looks me straight in the eye.

"Anyone who makes such an inquiry is either ignorant or trying to fool themselves. Do you agree?"

"What do you mean?" I say.

He shakes his head gently. He looks tired, old.

"You're not ignorant. You had your suspicions. Founded suspicions. And you knew that I would never be able to verify them. That it doesn't work that way. You knew I would give you an empty answer. Something that is not a lie and not the truth. Still you asked. Still you asked who killed your girlfriend, the mother of your daughter. You asked me when you didn't even know who I was."

"I was desperate," I say carefully. "I was willing to do anything."

He shakes his head again and opens his backpack, pulls a beige folder out of it. Balances it on his knees. I close my eyes. Lean back, feel the blood pulsing through my body.

"You asked me because you knew that my answer would be empty. That it would be possible to interpret however you wanted to. You wanted to be able to choose the easy way. Lie or truth. You chose the path of least resistance. Who am I to judge you for that?"

I don't say anything. Barely even breathe.

"And maybe I should let it be. What good will it do now?" he says. "To bring up the past? It has been such a long time. But this life turned us into instruments. Nothing more. Constantly ready to act on whatever they chose to share with us. Constantly ready to switch sides, switch ideology, or methods."

I nod, my eyes still closed. There is no difference. We're all the same.

"And now it's over for both of us. Life as we had imagined it. Maybe it's time to stop lying to ourselves too?"

206

He lifts the folder and drops it in my lap. It weighs almost nothing. The truth weighs almost nothing. I don't open my eyes until I hear the car door close behind him, until I hear the echo of his footsteps through the empty garage. I don't need to open the folder. I already know what it contains.

MAHMOUD WAS ABSOLUTELY CERTAIN. WHEN he'd turned around quickly on the platform, he'd caught a glimpse of the girl from the Brussels airport. She had been walking calmly among the other passengers twenty yards behind them.

He led them, his hand still on Klara's elbow, away from the platform. At the entrance to the terminal, he saw a sign with an arrow leading to the storage lockers. One floor down. Next to the rental cars. Mahmoud felt the adrenaline mixing with his blood, but tried hard not to let it show that he'd discovered his pursuers.

"How did you pay for the tickets in Brussels?" he whispered to Klara.

"Um, with my debit card, I think."

He nodded.

"Shit. I should have warned you. Fuck. It seems like they're able to follow everything we do. They must have seen that you bought the tickets and followed us onto the train."

Klara said nothing. Just nodded. She didn't look scared, only focused.

"You have the phone we bought in Brussels?" Mahmoud said.

After Klara had returned with the train tickets, Mahmoud had bought two cheap burner phones, so that if they had to split up they'd still be able to stay in contact.

"Yes," she replied. "In my purse."

"Good. We're going to have to take a huge risk. I think our best chance is to split up."

Mahmoud turned his head and looked straight into her eyes. She met his gaze.

"Okay," she said.

In the first few weeks of his ranger training Mahmoud had learned that you never know exactly how a person might react to extreme stress. Some become unreasonable, irrational, lose their self-control. Those who seemed to be natural leaders might suddenly become paralyzed. For others, their calm and focus increased with the degree of stress. Somehow he'd probably always known he wouldn't have to worry about Klara. Still, the realization left him feeling relieved and strangely moved.

"And you have the locker ticket too?" Mahmoud said.

"In my wallet," she said.

"Good. Here's what we're going to do. We'll walk out to the taxi stand, like everything is normal. If there's a line, we'll just wait calmly in it. When we get a taxi, you'll jump in first. As soon as you get into the car, you'll scoot right through the backseat and out the other side. Okay?"

Klara's eyes darted around nervously. She swallowed hard. She too was feeling the adrenaline.

"Okay."

"I'll drive away in the taxi and draw off our pursuers. You stay out of the way for a while, then hopefully you'll be able to empty the storage locker and take the subway as far away from here as you possibly can. I'll call you in a few hours, and we'll meet up again."

"And if I can't shake them? What do we do?"

"Then we'll figure something else out. But this is the plan. Right now, it's all we've got."

"Remind me never to travel with you again," Klara said.

Mahmoud stopped, turned toward her, took her face in his hands and pulled it toward him, pretending to kiss her tenderly on the cheek.

"You can do this, Klara," he whispered. "We can do this, okay? What was it your grandfather used to say again? Rock and salt? That's what you're made of, right?"

They'd nearly reached the taxi stand. Mahmoud felt his pulse racing even faster. It was a crucial moment. Sink or swim.

"Wait," he said to Klara.

He took off his backpack, bent down, and pretended to rummage in it while looking over his shoulder. The blond girl was moving in a wide arc in the same direction as them. On the opposite wall, he saw a man of about thirty-five moving in a similar pattern. He seemed to fit the profile. Physically fit, loose cargo pants. Ski jacket and a duffel bag. Bluetooth headset in his ear. Most likely an American. So there were two at least. He couldn't see any more.

"There are two of them at least," he whispered to Klara without looking at her.

"A blond girl with a ponytail in a dark blue Canada Goose jacket. And a guy wearing cargo pants and a grayish red ski jacket. Baseball cap. Both of them have headsets in their ears. Pretend you're stretching, while I fiddle with the backpack."

Klara did as he said. Stretched, and took the opportunity to scout the terminal.

"I see them," she said. "I recognize the girl. She was in my apartment."

Her voice was strained. Her face tightened.

"Focus, Klara," whispered Mahmoud. "Focus. It's all about technique. There is no emotion here, you understand? No feelings. In and out of the taxi. That's the plan."

Klara nodded calmly, collecting herself.

"Good. Here we go," Mahmoud said, and stood up.

The street outside the station was chaotic; full of smoke and cars and business travelers crossing at random pulling suitcases and families with backpacks and maps and crying children. At least there was no queue for the taxis. They walked up to the first one with determined steps.

"You know what you're supposed to do?" he hissed.

"Don't worry. Just do your part, and I'll do mine," she replied.

Mahmoud opened the car door, and Klara jumped into the backseat of the taxi. She glided across the worn and cracked leather seat, slightly hunched over, and opened the door on the other side just enough to be able slip out into the street. She didn't even turn around to look at Mahmoud.

"Louvre," Mahmoud said to the taxi driver.

It was the only thing he could come up with in the heat of the moment. The driver turned and looked over his shoulder, obviously confused by the young woman first jumping out into the street and now crouching behind his left rear wheel.

"Drive! Now!" Mahmoud said in English.

The driver shrugged and put the car into gear. They rolled out into the Parisian traffic. Mahmoud turned around in his seat and saw the guy in the cargo pants jumping into a small dark blue Volkswagen Golf, which must have been waiting for him across the street. So there are more than two, thought Mahmoud. The airport girl was standing in the taxi queue with a finger pressed against her headset. Mahmoud couldn't see Klara, but unless the airport girl had seen her—and there was no indication she had—Klara had probably made it.

KLARA RAN, CROUCHING ALONG THE line of taxis until she felt like she must be outside the field of vision of her pursuers. From the corner of her eye, she could see Cargo Pants jogging across the street. Klara snuck between two parked cars, so he wouldn't see her. Her heart was racing. A dark blue Golf came rolling up the street, and the man jumped into the passenger side, then the car seemed to take off in pursuit of Mahmoud's taxi.

Cautiously, Klara peeked between the cars. Ponytail was still standing in front of the side entrance to the station. It looked like she was talking to someone on her headset while scouting the surroundings. It was definitely the girl in running clothes that she'd seen come out of her front door. Klara felt sick, as if she might vomit. How long had they been spying on her? She took control of her breathing. Forcing herself to breathe deeply and evenly. No feelings. Shove aside your emotions. Shove away your thoughts.

She knew she had to make her way into the station again to access the luggage lockers. Still crouching slightly, she started moving down the street behind the cars. When she got to the corner of the station, she peered back along the sidewalk. Ponytail had disappeared. Klara took a red knitted hat out of her purse and pulled it down over her ears. She carefully tucked all of her dark hair under its edges. When she was done, she took off her dark blue coat and hung it over her bag. She shivered. Her gray cardigan, which had cost her a fortune in Antwerp, was not primarily designed for warmth. Paris was as cold as Brussels, but it couldn't hurt to alter her appearance as much as possible.

She gathered herself and started walking toward the main entrance. A steady stream of Friday commuters was flowing through the station, and Klara let herself be swept along by the wave. She followed the signs to the storage lockers and took the escalator down one floor.

In order to enter the lockers area she had to pass through a security screening. All bags were x-rayed by a grim-faced guard. A short line had formed behind the turnstiles. When it was Klara's turn, she put her shoulder bag and coat on the belt.

"Excuse me," she said and turned to the guard, "could you tell me where I can find C193?"

She had to make an effort to breathe normally. The guard looked attentively at her before answering.

"Section C is over there, mademoiselle."

Klara thanked him and retrieved her things from the conveyor belt. Maybe, just maybe, luck was on their side.

———

It took her no more than a minute to locate the locker. It was small, the smallest kind available, and square. Maybe two feet by two feet.

She leaned forward and entered the code that was on the receipt. She held her breath. A red light shone beside the locker door. A short message in French appeared on the display. Wrong code.

Klara felt the floor sway beneath her feet. Wrong code. She took out the receipt again, slowly pressing the six digits once more.

It took a few seconds for a green light to come on, another few seconds for the door to swing open with a mechanical click. Klara bent forward and peered into the small space.

A slim nylon bag was the only thing inside the locker. Squatting, she gently pulled it out into the bright light and unzipped it. The bag contained a small, aluminum-colored Apple computer. A MacBook Air. The smallest available. Klara zippered the bag again and closed her eyes for a second. Beautiful, beautiful luck. She stood up and started walking back toward the exit. Something at the periphery of her vision suddenly caught her attention. A movement outside the glass wall separating the rental car counters from the baggage room. She turned her head and caught what was possibly Ponytail's silhouette.

"Shit," she hissed.

But there was no turning back now. Rock and salt. She pressed her way through a group of travelers checking their bags and backpacks, and kept her eyes fixed on the glass wall. Nothing there. Maybe she'd imagined it. She threw the nylon bag over her shoulder as she walked out of the luggage room. No feelings, she thought. Get up to street level and take a taxi. Call Mahmoud. One thing at a time.

It was at that moment that she felt it. At first only faintly. But it was unmistakable. Artificial cherry. American chewing gum. She spun around. And there, only a few feet away from her stood Ponytail.

She knew instinctively that it was the wrong thing to do, but she couldn't help herself. Adrenaline rushing through her, she pushed her way through a group of Japanese tourists and ran, panicked, toward the escalators. She didn't turn around, just ran as fast as she could up the stairs, through the waiting room. Away, away, away.

IT WAS NEARING RUSH HOUR. Both Mahmoud's taxi and the Golf, a few cars behind them, were stuck in the bumper-to-bumper Parisian Christmas traffic. Mahmoud was trying to hold his stress at bay. There was nothing worse than having no control over your situation, being at the mercy of other people's choices. In his head he went through his options. He could disappear down into the Métro again. In the long run, he'd be able to shake off his pursuers there. But it was a time-consuming task. And he was worried about Klara. Why had he given her the assignment of checking the locker?

He hadn't counted on Ponytail from the airport staying behind. His plan had been impulsive. It filled him with anxiety. Maybe they had seen Klara sneaking out of the taxi and regrouped? He tried to call her again, but got an automated message in French. Probably she was busy with the storage locker and hadn't heard the signal. But he couldn't help imagining far worse scenarios.

Mahmoud turned around. The traffic inched forward. The Golf remained about eighty feet behind them. It was time to make a decision. He had to shake off his pursuers and find Klara. Take a chance. It was the only way.

"What street are we on?" Mahmoud said to the taxi driver.

The driver turned around and looked at him with his hangdog eyes.

"Rue La Fayette," he said.

"Where? Which intersection?"

"Almost at rue de Châteaudun. But in this traffic it'll take us twenty minutes to get there," the driver said.

He sounded defeated. Mahmoud turned around again. Traffic was at a complete standstill. He glimpsed the Golf behind them. He took out his prepaid phone, dialed three digits, and waited for the signal to go through.

It took less than seven minutes before Mahmoud heard the sirens of two police motorcycles. He turned around to look out the rear window. They were driving between the gridlocked lanes and stopped a car's length behind the dark blue Golf. The cabdriver rolled down the window and stuck his head out to see what was going on. Cold air filled the car. Around them bored drivers turned their heads toward the Golf. Mahmoud leaned forward to the taxi driver and tapped him on the shoulder. The man turned around irritably.

"I'm getting out here," Mahmoud said.

He handed a ten-euro bill to the surprised driver.

"Keep the change."

Mahmoud glanced over his shoulder. A police officer in graphite blue Kevlar armor had climbed off his motorcycle and was walking calmly, his hand on his gun, toward the Golf.

This was his chance. Mahmoud opened the door of the taxi and slid gently onto the cracked concrete. The air smelled of exhaust and winter. He crawled among the cars until he got to the sidewalk. The sky was low and gray. As if it hadn't yet decided what kind of storm to unleash. It must be a little above freezing; rain was almost as likely as snow. Before running down the stairs to the Métro station Cadet, he turned around one last time. Traffic was moving, but the Golf was still there, with its hazard lights flashing. The police had forced Cargo Pants and his driver out on the street, and they seemed to be arguing heatedly. Cargo Pants craned his neck, trying to keep an eye on the taxi. Had he seen Mahmoud leaving it? It didn't matter, the Americans would have their hands full for a few minutes convincing the police that they hadn't threatened another vehicle with a gun. By the time they succeeded, it would be too late. As he reached the bottom of the stairs, he felt his phone vibrate in his pocket. Klara.

KLARA WAS SHAKING FROM THE cold, though she'd put her coat on again when she'd come down into the Métro. She pushed her hands deep into her pockets and looked around for the hundredth time. She'd really thought it was over for a moment, when she'd met those eyes at the Gare du Nord. That it was the end. The fear she'd felt. The panic. Because the girl with the ponytail had seen her too. But there'd been too many people between them, and Ponytail hadn't been able to catch up with Klara, who had taken the escalator two steps at a time, and ended up in the transit hall. Without turning around, she'd flung herself down the nearest Métro stairs, jumped onto the first train that pulled into the station, and ridden it to the end of the line. But it had been a close call. Far, far too close.

"You look stressed, Klara," Mahmoud said. "Are you okay?"

Klara winced when she felt Mahmoud's cold hand against her cheek.

"Where the hell have you been?" she said.

They had arranged to meet fifteen minutes ago. A quarter of an hour of paranoia and torment. Mahmoud smiled slightly, his eyes searching the station.

"I've been here a while," he said. "Thought I'd scan the surroundings before I showed myself."

"What?" Klara said. "You let me stand around like some fucking bait while you figured out if it was safe enough?"

Klara felt her stress turn to annoyance. Who the hell did he think he was? But Mahmoud just shrugged.

"Sorry," he said. "It would have been better to meet somewhere else if things didn't look good."

His brown, cool eyes scanned the station once again. There was an impatience in his expression that made him seem arrogant, almost callous, but he was neither. He'd just moved on to the next page. Always one step, one move ahead. That was what had attracted her to him in the beginning, and what had also sometimes frustrated her.

"Was there anything in the locker?" he said.

Klara raised her arm to show him the bag hanging over her shoulder. She patted it and nodded.

"A computer," she said. "It didn't go entirely smoothly."

She told him about Ponytail and her escape in the station. Mahmoud nodded calmly.

"I'm sorry that you got involved in all of this," he said.

Klara just nodded.

"Oh well," she said at last. "I guess it's my own fault. How did you escape them, anyway?"

Mahmoud smiled proudly.

"I called the police. Said I saw someone waving a gun in a dark blue Golf. It took five minutes for the cops to get there. They couldn't very well chase after me then. I'm a bloody genius."

Klara glanced at him. For the first time, he looked as she remembered him. Full of initiative and mischievous, charming arrogance.

"So you have a plan?" Mahmoud said.

Klara hadn't wanted to tell him over the phone. It felt like it would be easier to explain it to Mahmoud face-to-face. She grabbed his arm gently and started to guide him out of the station. Out on the street big, wet snowflakes, lit by the yellow streetlights, were falling through the exhaust and melting before touching the ground.

"Okay, so this is the thing," she began. "I have a boyfriend in Paris. Or not really a boyfriend, but something like that. A guy. Or a man, I guess."

Mahmoud smiled an annoyingly ironic smile and looked away.

"Not a guy, but a man? I get it. How old is he?"

Klara pretended not to notice.

"He lives on Victor Hugo. Maybe he can help us."

"Maybe?" Mahmoud said.

A concerned, surprised wrinkle in his forehead.

"Yes. He's home now, I called him. Alone," she added.

"Alone?" Mahmoud said.

He turned toward her. There was a sympathetic note in his voice now. His eyes were no longer cool, but tender. Soft darts from the past. Promises whispered at the Carolina Rediviva library, on wet bridges over the Fyris river at dawn, after sleepless nights, two bodies side by side on a narrow bed in a run-down dorm room. She'd forgotten how she'd loved Mahmoud. He was the only man she'd ever loved. How could you forget something like that? She turned her face up and felt the snowflakes landing like tears on her cheeks.

"He's married," she said. "And has a daughter."

She regretted saying it. It felt too hard to explain. She didn't know what words to use to describe what had happened in Cyril's apartment that morning. It already felt distant, unreal. But Mahmoud just nodded.

"And how do you think he can help us?" he said.

"I don't know. Maybe we can sleep there tonight. Check the computer that was in Lindman's locker? I don't know. If you have a better plan just say so. But our relationship isn't really—how should I put this—official?"

"Can we trust him? I mean it's a pretty big deal to waltz in with your ex, the murder suspect."

"We've been discreet," Klara said.

She shook her head, trying to clear her mind, trying to make everything fall into place.

"I'd begun to trust him. Until I found a photo of him with his family this morning. And now I guess it's more in his interest that our relationship doesn't come out than in mine. "

"Oh my God," Mahmoud said. "You found out this morning that he had a family?"

Klara nodded. She felt so small, so stupid and naive. Mahmoud said nothing but gently put his arm around her, pulled her close. Klara felt the heat of him through the snow, through their clothes and jackets.

"I'm sorry, Klara," he said. "Really sorry. But yes, we have to take a look at this computer and calm down. Do you think you could manage going to his place?"

She nodded.

"Yes," she said. "Absolutely. Protecting a wanted ex-boyfriend with a, well . . . *complicated* sexual orientation is the least you can expect from a conservative politician, right?"

December 20, 2013

Brussels, Belgium

GEORGE TOOK ONE LAST BITE of his chicken vindaloo and put the plastic fork down in the foil box with a grimace, after which he stuffed a dry piece of naan bread into his mouth and chewed thoroughly, trying to minimize the paralyzing heat. Couldn't Reiper and his people at least order in some proper food? He felt tired and fat. How long had it been since he'd gone to the gym?

And why couldn't he just go home? Instead they were making him book travel arrangements and hotel rooms in Paris. Like some fucking secretary. Pointless to ask what the hell was going on. Josh, the fucking sociopath, just smiled his superior smile and said things worked on a need-to-know basis. What an ass he was, Josh.

And no one from Merchant & Taylor would return his calls. Soon it would be the weekend. Not very likely he'd hear from Appleby then. This was fucking insane. He'd put his soul into becoming someone at that company. Had worked his ass off for the first time in his life. He was a rising talent, a man for the big customers, for broad strategies. Hadn't Appleby himself said as much over that amazing dinner at Comme chez Soi? Was it possible that had happened only yesterday? Now he felt completely disconnected.

Dismissed. Not even worthy of having his calls returned. He considered firing off another message to Appleby but stopped himself. He didn't want to appear desperate.

Instead he got up to turn on the ceiling light in the little maid's room they'd put him in. The remains of the Indian takeout disgusted him, the scent of cumin and chili making him nauseated. He crumpled up the foil trays and shoved them into the thin plastic bag Josh had given him a half hour ago. There had to be a garbage can in the kitchen.

The hall outside his room was dark, and George couldn't find a light switch. Inside the living room, he heard muffled, mumbling voices. A narrow streak of light streamed out under the closed door. With the bag still in his hand, George crept across the floor. He held his breath as the floor swayed and creaked under him. Finally, he put his ear gently against the door.

"And everyone knows the game plan? Code Black. We leave no trace. No survivors. That has to be absolutely clear. We can't afford any more mistakes."

It was Reiper's voice, dry and matter-of-fact. George thought for a second he might fall backward, might faint. It felt like the oxygen in the air around him had thinned out, and he had to fight to breathe.

No survivors.

He couldn't believe he'd heard correctly. He backed away from the door.

No survivors.

He tripped back into the maid's room, dropped the plastic bag. A disgusting sludge of orange chicken vindaloo oozed onto the floor. With trembling hands, he fished his wallet out of the inside pocket of his jacket. Dug with his fingers in one of the soft calfskin pockets. Emergency rations. He grabbed the small bag. Poured the cocaine onto the computer desk with trembling fingers and drew it up his nose with a few quick snorts. Closed his eyes and felt himself almost lift off of the chair.

No survivors.

THE FIVE-STORY BUILDING ON AVENUE Victor Hugo, number 161 in the sixteenth arrondissement, was everything Mahmoud had always expected of Paris. A white plastered facade with tall, mullioned windows and green shutters. The whole neighborhood seemed to consist of old money and well-tended flower boxes. Klara rang the little bell next to the front door.

"It's me," she said in English when it crackled.

The door opened with a growling sound, and they stepped into an echoing stairwell. Frescoes depicting flowers and garlands covered the walls. A warm light streamed down from an enormous light fixture on the ceiling. Klara went over to the ancient elevator and pressed the button.

"Not the elevator," Mahmoud said.

He pointed toward the stairs.

"I want to make sure that no one is waiting for us on our way up," he whispered.

Klara nodded in reply.

Cyril lived on the top floor of the house. They climbed briskly up the stairs without talking to each other. Cyril's door was ajar. Mahmoud looked at Klara, who shrugged and attempted an unconvincing smile. Just as she was turning toward the door to push it open, her cell phone beeped. Two distinct beeps. The classic signal for receiving text messages. Mahmoud couldn't believe his ears.

"What the hell," he hissed. "You haven't turned off your phone?"

He felt the panic come rushing in.

"Have you been using it since we got here?"

Klara's face was pale as she stuck her hand in her purse to fish out her phone.

"I just had to get Cyril's number. But I called from a pay phone. I must have forgotten to turn it off."

She looked terrified.

"Have they been able to follow us now?"

"No idea," Mahmoud said. "But we can't afford this."

They were interrupted by the door being opened. Cyril stood in front of them, impeccably dressed in well-tailored chinos and a Ralph Lauren shirt. His hair was damp, as if he'd just come out of the shower.

But it only took Mahmoud one quick look at his face to know something was terribly wrong. He was pale and his eyes kept roaming toward the stairs. He obviously didn't know what to do with his hands. At first he held them out toward Klara, only to withdraw them. He tried putting his left hand in his pocket and took it out again. This was no longer a young, promising French politician standing in front of them, but a broken man.

"Klara," he said and tried a shaky smile. "What are you doing here? You were so mysterious on the phone. Who's your friend?"

Mahmoud turned toward Klara, who hadn't answered. She was reading something on her cell phone. Her eyes were narrow.

"Klara," Cyril said again. "Come in, don't stand out there for God's sake."

Klara slowly turned her eyes from her phone to Cyril. It took her a second before she opened her mouth to speak.

"Oh my God," she said at last.

Her eyes were empty, bottomless, all emotion completely erased. Mahmoud knew that look. He'd seen it only once in his life. Three years ago at Arlanda airport. Just before Klara had picked up her bags and gone to check in without turning around.

"What have you done, Cyril?" she said.

Cyril swallowed. Instinctively, Mahmoud almost felt sorry for him. He was obviously not accustomed to being at such a complete disadvantage.

"Klara! You don't understand! They said you were being held prisoner by a terrorist, and that I should contact them if you came here."

Klara shook her head but didn't release Cyril's gaze.

"They said they had photographs, sound recordings. Of you and me. That they'd filmed us together in your apartment. They'd release them if I didn't cooperate. Klara, you have to understand! You always knew what we had was temporary? I have a family, a child. You must have understood that?"

Mahmoud had no time to react before Cyril was moaning and gasping for air on the granite floor, both hands over his crotch. Klara's kick had been as explosive as it was precise. She squatted down beside him, and swept a jet-black lock of hair from her eyes.

"Where are they?" she whispered. "Inside the apartment? On the street? Answer, or I swear I will kill you."

Cyril looked up at her. His eyes were moist and he whimpered faintly, like a dog.

"They're not here," he hissed. "I don't know where. On the street, maybe, I don't know, I promise."

"Where's your car?" Klara's voice was steady and as cold as the rocks of the archipelago.

"In the inner courtyard," he said.

"Give me your keys and your wallet."

Cyril hesitated and looked up at her in surprise.

"Come on, Klara, we can surely solve——"

She silenced him with a slap across his cheek. Cyril swore and tried to grab her hands, while rolling over on his side. But Mahmoud stopped him with a kick just below the left knee. Cyril howled and rolled onto his back.

"Give her the keys," Mahmoud said. "Come on, can't you see she's serious?"

Cyril motioned toward the apartment.

"On the hall table," he said, defeated. "Both the keys and the wallet."

Mahmoud stepped over him into the apartment.

"What's the PIN code for your cards," Klara said.

"Now!"

Cyril muttered a four-digit code.

"You better hope you're telling the truth," Mahmoud said as he came back out onto the landing with the wallet and keys in hand.

Klara stood up and brushed off her pants. Mahmoud grabbed her hand and led her away from Cyril. But just before they reached the stairs, she let go and went back over to Cyril, who had managed to rise to his knees. She bent down, grabbed his chin, and bent it upward, forcing him to look her straight in the eye.

"By the way," she said with a voice that was completely empty of emotion. "It's over, asshole."

December 20, 2013

Paris, France

MAHMOUD THREW OPEN THE DOOR to the courtyard, their footsteps still echoing behind them in the stairwell. A lonely lamp lit the small, narrow parking lot. It was snowing more than before. A thin layer covered about a dozen cars in front of them.

"Which one is his?" Mahmoud said.

"A blue Jaguar."

"Discreet."

It took no more than a few seconds to find it. Mahmoud unlocked it and hopped into the tobacco-colored, worn leather seat. Klara sat down next to him.

"Oh my God, Klara," Mahmoud said and turned toward her. "What did it say in that message you got? I mean, you turned into Lisbeth Salander up there."

Klara stuck her hand into her pocket and took out her BlackBerry. She held it up to Mahmoud. The message was short: THEY'RE GOING TO KILL YOU. STAY HIDDEN. / GEORGE.

"George?" Mahmoud said.

"I only know one George." Klara said. "A Swedish guy I met a few times at parties in Brussels. He looks like a Wall Street jerk and works for a lobbying firm. I really have no idea what he has to do with any of this."

She shook her head, as if trying to wake up from a dream.

"It's so sick," she said. "I could see that something was wrong as soon as Cyril opened the door."

Mahmoud just nodded. His brain was filled to the breaking point, impossible to penetrate. He also shook his head.

"We have to get out of here," Klara said. "Who knows how much time we have."

Mahmoud turned the key, and the Jaguar started with a growl. The wipers scraped the thin layer of snow from the windshield. In the hidden storage compartment between the seats Klara found a remote control for the gate facing the street, while Mahmoud maneuvered the car out of its parking spot. He drove up to the gate and stopped, then turned to Klara.

"There's no way of knowing what's on the other side of that door," he said.

She just stared straight ahead and nodded, something intractable in her ice blue eyes.

"Might as well find out," she said and pressed the single red button on the remote.

The gate responded with a humming sound, and started to rise slowly.

Mahmoud revved the engine and threw another glance at Klara.

"You're tougher than you seem," he said.

"Just you wait," Klara replied.

Before the door was fully open Mahmoud pressed down on the gas pedal and released the clutch. The car's six-cylinder engine rumbled, the tires spun a few times before taking hold. There was only a centimeter or two to spare between the car roof and door, as they shot out onto Avenue Victor Hugo. Sparks flew as the bumper scraped against the curb. The tires skidded on the slushy asphalt, and Mahmoud struggled for control of the steering wheel. Cars honked and braked. Some pedestrians looked out from under their umbrellas to see what was going on. Soon Mahmoud and Klara were driving down the street at high speed. Melting snow ran in rivulets down the windshield.

"Is anyone behind us?" shouted Mahmoud.

Klara turned around, craning her neck to see.

"I don't know. The damn snow. I can't see out the rear window. Yes, wait! A black van! It was parked on the sidewalk when we arrived. They're after us. Fuck!"

There was less traffic now. Mahmoud remained in second gear and maneuvered the Jaguar into the left lane. Floored the gas. Passed two cars and slipped back into the right-hand lane. He barely heard the honking of oncoming traffic, didn't notice their fists and middle fingers. The only thing that mattered was getting away.

"What about now?" he shouted to Klara.

Klara turned around in her seat again, straining to see.

"I can't see them."

Sirens were blaring somewhere. In the rearview mirror Mahmoud saw the faint blue lights of police cars.

"Are those coming after us?" Klara said.

Mahmoud shrugged, focusing on the road, the wet asphalt, the snow that wouldn't stop falling.

"Who knows? Maybe your boyfriend got fed up and reported us for stealing his car."

"He's not my boyfriend. Anymore."

They were approaching an intersection. Mahmoud saw the traffic lights turning yellow. He changed lanes and floored the gas pedal. Sink or swim. He barely noticed a car veering onto the sidewalk to avoid them. The sirens were blaring behind them. The black van. Still in the left-hand lane he drove straight toward the red light. The oncoming traffic seemed to be standing still, paralyzed by their recklessness. He spun the wheel. An intersection was approaching at breakneck speed. To the right there seemed to be an alley that led, straight and narrow, like a tunnel through some well-polished Parisian balconies. He put all his money on that one card and swung hard to the right. The tires screeched on the asphalt, but didn't lose traction. The sound of sirens subsided.

"Where are they? Do you see them?" Mahmoud shouted at Klara. He had no idea what he was doing.

"Over there!" she said, pointing to the left. "A grocery store with parking underneath. Drive down there!"

Mahmoud saw the sign. SUPERMARCHÉ CASINO. An arrow to a parking garage. Fifty yards. He didn't slow down until he started turning the wheel. The car jumped and shook as it went over the low curb. The grocery store appeared to be open. A bar was down in front of the entrance to the parking lot. Mahmoud stopped, rolled down the window, and pressed the green button. It took forever for the bar to rise. They rolled down a curved ramp and into the garage.

"Where are they? Do you see them?"

Mahmoud's eyes were fixed on the rearview mirror.

"Nothing so far," Klara said.

———

The garage was another world. Small families were pushing shopping carts toward their station wagons under cold fluorescent light.

Children and parents. The absolute normality of it was almost shocking. Mahmoud had forgotten that there was such a thing as a normal, real world. A world where he wasn't wanted for murder. A world where he wasn't threatened with automatic weapons, didn't beat up promising French politicians, didn't watch old army buddies get shot in the head. He parked the Jaguar in a vacant spot. Calmly. Like any normal Parisian Friday shopper. After he turned off the engine, he rested his head against the steering wheel. Its walnut frame was cool and soothing against his forehead. He released his desperate grip gently. His knuckles ached.

Klara had already opened the passenger door.

"Come on, damn it," she shouted into the car. "We don't know how much time we have."

December 20, 2013

Paris, France

THEY COULDN'T FIND THE STAIRS fast enough, so they took the elevator up from the parking lot, crammed into opposite corners by shopping carts. Bing Crosby sang "Silent Night" over the crackling speaker. The elevator walls were covered by ads for deals on foie gras, oysters, and champagne. Parisian Christmas food. Klara glanced at Mahmoud. He was grinding his teeth, his eyes locked on the worn elevator door in front of them.

Klara was also focused and on edge. She felt aware of every muscle in her body, and every thought was clear and simple, concentrated.

The doors opened and the shoppers and their carts detached themselves, leaving the oversize elevator one by one. Finally it was just Klara and Mahmoud left. They looked at each other. Klara shrugged.

"Let's go."

They stepped out under the fluorescent lights in front of the checkout counters of the Supermarché Casino. And nothing happened. Just Christmas decorations and Friday shoppers.

"Did we make it?" Klara said.

Mahmoud looked around, tense, almost crouching, as if he couldn't believe his eyes.

"It almost seems like it," he said. "Maybe they got stuck back at the red light."

They began moving hesitantly toward the exit.

"No black van," Mahmoud said, peering out of the windows.

When the automatic doors slid open, Klara saw her immediately through the heavy snowfall. Across the street, flooded by the light from the streetlamps. Those eyes from yesterday, from earlier today. Ponytail. No more than thirty yards away from them. And she saw them too.

"They're here!" screamed Klara as she turned and grabbed Mahmoud's arm to pull him back into the store.

"They're here!"

But Mahmoud's arm felt heavy. Pulling her down toward the floor instead of inside toward the store. The automatic doors on the street side closed silently.

"Come on, we have to get out of here!" she screamed, crouching down, and grabbing his arm.

The glass doors exploded in a shower of small crystals. Time stopped. Klara threw herself onto the floor in front of the cash registers. Behind her a shelf of sparkling wine, displayed enticingly at the entrance, collapsed. Crushed bottles mixed with the glass from the door. The sweet smell of cheap wine. Screams and chaos. Customers threw themselves to the floor in panic all around her. From the speakers Bing Crosby sang, "*Jingle bells, jingle bells, jingle all the way*." Klara kept pulling on Mahmoud's arm.

"Come on! Come on!"

She turned toward him. Mahmoud lay on his back in the middle of the crushed glass. His brown eyes were wide open and blank in the unforgiving fluorescent light. On his forehead, just above the right eye, Klara saw a small black hole.

It was only then that she saw the blood.

Huge amounts of red, sticky blood spreading like a living mass, like a halo, around the back of his head, mixing with the spilled wine.

"Moody, Moody, come on, come on!"

She tugged at his arm, trying with all her might to get him to the protection of the checkout lanes or anywhere else. As if there were any kind of protection. Everywhere people were screaming, carts were being overturned, goods were being crushed against the concrete floor. He was too heavy. She couldn't budge him.

Instead she bent over his face, down to the neck she'd kissed so many times, so long ago. Her jeans were soaked with his blood, and stuck to her knees. Broken glass cut into her palms as she laid her cheek against his mouth. Groped with her fingers against his neck. But there was nothing there. No breath. No pulse. Only his brown eyes, from which all life had vanished.

Her adrenaline was pumping. Was this it? she wondered.

She raised her eyes. She could see a man and woman running through the falling snow. Something heavy and black in their hands. Weapons.

"Moody! Moody!"

Panic. Shock. The first, almost unidentifiable, feeling of a sadness so deep it scared her far more than the murderers outside. It took her a split-second to decide not to die. A flash through her mind. An unprecedented clarity. She'd never stopped loving Mahmoud. She had repressed it but not forgotten. And she couldn't let it end here. Shot down like a dog, extinguished, spilled onto the dirty floor of a grocery store. Portrayed as a murderer and a terrorist. It couldn't end here.

"I love you, Moody," she whispered with her lips against his.

Then she released his arm, got up, and ran past the checkouts, past the crouching customers, into the store. Somewhere in the background, she heard the sound of sirens.

She ran through the glass and the wine and the chaos. She couldn't hear the screams and sobs. Her head was completely empty as she zigzagged through the shelves. She didn't look back.

Farther into the store a strange calm reigned. Customers moved cautiously in the direction of the cash registers, uncertain of what was happening. At the back of the store stood an unmanned deli counter. All the staff seemed to have moved toward the entrance. Klara rounded it and ran through a pair of swinging doors into a messy stockroom. A man in a white apron and hairnet, who apparently hadn't noticed the chaos at the other end of the store, shouted at her. Klara barely registered him; she had eyes only for the green emergency exit sign. The bloody jeans clung to her legs.

She pressed the handle of the emergency exit door with her elbow, trying to avoid driving the shards of glass any deeper into her palms than they already were. The door led out to a loading dock at the back of the store. A thin layer of snow covered the ground. The snow was falling fast and diagonally in the twilight. A short hop down from the loading dock, and she was in a courtyard. The bloody soles of her shoes left red tracks as she ran across the snow, out through an exit with a yellow traffic bar, and onward to a side street where the snow had already melted away. She turned left. It wasn't until after she had run a hundred yards across the pavement that she looked back over her shoulder. No one was following her.

A SINGLE STROKE. TWO. THREE. BREATH. I close my eyes and shut out water, thoughts, memories.

A single stroke. Two. Three. Breath. I'm a torpedo that never exploded. A dud.

I break the rhythm, swim four strokes without breathing. Then five. Six.

I turn at the far end, the soles of my feet touch the tiles for a moment. The force of my push moves up my calves and my thighs. I feel how my energy is converted, how the power turns to meaningless speed. I stay underwater much longer than is efficient. Half of the pool, longer. Long past the point where the momentum is overcome by the resistance of the water. And farther still.

I continue downward. Allow the speed to slow further, let my legs stop kicking, my arms rest. I empty my lungs. The pressure on my eardrums. The sound of air bubbling out of my nose, my mouth, as I sink. The roughness of the pool bottom against my chest. The slippery, shiny paint of the black lines. Lungs tightening and shrinking in simulated, fruitless breaths.

But it doesn't help. Not even that helps. The thoughts. The memory. I said my prayer. My only prayer. Nothing helps.

Afterward I lie bent over the edge, heaving, hyperventilating. It's been three hours since I found my daughter's name in our databases. Three hours since my prayer ceased to be answered. Three hours since I could no longer hide from my past.

———

I sit in the Mazda, waiting for something, anything, to fall into place. I hold the steering wheel so tightly that my knuckles whiten. It feels like if I let go of the steering wheel I'll be swept away. All that I chose not to see. Now it breaks over me like a tidal wave. The shame is so strong it pushes me back against the imitation leather seat.

On my screen in Langley, I saw the inquiries and reports about my daughter from Paris and Brussels. I read everything I could find. Everything my clearance allowed. There wasn't much. Open media. Summary. Nothing about us. Nothing about the background or reasons. Nothing about the shadows. But I know anyway. Their fingerprints are unmistakable. The Arab boyfriend and the silencers on their guns. Files in our register that I don't have access to. The fact that there even are files I can't access. Code names and classified documents. Secrets piled on secrets.

In the glove box is the thin manila folder I never opened. My leverage. My only chance to save her, to save myself. My past for her future.

———

My steps rustle across the frosty grass. Tasteful spotlights illuminate the glued-on granite, the white wood, the hollow Masonite columns in imitation Colonial style next to the slate stairs. The pre-fabricated American dream. A paper-thin Potemkin house at the far end of the economic reach of the middle class. A testament to success that looks like it could be blown away by the first strong gust of wind.

I stand at the foot of the stairs and look up at the dark windows. The beige folder in my hand. I have been a dead thing. A broken branch in the river of history. Docilely, I've let myself be swept along by the slightest current. It's over now. A strange calm descends upon me as I ring the doorbell.

Susan opens the door surprisingly quickly, considering it's nearly midnight. She's still wearing office clothes, skirt and blouse, as anonymous as any middle manager. Her face is still tight, stressed, and inscrutable, not adapted to the home. Maybe she just walked in the door.

She insists that we take her car, and we drive in silence through the wide suburban streets, under the bare maples, past the endless football fields and baseball cages of an enormous school, past the dark houses and sealed McMansions sinking under the weight of their twinkling Christmas decorations. Through the slumbering, American dream.

The highway is deserted, an echo, and we say nothing, temporarily mesmerized by the rhythm of the tires over the seams in the concrete. On the radio, someone calls in screaming about the president, the Muslims, the Supreme Court. Susan moves her thumbs over the leather-wrapped controls on the steering wheel and the idiot's voice dies out. We drive south on 245. Toward DC. Her eyes are fixed on the farthest point in the cone of light coming from the car's headlights. I sense something ambivalent in her gestures. Perhaps she's weighing secrets against secrets, lies against lies. The truth. Moving them between scales to find the balance.

Finally she turns off the highway, down toward Potomac Park and stops at the FDR Memorial. We get out of the car, and the sound of doors closing behind us echoes across the park, out toward the water. We walk slowly over to the sculpture, where artificial light renders Roosevelt ghostly in his bronze wheelchair. We shiver in the cold sweeping in from the Tidal Basin. Around us monuments and their remote reflections shine in the still, black water. Narcissus. Is that what we've become?

"So," she says at last. "What was it you wanted to talk to me about?"

She looks small, gazing out over the water. It occurs to me that we've all made our own compromises, our own senseless choices. Maybe she made more than most. She was a manager before there were barely any female employees in the Agency. How many bodies did she step over, ignore, hoard for use when the occasion required it?

I prepare myself, amazed at my own calm. Start right in.

"Who did I kill in Beirut?"

December 20, 2013

Paris, France

KLARA PLUNGED A PAIR OF scissors into the thick hair just below her ears. Five quick snips and a hairstyle that cost her eighty-five euros at Toni & Guy in Brussels's EU Quarter became a distant memory.

She continued upward and forward, while turning her head to look at herself from the side in the dirty hotel mirror. She caught the wisps of hair with her left hand and threw them in the trash next to the sink. She'd paid for the tiny hotel room with money taken out in a completely different part of the city using Cyril's ATM card. The code had proved to be correct. The cowardly bastard. She'd taken out two thousand euros, apparently the daily maximum for withdrawals. It was a cheap price to pay for betrayal. Then she'd ripped the cards apart and tossed them into the trash.

It took her fifteen minutes to transform her shoulder-length hair into a short, boyish haircut. She leaned forward and doused her hair with the icy water from the tap, before emptying nearly an entire bottle of hair bleach into her hand and massaging it into her scalp.

All she wanted to do was cry. All she wanted to do was to lie down on the worn, flowered sheets in the rock hard bed, close the curtains, and sleep. Sleep, sleep, sleep. Never ever wake up again.

All she wanted was to escape, or give up, or just close her eyes and turn to nothing. To cease to exist. But the tears refused to fall. And every time she closed her eyes, she saw Mahmoud's wide eyes, smelled the scent of cheap wine, felt the silent bullets whizzing past her face. Why couldn't she just cry?

When the bleach started burning her scalp, she unwrapped the hotel room's frayed and thin towel and climbed into the yellowish tub to wash her hair. There was no shampoo, so she used someone's forgotten soap. When she was done, she dried off and gazed into the mirror again. To say that she was blond would be an exaggeration. Light brown instead of jet-black. But with short hair. Perhaps the difference was enough. A halfhearted, clichéd attempt at metamorphosis. It might be ridiculous, a waste. More ritual than disguise. She couldn't save Moody. But she could save his memory.

She left the mirror and walked over to the little MacBook open on the bed behind her. It was locked with a password, impossible to bypass. An electronic sphinx. Hidden in its binary maze was something people were willing to kill to keep hidden.

She wanted to break it open, tear apart the hard drive and throw its contents onto the bed. Do whatever it took to gain access to what was inside. Instead she closed her eyes and leaned back. Almost immediately she sat up with a start.

Jörgen! Of course. Jörgen Apelbom and his hacker contacts. Maybe he could help her? She looked at the clock. It wasn't even eight-thirty. Without another thought, she threw on her clothes and ran down the stairs.

The sleepy Spanish exchange student surfing on his laptop behind the small table that constituted the reception didn't seem to recognize her at first.

"I'm staying in room twelve," Klara said. "I dyed my hair."

She took out an international phone card she'd bought in order to call Gabriella and walked over to the pay phone in the corner facing the street. She could feel the student following her with his eyes but ignored him. Jörgen answered after one ring.

"Jörgen," Klara said. "This is Klara Walldéen. Did I wake you up?"

She heard Jörgen clearing his throat on the other end.

"Wow," he said. "Wow!"

"Why 'wow'? What do you mean?" Klara said. Maybe this was a stupid idea.

"I just saw your picture on *Aftonbladet*. You're . . ."

Jörgen cleared his throat again.

"You're wanted by the police," he said.

Klara closed her eyes and ran her hand through her short hair. Wanted. At the front desk the exchange student waved at her. She lifted her hand, gestured for him to wait.

"I have to ask you for a favor," she said. "And I truly understand if you can't help me."

There was silence on the other end for a second.

"Go on," Jörgen said at last. "What do you need?"

"Someone who can crack the code to a computer. A Mac. Someone who's discreet. If you know what I mean."

"Someone who can crack a code?" Jörgen asked.

He sounded cautious, thoughtful.

"Never mind," Klara said. "I'm sorry that I even called you. It was idiotic, I really don't want to drag you into anything."

"Where are you?" interrupted Jörgen. "In Brussels?"

"It's probably better if you don't know, okay? But if you can find someone in Brussels, that works for me."

"Where can I reach you?"

Klara gave him the number to the burner phone they'd bought in Brussels.

"But, please, don't give that number to anyone, okay?"

They hung up. On the way up to her room, she thanked the exchange student but ignored his attempt to talk. She took off her jeans, still wet from her attempts to wash Mahmoud's blood out of them in the bathtub. The bed was hard, and the cold streamed in from the window facing the street. It didn't matter. She couldn't sleep anyway.

═══

Klara was sitting on the windowsill, head leaning against the window, when the phone sounded on the bed. She'd been sitting quietly in the dark room as the snow gave way to a serene, drumming rain. When she stood up, she saw her face in the black glass. The short, badly dyed hair. The weary eyes. The same change she'd seen in Mahmoud. The proximity to violence, the paralyzing fear. And something more. Something deeper, darker than the night outside. Something that she'd still barely even touched. The unfathomable, overwhelming grief. She steered her thoughts in a different direction, forcing herself away from the tempting darkness, that selfish, self-pitying, velvety feeling that would shut everything else out.

"Not now," she whispered to herself. "Not tonight. Not until this is over."

The message had been sent from an unknown number. Good, thought Klara, he didn't use his own phone. Would they still be able to trace their contact? Maybe, it was impossible to know. The message was short:

PRINSENGRACHT 344, AMSTERDAM. TOMORROW AFTER 10:00. HE

CALLS HIMSELF BLITZWORM97. SAY SOULXSEARCHER SENT YOU. NO
NAMES, NO PHONES. 200 EUROS. WILL THAT WORK?

That was all. Like a confirmation for a doctor's appointment.
Though it was an unusual name for a doctor.

YES, replied Klara. THANK YOU.

After she sent the message, she shut off the phone and removed
the battery. Then she put on her jeans again. They were still damp.
But it didn't matter. She couldn't stay here one second longer. If
they'd somehow tracked her phone, they'd be here any minute. On
her way out she threw the phone and the battery into the trash can
by the door. She stopped in the lobby at the dirty computer the hotel
kept for guests. The buses to Amsterdam left from the other side
of Paris. The next one was the night bus, leaving at 11:00 P.M. She
glanced at the computer's clock. 9:30.

To Amsterdam.

S USAN TURNS AROUND SLOWLY. OUR eyes meet. Her eyes are empty, lonely, gray.

"Is that why we're here?" she says. "To rummage through the past?"

I say nothing.

"My God," she continues. "It's been almost thirty years. You know who he was. Basil el Fahin. Bomb maker for Hezbollah. You saw his—"

"I know who you said he was," I interrupt. "I know damn well who you said he was."

My voice is filled with adrenaline, completely unstable. It scares me, that voice. I take control of it. Subdue it. Run my hands over my face.

"I know what you said. But he didn't kill Anna. You weren't telling the truth."

Something in her posture changes. She bends her back like a bow, her features tighten for a moment, then she forces them to smooth out again. All these signs. All these lies.

"Pull yourself together," she says. "What's the matter with you? Did you drag me out here in the middle of the night just to spout your crazy theories?"

But there's something there, a gap in her pretend irritation, a tear in her feigned frustration. Something else, something deeper. I see it in her eyes. The way they rove and jump. Maybe it's harder to lie to a liar. But there's something more. As if part of her wants to tell me. Part of her thinks there have been enough lies. There's a possibility there, an opening.

I take out the folder, hold it out in front of me, toward her. It is a knife to stick into the crack, to pry it open.

"Give up," I say. "Please, Susan, I already know everything. See for yourself. Everything is in there."

My voice is calm now, under control. I clear my throat and wave the folder encouragingly at her. She lets her arms hang at her sides. We stand like that. On our respective scales. It wouldn't take much to shift the balance. She takes the folder. Holds it in her hands without opening it.

I don't know how long this moment of odd, icy intimacy lasts. Maybe just a second. It's broken by a car alarm blaring somewhere in the distance. I wait until it stops.

"The Agency killed Anna," I whisper. "You killed Anna."

Susan takes a step back and sits down on the icy bench without drying it off. She puts the folder in her lap and seems to lose herself in the black water facing us.

I squat in front of her. I can't breathe. She turns her face toward me, looks at me. Her eyes are suddenly pure, naked. Temporarily without deceit and delusion. She takes a handkerchief out of her purse. Turns away, wipes something from the corner of her eye, blows her nose.

"But you must've always known?" she says.

Her voice is thin now. I don't say anything. It's shocking to see her like this. Suddenly so vulnerable. Suddenly so young, almost like a girl, a child. She, like me, made her journey through the shadows all alone. Two bullets of the same caliber but on different trajectories. Her trajectory went upward and out. Mine was always directed toward myself. Susan and her dreaded intellect, her unforced, natural authority. How much shit has she taken? How much emptiness does she store inside herself? When she starts talking, it's not to me but to herself, to the monuments, to history itself.

"It wasn't supposed to go like that, of course. But I didn't know that. Not then. None of us did. Our operation in Damascus was a Russian nested doll, and you were just the outer layer. I was so new, so inexperienced. You were my first responsibility, my first agent to coordinate. I hadn't even been in the field except in Paris, and that hardly counts. And I have no idea why no one informed me that we were supplying weapons to the Syrians. It was so naive of me not to make the connection. But I didn't know then that there would always be other levels, always other decisions made by someone else, in another context. Mistakes are made and have to be atoned for. Debts have to be repaid. The weapons we supplied to the regime were a down payment on another deal we'd made long ago. Someone else's empty, poorly devised compromise. That was how the cold war worked. One hand never knew what the other was doing. I learned, over time."

I straighten up, gently, afraid to disturb her story, her confession. I sit down on the bench beside her.

"And then you found out who was supplying the arms, and I knew it was true, that it was for real. I took it up with Daniels, who was the chief operating officer. All he said was: 'Good job, darlin', we'll take it from here.' That's when you know it's really bad. When they say 'we'll take it from here.' And now I'm the one who says that."

She smiles wryly and shakes her head slightly, letting her eyes wander over the black water to the cold, white columns on the other side.

"It wasn't my decision to eliminate you to protect the bigger secret. Those weren't my orders. Not that it matters, but no one told me until afterward. Honestly, I don't know where it came from. Daniels maybe. Or even higher up. And I don't know who placed the bomb. But I know it was us."

Finally, here we are, encircled by what I always knew, what was always right in front of me. What I chose not to see. Finally we find ourselves in the middle of what I spent half a lifetime trying to escape. A wave of dizziness hits and I lean against the bench for support. My own cowardice is so palpable, so terrible in the light of what might be the truth. But I force my self-hatred aside. We have to go further, all the way up to the surface.

"Why did you let me live after you knew the bomb had failed?"

Why did you let me live? It's such a strange thing to say. The words almost stick in my throat. Susan shrugs.

"What were we supposed to do? Execute you in Langley? A car accident in Delaware? It would have been too obvious, of course. If you'd died like that, after the bomb? It would have come out. And we weren't sure if you understood the connection. If you'd taken some kind of precautions after the bomb. At the same time there was surely someone higher up who must have realized that we couldn't just go around killing our own agents for doing their jobs. The whole thing was a mistake from beginning to end. A terrible mistake. And then it turned out you were loyal. More than loyal."

My heart stands absolutely still. The heat and the concrete, shards of glass. Your tired eyes, your greasy hair in my car. The baby's barely perceptible breath against my chest. A mistake. The banality of it. The banality of having avoided that thought for my whole life. I feel the outlines of a horrible anger. Meanwhile, time is escaping me. This is just one part. History is only one part. Perhaps there's still room for a future.

"And Beirut?" I say. "Who did I kill in Beirut?"

"A bomb maker for Hezbollah. Just like we told you. We'd been looking at him for a long time and had just received new intel that he was in Beirut. We fabricated the information that he was behind the murder of your girlfriend. It was an opportunity to achieve our operational goals and rewrite history. It solved our problems. And it gave you what you wanted, right? It gave you your revenge. It was a win-win situation. Except from a moral perspective. But, well, you understand?"

She smiles halfheartedly again, sadly. Maybe she thinks like I do, that we weigh evil against evil; it's the equation that led us here. Relativity guided us here. An equation that makes perfect sense until the veil is pulled back, and all we see is the madness. She turns to me.

"Why now?" she says. "Why suddenly decide to see what's been right in front of you all this time?"

All I feel is an immense emptiness. All I know is that I want a drink.

"I need a drink," I say.

"I didn't think you were drinking anymore." Susan says.

There's nothing they don't know about me.

December 20, 2013

Stockholm, Sweden

THAT'LL BE TWO HUNDRED SEVENTY-FIVE kronor," the taxi driver said, leaning forward to get a better look at the impressive 1920s mansion glistening in soft floodlighting.

"It looks like a castle," he said.

Gabriella fished out her wallet and handed him her company credit card. Klara had called her half an hour ago. Terrified and in shock. A small, pitiful voice. It was a nightmare, a strange, perverted fantasy. Mahmoud shot in front of her eyes in Paris. Klara now wanted by the police, her picture on the front of all the tabloids. Doctor Death and the beautiful political secretary.

"Will you represent me?" Klara had asked. "Tell me what to do."

Thoughts had flashed through Gabriella's head. Confusion and fear. The feeling she might be out of her depth. Way out of her depth. She thought of what Bronzelius had said. That what happened to Mahmoud had been a misunderstanding, that Säpo seemed to know that. But who had been hunting Mahmoud and was now out to get Klara?

"Come home," she said at last. "Come home, and we'll solve this. Somehow."

She had no idea if that was the right decision. Maybe she

should have told Klara to contact the French police? According to the media, she was only wanted for questioning. But Gabriella didn't dare take the chance. She'd called Wiman as soon as she'd hung up.

She took back her card and jumped out of the cab. The clock on her cell phone showed 12:12 A.M. An unusual time to visit your boss at his home. But it was Wiman who'd suggested it. It felt good somehow. That Wiman cared about this.

His house was undeniably magnificent, she reflected as she walked up the beautifully laid cobblestone path that led to the entrance. Gabriella had heard the stories. The house was legendary among the young lawyers at the firm who'd been honored with an invitation. It was a perfect, cream-colored cube, two stories, maybe three thousand square feet. The house sat on a small hill, which made it feel somewhat secluded, as if it were too exclusive even for Djursholm, Stockholm's most upscale suburb. The wind howled through the bare oaks.

The doorbell emitted a deep *ding-dong* when she pressed the little white button next to the double doors. It didn't take more than a few seconds for them to open.

"Gabriella, welcome. Come in," Wiman said.

He was, despite the hour, dressed impeccably in his usual style. A dark suit with a red handkerchief in the breast pocket. White shirt. The only compromise was his lack of tie. He was holding a whiskey glass with a rounded bottom. The amber liquid seemed to glow in the dull light from inside.

"Sorry to bother you so late," Gabriella said. "It certainly wasn't my intention, we could have discussed this tomorrow. I just wanted to keep you informed."

Wiman waved impatiently with his hand and led the way across the marble floor of the hall.

"I invited you here, Gabriella. If I had wanted to wait until to-morrow, I would have said so."

He led her into what seemed to be an office or library. Did people still have private libraries? Gabriella looked around in wonder. Three tall windows, facing the water, took up the long side of the room. In the darkness, she could only imagine the water, but she assumed the house was on a seafront property. A window on the short side also presumably looked out over the water. The rest of the walls were covered from floor to ceiling with books. A fire was burning in the fireplace next to the door they'd just come through. How much did a house like this cost? Twenty million kronor? More? Is this what you could expect if you became a partner?

"Wow, what a fantastic house," she said.

"It's from the turn of the century," Wiman said, completely un-fazed by the compliment. "But it was rebuilt in the twenties in the Italian style. And I've done some renovations, of course. Can I of-fer you something? A cognac? Red wine?"

He gestured toward a small, but well-stocked mahogany cart that stood in the corner by the windows.

"I'll have a whiskey," Gabriella said.

She suddenly felt that a drink was just what she needed.

Wiman went over to the cart and poured a hefty amount of whis-key in a glass similar to his own. Before putting the bottle back, he refilled his own glass.

"Water?" he asked.

Gabriella shook her head, and Wiman handed her the glass be-fore they sat down across from each other in the Bruno Mathsson armchairs in front of the fireplace. The room was dark, lit only by the fire and the subdued floor lamp beside the bar cart.

"I was sad to hear about your friend. I'm sorry," Wiman said and took a small sip of whiskey.

Gabriella took a much larger sip and leaned back against the sheepskin of the armchair. She wasn't going to cry, not here, not now.

"Yes," she said instead. "It's terrible. Shocking. I don't think I've really grasped it yet."

She couldn't help it. A tear escaped the corner of her eye and ran down her cheek. It was still so fresh, so utterly incomprehensible.

Wiman said nothing, just stared into the fire. He looked older. Haggard. As if something was weighing on him. Gabriella had never seen him like this. Usually his face seemed made of Teflon, completely resistant to emotions.

"And now you've been in touch with Ms. Walldéen? Who, according to the media, was with Mr. Shammosh when he was shot in Paris?"

Wiman got up and put a birch log onto the fire, which crackled as the bark started to burn. Gabriella heard the wind whistling through the ancient trees outside. She wiped the tear from her cheek and ran her hands through her hair. She nodded.

"Klara called me a little while ago and asked me to represent her. And I intend to do so, of course. That is, if she even needs representation. She's not suspected of anything, as far as I know."

"And where is she now?" Wiman said.

"I don't know. She didn't want to tell me over the phone. But I asked her to come back to Sweden. It felt like the right thing to do. So that we can sit down and go over what happened before she contacts the police. She's in shock, of course. Completely in shock."

"What is this about?" Wiman's tone bordered on impatience. "Why were Shammosh and that other Swede murdered? It's extremely important that we find out what's behind all this."

"I don't know," Gabriella said. "I honestly have no idea. And I'm not sure if Klara knows either."

"Is that the impression you got? That she didn't know why they were being hunted?"

"Yes," she said. "Or no. I don't think she knows what's going on. Or at least she didn't tell me."

Wiman nodded slowly.

"Exactly what did she say on the phone? Try to remember verbatim."

Gabriella reconstructed their short conversation as best she could. It was soothing to be questioned by Wiman. Safe, somehow. A lawyer's icy focus on details. It helped her to achieve some distance.

"And when she comes to Sweden?" Wiman said, after she'd finished describing the call. "If she comes to Sweden, that is. What's the plan then?"

"She mentioned that she knows someplace in the archipelago where she can hide while we figure out what's going on. Outside Arkösund. And I guess that was really the reason I wanted to talk to you. What should I do? What should I say? The media will probably have their own version of the story by tomorrow."

Gabriella downed the last of her whiskey and felt it warming her from the inside.

"Forget the media for now," Wiman said.

He took Gabriella's empty glass and went to the bar to refill it.

"The only thing you need to focus on right now is getting her to Sweden. Keep her hidden while we figure things out. Keep me informed of exactly where you are, okay? It's important that we stay connected."

Wiman handed the whiskey glass to Gabriella.

"Give me all the details as soon as you have them," he said. "No fucking solo flights now. I mean that."

Gabriella nodded and gulped down the whiskey in a single burning mouthful.

"I should really call a cab," she said and picked up her phone.

December 20, 2013

Washington, DC, USA

TWENTY MINUTES LATER WE'RE SITTING in a hazy bar in Georgetown, in a booth near the back, the burgundy vinyl seats slippery against my chinos. It's a place for those of us who are serious about our alcohol. My first Rusty Nail tastes smooth and nostalgic against my lips. The second plants my feet firmly on the ground, makes history fade temporarily. I set the glass down on the dark, well-worn table.

Susan is sipping her club soda. Spinning her highball glass so the ice clinks against the edges. The sound blends together with a song I vaguely recognize. That warm guitar, those lines about the mist-covered mountains. In the dim light she looks translucent, almost ghostly. She's followed me here. How much further?

"So why now?" she says.

We have arrived. We have followed the complicated tentacles of history all the way here. All the way to the surface. To a point where everything is about forgetting, forgiving, saving what can be saved.

"My daughter," I say. "It's about my daughter."

Her expression doesn't change. She takes a small sip of her drink.

"Klara Walldéen," I say. "She's in our register. I want access to everything about her. All of our reports, all real-time data, every-thing. And I want it now. Immediately. Tonight."

Susan just looks at me. The neutrality of her look is paralyzing.

"And if you were to get it?" she says. "If you were to gain access to what you want? What would that change?"

I drink what's left of my drink in one gulp, until the ice cubes hit my teeth. I lean back and feel how the room is shrinking around me. How the world outside is growing. I feel the warmth of the al-cohol and the grief from my past. I feel the anxiety and the thrill of the hunt. I feel the power of every wrong decision outweighed by the power of a single possibility to set something right. At a certain point relativism can no longer save a person's soul. I have so much to make amends for.

"What is this about?" I say. "What has she gotten involved in?"

Susan's eyes look right through me.

"Why have you never mentioned your daughter?"

Even though I know I shouldn't, that I've already gone too far, crossed a line, I wave to the bartender and see him nod and reach for a glass, filling it with ice, whiskey, Drambuie.

"I asked first," I say.

"Did you think you could protect her? By hiding her?" she says.

There's something almost sad about her now. Her pale complex-ion against the burgundy backrest of the booth. The darkness of the room. The first outlines of dark circles under her eyes that her subtle makeup can't hide. It's late, but we're both accustomed to sleepless nights.

"You understand, of course, that we already knew all of this when you came in from Damascus thirty years ago? We knew you left her at the Swedish embassy a few days after the bomb. We knew she grew up with her grandparents in the Swedish archipelago. I've known about your searches in our databases since you started them ten years ago. There's nothing we don't know."

It's an out-of-body experience. Staggering. To come face-to-face with your own delusions. To finally stand naked in front of yourself. Floating high above your own body, your own constructed world. I feel my fingers trembling and fight the impulse to down the drink the bartender just put in front of me. I take a sip. The clink of ice. Everything she says, I actually already knew. I take another sip of the drink. Lean my head back, giving in, and down it. Let the sweet liquid rush through me, lend me some kind of fragile strength. The only secret I had actually fooled myself into believing. Not even that. I fumble with the manila folder Susan set on the table between us.

"It doesn't matter," I say. "I don't care what you knew. Give me the information about Klara, Susan. It's over for me now. It's done. I'll go to the *Washington Post* with what I know and what I can prove. I swear to God, Susan. It's enough now. Give me the chance to correct what I can."

Susan sets her glass down silently and reaches across the table for the folder. Quietly, she opens it. The papers inside flutter in the draft from the door to the bar, spread across the table. Ten. Twenty. Maybe thirty pages. All of them are completely blank. Just white letter-size paper. Nothing else.

———

We're sitting in the car. Susan drives quietly through the sleeping city while telling me all about Klara and Mahmoud. All about the mistakes, the loss of control. All about the usual, hopeless everyday of our world. One more operation that went beyond rhyme or reason.

When she's finished, she makes a call and asks some nameless assistant at a safe distance to book my trip. She parks the car carefully in front of my apartment complex. Turns her wrist and takes a look at her simple, expensive watch.

"Four hours until your plane leaves," she says. "You need a shower and a pot of coffee. Do you still have an alias you can use?"

I nod, thinking of the two Canadian passports under different names lying in my safe. I thought that was all over. That the game had ended. But there's always one more move. Always one last chance.

"Why, Susan?" I say. "Why are you doing this for me?"

The Ford's engine hums. A few snowflakes dance under the streetlamps outside.

"Maybe I owe you this?" she says. "Maybe you're our best chance to solve this now? Does it matter?"

I open the car door. The alcohol turns me into gas, allows me to float out of the car. Nothing matters. Nothing except the next move.

ON THE HALF-EMPTY AND POORLY cleaned night bus to Amsterdam, fatigue finally overtook Klara. The Eurolines bus out of Paris had been her best option. No ID requirements, and it was unlikely there'd be passport control in Amsterdam. Eurolines—the excruciatingly sluggish cross-continental circulatory system of Europe's poor—was an exact reflection of the middle class's clinical network of train and flight routes. The same destinations, but different people. Instead of Samsonite-rolling business travelers and rosy-cheeked families, buses transported Polish carpenters with vodka bottles and toolboxes, Muslim women traveling alone with head scarves and meticulously packed cheap, plastic suitcases. Maybe a student with severe liquidity problems and a sweetheart in another part of the continent. Klara stretched out across two seats, using her handbag as a pillow and with the shoulder strap of the computer bag wrapped several times around her left arm. She was asleep before the bus even left downtown Paris.

═══

Klara didn't wake up again until the bus stopped outside the Amstel station in central Amsterdam. It was still dark outside and a harsh wind flooded the bus as the doors opened with a hiss. Klara put on her coat and pulled the knitted cap over her ears. Wiping the sleep from her eyes, she peeked out the window, half-expecting to see a throng of police. But the bleak pavement in front of the 1930s building was completely vacant, except for a single city bus standing with its headlights off under a broken streetlight. Klara joined the motley group of passengers moving out of the bus. The station clock read almost 7:00 A.M. Three hours to go.

═══

Amsterdam's streets and canals were deserted as Klara wandered through the city. The wind whipped right through her. It had been blustery every time she'd been to Amsterdam—a constant, chilling reminder of how flat Holland was.

She felt impatient, almost manic. Keeping the thoughts of Mahmoud, the blood, and her impending grief at bay took whatever strength she could muster. At times it felt like her head, her chest, and her heart might burst with a force so violent, she'd be scattered across Europe. She stopped and closed her eyes for a moment. She forced herself to stop thinking about the horror of Paris and instead focus on a place where she was, if not happy, at least safe. She visualized her grandmother in her living room, the crackling fire in the stove, the lace tablecloth and the finest Gustavsberg porcelain. The taste of saffron buns and the sound of an approaching storm. She knew it was far from a permanent solution; it was a temporary bandage on the stump of an amputated leg, but it stanched the bleeding for the moment.

———

She'd expected that someone calling himself Blitzworm97 would live in a rougher neighborhood than Prinsengracht proved to be. Maybe in a garage in some concrete suburb, where he—slightly overweight, wearing a *Star Trek* T-shirt, drinking Jolt Cola—spent his time hammering out plans for the destruction of the world's financial centers through a highly targeted cyber-attack. Anywhere but here among the picturesque canals and Christmas decorations of central Amsterdam. Did she really have the right address? But she'd checked it a hundred times before getting rid of the phone, and there was only one Prinsengracht in Amsterdam.

Number 344 appeared to be a single-family home. The large, gleaming windows overlooked the canal. She could see a clinical, stainless steel kitchen inside, where a gray-haired man of about forty-five, in an immaculate, navy suit, sat on a barstool, drinking coffee with a newspaper in front of him. It was the perfect image of a successful European man, taken from the pages of the How to Spend It section of the *Financial Times*. Klara felt her heart sinking in her chest. Damn. There was absolutely no way he could be Blitzworm. Something wasn't right.

She walked past the house quickly and sat down at a café a few blocks away. She ordered a cappuccino and two croissants. She was suddenly very hungry. When was the last time she'd eaten? She felt confused, worried. The man in the window hardly looked like he was in need of two hundred euros. His tie probably cost more than that. But this was her only lead.

At 10:15 Klara swallowed nervously and rang the doorbell of Prinsengracht 344. She was sweating despite the winter cold. The clouds hung low over Amsterdam, and a nasty drizzle dampened her face. It took almost a minute before she heard footsteps on the stairs inside the house. Ten seconds before the door opened wide.

A skinny girl of about fifteen stood in front of Klara. High cheekbones and clear blue eyes. A slim, greyhoundlike face, with a mouth that seemed way too big. Long, gangling arms. Baggy jeans and an oversize Justin Bieber T-shirt. Everything about her was out of proportion. Awkward. Klara suspected, judging by those cheekbones and those eyes, that she'd look quite different by the time she got through her teens. The girl was chewing gum. Of course.

"Hi," said Klara in English, unsure of how to proceed.

The girl looked at her. A childish, arrogant smile on her lips.

"Yes?" she said. "Who're you looking for?"

She spoke American English. Almost without an accent.

"Sorry," Klara said. "I must have the wrong address."

The girl continued looking at her without making any attempt to close the door.

"I'm sorry. Please excuse me," Klara said, starting to turn around.

"Come in," said the girl. "You're SoulXsearcher's friend, right?"

Klara stopped in midmotion.

"Yes," she said. "I suppose so. Are you Blitzworm97?"

"Were you expecting somebody else?" the girl said as Klara hesitantly stepped into the bright, Philippe Starck–inspired hallway. A tall vase filled with fresh white roses stood on a white rococo table under what could be an authentic Miró.

"I don't know," replied Klara.

"A guy, maybe?" the girl continued. "Sorry to disappoint you."

She pointed to the stairs at the other end of the hall.

"My room's on the top floor."

She led the way up three flights of stairs. A door led into a large, somewhat schizophrenic room with sloping walls and two dormer windows. The tasteful, minimalist decor continued up here. White walls and a dark, well-maintained wooden floor. Exposed beams and windowsills in black marble. But someone—probably Blitzworm97—had done their best to create a less sophisticated and more urban environment in the room.

Large parts of the walls were covered with photos and posters. Eminem, Tupac, Bob Marley. A blown-up print from Instagram of what looked like Rihanna smoking a joint. Graffiti was sprayed over large canvases. Pictures of marijuana leaves. A couple of well-worn skateboards stuck out from under the bed. And the whole of one side of the room was covered by an impressive array of computers and monitors. The Laura Ashley sheets on the Hästens bed were unmade. Thongs, socks, and plates of leftovers were scattered across the floor.

"I guess the Bieber shirt is ironic, then?" Klara said, smiling.

"Bingo," the girl said drily.

Blitzworm97 sat down on her bed and pulled out a small bag of marijuana and some rolling papers from a drawer in the bedside table. Without a word, she started rolling a joint. There was something so self-consciously rebellious about it that Klara had to hide a smile.

"So, Blitzworm," she said. "Do you want me to call you that, or do you have a real name?"

"You can call me Blitz if you want. Or Blitzie. Whatever."

She lit the joint and took a few deep drags.

"You want some?" she said, and held it toward Klara.

"Sure, Blitzie," Klara said and took the joint.

She couldn't even remember the last time she'd smoked marijuana. At some point just after moving to Brussels, she supposed. She'd never really liked it that much. But just now, at ten in the morning with a rebellious teenager in Amsterdam, it seemed fitting.

"Aren't you a little young for this?" Klara said, blowing smoke up toward the ceiling.

Blitzie grabbed the joint back and took a greedy, defiant drag.

"This is Amsterdam, okay? Nobody cares."

Klara nodded. Maybe that was true.

"You have a nice house," she said.

"Who cares?" Blitzie said. "My parents are disgusting capitalists. I hate them."

This time Klara couldn't hide her smile. Maybe it was the marijuana that made her warm and almost calm. She felt like going over and putting her arm around Blitzie.

"It'll pass," she said.

Blitzie shrugged.

"How do you know SoulXsearcher?" she said.

"We work together," Klara said. "We're friends, I guess. How about you?"

"Internet," Blitzie said, nodding toward the computers. "He knows people I know. Hackers. Real hackers. They trust him, so I trust him."

"So you're a hacker?" Klara said.

Blitzie nodded and leaned back while slowly exhaling smoke.

"I created Blitzworm."

She looked at Klara, as if expecting her to be deeply impressed.

"Oh," Klara said. "Sorry, I'm not a hacker. I don't know what that is, I'm afraid."

Blitzie looked disappointed.

"I hacked MIT's server. Massachusetts Institute of Technology. The world's best school for code. Left my résumé on their intranet. It was kind of a big deal. They offered me a spot there when I'm done with school. But I don't care."

"Wow," Klara said. "Why don't you care? Wasn't that the whole point of giving them your résumé?"

"Nah, I don't care about their fucking preppy school. It's just a bunch of Koreans there anyway."

Klara shook her head. The marijuana had made her a little slow. How had they drifted into this? She wasn't a career counselor.

"Okay," she said. "Listen, Blitzie, I have a computer I can't get into. Jörgen, or SoulXsearcher, said you could help me with that?"

Klara pulled the MacBook out of its bag.

"Why don't you take it to a Mac store, they'll help you?" Blitzie said, with a wicked little smile.

Klara sighed. "Come on, do you want two hundred euros or not?"

"The price has gone up," Blitzie said as she relit the joint between her fingers. "I want three hundred euros."

B EING BACK IN SWEDEN JUST made the situation that much more bizarre, more incomprehensible, more nightmarish. In the small private jet, George had almost felt at ease for a moment. Despite everything, it was fucking awesome. Digital Solutions' black van driving right up to a plane ready to go on the runway. No passport or security checks. Just out of the vehicle, up the stairs, then sinking down into the leather seats. For Josh and Kirsten and the rest of Reiper's people, it seemed to be no big deal. Maybe that's how they usually traveled.

But George had dreamed about a situation like this, had hoped for a client who had that kind of lifestyle, those resources. His colleagues had told him about working for banks or Internet companies where consultants sometimes flew with senior management, and George had longed for the day when that would happen to him. Private jet. The ultimate confirmation of inconceivable success. But now, in the company of Reiper's gang of murderers, or whatever the hell they were, he couldn't fool himself any longer. The stress wouldn't go away. And he didn't even have a hit of coke to lighten things up a little.

Besides, the mood had turned after Paris. Reiper had gone com-

pletely ape shit. George had, with a growing sense of utter disbelief, watched the news about the murder of Mahmoud Shammosh.
The hunt for Klara. It made him want to throw up. He was involved
with this. How the hell had that happened?

But Klara at least seemed to have gone underground completely,
as far as George could tell from the fragments he'd picked up. No
cell phone, no withdrawals at ATMs, nothing. But then he had to
translate a conversation between her and her friend, a defense attor-
ney whose name George vaguely recognized. They were tapping
her phone too, apparently.

George had hesitated, thought about lying. But he didn't dare.
Not after their ruthlessness in Paris. Not after it became clear that
Digital Solutions were murderers. Cold-blooded, ruthless, professional killers. So he had sold out Klara a second time. Told them it
seemed like she was on her way to Sweden. What a spineless little
cunt he was.

On Reiper's orders, George had rented a house in Arkösund.
They seemed confident that she'd be showing up there. Thirty-five
thousand a week was an exorbitant price, but Reiper didn't seem to
care, and at least it was a nice house. Built around the turn of the
last century, it was yellow with white trim and had a veranda that
faced the sea and the marina. Reiper's people had immediately set
up a pair of large binoculars on the porch and seemed to be guarding the harbor in shifts around the clock. No one had bothered to
tell George what they were looking for, but he could guess.

He was basically a prisoner. Reiper hadn't said anything, but it
was obvious that he couldn't just leave. They locked the front door
and took the key out of the lock. And he was rarely alone, it seemed
like someone always remained in his vicinity. Reiper had taken his
cell phone after the Paris incident. He hadn't said anything about

it, but George lived in constant fear that Reiper knew he'd warned Klara.

George considered turning on the TV again but didn't want to hear any more endless news updates about Shammosh and Klara. Instead he looked through the house's only bookcase, which consisted exclusively of well-thumbed Swedish crime novels. Just like any other summerhouse. There was a complete set of a crappy women's magazine called *Amelia* in a rack next to the fireplace. George picked up the latest issue. "Malou von Sivers—'How I pamper myself every day'" read one of the headlines. With a sigh of resignation, he put the magazine back, slouched down in the sofa, and closed his eyes.

"It's hard work doing nothing. It wears you down."

George opened his eyes and turned his head. Kirsten was reclining on the couch opposite him. In the gray morning light, he only saw her silhouette. He must have dozed off because he hadn't heard her come into the room.

"That's for sure," he said and smiled. "I must have fallen asleep."

He sat up a little halfheartedly on the couch, straightening the dark blue sweatshirt that Josh had lent him. Reiper hadn't let him go home to pack before they left. Instead, George had to make do with the clothes he'd been wearing, and a pair of jeans and a few shirts that Josh had reluctantly tossed at him. Someone had bought him some tighty-whities and socks in a supermarket somewhere. He felt like an idiot. But he blended in well. Everyone at Digital Solutions went around dressed like American college kids. Workout clothes or jeans.

"I guess so," she said. "It's tough for all of us. So much anticipation and waiting. But that's part of the job."

"Part of the job?"

George did his best to fix his hair as inconspicuously as possible. Kirsten wasn't his type. Her lips were too thin. Far too little makeup, if any at all. And always a ponytail. Sure, her body was extremely fit, though she hid it behind sweatshirts, but it seemed sculpted for athletic rather than aesthetic purposes. Whatever, she was the only woman on Reiper's team. And diversions were in short supply around here.

"And what is the job, anyway?"

Kirsten smiled at him. She had a small, irregular dimple on her right cheek. It made her look cute. Not at all like a professional killer.

"Damage control," she said. "At the moment it's damage control. Your old friend had the misfortune of getting a hold of information she's not able to handle properly. We can't take any risks. It's highly probable that the negative consequences would be uncontrollable. Unfortunately."

"The negative consequences would be uncontrollable?" George winked at her. "Do you always talk like that?"

Kirsten shrugged.

"What do you want me to say? That we, all of us, will get fucked in the ass—and not in a good way—if this information gets out? Does that paint enough of a picture for you?"

She looked at him with an expression full of quiet confidence and a superiority bordering on pity. As if she belonged to a more advanced life-form and had to remind herself that inferior beings didn't have the same intuitive access to information that she did.

"Yeah, yeah. Reiper has tried to explain that," he muttered. "But to murder them? My God."

"We're not murdering anyone," Kirsten said calmly. "We're fighting a war, all right? Soldiers don't murder, they fight for their country's survival. And that's what we are. Soldiers. What we do keeps the world turning. We make sacrifices so you and your anemic colleagues can go to work every day and continue your fucking bullshit. Murder? Who the hell are you to sit here and talk about murder? We do everything we can to make sure nobody loses their lives. Maybe you don't believe me? Maybe you think we enjoy it?"

Her intelligent eyes scrutinized George. A small wrinkle appeared in her otherwise smooth forehead. That purely physical self-confidence. She could be an Olympic runner or a young, athletic doctor. Anything, but not what she was. What was she? Soldier? Spy? Murderer?

"But that's the way these kinds of operations pan out," she continued. "It's like any battle. You decide your tactic, plan how everything will be carried out down to the minutest detail. But as soon as the first shot is fired, you might as well just toss out your plans."

"And what about me?" George said hesitantly. "It's almost Christmas. How long am I going to have to stay here?"

Kirsten cocked her head, a bit of warmth in her eyes now, as if she understood that this wasn't George's war. That he hadn't chosen to be here.

"I'm sorry," she said. "You'll have to remain here until further notice. Reiper's analysis is that we can't afford to let you leave in the middle of the operation."

She straightened up and winked at him.

"So it's just as well that you make yourself at home. Maybe you can make some Swedish meatballs. It's time for my shift."

She smiled at him again and went out to the porch to take over the binoculars.

KLARA LAID THREE HUNDRED-EURO BILLS on the small coffee table.

"If that's what you want," she said. "But no more bullshit, okay?"

Blitzie grabbed the notes and stuffed them into the pocket of her jeans.

"Do you really need the money?" Klara said. "I mean with such disgusting capitalist parents?"

She smiled gently toward Blitzie, who just pursed her lips.

"They want me to have what they call a normal childhood," she said. "Forty euros a week. As if that makes you normal."

She turned back toward the computers on her desk and seemed to lose herself in some kind of discussion forum. She hadn't bought those computers on forty euros a week, thought Klara. Maybe there were different levels of normal.

"Okay," Blitzie said at last. "Let's see?"

Klara handed the computer over to her. Blitzie grunted as her fingers flew over the keyboard.

"Can you unlock it?" Klara said.

Blitzie looked up at her with marijuana-glazed eyes.

"I can open anything, okay? It's just a matter of how long it takes."

"And how long do you think this will take?"

Klara wasn't sure how much longer she could hold this expanding lump of stress and sadness beneath the surface.

"Jeez! Settle down. Let me get going, and we'll see."

Blitzie paused and studied Klara with a new expression in her eyes. The smile had disappeared.

"Your name is Klara, right? You're wanted for murder or something in Paris? You're, like, on the run."

It was a statement, not a question. Blitzie was obviously a genius, but she seemed far from predictable. Klara nodded.

"Perhaps."

"So, did you kill somebody?"

Klara felt a sudden shard of anger break free from the anxiety and travel up through her body. Why the hell did she have to sit here with some spoiled prodigy and answer questions about the very thing she was trying so hard not to think about?

"I didn't kill anyone," she said. "And I'm not fucking wanted for murder, am I? If you really want to know, my ex-boyfriend was shot in the head by people I don't know. I was holding his hand."

Klara didn't even notice that she'd raised her voice. Tears were flowing down her cheeks.

"I was holding his hand when they shot him. He got so heavy. He pulled me down onto the floor. And I just left him there. All alone."

She couldn't continue. The lump in her throat was growing and she turned away. She didn't want to sit here and cry, didn't want to think about what had happened. She just wanted the goddamned password, and then to keep moving on, away. Never slowing down.

Blitzie put the computer on the floor and sat down next to Klara on the low sofa. She curled one of her skinny arms around Klara's shoulders. With the other hand, she stroked Klara's cheek.

"Sorry," she said. "I'm sorry. I didn't mean to. I'm not so good with emotions and stuff, you know. Maybe I'm autistic or something. "

Klara dried her tears, pushed her hands through her short hair. She turned to Blitzie.

"You're not autistic," she said. "You're just a teenager."

She took a deep breath.

"Can we forget about me and just focus on the computer right now?"

Blitzie let go of her shoulders and picked up the MacBook. After rooting around a little on her cluttered desk she found a USB stick, which seemed to satisfy her. She plugged it in and restarted the computer. Her slender fingers flew over the keyboard again.

"There," she said at last. "Now all we can do is wait. I'm running a program that I modified a bit. We'll find the password, but it might take a while. Do you want a beer?"

They were on their second Heineken, and their second joint, alternating between a *Jersey Shore* marathon on MTV—which Blitzie supposedly hated but still insisted on zapping over to—and news channels. There seemed to be an infinite number of channels. The morning drifted slowly into afternoon.

Blitzie's "capitalist pig" parents ran a hedge fund and were apparently information junkies, so they had every TV channel imaginable. It seemed that Mahmoud's murder had been pushed off of all the European news. But when Blitzie went down to the kitchen to get some snacks, Klara clicked up to higher numbered satellite channels and found to her surprise SVT24, a Swedish Public Television station. She felt slow and apathetic from the marijuana and beer. But at the moment, being stoned was far better than actually being awake.

A newscast was under way when Blitzie stepped into the room with a tray full of nachos and salsa.

" . . . and with us in the studio today, we have Eva-Karin Boman, Social Democratic member of the European Parliament. Welcome, Eva-Karin."

Klara turned up the volume on the huge TV and struggled to focus. The camera zoomed in on Eva-Karin's heavily made-up face. She looked strained.

"For the last few days we've been following the developments surrounding a Swedish Ph.D. student who's wanted by Interpol for terrorism," began the male anchor, looking solemnly into the camera. "Last Friday night he was shot to death by unknown assailants during a gun fight. At the time he was accompanied by a Swedish woman, Klara Walldéen, who is now sought in connection with his murder by the French police."

The anchor paused and the camera zoomed out to include Eva-Karin.

"Klara Walldéen has been working for you for several years, Eva-Karin. Why do you think she's gone into hiding?"

Now, the camera zoomed in on Eva-Karin's face.

"I really don't know, Anders. You'd think the normal reaction for anyone who's been through what Klara seems to have been through would be to voluntarily seek out the police. When you consider the fact that she chose not to, and has even gone into hiding, well, it's not surprising that questions arise."

"What kind of questions do you mean?"

"Questions regarding her dealings with convicted terrorists, for example. Of course, this isn't something I've ever had the occasion to discuss with Klara. Her role in my office has been as a secretary . . ."

Klara stood up from the couch. She was shaking.

"Convicted terrorists! Secretary!" she screamed in Swedish. "What the hell do you mean?"

It was obvious the news anchor was thinking the same thing.

"The Swede who was shot wasn't a convicted terrorist, as far as we know."

"As far as we know," Eva-Karin said. "And we don't know what kind of network he was a part of or what Klara's connection has been to all of this. All I can say is that if she doesn't have anything to hide, I urge her to seek out the French police immediately."

Klara switched off the TV and threw the remote control across the room. The batteries scattered across the dark floor in every direction. She hadn't expected much of her boss, but that she would actively go to a news station in order to smear her was a bit much even for Eva-Karin.

Blitzie seemed totally indifferent to Klara's outburst and had sat down in front of the computer without Klara noticing.

"Fuck," she muttered as her hands traveled over the keys. "This fucking code will take weeks to crack."

Klara felt something warm and large growing inside her. A burning tension across her temples and behind her eyes. Like when she was little and was suddenly overwhelmed by an injustice or sadness. She bent her head back, trying to take control of the impending crying jag. It would take several weeks to find the code. How would she manage to stay hidden for weeks? Mahmoud's wide-open eyes, the blood, the photo of Cyril's family, and the shadows running through the falling snow outside the store in Paris—all of it was spinning in front of her. Everything ran through her like a violent river. She couldn't take more, couldn't bear more. She sobbed loudly. The tears ran hot and heavy down her cheeks.

But then she felt Blitzie's bony little finger stroking the back of her hand. Klara forced herself to look at her through a blurry filter of tears. Blitzie looked so small. So worried.

"Don't cry," she said. "Please. I think I have an idea. But it's complicated. "

G ABRIELLA SHIVERED AND PULLED HER hat down farther over her ears. She hopped in place to keep warm. When that didn't help, she pulled out a pack of Benson & Hedges and a matchbook from her pocket. It took three matches for her to get the cigarette lit. She was out of practice. It had been a long time since she'd smoked in the morning. Actually she'd never really been much of a smoker. Only now and then with Klara and Mahmoud during exam weeks or in pubs in London. But under the current circumstances it seemed appropriate. She took a few quick puffs and let her eyes wander over the city.

Even after dark, the view from the Katarina Elevator was exceptional. Stockholm glistened in the early morning, through the chimney smoke and snow crystals. The traffic had already started piling up. She could hear the muffled rumble of it beneath her. The metro tracks looked like Christmas lights as trains rushed back and forth between the islands of Södermalm and Gamla Stan. Even though she only lived a few kilometers away and could almost see her office down on Skeppsbron from where she stood now, she rarely came up here. It felt like the Katarina Elevator was for tourists. Or teenagers. Or alcoholics. Anyone except her. She turned and looked back toward the footbridge. No one there. She was completely alone. It was five minutes before eight in the morning.

Five minutes left. It had been almost twenty-four hours since she'd received the message at princephillipmitchell777@gmail.com, the address Klara had asked her to set up. Prince Phillip Mitchell's "I'm So Happy." How many times had they listened to Klara's scratched single? The Holy Grail of soul that Klara had found at the bottom of a crate of discs on Vaksala Square during their first term at Uppsala. She'd only paid ten kronor for it. In an online auction you'd pay well over a thousand kronor if you were even lucky enough to find it. Klara only needed to tell Gabriella to create a new Gmail address using the name of the singer of the world's very best song followed by three sevens for Gabriella to know exactly what she meant. And if someone had been listening to their conversation, no one would ever know what Klara was referring to.

The message she'd received from an anonymous Hotmail address hadn't been signed and had consisted of detailed instructions on how Gabriella should ride subways and taxis around half the city before she made her way to the Katarina Elevator. How she should constantly check to make sure she wasn't being followed. How she should be there at exactly 8:00 A.M.

Which was exactly what time it was now, Gabriella realized when she glanced at her watch. And at that very moment she heard the elevator bounce into place and the doors opening. When she turned toward it, her anticipation increased. But instead of Klara, she saw a slim teenager in baggy clothes, a baseball cap, and a hoody under a way too big, black jacket. A skater, maybe. Gabriella sighed and turned back toward the railing. As if it were the most natural thing in the world to stand 125 feet above Stockholm, on an early morning the day before Christmas eve, admiring the view.

"Wow, either you're mad at me or my disguise is a lot better than I'd hoped," the skater said.

Gabriella spun around and looked straight into Klara's bright blue eyes, peeping out beneath a black cap with MIT printed across the forehead. She wasn't wearing any makeup and her cheeks seemed sunken. Her face was gray in the darkness, her lips colorless. A small, pained smile flashed across her face.

"Klara!"

Gabriella had to stop herself from shouting it out. She enfolded Klara in a hug. Their jackets rustled against each other. Klara's cheek was ice-cold.

"Klara, Klara," whispered Gabriella.

It was all she could get out. Everything she might possibly say felt irrelevant. Instead she held Klara close and as hard as she could, as if wanting them to become the same person for a moment. Klara's tears wet both their cheeks. Finally, they let go of each other. Klara made a futile attempt to dry her tears, but they didn't seem to want to stop flowing.

"Sorry," she whispered. "I'm sorry, it's been a couple of very long days."

Gabriella stroked her cheek.

"What happened to your hair?" she said. "You look like k.d. lang."

Klara looked up at her and laughed. Just once, then the dam burst and it was impossible to tell if she was crying or laughing.

"k.d. lang?" she said, the tears still running down her cheeks. "Is that the best you can come up with? k.d. lang! Does anyone even remember her? Canada's National Lesbian. My God."

Gabriella laughed too.

"Yeah, but in a good way," she said.

"In a good way? How? Can you look like her in a good way?"

Their laughter subsided and they looked around, suddenly becoming aware of where they were.

"You followed my instructions?" Klara said.

Gabriella nodded.

"Your spy instructions. Of course. I've been riding all over town since six o'clock this morning."

Klara looked around again; a hunted, deeply uneasy look had returned to her eyes.

"Let's hope we're alone," she said. "Did you get hold of a car?"

Gabriella nodded.

"Borrowed one from a colleague yesterday. He thinks I'm going to IKEA. I can keep it over the Christmas holidays."

"And you've taken the battery out of your cell phone?"

"Yes, and I've gone through all my clothes in search of a transmitter or whatever it was you called it in your e-mail."

Klara nodded.

"Come on," she said. "Let's go down again."

Södermalm was still deserted as they crossed Slussen toward Hornsgatan, where Gabriella had parked her borrowed Saab. Gabriella took Klara's hand and pulled her closer. There was so much to talk about, so much to try to understand, so much incomprehensible grief to share. So many important questions. But she couldn't bring herself to ask them. Not yet.

"How did you get here?" she said instead.

"Bus," Klara said. "It certainly took long enough."

"And where did you get a hold of those skateboarder clothes?"

Klara looked back over her shoulder, her eyes searching the street.

"A long story. A teenage hacker in Amsterdam gave them to me.

I'll tell you all about it. I'll tell you everything, as soon as we get in the car."

A thin layer of frost had already settled over the windshield of the black car. Gabriella didn't bother to scrape it off. The wipers would take care of it. With one touch of a button, she unlocked the car, which responded by flashing its lights.

"I'll drive," Klara said. "I know where we're going. And you'll be busy listening to me."

It took them two and a half hours to reach Arkösund.

Klara had driven calmly and talked almost incessantly. About Mahmoud. About every terrible thing. The tears had fallen silently down her cheeks, but she'd refused to let Gabriella take over the wheel. It was as if she needed the distraction, the concentration of driving. It was so unreal. So nightmarish. Mahmoud's murder. Cyril, that two-faced rat. The hunt and the computer. Blitzie's far-fetched plan.

"So you don't know what's on the computer?" Gabriella said at last. "We don't even know why all this is happening?"

Klara shook her head silently.

"And our only way of finding out is through a plan hatched by a stoned, sixteen-year-old hacker in Amsterdam?"

Klara nodded again and smiled a hopeless little smile.

"But she's really freaking smart," she said. "Blitzie is a really freaking smart, stoned, sixteen-year-old hacker, okay?"

Gabriella smiled back.

"Yes," she said. "I'll admit we don't have much else going for us. Maybe we could work something out with that Bronzelius guy from Säpo?"

Klara giggled, shaking her head.

"Fucking hell," she said. "We really don't have that much going for us, do we?"

Finally Klara parked the car in a parking lot in a small village Gabriella assumed was Arkösund. Farther down the road she could make out a dock and beyond that black cliffs and sea. The engine stopped. Klara took the key out and gave it to Gabriella.

"We're here," she said. "Arkösund."

They sat in silence for a second, quietly watching the snow blow ever more furiously against the windshield. It was still melting where it landed, but not for long. Soon it would start piling up.

"Seriously," Klara said. "I understand if you want to go back now. I can't ask you to stay out here with me, when I don't even know what I'm doing. And it's Christmas, after all."

Gabriella looked at Klara as if she hadn't really heard or understood what she'd said. Then she shook her head.

"What are you talking about? Going back? Now? Stop it."

Gabriella opened the door and stepped out into the cold. The large snowflakes landed on her face, her hair. She bent down and looked expectantly toward Klara, who was still in the car.

"Come on. Here we go. Where are we meeting your old friend?"

Klara followed her out into the winter darkness. She pointed down toward the marina.

"Down there. In fifteen minutes. Or in twelve minutes to be precise."

"Twelve minutes? That's very precise," Gabriella said.

"At eleven o'clock on the dot. He'll bounce onto the pier and stay just a few minutes. If we're not there he'll come back at six o'clock tonight."

Klara threw the laptop bag over her shoulder and pointed down toward the harbor.

"Come on," she said. "We'll run down to the harbor. I'm freezing to death."

It took less than five minutes to reach the deserted marina. An icy wind swept in from the sea, and Klara led them into the shelter of a darkened gas station. They shivered and flapped their arms for warmth.

"Just a few more minutes," Klara said.

"You seem to have complete confidence in Bosse," Gabriella said.

She remembered that Klara had talked about him before. The boy Klara had grown up with on islands far out at sea, going to and from school with him from first to ninth grade. But everything about Klara's childhood had always seemed so foreign to Gabriella, so exotic. Taking boats and hovercrafts to school, hunting and fishing. Romantic and sepia toned, an orphan fairy tale. So different from Gabriella's own secure and completely ordinary childhood in an upscale Stockholm suburb. Klara didn't talk that often about the archipelago. It was what it was. But Gabriella knew that no matter how single-mindedly Klara struggled to get away, something was always calling her back. Maybe even more so since she'd moved to Brussels.

Suddenly from across the bay came a muffled chugging sound, a deep heartbeat, a bass line.

"Get ready," Klara said. "He's only a few minutes away."

GEORGE TOOK A BITE OF bread covered with aged Herrgård cheese and tried to at least enjoy having access to the ingredients of his favorite breakfast. Kirsten had taken him along to a grocery store yesterday in some musty little one-horse town called Östra Husby. He assumed they wanted him to do the talking so as not to draw attention to themselves. Americans were unusual out here in the boonies, especially at this time of year. In the car on the ride there he'd daydreamed about just grabbing the first fucking farmer he saw and telling him to call the police. But Kirsten seemed to know exactly what he was thinking. When he parked the car, his heart racing, escape plans like oxygen bubbling through his veins, she calmly placed her hand on his elbow.

"I like you, George," she said.

She looked sincere. Wasn't there something kind of hot about her after all?

"But no fucking ideas now. Don't doubt for a second that I'll shoot you in the back if you try something."

She'd lifted the edge of her lined jacket and he'd glimpsed a large, gray automatic pistol in her waistband. George's heart had skipped a beat. The idea of her potential fuckability had vanished along with any thoughts of escape. She was a murderer. He shouldn't forget that. Instead he'd concentrated on freshly squeezed orange juice, bread, and Herrgård cheese. Cheez Doodles. Beer. Frozen pizzas and hash browns.

He shivered in the tastefully decorated, modern country kitchen. No matter how high he turned up the heat, the villa remained ice-cold. The coffee had already cooled in his cup, and one of the Americans had drunk the rest of the pot he'd put on when he woke up. To be precise, he didn't actually wake up; he'd barely slept at all. His anxiety and bad conscience were growing like a cancer inside him. He stood up and stretched his stiff limbs. If they would just leave him alone for a minute, he'd smash a window and run. Fuck Reiper's cheap blackmail. Fuck all the crimes he'd committed. Fuck the fact that they might shoot him in the back. Fuck it all. He'd just run away in his socks. But in the room upstairs where he slept, they'd put padlocks on the window, and Josh or someone else always slept in the other bed. And even down here the windows were locked. The front door was bolted. Always someone nearby. They were professionals. No doubt about it.

All he could do was go back into the living room. Turn on the Xbox that they'd set up to pass the time and play a few more rounds of Halo 4 or Modern Warfare 3. Just empty his mind. No thinking about the past, no thinking about the future. Just push down the buttons on the control and give his virtual enemy a taste of his angst.

He'd just sat down at the console and clicked past the first menu in Halo, when he heard Kirsten, who had the morning shift at the binoculars on the front porch, raise her voice.

"Code Orange," she said in a loud, restrained tone into her Bluetooth headset, which everyone besides George was equipped with.

"I repeat: Code Orange. Identification seventy percent. Suspected target plus one embarking a small vessel at the pier. Take your positions."

She'd barely finished her call before the house exploded with life. The stairs rumbled as Reiper's men threw themselves into the hall, most of them already dressed for combat. In the hall they pulled on their black Gore-Tex jumpsuits and winter boots. George got up and walked slowly out toward Kirsten on the porch. She was leaning over the binoculars and reporting continuously into her headset.

"The vessel landed and is already backing away from the dock. Two targets embarked onto the bow and seem to have hit the deck. The vessel is a small fishing boat. Approximately eighty horsepower. Estimated maximum speed of twenty knots. A person in the wheelhouse. No visible weapons. Standby for bearing and course."

At first George didn't notice that Reiper had crept out onto the porch through the other door and was pulling on a thick, black jumpsuit. He already had a black knit hat rolled down over his slush gray eyebrows.

"You're not a hundred percent that was Walldéen?" he said quietly.

"Not a hundred," Kirsten said, without looking up from the binoculars.

The front door slammed. Through the front porch glass George saw two black-clad men with duffel bags jogging across the grass down toward the dock that belonged to the house. The small covered motorboat that had been moored there since they moved into the house had already rumbled to a start.

"But almost?" Reiper said.

"As I said, seventy percent. The target was dressed like a young guy, and it's hard with details in the snow. But the person was in the company of a woman who could be Gabriella Seichelman. They were hidden behind the gas station. And I didn't see the boat until the last second. It came in at a weird fucking angle with its lights switched off."

Reiper seemed to be thinking, but for no more than a second.

"We can't afford any more mistakes. We need to be one hundred percent sure before we intervene," he said and pressed a button on his headset. "Start Plan B and await team leader. Do not intervene under any circumstances until we have complete identification."

He turned to Kirsten again.

"Well then," he said. "We'll follow them via radar and see where they go. I assume they're smart enough not to hide at Walldéen's grandparents. It doesn't seem like it was their boat picking her up either. Do we have any info on who it might have been?"

Kirsten shook her head.

"Nothing. As you know, we haven't received any information at all about that."

Reiper nodded, and when he turned to walk down to the boat, he seemed to catch sight of George. Without so much as acknowledging his presence, Reiper turned to Kirsten again.

"And you'll keep an eye on our Swedish lodger?" he said. "Josh has prepped the bedroom."

"It's cool," Kirsten said, without looking up. "We'll follow protocol."

And with that, he was gone. George followed his silhouette for a moment through the windowpane until it disappeared into the snowfall. A minute later he sensed more than saw the motorboat slowly leaving the dock and gliding out into the steel gray water with unlit navigation lights.

"George," Kirsten said, turning to him. "We're entering into an operational phase, and it's in your best interest that you don't know what happens. Believe me. So I'm going to lock you in the bedroom."

George sighed. He hardly had the energy to protest. The anxiety in his chest was sucking all the life out of him.

"Seriously?" he tried anyway. "Kirsten, damn it, is that really necessary?"

She stood up and pointed to the door out to the hall.

"Don't be a baby," she said quietly, her head tilted to one side. A smile at the corner of her mouth. "We don't have all day."

"Whatever," George said, and shrugged.

I T WASN'T UNTIL THE BOAT had turned around 180 degrees and started heading straight out from the pier at Arkösund that Gabriella dared to turn her face to look at Klara. They were both lying flat on the damp plastic deck. Gabriella could sense the waves below them. She bounced around as the boat started to gain speed. The wet snow ran down her cheeks.

Klara met her eyes. Gabriella could see her lips moving, but her voice was drowned out by the sound of the accelerating engine.

"What?" shouted Gabriella.

Klara raised one hand and pointed toward the wheelhouse.

"Let's go in, I'm freezing to death out here!" she shouted.

They got to their knees and crawled across the deck. The door opened from the inside, and they stumbled into the small wheelhouse. A huge man wearing well-worn rain clothes enveloped Klara in a bear hug before they even crossed the threshold. He looked at least ten years older than they looked, but Gabriella knew that he was almost the same age as Klara. Maybe those extra years could be blamed on his large bald spot, together with the fact that he'd retained his thin, white-blond hair around the sides. It was an unusual hairstyle nowadays, devoid of vanity. He was six and a half feet tall and must've weighed well over two hundred pounds. Klara disappeared into his vinyl-coated embrace.

"What the hell, Klara!" he said in a thick Östergötland dialect. "What sorta mess have you gotch yerself into now?"

Klara disentangled herself from his arms and bent over to look through the aft valve.

"I'll explain, Bosse, I promise. Later. First we need to get somewhere safe. Did you see if another boat was waiting when we arrived?"

"Naaaay," he said, and pressed the throttle farther down as they left the bay behind.

The boat bounced on the small waves as if running over corrugated steel.

"But it ain't easy to see much a' anything in this weather."

Klara nodded. Through the aft valve she saw the snowfall intensifying in the dim, gray light of day.

"Bosse," she said. "This is my best friend, Gabriella."

Gabriella wiped the melted snow off her face and held out her hand, while struggling to stay upright in the oncoming storm.

"I'm Gabriella," she said. "It's lovely to meet you."

Lovely to meet you? As if she were at a party with Klara's old friends instead of on an ice-cold boat fleeing from God knows what.

Bosse pulled her to him and gave her a hug like the one he'd given Klara.

"Truly!" he said. "Hope it wasn't you who's dragged Klara into all this trouble."

"No, you couldn't really say that," said Gabriella. "The opposite, really."

"Damn," Bosse said and turned around. "You've been flyin' under the radar your whole life, Klara. No trouble in school, good grades, law school, the whole shebang. And now they're sayin' you associate with terrorists? And you used to rag me for selling a little moonshine in Sanden?"

"I guess I've lost the moral high ground now," Klara said. "But speaking of radar, you don't have any do you?"

She looked around the small cabin.

"Radar? Don't you think I'll find my way through the islands on my own? How many times have I driven you out here? You yourself could do it in your sleep. Why the hell would I need radar?"

"Not for navigation," Klara said. "But I'd like to check if we're being followed."

"Followed?"

Bosse raised his bushy eyebrows and shook his huge head in disbelief. He took a good look at Klara.

"What's happened to your hair?"

"She left it in Paris, apparently," Gabriella said. "Where are we going anyway?"

"To Bosse's inheritance," Klara said. "It's called Smugglers Rock. I don't even know if that's its real name. His family has a little cabin out in the archipelago. They were smugglers, right Bosse? And that was where they kept their goods? Bosse's family has never really been ardent supporters of this country's alcohol monopoly."

Bosse smiled proudly.

"Quite the contrary," he said. "If it weren't for the monopoly, we'd have no market. Not for my homemade stuff or for Grandpa's Russian contraband. He used to call it the warehouse. Klara and I'd go out there in the summertime, right Klara? Do some fishing."

Klara nodded.

"And I went out there to study during my second semester in Uppsala. There are definitely no distractions. Just a tiny island. It feels like you're closer to Finland than to Stockholm when you're out there."

"It's a bit rough out there. No water or electricity," Bosse said. "But I dropped off supplies yesterday so you should do all right."

The farther out in the archipelago they got, the more barren and wild it was. The lush islands in the inner archipelago began to give way to steel gray rocky islets with low shrubs and brush. No red houses anymore, just hard, cold sea and granite.

Klara stood for a long time, studying the contours of the islands.

"Home?" Gabriella said and took her hand.

A tear in the corner of her eye was quickly wiped away. Klara nodded.

"Wouldn't you rather go to Aspöja?" Bosse said.

"I can't risk it," replied Klara. "If there's anyplace that's being watched it has to be Grandma and Grandpa's house. But no one knows about Smugglers Rock. And there's no cell coverage, no broadband, not even GPS works very well out there. It'll give us time to think things over."

They continued in silence. Gabriella sat down on the floor and leaned back. It was remarkable that Bosse felt no need to cross-examine Klara about what she'd been through. Instead, he seemed satisfied that she was there. There was a sense of security in that silence, she thought as she struggled to keep her eyes open. The hypnotic song of the engine and monotonous stuttering of the boat over the waves drove her inexorably toward sleep.

She was awakened by Klara's voice.

"Bosse," she said. "Full back, dammit. There's smoke coming out of the chimney on the island!"

Gabriella sat up, immediately wide-awake. Klara was standing next to Bosse with binoculars in front of her eyes. It certainly looked like smoke coming out of the chimney of the little cabin, barely discernible on the tiny island in the archipelago.

LOCKED INTO THE BEDROOM LIKE an animal. A tiger in a cage. Or not even that. More like some tame fucking lapdog that would do anything for his dinner, his walk, his master's affection. George lay on the bed with his clothes on, pulled a blanket over himself, and buried his face in a pillow.

For the first time in a very long time, he felt like crying. How had he ended up here? Just a week ago, he'd been on top of the game in Brussels; his only worry was how annoying spending Christmas with his family in Stockholm would be.

And now. Now he'd give an arm just to call his old man. If he'd had a phone, he would call immediately and tell him everything. About Reiper and his gang. About the cocaine. About Gottlieb and the stupid mistake he'd made in his immature pursuit of quick, easy money. Money! What a fucking joke.

"I'm coming home," he would sob. "I'm coming home, and I'm going to make things right, make you proud."

The old man would be disappointed, sure. Everything George had done was the complete opposite of his family's ideals. But his father would understand. Or if he didn't understand, at least he would forgive? Surely he would? George sobbed long and loud.

"Fuck!" he screamed into the pillow. "Fuck! Fuck! Fuuuck!"

How much longer would this go on? Reiper and his gang were out in the archipelago somewhere, obviously chasing what—with "seventy percent probability"—was Klara Walldéen. He didn't doubt that they would find her and that, assuming it was Klara, they'd kill her too. Just like they had apparently already killed at least two other people. As far as he knew. They didn't seem particularly affected by it. The dead were just *collateral damage*. Negligible victims in a war that he had no idea who was fighting or why. How many others had they murdered? How many others had become collateral damage?

And what would happen after that? When they came back? Would they just shake hands and thank George for his good work, before paying his rate into Merchant & Taylor's account, plus 20 percent to him personally? After everything he'd seen and heard?

Slowly it dawned on him. The truth had been staring him down the whole time, and he had refused to see it. If there was anyone in all this who could be called collateral damage, it was he. Oh my God! They were going to kill him too. Had they known that from the start? Had Appleby known? That there was a risk? Had they just sent him straight into the jaws of the devil? That dinner at Comme chez Soi, the final meal of a dead man walking?

George sat up in bed, his head spinning. He rose to his knees and leaned against the windowsill and pulled on the latch, but it was held fast by a huge padlock. Outside, the melting snowflakes ran in rivulets down the windowpane. Could he break the glass? He leaned forward, looking down toward the ground. Third floor. It was five or six meters down to the lawn. If he somehow managed to climb out and hang on to the windowsill, it would still be four meters down to the ground. Kirsten would hear the glass breaking and she wouldn't hesitate to kill him as he limped through the gray, windy morning with a sprained or broken foot. With another sob he let go of the latch and buried his face in his hands.

The house was completely quiet. The only sound was the rising wind howling over the roof tiles. George opened his eyes again and looked around the small, flowery bedroom. Two unmade beds. A dresser where Josh had unpacked all his underwear, workout clothes, and jeans in neat piles. Restless, George got up and went through the drawers. He didn't even know what he was looking for. Whatever it was, it wasn't among Josh's Calvin Klein underwear and Abercrombie & Fitch T-shirts.

The low, thin door to the built-in closet was unlocked, and George opened it to peek into the darkness. Cold, stale air washed over him. Just as he was closing the door again, he heard a crackling noise and what sounded like a muffled voice. He opened the door again and tried to adjust his eyes to the darkness. On the left side, just inside the door, he saw a flash of pale green light.

George crouched down and ran his fingers over the unfinished wood floor. The green light was coming from a small electric charger. He grabbed hold of it and lifted it up into the light. In the charger sat what seemed to be a small radio and a Bluetooth headset, of the same model that Reiper's people kept in their ears. He couldn't believe his eyes. They must have left in such a hurry that they'd forgotten the spare set charging in the closet. The headset crackled again, short staccato sentences answered by short staccato sentences, and George glanced at the locked door to the bedroom. You could hear everything in this house. He'd hear if Kirsten came up the stairs. He fastened the tiny device around his ear with trembling hands and sat down on the floor, with his back to the door.

KLARA HADN'T BEEN MISTAKEN. THE storm limited visibility, but smoke was definitely coming out of the chimney of the cabin. She let the binoculars fall and turned to Bosse, paralyzed by fear. How had they found their way here? To her only hideout? Bosse didn't slow down, just met her gaze calmly. A smile at the corner of his mouth.

"Take it easy, Klara," he said. "I was by here and lit the fire before I went in to Arkösund to getch ya. Couldn't very well let you sit in the cold, could I?"

"Damnit, Bosse," Klara said grimly. "You scared the life out of me."

She turned to Gabriella, who'd woken up from her slumber.

"Dear lord," she said. "You're really on edge. I was about to have a heart attack."

Klara sighed deeply and felt her heart rate returning to normal.

"How much wood did you push into that stove if it's still burning?" she said and turned to Bosse.

"I'd say enough," Bosse said contently.

A few minutes later Bosse pulled up to the rounded cliffs of Smugglers Rock. Klara was standing on the foredeck and hopped straight
down onto the rocks with ease, lashing the bow line around one of
the rotting poles of the battered jetty. She had to hunch over in the
wind and sleet. With a hand on her forehead to protect her eyes,
she squinted past the rocks toward the small cabin. It had once been
barn red like everything else out here in the archipelago, but storms
and sun had scraped and bleached the paint off until the century-
old fir planks were completely bare. It was a miracle the mullioned
windows were still intact. Bosse hadn't exactly lavished care on this
part of his inheritance.

They docked by the dilapidated jetty in the natural harbor, which
faced back toward the mainland. From the jetty it was maybe fifty
yards up to the little cottage. On the other side of the island Klara
could see the waves bearing down, already white and violent. It
would get worse through the afternoon and into the night. Beyond
the rocks stood only gray, merciless sea all the way to the horizon.
The first time Bosse had brought her here, she'd thought this place
must be what the end of the world looked like.

She turned and saw Bosse helping Gabriella down from the boat.
Gabriella looked tired and a little disoriented. Klara felt momentarily guilty for dragging her out here. But she didn't know how she
would have managed to deal with this on her own.

"Well, now," shouted Bosse through the wind and slush. "It's
gonna be a nasty night out here. A gale at the very least. And snow.
I'll think about ya when I'm snuggled up at home under my covers."

He laughed and put his arm around Gabriella.

"It's a bit different from your city life in a law firm, ain't it?" he said with satisfaction.

Gabriella looked at him, annoyed. Klara smiled to herself. If there was anyone you shouldn't underestimate, it was Gabriella. No matter what. Klara took her by the arm.

"Gabriella is no ordinary lawyer, Bosse," she said. "She's my friend."

"Well, well," Bosse said. "You've also gone and become a lawyer. And you're not payin' any taxes to boot."

He shook his head and took the lead up to the cottage.

"He grows on you," whispered Klara.

"I'm sure," Gabriella said with a smile. "But let's just say that the two of you have evolved in slightly different directions?"

Bosse opened the door to the cabin and they hurried inside and out of the storm. The house consisted of just one room of about three hundred square feet, open to the roof. At one end a rickety ladder led up to a sleeping loft. In front of the fireplace stood an old saggy green sofa. The walls were untreated pine, just like the floor. Under the loft stood a makeshift kitchen, consisting of a gas stove and a couple of coolers. Bosse hurried over to the stove and threw a few logs on the fire.

"You should have enough to get by," he said. "And I filled the gas stove. You'll find some milk and cheese in the coolers. Some hash browns, eggs, and red beets. Smoked salmon. Some potatoes. It'll last ya' few days at least. And I brought ya some a' this, too."

He pulled out an old 1.5-liter Coke bottle with a peeling label, which contained some kind of clear liquid.

"Oh?" Gabriella said. "And what is that?"

Klara shook her head.

"Well hell, Bosse," she said and turned to Gabriella. "That there is Bosse's finest vintage. Moonshine from his very own still, I'd guess?"

"That's right!" Bosse said. "An island specialty. There's no better liquor than this here liquid gold. It's Christmas! You'll need something tasty, right?"

He looked at his wristwatch.

"All right, you've got what ya' need. I'll come back tomorrow, weather permittin'. But at the moment I've got things to attend to."

"Get going then," Klara said, suddenly relieved to be alone with Gabriella. "We'll be fine."

She went over to Bosse and gave him a hug.

"Thanks for everything," she said quietly. "You've saved my life again."

Bosse looked embarrassed and shrugged.

"Oh, come now. I only wish I could do more."

"You've done enough," Klara said.

Bosse went to the door and stopped with his hand on the door-knob.

"By the way," he said. "Just in case. I brought your gun."

He pointed toward the stove, where Klara's shotgun was lying next to a few boxes of cartridges.

Klara went over and patted him on the cheek.

"That was nice," she said. "But if I end up needing it, it will probably already be too late."

F ROM WHERE GEORGE WAS SITTING, on the floor with his back against the locked door, he could hear the old house creak and complain about the winter storm like a tired old man. The headset had been silent since he'd put it on. Someone had undoubtedly been speaking in it when he took it out of the closet, but since then it hadn't made a peep. George had checked the battery and volume several times, but everything seemed to be in order. He could only hope that the last orders he'd heard hadn't been instructions to change frequency.

But maybe it didn't matter. He still didn't know what he'd do with any information that he managed to get hold of. He was a prisoner. And a cowardly prisoner too. Apparently he lacked both moral courage and any real survival instinct. How else to explain being drawn deeper and deeper into this mess without doing anything about it, neither trying to escape nor to stop what was about to happen to Klara? He was in so deep that he couldn't even figure out how to get out of this room. Again, he buried his face in his hands and let out a long moan.

Then he heard Reiper's voice in his ear, so clearly that he jumped and, with his heart racing, started to turn around before realizing the neutral, unsettling voice was coming from the radio.

"Beta one to alpha one," Reiper said.

It took a second before Kirsten's voice came on.

"Come in. Alpha one here, over."

"Switch to channel five. Copy, over."

"Copy that. Switching to channel five, over."

"Roger, see you there, over and out."

"Over and out."

George fumbled with the radio. Channel five, channel five, channel five. He found a control labeled CHANNELS. A few keystrokes later, the radio display indicated he was on channel five. It didn't take long before Reiper's voice came on again.

"Beta one to alpha one."

Barely a second later, Kirsten's voice sounded through the earpiece.

"Alpha one here, over."

"We're in the shelter of an island at the following coordinates."

Reiper rattled off a long sequence of digits. George stood up and ran over to Josh's bedside table. Josh did Sudoku before going to sleep; there should be a pen next to his bed.

"I repeat," Reiper said and stated the coordinates once again.

George repeated the numbers aloud to himself until he finally found a promotional pen from Merchant & Taylor. He raised his eyebrows. Where the hell had Josh gotten a hold of that? He couldn't recall having any with him. Whatever. Fully focused, he managed to scribble the long combination of numbers on a page of Josh's half-finished Sudoku.

"I repeat," Kirsten said and read out the digits again.

George checked them against his row and noted with satisfaction that he had gotten them all right.

"Roger that," Reiper said. "The target is installed at the following coordinates."

A new series of numbers followed and was confirmed. George also copied them at the bottom of the Sudoku page.

"We'll wait until dark and then we launch an operation to identify the target. Once we have full identification, we'll continue with the original plan."

"Roger that, over."

"Everything under control on your end? Over."

"Everything according to plan, over."

"Good, over and out."

"Over and out."

George sat down on the bed again. He looked at the numbers he'd written down. So now he knew where Reiper was. He knew where the target, Klara, with 70 percent probability, was. So what? As soon as darkness fell Reiper's people would identify her. And then kill her. And probably also her friend who had evidently been with her on the boat in Arkösund. And here he sat, locked in a drafty bedroom, most likely awaiting his own execution.

This time he didn't bury his face in his hands as hopelessness streamed over him. Instead he put the radio and headset back into the charger in the closet where he found them. Then he went up to the locked door that led out to the landing. He took a deep breath. It was time to take control of the situation.

"Kirsten!" he shouted as loud as he could while pounding on the door. "Kirsten! I need to go to the bathroom! Come on! Open up!"

It took a minute before George heard the stairs creak, and he stopped pounding on the door. He turned and looked out the window at the gray lawn, the gray, sprawling apple trees. Behind them he sensed the waves beating against the smooth rocks. It was getting dark already. He glanced at his Breitling watch. It was almost three o'clock. With his heart pounding in his chest he shouted again.

"Kirsten, what the hell, I really need to pee!"

"Calm down." Kirsten's voice came from the floor below.

A few seconds more, then the sound of a key in the lock.

"I want you to go and sit on your bed before I unlock this," Kirsten said through the thin wood. "So, step away from the door."

George groaned.

"Come on! What the hell do you think I'm going to do? Attack you?"

A mixture of disappointment and relief washed over him as he moved away from the door to his bed. His first idea had been to pounce on her as soon as she opened the door. Surprise her, wrestle her down to the floor, and take the gun away from her before she knew what was happening. It wasn't a particularly well thought out plan, and he wouldn't have had a chance. She was probably both stronger and smarter than he was. In addition, she most certainly fought dirty. It was just as well that the possibility had been precluded right away.

"Okay," he said. "I'm sitting on the bed."

The key turned in the lock, and Kirsten stood in the doorway. She looked focused, her cheekbones were even more prominent than usual, her mouth set in a thin line.

"Keep your hands where I can see them," she said. "And put these on."

She threw a pair of matte black handcuffs next to him on the unmade bed. She didn't move from the doorway.

"Seriously!" George said. "Handcuffs? Are you serious? Isn't it enough that you've imprisoned me? Don't you even remember that this started out with you as my client?"

"Stop fucking around," interrupted Kirsten. "Just put those on. And be grateful that I'm breaking protocol. Because the rules state you should have a hood and earmuffs on when you're out of the area of confinement. So you can consider this a favor."

"Rules?" muttered George. "What fucking rules? When did this turn into Guantánamo?"

Kirsten didn't answer, just gestured to George to hurry up. He put on the handcuffs with a sigh. They closed silently and alarmingly tight around his wrists.

"After you," Kirsten said. "You know where the toilet is. I'm a few steps behind you. I'm sorry, George. I really don't think you're going to do something stupid, but we have rules for how we do things around here."

George nodded mutely and took a tentative step down the stairs. His head was spinning. Maybe this was his only chance. Why had he been so impulsive? Why didn't he have a plan? Why was he such a fucking idiot?

There was a guest bathroom in the hall at the foot of the stairs. That's where Kirsten was leading him. Maybe he could convince her to let him sit in the living room for a while? To avoid the boredom of the bedroom? Once there, he could think about what to do. He took each step carefully, slowly, trying to win time. The staircase spiraled downward.

It was when he finally saw down to the entrance that his opportunity appeared, his only tiny, tiny chance. He suddenly felt giddy from both possibility and fear. On the windowsill at the foot of the stairs, there was a black iPhone charging. From her position three steps behind George, Kirsten hadn't seen it yet.

In the course of a second he decided to bet it all on this one card. With a scream he pretended to stumble, two quick steps down in a pretense of regaining his balance, then he threw himself forward, twisting so that he fell sideways down the last few steps.

"Aaaaaaah," he cried.

He felt the worn wood of the stairs on his hip bone. His shoulder hit the parquet floor in the hall. But the only thing he saw was the phone and the charger. He managed to twist and stretch his arms toward the window as he landed. He grabbed the cord of the charger between his fingers and yanked as hard as he could. The phone was pulled down from the windowsill and landed on the floor. George's head hit the heater and he felt something wet and sticky dripping into his eyes. He must have split an eyebrow. Through a reddish haze, he saw the phone in front of him on the floor, still spinning after the fall. He stretched his bound hands out for it and grabbed hold of its cold, smooth surface.

"What the hell!" he heard Kirsten hiss behind him.

Her feet thudded down the stairs. George leaned forward, one shoulder to the floor, and, using both his hands, he pressed the phone inside his waistband, down into those damn tighty-whities he'd gotten from Josh. For the first time since he got them, he was grateful they weren't boxers. The phone would stay put in his underwear. He did his best to pull down the huge, borrowed sweatshirt to conceal his crotch.

Kirsten was behind him. I'm going to die, thought George. This is when I die.

"What happened?" she said with something like genuine concern in her voice.

"I stumbled," George wheezed. "And these fucking handcuffs didn't help."

Kirsten crouched down beside him and George rolled onto his back with his hands over his crotch.

"You're bleeding," Kirsten said. "You've split an eyebrow. Nothing serious. But you'll have to tape it. Come on, go into the bathroom and fix yourself up."

George got up on his knees. His whole body aching, his eyebrow pounding. Was it possible? Was it really possible that she hadn't seen the phone? He hardly dared to breathe but still managed a small smile.

"Sorry," he said. "Seriously, I didn't mean to fall and hurt myself."

"Yeah, good thing we didn't put you in a hood, you would have fallen right through the window," she said drily. "Get up."

George stood up cautiously. He pinched the bleeding wound and started walking toward the bathroom.

The phone was cold and hard against his genitals. Was this what a last chance felt like?

December 23, 2013

Stockholm and Arkösund, Sweden

I'T'S THE SAME AIRPORT, BUT a different time. Wood and glass and Starbucks. A confidence that didn't exist here twenty-five years ago. *WELCOME TO THE CAPITAL OF SCANDINAVIA*. Smiling people. It doesn't resemble a funeral anymore. But the darkness is the same, as I maneuver my rented Volvo out onto the highway with jet lag breathing down my neck. Even the car design has changed. They are no longer coffins, more like water, with their flowing lines and tinted glass. Here's where I'll start to retrace my own footsteps and continue on where they end.

I drive over the same asphalt, through the same dense web of forest, over the same bridges and wet fields. The same road where everything is exactly as I remember it, and the only thing new is me. This is where I'll suffer the consequences of my actions. This is where I'll take hold of the story and change its course.

It's been twenty-five years since I drove this road that one time and yet I remember it, never once glancing at the car's GPS. Snow hangs in the air when I stop and buy coffee to keep from falling asleep. Microscopic crystals glitter weightlessly in the light from the SHELL SELECT sign. Hard, compact steam billows out of my mouth. The cinnamon buns are bigger and sweeter. The coffee is no longer watery, but bitter and mixed with steamed milk. I throw half of it into a modern-looking trash can, covered with technical and complicated instructions for recycling, and continue driving down the almost deserted, black road. It's difficult to stay within the speed limit. Impatience, fear, lack of time. They're all hunting me like I'm an outlaw. All I can think is that I regret everything. That maybe there's nothing I don't regret.

Somewhere near Norrköping I turn off the highway, onto small winding roads, and am engulfed in a darkness so intense that I have to slow down, a darkness so thick that it barely lets the light of the headlights through. Every single car I meet is an explosion that shakes my world for a moment until it passes. It shouldn't surprise me, I've seen it before. But my history is false, full of constructions and justifications. Not even my memory of the dark matches reality.

This time I turn off before Arkösund. I avoid the obvious. I'm not sure how much my enemies know. The forest has thinned out and has been replaced by rocks and gnarled bushes. The black windows of empty summerhouses gleam in the headlights. The wind sings against the car and the windshield wipers skid in the rain or watery snow. If the clock on the instrument panel didn't prove that it was late afternoon, I'd think it was the middle of the night. The asphalt turns into gravel, and finally the road ends at a dock where I see a single, open boat bouncing against its fenders in the wind.

I slow down and stop the car by the dry reeds. Pull up the hood on my Gore-Tex jacket and step out into the storm. I lean over the trunk of the Volvo and pull open the sluggish zipper of the rubber duffel bag, which was already in the car when I picked it up. Double-check the Swiss automatic rifle that lacks both model name and serial number. Double-check the magazines. When I'm satisfied, I pull out a lined, waterproof jumpsuit, hat, waterproof gloves, the GPS with nautical charts already loaded and the route already plotted.

The small rubber boat is just where I was told it would be. Hidden in the bushes ten feet from the dock. Susan has worked fast. Prepared well.

I place my pack in the boat and attach the GPS to the control in front of me. Pull the light boat down to the edge of the water where I'm able to step in without getting wet. The snow flurries into my eyes. The wind is raging across the bay. Even this far in, the waves are white in the night. Farther out it will only get worse.

I look at the electronic chart and make adjustments so my route will be leeward and avoid the open water. It takes me a few tries to get into the rubber boat, which is rocking wildly in the wind. I take off my gloves and put my hands inside my jacket. My frozen fingers find their way to the zipper of the inside pocket. I open it and feel the locket's aging silver against my fingers. For a moment I'm tempted to take it out so I can see you again. It's been so long since I saw you. But it's too dark, too windy. I can't afford to lose it. My key, my shibboleth. Instead I close the jacket and push off from the beach. The sea is just as dark as everything else. The red route on the GPS's nautical chart shines its lonely light in the rain, in the snow, in the wind.

WHEN KLARA FINALLY WOKE UP, it was already dark. She sat up on the thin mattress and looked around in the soft, warm light from the stove's smoldering fire, for a moment unsure of where she was. The wind shook the house, twisting around and through it, and came hissing, headlong over the metal roof and past the worn joints. Between the gusts, she heard the waves beating over the rocks just twenty yards from the house. Klara rubbed her eyes, remembering where she was.

How long had she been sleeping anyway? As soon as Bosse had left, an immense weariness had enveloped her as she felt the security of the sea and surrounding islands. Bosse and Gabriella. Gabriella? Klara crept shivering out of the sheets and over to the edge of the loft. Gabriella lay on her back on the couch, sleeping in front of the stove with a worn, red plaid blanket thrown over her legs. There was something peaceful, something so mundane and comforting about that scene.

"Gabriella?" Klara said gently. "Are you asleep?"

Gabriella grunted, turned onto her side, and blinked her eyes.

"It seems so," she said, shivering, and pulled the blanket over herself. "Ugh, it's so cold. What time is it?"

Klara turned her wrist and took a look at her watch.

"Nearly eight," she said. "Oh my God, how long have I been asleep? Six hours?"

"Well, you zonked out pretty quickly," said Gabriella. She paused, and seemed to be listening for something.

"What a wind!" she said.

"Yes, Bosse wasn't exaggerating when he said it was blowing in."

Klara suddenly realized she was extremely hungry. The last thing she'd eaten was a dry ham sandwich at a gas station on the way down from Stockholm. She found her jacket and her jeans on the floor, and pulled them on before making her way over to the steps that led down to the cabin's only room.

"Salmon sandwich?" Klara asked.

No sooner had the words left her lips than she froze in midmotion on the ladder. Cautiously, she turned her head and met Gabriella's wide-open and wide-awake eyes. She'd heard it too.

Maybe it was the storm howling over the roof. Maybe it was a seabird in distress. But it had sounded like a human voice. Just briefly, almost hidden by the wind. Very close. Klara felt paralyzed. How was it possible?

"What was that?" whispered Gabriella.

Klara regained control of herself and climbed down the last few steps.

"I don't know," she said. "Maybe just the storm?"

While she was whispering, she tiptoed quickly into the cabin's kitchen area. The shotgun still stood where she'd left it, leaning in the corner beside the makeshift counter. On the floor beside it lay two square cardboard boxes of cartridges. The steel of the gun felt cold and familiar when Klara picked it up. She squatted down and opened one of the boxes, cracked open the gun, and loaded a shotgun shell into each barrel. The gun closed with a muffled click.

She gestured for Gabriella to leave the couch and come over to her. The faint glow of the stove didn't reach all the way into the kitchen, and Klara only sensed the outline of Gabriella's crouching figure as she took a few quick steps across the floor. She felt Gabriella's hand on her elbow, her rapid breathing on her neck.

"What do you think?" whispered Gabriella. "It sounded like a voice, right?"

Klara shrugged.

"Maybe. Impossible to say."

But it had definitely sounded like a man's voice. A short order given just a little too loudly in a moment when the storm was catching its breath.

"What should we do?"

Klara heard a shade of anxiety in Gabriella's voice. It was an anxiety that had the potential to escalate. The seed of panic. It was something Klara had learned to recognize far more intimately than she would have liked in the last week. And she knew that it needed to be checked immediately. She turned to her friend and let go of the gun for a moment to take her hand.

"Gabriella, listen to me," she whispered. "We cannot afford to lose focus, okay? We can only think about what is happening right now. Not yesterday or tomorrow or even ten minutes from now. Just now, just the next movement, the next step. Do you understand? Can you try to do that? Keep your fear at bay."

She heard Gabriella swallow.

"Well, yes," she hissed. "What do you think? That I'm going to have a panic attack? Come on."

Of course. She was an idiot to underestimate Gabriella. Of course she was just as capable, or incapable, of handling this situation as Klara was.

"Good," she whispered. "Can you make your way to the window and try to see what it was? I'll keep an eye on the door. "

Klara felt the warmth of Gabriella's body depart as she shuffled across the floor toward one of the two windows facing toward the archipelago. If someone had landed on the island, they'd do it on the leeward side and not where the waves were beating too high to get ashore. The door, which Klara never looked away from, opened in the direction of the open sea. Behind the rain and wind Klara could hear the waves heaving over the cliffs.

It took maybe ten seconds before she heard Gabriella's whispering voice again.

"Klara, come here, it's probably best you see this for yourself."

With a firm grip around the barrel of the gun, Klara quickly crept across the floor to the window. She squatted down next to Gabriella.

"What? What is it? " she whispered.

But Gabriella didn't have time to respond before she saw for herself. On the same path that they had walked this morning. The weak skittering glow of a flashlight.

GEORGE LOCKED THE DOOR TO the guest bathroom behind him and turned on the light. The small space had no windows, which was probably why Kirsten had left him alone in there. He looked at himself in the small mirror above the sink. He looked like shit. Half of his face was covered in bright red blood. The upper half of the sweatshirt was as well, and he could see the blood continuing to pump out of the little gash above his eyebrow. George had to swallow his queasiness, fight his body's impulse to vomit. He hated blood. Especially his own. But he couldn't think about that right now. He squeezed the gash and bent over to wash his face as best he could.

"You look fucking terrible," Kirsten said when he opened the door and stepped out of the bathroom.

She smiled apologetically at him and handed him a round box. He took it with his shackled hands.

"First aid tape," she said. "So you don't get blood all over the house."

"Thank you," George said.

She gestured toward the stairs.

"I'm afraid I have to lock you in again, George."

This time George didn't drag his feet. It took effort not to appear too eager to get back into his cage.

Sitting on the bed, he heard Kirsten's footsteps disappear down the creaking stairs. After some fiddling, he managed to open the tape and at least temporarily stanch the flow of blood above his eyebrow. Kirsten hadn't bothered to unlock his hands and just shook her head when he suggested it. He hadn't insisted, terrified that she'd sniff out that something wasn't right.

He stood up, pulled the phone out of his underwear, and poked the Sudoku out from its hiding place behind the radiator. After having ascertained as best as he could that Kirsten really had disappeared down the stairs, he sat on the bed and unlocked the phone. With trembling fingers, he pushed the numbers 112.

It rang four times. George's pulse raced as he waited while simultaneously trying to hear if Kirsten had decided to come back up the stairs. Finally he heard a calm, female voice.

"112. What is your emergency?"

George felt light-headed, his mouth dry. Why hadn't he contacted the police in Brussels, long before everything got derailed?

"My name is George Lööw," he said. "And I'm kidnapped. I guess."

"Where are you right now?"

The voice was calm, apparently unmoved by the inherent drama of the word *kidnapped*.

"In Arkösund, I think. Is there a place called Arkösund? In the archipelago outside Norrköping somewhere. I've been locked up in a yellow house by some Americans—"

"Help is on the way," interrupted the voice. "Stay on the line. I'm connecting you further, you understand? Do not hang up."

There was a click and the voice was replaced by empty, atmospheric noise. Ten seconds. Twenty. Thirty. George listened at the door. Still nothing. Then there was a voice on the other end. A man. A calm, confident Swedish man.

"My name's Roger," the voice said. "I'm part of Säpo's antiterror unit."

"Umm, hello," replied George somewhat uncertain.

"Where are you?"

Säpo. That's more like it, thought George. He repeated everything he knew. That he was imprisoned in a yellow house in Arkösund. He tried to explain where the house was in relation to the harbor.

"Stay there. Don't try to escape or flee. We'll take care of this. How many people are guarding you?"

"Right now, just one person," answered George. "I'm locked in. Everyone else is out on a boat looking for Klara Walldéen. You know, she's the one who's . . . wanted?"

"How many people are there?"

"Five, I think."

"You said you knew where they were? That you knew where Walldéen was?"

There was something tense in his voice. Something that George couldn't put his finger on. With the phone wedged between shoulder and cheek, he grabbed hold of the Sudoku with his shackled hands. He read out the coordinates.

"Good," the man said. "Have the phone nearby in case we need to contact you again. But don't endanger yourself by making any more calls. It's possible that they might be able to trace it."

"Of course," said George. "What happens now? You have to help me!"

"We'll take care of this," said the dry, confident voice.

WHAT IS THAT?"
Gabriella's voice could barely be heard above the squalls. "A flashlight?"

Klara felt her body tense. The adrenaline was rushing through her.

"It looks like a flashlight, right?" she said again. "Is it Bosse?"

Klara shrugged.

"He wasn't coming back until tomorrow. And he knows better than to be out in this storm."

"What should we do?" Gabriella said.

Klara turned toward her. Saw her own terror reflected in Gabriella's eyes.

"I don't know."

She grabbed the barrel of the shotgun with one hand while releasing the safety with the other. She took a deep breath. A few minutes passed. Life narrowed to her trembling fingers and throbbing temples. To waiting and tense muscles, ready for flight.

Then someone knocked violently at the door. Fast, heavy blows. The beam from a flashlight shone in the window. The cone of light traveled across the floor. Somewhere a voice was drowned out by the storm, impossible to make out. Klara braced herself against the wall and gestured to Gabriella to crouch beside her. Her index finger trembled as she wrapped it around the trigger. The pounding on the door resumed. And when the storm quieted for a moment, she heard the voice again.

GEORGE FLINCHED AS HE HEARD the lock turning on his prison door. When he looked up, Kirsten was standing in the doorway. He raised his eyes, genuinely terrified. How was it possible that he hadn't heard her on the stairs? In the gloom her face looked grim, focused. Whatever solidarity and goodwill might have been there before had completely vanished. The way she looked at him was so ice-cold that George had to look away. His hands were shaking. What the hell had he done? From the corner of his eye he could see that Kirsten was holding the large, gray gun in her hand. A long, narrow cylinder was attached to the tip. A silencer.

"Give it to me," said Kirsten.

Her voice low and very calm as she walked slowly across the room toward George.

"Give what to you?" he said.

His voice sounded so small. Kirsten stopped a few yards away from him.

"The phone, you idiot," she said. "Surely you didn't think it was going to be that easy. Just steal a phone and call the police? Haven't you understood anything?"

She raised the gun at him. The silencer nearly touched George's forehead. The hole in the barrel looked enormous.

"It's too late," said George. "I've already called the police. They're on their way. Whatever you do to me, it's too late for you."

His voice was no more than a whisper. Kirsten swallowed.

"What made you go and do that?" she said. "What did you think? That we were goofing around out here in the archipelago on our own, without any protection? Did you really believe that? Are you truly that fucking naive?"

She shook her head. As if the scope of his ignorance was impossible for her to grasp.

"Our operation is sanctioned on the highest levels, and the Swedish police have instructions not to intervene out here. The only thing your call led to was a phone call from the Swedish Security Service to us. Sorry to disappoint you, George. This is how the war on terror is fought on the ground. So give me that fucking phone. Now."

All of his hope evaporated instantly to be replaced by an almost paralyzing despair. But simultaneously something else took root in him. A fury, a frenzy as unexpected as it was liberating.

All of these layers of lies and secrets. All he had suffered in the past week. Was it really possible that these bastards could just do whatever they wanted? That there were absolutely no rules they had to abide by? No one to hold them accountable or ask what the hell they were doing?

Kirsten waved her hand impatiently.

"Give it to me," she said.

"No," he said and shook his head. His mouth was so dry the words almost stuck to his tongue.

"What?" said Kirsten. "What do you mean no?"

"I will not give you the phone."

He could barely breathe. She was going to kill him. One of them was going to kill him no matter what. Suddenly it felt extremely important not to play along anymore. To quit cooperating. Whether it made a difference or not.

George tried to swallow and forced his gaze away from the huge muzzle of the gun, up toward Kirsten's face. A muscle twitched, barely noticeable under her left eye. The big mouth was no more than a line. The eyes small and focused.

"Do you think that phone even matters anymore? You really are a bigger idiot than I imagined. Don't you get it? Your death sentence has already been signed."

Her voice trembled and slid. She blinked several times in succession. George braced himself. The adrenaline surged through him when he saw her grip tighten on the gun. Her index finger hooked around the trigger. The steel of the barrel was cold and heavy against his cheek. Something warm was spreading across his crotch; he had wet himself.

"Close your eyes," she said.

Her voice cracked and a small trickle of sweat ran down her temple. George kept his eyes locked with hers. There was something there. Something he discerned through his haze of adrenaline, through his mortal terror. Something that wasn't there before. A crack, a fracture, a hesitation. Even a seasoned hunter doesn't like putting down a pet.

"Shut your eyes, for fuck's sake!" she shouted.

"No," whispered George.

A second, infinitely long. The only sound came from the storm. And George's heart. Then a crackling in Kirsten's earpiece. They both awoke from their shared trance, and she grabbed the earpiece to press the answer button.

She looked away from George for a split second.

What happened then was a result of mechanics. Of a desperate, inborn, overwhelming will to survive.

George threw himself to the side on the bed while simultaneously grabbing the barrel of the gun with his handcuffed hands and spinning it away from himself. Felt the blast of wind and the stinging pain of a bullet tearing off the outer tip of his right earlobe. There was a whistling inside his head, as if someone had turned the sound of his pulse up to max. Somewhere beside or below him he could hear Kirsten shrieking. They crashed down onto the floor. It felt like wrestling underwater, in zero gravity. George no longer knew what was up or down. What was thought and what was instinct. All he cared about was the barrel of the gun. All he saw was the muzzle.

He bent and pulled, twisted and punched. Another silent shot went off, the barrel warm from the explosion. George slapped the hand holding the gun toward what he assumed was the floor. It could just as well be the ceiling. Or the wall. The world was helter-skelter. A kaleidoscope.

Again: coughing. And then the hand holding the pistol let go. A drawn-out scream, somewhere beside him. Hands clawing him across the face, arms, and chest. Nails searching for his eyes. George managed to free his arms and raised them over his head. The barrel was still warm when he brought the butt down on what he assumed was Kirsten's face. As hard as he could. First one time, and then another. Then a third time. The crunch of facial bones breaking. Like biting into gristle.

The attack against him subsided. Those strong arms lost their resolve. George raised the butt again. It was as if he were blind. Deaf. An organism focused solely on destroying its enemy. But the fog, the paralysis, gave way before he struck again. He was sitting on Kirsten's chest. Her battered face. That slurping sound as she drew breath through broken bones, through blood. He looked away, and pushed himself up to his knees. His hand trembling, he rested the barrel of the gun against Kirsten's forehead.

"The keys," he said. "The keys to the handcuffs."

Kirsten fumbled in the pocket of her cargo pants and a small bunch of keys fell with a jingle onto the wooden floor.

"The keys to the other boat at the dock?"

Kirsten shook her head. "What the hell are you going to do? Rescue your princess? Who do you think you are? Rambo?"

Her voice was thick with strain, blood, defeat.

George didn't hesitate a moment before turning the barrel away from Kirsten's face and firing a shot into her thigh. He was surprised by the kickback and nearly fell backward. Kirsten screamed.

"The keys to the boat," said George again.

Kirsten snorted, shook her head, growled like an animal.

"In the cabinet beside the front door," she hissed. "You'd probably find them anyway."

George got up and managed to remove the handcuffs. He didn't dare look at Kirsten, moaning on the floor. Was it really possible that he was responsible for all of this damage? He was filled with shame and anxiety. A woman. He had beaten a woman. A woman that he, until a few minutes ago, had at times almost had an amicable relationship with. With extreme effort, he forced those thoughts away and pulled the sheet off the bed. He methodically tore it into long, four-inch thick strips. Without looking at Kirsten, he laid them on the floor beside her.

"You can wrap those around your wounds," he said.

Then he stood up, walked out the door, and locked it behind him.

T HE PERSISTENT POUNDING ON THE door. The voice outside, torn apart by the wind. At first impossible to understand.
Then, quite suddenly, completely clear. Klara felt her paralyzing terror ease.

"Grandpa!" she cried.

She turned to Gabriella with relief in her eyes.

"It's Grandpa! Oh my God!"

She put the gun on the floor and ran her hands over her face.

"Holy shit, that was close," said Gabriella. "I thought we were
going to . . . I don't know what I thought."

Klara had already jumped up and taken a few steps toward the
door.

When she opened it, the wind caught it, and she had to fight not
to be pulled out into the cold. The snow whipped in through the
opening.

"Grandpa!" she screamed over the wind. "What on earth are
you doing here?"

Her grandfather was wearing his neon orange storm gear. A
sou'wester that was so worn out that it was almost black hung down
over his eyes. Something flashed behind him. A second flashlight.

Klara peered over his shoulder and glimpsed a dark silhouette in the darkness. Her grandfather grabbed hold of her elbow and gently led her back into the relative warmth of the cabin.

"Klara," he said, calmly. "I was hoping you'd come visit us for Christmas."

He gave her a tired, small smile as he took off his sou'wester and led them toward the stove. Christmas. Klara had completely repressed the fact that it was even December.

"What?" she said. "What day is it?"

"The day before Christmas Eve," said Grandpa. "Klara, sit down."

She turned her head and saw that the other man—the silhouette—was moving, cautious and unsure, over the threshold. He, too, was dressed in storm gear, considerably more modern and technologically advanced than her grandfather's. He set a dark duffel bag down on the floor inside the door and remained standing.

"Who is that?" she said.

Her knuckles whitened around the butt of the rifle, her index finger resting on the trigger.

Grandpa unbuttoned his raincoat and let it fall onto the wooden floor.

"To be honest, I don't really know," he said. "But I've got my suspicions."

He sat down on a wooden chair and motioned for Klara to have a seat on the couch. She sat down gently, never taking her eyes off the man by the door.

"He's American, I think. And he showed up on Aspöja about an hour ago."

Klara felt the panic knot up in her chest. She propped the gun up in her lap, grasping it with both hands.

"Oh my God!" she said. "You couldn't have known, but . . ."

Grandpa put an icy hand on her knee and shook his head.

"He knew your mother, Klara. He's proved it in more ways than one. I would've died rather than bring him to you, if I suspected he was hiding anything."

"But how did you even know where I was?"

Grandpa looked at her and winked.

"I have my ways, you know," he said.

"You can never trust Bosse," Klara said.

Grandpa turned to the side and smiled at Gabriella.

"Hello there, Gabriella," he said. "It's been a while."

Klara didn't even hear them. Her eyes were fastened on the man standing beside the door. With a thick glove he brushed the wet snow from his hood and pulled it from his head.

He looked like he was in his sixties, with the efficient build of a marathon runner. His hair was cut short but was dark and as thick as horsehair. Grizzled stubble covered his furrowed cheeks and chin. Brown eyes and olive skin. Maybe he had Mediterranean or Arab ancestry. Klara met his gaze, but he turned away. He didn't frighten her; instead, he gave off an impression of deep sadness. As if he'd spent far too long far too alone with a great sorrow.

December 23, 2013

Sankt Anna's Outer Archipelago, Sweden

I STAND IN THE WET SNOW, allowing the storm, the falling snow, to swirl around my Gore-Tex-covered body; allowing myself to bend with each gust of wind. I close my eyes while the old man pounds on the door, shouting against the wind in his singing dialect. The storm drowns him out, tearing his words in every direction, breaking them into atoms, into chunks of vowels, consonants, which swirl randomly out into the snow, into the sea.

When the door opens, it's as if I go blind, as if my eyes momentarily refuse to accept the signals my mind is sending them. Perhaps it's a defense mechanism? The last one remaining, the definitive, the least refined. Mechanics instead of psychology. A blunt weapon to protect myself against finally facing the product of my betrayal. But in the end, of course, there's nowhere to hide and my eyes adjust to the light.

Through a screen of snow, I see her in the glowing rectangle of the door. She stands on the threshold, thin and haggard, struggling to keep the wind from grabbing hold of the door. A shotgun that looks huge in relation to her thin body lies across her arm, and there's something about how she's holding it, or almost doesn't seem to be holding it, that gives the impression of a casual, natural competence.

I squint and see her eyes. They glisten like water in the darkness. They are your eyes. I have no defense against the realization that in her heart beats my heart. In her blood flows my blood. The idea is too enormous. The storm has moved into my head and is gaining in strength. Everything I've thought. Everything I haven't articulated even to myself, but that has been growing inside me all of my adult life. All of it is just wreckage now. A casualty of this storm. I left her all alone. Have mercy on me.

———

I see the old man take her gently by the arm and lead her into the little cabin. She sits on the couch in front of the stove. He takes off his snowy sou'wester. His boots leave wet tracks on the untreated wood floor. I move cautiously into the room. Lower my hood, set my bag down on the floor in front of the door. Wet snow drips silently.

Another young woman is standing by the stove. Her eyes move back and forth between Klara and me, and she runs her hands through her big red hair repeatedly. She's doing what she can to keep the shock in check. Probably she thought we'd come to murder them.

The old man is speaking quietly in his bizarre language. I don't know what he's saying, how much he knows or suspects. All I've spoken to him are the few words I learned in his language, before seeking out him and his wife.

I knew your daughter. Klara is in grave danger. I'm here to help. And then I gave the locket to his wife. The picture of her daughter. Her eyes when they met mine: pale blue, like a winter sky. The same eyes that I will never forget. Why did they decide to trust me? It was as if they instinctively knew who I was. As if they'd been waiting for me.

The old man has stopped speaking and the young woman, who is my daughter, if I can even allow myself to think that word, turns to me at last. I hear the waves crashing over granite; the wind never wanes. The eye of the storm. I never thought I would make it here. I've reached the outermost edge of my plan. What remains is chaos, chance, truth. Her voice is deeper than I'd expected. Her English is British and natural.

"So," she says. "My grandfather says you knew my mother? You've certainly chosen an odd time for a visit."

GEORGE STUMBLED DOWN THE STAIRS, almost dropping the heavy gun, and grabbed the railing to regain his balance. Nausea, shock, blood. The image of Kirsten's battered face, and the knowledge that he was the one who'd beaten her. He just barely made it to the bathroom in time to vomit.

Two steady, unstoppable convulsions. Eyes tearing up from the stench of vomit, urine, and blood. His head was pounding, his face pounding, his whole body was pounding and bleeding.

When it seemed he had nothing left inside, he sank down next to the toilet with his back against a tastefully renovated, natural stone wall. Above him he heard a shuffling noise. The handle of the bedroom door was being turned. He held his breath. He knew he'd locked the door and taken all the radio transmitters for fear that Kirsten might contact her cronies. After a minute, it was silent again. Had he killed her? Surely he hadn't killed her? She'd spoken to him and had apparently been moving around up there. But the silence was terrifying. Maybe she was bleeding to death?

He didn't know how long he'd been sitting still when he finally noticed his teeth were chattering from the cold. He forced himself to his feet and pulled his shirt over his head. It was heavy with blood.

He peeled off the urine-drenched pants and underwear. Naked now and still shivering, he stood up and looked at himself in the mirror. My God. He stepped into the large shower and turned up the heat. As the water washed over him, it mixed with his tears.

———

He forced himself to get out after only a few minutes. There was no time to lose. At least his legs were steadier now. He found the roll of first aid tape in his pocket. Retaped his eyebrow. Put tape over the torn earlobe. In the mirror, he looked like a half-wrapped fucking mummy.

Still naked and shivering with cold, he went into one of the white, tasteful bedrooms where Reiper's men slept and indiscriminately tore through drawers and shelves until he found someone's clothes. More jeans. More T-shirts and sweatshirts. The wrong size, but clean and warm. He dressed himself in double layers. Still, his hands wouldn't stop shaking. Underneath a pile of underwear, he found an extra magazine that looked like it would fit Kirsten's gun. He slipped it in his pocket and went down the stairs.

His head was spinning. Run. Run. Run. It was all he could think. Just pull on a jacket, open the door, and run straight out over the snow. Away from here. As far away as he could get from Reiper's ruthlessness and Kirsten's disfigured face.

But then what? Where would he go? Where would he hide? And what if Kirsten was right that the Swedish police had sanctioned what Reiper and his gang were doing? He'd hardly be safe at home on Rådmansgatan.

And then there was Klara. He barely knew her. It wasn't his style to give a damn about other people. Everyone had to take care of themselves. But he was the snitch. He had dragged her into this. Even though he really wanted to, there was something about this that he couldn't let go. He knew where she was. Maybe he could warn her? What choice did he have?

A thick oilskin coat was hanging on a hook in the hall. He heaved it over his shoulders and put the gun in his pocket. The coat was one size too small. Fuck it, whatever. There were gloves and a hat on the rack. He moved quickly, as if fear or doubt might overwhelm him if he relaxed for even a moment.

The keys were indeed hanging in the cabinet next to the door. He fished out the iPhone and resisted the impulse to call someone, anyone. Most of all his old man. But he couldn't take the risk of getting caught again. With a few stiff pokes to the screen, he loaded the maps application.

A few seconds later, he'd managed to input the coordinates he'd got from Reiper. Navigating by Google Maps? And in a storm? It was pure insanity. But it was all he had. The map showed a small island in the archipelago. He zoomed in on the satellite image. Something that might be a little cabin stood on the island. Was that where he was going? Was that where Klara was? The phone's battery was almost completely charged. It should suffice.

When he opened the door, snow whirled into the hall. He pulled down his hat over his forehead and jogged across the lawn down to the dock. His footsteps were nearly covered by snow by the time he jumped into the small boat and turned on the fuel valve. Childhood summers in the archipelago had at least taught him how to drive a boat. Still, it took him three tries to get the engine running.

December 23, 2013

Sankt Anna's Outer Archipelago, Sweden

DON'T ANSWER HER. I HAVE no answers and no words to express myself. All I know is that the truth has finally caught up with me. That the lies were never complete. Her face is exhausted, beautiful. Yet there's something implacable in her expression. Something strong and determined that I find confusing. An obstinacy I don't recognize from myself. It must come from you. I know it's yours. I avoid her eyes at all costs.

Unable to speak or explain, I make my way over to the window facing back toward the archipelago. I peer into the darkness. We don't know what our enemies know.

"Who knows you're here?" I say to her without turning around.

My reflection in the glass mingles with hers. Her hair is short, sloppily cut and poorly dyed. An amateurish disguise that doesn't hide the fact that she has the same raven black hair I once had. That her skin is my skin.

She tilts her head, pushes a lock of hair from her forehead, her eyes roving. It pains me to see her move so nervously. That hunted paranoia and sadness. Is there any human behavior I'm more familiar with?

"No one," she says. "No one knows I'm here."

I turn around. We don't have time for this.

"Come on," I say. "I found you. Your grandfather knew where you were. Try again. Who knows you're here?"

My words are too harsh. My voice trained for interrogation. Her face tightens, her voice is quiet, but it smolders.

"Who the hell are you to come here and make demands?" she says. "I don't even know who you are."

The words burn, and I almost flinch. She doesn't even know who I am.

"I'm sorry," I say. "I didn't mean to be so tactless. But we have very little time. I'll explain, but right now you'll have to take my word for it that I'm an expert on these situations. And besides, if I didn't want to help you, you'd already be dead."

She exchanges a look with her redheaded friend. Her friend nods gently.

"Okay," she says. "The only one who knows that I'm here is my friend who brought us here with his boat and then left. He'll be back at dawn to check that everything is okay. He was the one who told Grandpa."

I nod.

"Who else has he told?"

"He hasn't told anyone else. I can guarantee it."

"Believe me," I say. "Right now you can't trust anyone."

"I trust him," she says. "As much as I trust myself."

"Still he told your grandfather?" I say.

She doesn't answer. Her friend clears her throat. Her eyes bounce around the room; she is fiddling with her hands.

"And you?" I say. "Who have you told?"

I know all the signs. All the leaks, all the gaps. All the ways our bodies betray us.

"I mentioned it to my boss," she begins. "But he's a lawyer, and Klara is our client. There is no way he would tell anyone. He'd be thrown out of the bar association, if he were to disclose it to anybody. "

"You're Gabriella Seichelman, right? You work for Lindblad and Wiman in Stockholm? "

"How do you know who I am? " she says.

I don't respond. It doesn't matter. We don't have time.

"They know you're here."

I turn to Klara.

"The people who are hunting you know where you are. The reason they haven't attacked yet is tactical. They've waited for darkness. Maybe for the storm to die down. I would guess they're less accustomed to the sea out here than your grandfather."

I throw a glance out the dark window. It's futile. Needless. Just a reflex. Hunters are always invisible.

"But how is that possible? " says Klara. Her voice is skeptical, unyielding.

"I found you," I say. "The people who are hunting you are like me. Your location has been shared with too many people. I've figured out who your friend is."

I nod to Gabriella.

"If I know, they know. And, believe me, they have ways of getting information. Even from lawyers. Especially from lawyers."

I feel the stress growing inside me, and I force myself to take control of it. Pushing it down to the pit of my stomach. Even if they hadn't told me they'd been talking about their destination far and wide, I still would have known that our enemies are here. A sixth sense. A scent. A vibration in the air that has nothing to do with the storm.

"Stay away from the windows," I say.

I sit back on my heels in front of her. Looking directly at her. Forcing my way through the resistance. Forcing myself to look into her eyes. They're much more than just blue in the copper-colored glow from the fire. Sincere, defiant. Eyes meant for ideals, not compromises. They're everything I remember and more.

"Klara," I say.

It's the first time I say her name.

"It's extremely important that you're honest with me. That you tell the truth. We, you, are in grave danger, as you know. Maybe we'll find a way to survive this, but only if you tell me everything you know."

She looks at me without blinking, without affect or one iota of recognition. But her restless hands betray her stress. Her jerks and tics.

"Why? Why should I trust you?"

"Because I've come a very long way to help you. There are several, very powerful interests at stake, and right now I'm the only one who cares about you."

"Why?" she says again. "Why do you care about me?"

I hold my breath. We don't have time. There is no time.

"I knew your mother," I say. "Something happened a long, long time ago, and I want to make it right. Or I can't make it right. But I want to do something to pay off my debt."

She says nothing. Her eyes continue to jump around the room. She fiddles with her hands. Her friend has sat down beside her. Taken her hand. From the corner of my eye, I see the old man squinting out through the dark windowpanes.

"Ask your grandfather to keep away from the window," I say.

She says something short in the language I don't speak and turns to me again.

"Do you have the computer?" I say.

The two young women exchange a quick, almost imperceptible glance. Klara nods.

"We have it," she says.

"What's on it?" I say. "Have you seen what's on it?"

Something is growing in her ice blue eyes. Something hard and completely indifferent. She has no reason to trust me. Still, it hurts.

"What do you think is on it?" she says. "You, if anyone, ought to know. Why else are all of you trying to kill us?"

"What do I think?" I say. "I can start by telling you what I know."

I see their concentration intensify. Maybe they really know nothing at all. So I tell them what Susan told me. The truth. Or what might be the truth.

"Mahmoud Shammosh's friend," I begin. "Lindman. He worked for a contractor of the U.S. government in Afghanistan. A company hired to take suspected terrorists and interrogate them using what we call unconventional methods."

I'm disgusted by myself. By my choice of words. I start over.

"What I mean is that this Lindman worked for a company that was acting indirectly on behalf of U.S. intelligence. Digital Solutions, we called it. Nothing strange in and of itself. It's a necessary part of our work, in order to avoid leaving our fingerprints everywhere. These companies usually consist of old, discarded field operatives and are controlled by shell corporations we create. This company . . ."

I stop, thinking how to phrase this next part, so that it's accurate. As accurate as it can get.

"Digital Solutions would interrogate terrorists that we tracked down. They were instructed to use harsher methods. Dogs and mock executions. Water. Methods that don't do lasting harm. Methods that are torture, no matter what we call it officially. The kind of methods the CIA used before Abu Ghraib. But something went wrong with this company. We don't know what exactly, but they started going beyond what was originally intended. Far beyond. It took a while before we found out about it. Electric shocks, deaths. Awful things. Indescribable cruelty."

"Why?" interrupts Klara. "If they hadn't been asked to do it, why did they do it then?"

Her eyes flash. Swinging between stress and doubt and something else. Something darker. I shrug my shoulders. How much can I tell her? How many more lies before my quota is finally full? Something cuts through me, like a metal blade, a physical urge to be completely honest. Still when I open my mouth all that emerges are half-truths.

"I don't know. Maybe they were numbed by the methods they were already using? Maybe they thought they could get more information . . . faster? And there are some people who don't need orders. Some people are just sadists."

Memories of Iraq and Afghanistan. The car battery and the shattered Iraqi prisoners in Kurdistan. Improvised interrogations in Beirut and Kabul. There are so many examples, so many justifications and explanations, so much suffering. So much to answer for.

"What I know is that we immediately shut this operation down when we found out what was going on. That was a few weeks ago. But some of the people responsible for the operation have a long history in American intelligence. They have contacts. Contacts and leverage. They know too much about too many processes. They know too much about too many people, high up in the organization. So instead of taking their agents home immediately, they gave them the assignment of cleaning things up afterward. And that's when everything went to hell. We believe the Swedish soldier Lindman came across some kind of data on this operation, which he intended to make public. We know that he worked for Digital Solutions in Afghanistan. I have no idea why he contacted Shammosh. But you asked what I think is on the computer? I think your computer is full of evidence of an operation which, if made public, would lead to irreparable harm."

The storm outside—maybe it's abated somewhat now. Perhaps there's less power, less determination in the gusts that shake the windows, roll over the roof, and push the water up over the rocks.

"Surely I don't need to tell you what would happen if this information were to become public?" I say. "What the consequences would be? When the U.S. is just about to leave Afghanistan? If this information comes out it would result in chaos again."

But there is more. There is always more. What Susan didn't tell me, but the scent of which, the trace of which, is obvious to me. The torture, the black-ops and psychopaths, all carefully placed within the realm of deniability. All meticulously arranged at arm's length, distraught statements already prepared and polished on somebody's hard drive. For us to be willing to pay this price for silence? There is something else on that computer. Something more. Always something more.

"But you haven't seen what the computer really contains?" she says.

"I've been told what it likely contains," I reply.

"You say it will lead to chaos," she says. "If it's made public. Well, then it will lead to chaos."

She's not blinking anymore. No jerks or tics. She's completely still.

"Maybe chaos is justified," she says.

"Is that what your friend Mahmoud would have wanted?" I say.

I don't have time to react before she hits me with all her might, with what must be a clenched fist, right above my left eye. A flash of pain, tears. I blink and put up my hands in defense, catching her other hand before she can hit me again. She's surprisingly strong.

"Klara," I say. "Calm down! Calm down. What are you doing?"

Her friend has stood up and caught Klara's arms. The old man strokes her hair, whispering to her.

"Do not say his name," she says. "If you say his name one more time, I'll kill you. Do you understand? I'll kill you. It's you, your friends, your fucking people who are responsible for all this shit! You! You fucking murderers! You have no right to say his name. You do not have permission to use his name. Do you understand?"

Her voice is a hiss, low like an animal. Her eyes are so full of pure, undiluted hatred that once again I have to look away. I hold up my hands.

"Sorry, sorry," I say. "I understand that you're under extreme stress."

"This has nothing to do with fucking stress," she sputters. "Do you get that! It has to do with the fact that you people murdered him. You shot him in front of my eyes. While I held his hand. He died in a pool of cheap fucking wine, in a fucking mall. And I just left him there. Do you understand that? Stress? *Fuck off!*"

"I just want to help you," I say.

"I don't care about Afghanistan," she says. "I don't care. I don't care how many die. How many Americans die. How many schools are never built. Hospitals or whatever the fuck. I don't care! Will that take away the moment when he died? When you people shot him like a dog? Will it change anything for him? For me? Will it?"

I shake my head.

"But you can minimize the suffering," I say.

She's silent for a moment. Locking her eyes with mine. It requires superhuman effort not to look away. When she speaks, she's completely calm.

"But I want there to be more suffering," she says. "Right now all I want is to detonate a bomb in the middle of all this shit. I want to see all of you suffer. I want to see you die. Do you understand that?"

December 23, 2013

Sankt Anna's Outer Archipelago, Sweden

IT HAD TAKEN TEN MINUTES for George's eyes to adjust to the darkness, still he was blinded again every time he looked at the glowing map on the phone, so he did his best to limit how much he looked at it. Instead he tried to map out his path on some old laminated charts he'd found stuffed under the steering console. He was squatting, propping the chart up against the steering wheel. The boat lurched and shuddered. The storm drowned out the sound of the engine.

He maintained a steady speed. Fast enough so that the boat glided and bounced across the waves, but not so fast that he lost control. Wet snow and brackish water poured over him, drenching him, freezing him to the bone. But it didn't bother him. It was as if he were in another world where neither weather nor wind could touch him.

He had no plan. Yet strangely he felt more relieved and less anxious than he'd felt since first meeting Reiper. It was only a few days ago, but it felt like a year. A lifetime. He held his fate in his own hands. He'd switched sides. He was no longer a mercenary in Reiper's army of assassins. He was going to strike back.

"Yippieekayeee, motherfuckers!" he yelled as loud as he could, straight into the storm.

After about a half hour George slowed and steered the small boat into the relative shelter of a small, juniper-covered cliff. In a hatch under the rear seat was a small, rusty anchor, which he heaved overboard so he wouldn't drift away. He huddled up as best he could and took out the phone. The boat rocked in the waves. The snow melted and ran down his face. There was only a sliver of cell coverage. A little farther out, and he wouldn't be able to use it anymore.

He compared the satellite image with the chart and felt his pulse start to race. If he was reading it correctly, he was less than one nautical mile from the island where Klara, according to Reiper, was hiding. Reiper's gang must be somewhere nearby. He quickly typed in the reference numbers they'd given for their own position, and the needle on the digital map moved slightly eastward.

George heaved a deep sigh. He'd been so focused on his own actions he hadn't even thought of the risk of running straight into Reiper and his minions.

And now what? What should he do now? He heard Kirsten's rattling voice, saw her mocking smile before him.

"Who do you think you are? Rambo?"

He pushed away the image of her battered face. But her voice stuck fast. He was no Rambo. Of course not. He held the phone in his frozen hands and considered calling someone again. But his last call had led to disaster. And if the police weren't on his side, whom could he call?

George's only advantage was that he was absolutely sure Reiper hadn't considered him a threat. By now they must wonder why they weren't hearing from Kirsten, though he doubted they'd ever suspect George was behind it. In their eyes he was a suit, a wimp, a useful idiot. And that was his only possible advantage. It was sink or swim.

He took Kirsten's gun out of the deep pocket of his oilskin coat. It was so black it seemed to absorb what little light reflected off the newly fallen snow. He found the small catch that opened the magazine and reloaded it with the full magazine he'd found in the house. Then he slid the gun back into his pocket and turned off the phone. It was time.

WE DON'T HAVE TIME FOR this," said the man.

There was something almost pleading in his voice. A trace of hopelessness in a tone that until just now had been sensible, sober.

Klara didn't drop her gaze. The emptiness within her refused to go away, but for a moment it had been overshadowed by the adrenaline, the phosphorescent rage. The knuckles on her right hand ached where they'd met his temple. Everything she'd kept inside since Mahmoud's murder had suddenly overwhelmed her, sent her spiraling out of control.

But now she felt the fury start to recede; the world around her began to regain its contours. She tried to hold on to that wonderful anger, tried to focus on it to keep it from slipping away, back into the depths, leaving her alone with her emptiness and grief. But she couldn't catch it. Like sand through her fingers.

She sat back down on the couch. Her head was suddenly so heavy; she had to rest it in her hands. Somewhere next to her, she sensed Gabriella. She felt her grandpa's rough hands on her neck. After what seemed like an eternity, she looked back up at the man.

"So," she said. "You say you're going to get us out of this alive. Then you'd probably better tell us how."

The man crouched down in front of her. There was a livid red mark on his cheek.

"You have a pretty mean right hook," he said.

A smile on his lips. Something in that smile was so familiar. So absolutely familiar. There were so many questions that couldn't be asked. So many thoughts that had to be postponed. Later.

"What should we do?" said Klara.

"I have to see what's on that computer," he said. "What's there is what you have to negotiate with."

He stopped for a moment before continuing. It seemed as if he was hesitating.

"My assignment is to get that computer and make sure you haven't made any copies of what's on it. My boss has given me the authority to promise that will be the end. That everything will be over when you hand over the computer and the information."

There was something about the way he said it. Some doubt or hesitation. Something that chafed.

"But I don't trust my boss," he said at last. "I don't trust anyone. If you give them the computer, you have nothing to bargain with. And if you have nothing to bargain with, you have no protection. So many have already died. It won't matter to them if you die too. Or, it will matter. They're not animals. But the risks posed by this information are obviously deemed too great. If you give up your only bargaining chip after all you've seen, all you know . . ."

He stopped. Turned his head. Something had caught his attention, and his eyes turned toward the window. He sat a second longer before getting up and crossing the room with surprising speed and grace. He took a camouflage-colored rifle out of the duffel bag. There was a metallic sound as he loaded the magazine. A click when he attached a telescopic sight to its top. He unbuttoned his jacket. Pulled up his hood.

"Wait here," he said. "Whatever you do, stay away from the windows."

And with those words he slipped out the door and disappeared into the darkness.

"What's going on?" whispered Gabriella.

Her grip of Klara's hand had stiffened.

"He heard it too," said Klara's grandfather. "A motor. It sounds like there's a boat approaching."

December 23, 2013

Sankt Anna's Outer Archipelago, Sweden

THE SEA GREW ROUGHER AS George swerved around the island where he'd sought shelter. The waves got bigger and more powerful. He increased his speed and felt the sea lifting his small boat. Heard the sound of the propeller spinning in midair before the boat plunged down into the next wave. The compact darkness.

George had the dizzying sensation that he was very close to losing control. With a desperate flick of his wrist, he put the engine in neutral. The water swept in over the foredeck. The boat tilted and was pushed back by the storm. His maneuver had only made things worse. His panic increased with each attack from new waves. George pushed the throttle forward, waiting for it to take effect, and moved the wheel in the right direction. Or in what he thought was the right direction. The boat lurched, but it didn't move forward.

When he was on the top of the cresting waves, he could discern what might be the island Klara was on. A faint, almost invisible glow might be coming from the window of a small cabin. It came closer with each wave. He couldn't make out any details in the darkness. Just a black mass, in the middle of all the blackness.

Until it was right in front of him. He put the engine in reverse, pulled the throttle as hard as he could. Heard the hull scrape against the rocks. He could feel how completely irrelevant the engine had become in the driving sea. The waves turned the boat sideways and pressed it up against the jet-black rocks.

"Fuck!" shouted George.

The boat banged and scraped against the rocks. The screech of the propeller's steel on granite cut through the storm.

"Fuck!"

He released the wheel and threw himself down on the deck. Crawled on all fours through the icy water on the foredeck. He could feel the rocks scraping and dragging at the fiberglass hull. It was only a matter of minutes before they'd cut right through the boat. Lying flat, George threw one leg over the boat's low rail. Stuck his right foot into a foaming wave and felt the slippery rock against the sole of his shoe. An inhuman cold. Around him was only blackness, foamy water, and darkness. The waves sucked the boat out, and he lost his footing before they tossed the boat into the rocks again.

He put his foot onto the slick stones once more, slipped, lost his footing, yet somehow managed to twist his body overboard. With a desperate grip on the railing, he swung his other foot out of the boat and into the sea. He felt his soles gliding helplessly over the sloping rocks. The current snatched hold of the boat and pulled it out. George pushed himself out and down into the water, thrusting the boat away with his hands. The waves crashed around him, the storm whistling and howling. He finally got a foothold on a flat ledge. Clawed and pulled to grab hold with his numb hands. Felt the rock cut into his fingers.

He kicked with his left foot and found a crevice at the waterline.

Flat on his stomach he pushed himself up, up. His hands fumbling for a grip. The boat thundered into the rocks, just a few inches away from him. He could hear the sound of rocks cutting through the hull, felt frothy water beat against his legs as he finally got a firm grasp on the rocks and managed to pull himself higher up the cliff. Just below him the boat, gashes in its hull from the rocks, was twisting around in the waves and already half-filled with seawater.

At the foot of a windswept juniper, George lay on his stomach, trying to catch his breath. He was alive. But not much more than that. He turned his head upward, toward the little cabin.

And once again the small flame of hope inside him died.

In front of him in the snow squatted two black-clad men. Dark clothes, black ski masks. They were holding small automatic rifles, the barrels pointed straight at him.

"George," Josh said. "You look like shit."

THE BOAT WAS COMING IN from the wrong direction. From the north, with the waves angled in front of it. Through the night-vision binoculars, I watch as it disappears into the troughs and then reappears on the crests of the waves. I can hear the sound of the motor through the storm. It's amateurish. More than that. It's insane, suicidal. When the boat reaches the cliff, it will be crushed. That can't be our enemies. Klara's friend? He knows these islands, this storm. He would never come from that direction.

I squat down. It all rushes through me. The good intentions and the devastating results. The fear. The void. Everything we plan. All our strategies and long-term goals. All barriers and defenses. Everything we do to minimize risk, to anticipate it. Ultimately, it's the unexpected, the inexplicable, the completely unforeseeable that destroys us.

There's something in the air. Something more than the snow and the storm. I turn the binoculars toward the cliffs where the old man landed his boat effortlessly in the middle of the worst of it. I see only its stern. The rest lies behind the rocks. But there's something more. A shadow, a silhouette. Pontoons or a hull. Maybe another boat? Perhaps our enemies are already here?

My pulse quickens. I lie flat and slide along the cliff, away from the cabin. Hugging the rifle with my right hand, I brush away the wet snow. Somewhere on the rocks, I hear the sound of a boat colliding with the granite. Hear someone shout twice. Like a bird crying through the storm.

I slither in a circle. If our enemies are already here, they too will be following the progress of this boat. Waiting to see what the unpredictable will mean for them. The small island is smooth and without mercy. Only a few stones, some shrubs, offer protection. I point my night-vision binoculars in the direction the sound came from. I see the boat, battered by the waves. Above it a figure is struggling to get up the cliff. Someone is climbing and slipping in the slushy snow.

"Who are you?" I whisper to myself.

The man grabs hold, pushing himself up from the waterline, up to safety. Lies flat on the mountain, perhaps catching his breath. He looks soaked. Frozen. Shipwrecked. After a moment, he turns his face upward and seems to stiffen. He's only about twenty yards away from me. What can he see that I can't? I move my binoculars up along the smooth rock. A couple of shrubs. A crevice in the rock. A movement, several movements. My hand cramps around the rifle.

Someone detaches himself from the shadows. A black figure. A hood over his head. Bent by the wind but with a gun at his shoulder. Behind him, another figure. No more? There must be another group.

But right now there are only two. That's all I know. And a third, an unknown. Is this my chance? The only thing I have is the element of surprise. Were it not for the man from the boat, they'd have taken us inside the cabin. How do I make the best use of this chance? The never-ending estimations. Calculations. The probability.

I pull the gun closer. Prop it up against my shoulder. It's been a long time since I found myself in a situation like this. I exhale. Blink to see more clearly in the snow. In front of me the black-clad man raises his weapon, pointing at the figure lying flat, helpless, on the cliff. The sound of the shot bounces off the rocks and disappears into the storm, into the snow.

December 23, 2013

Sankt Anna's Outer Archipelago, Sweden

GEORGE CLOSED HIS EYES. LAID his head against the rock, felt its cold wetness against his frozen cheek. Felt the snow swirling over him. It had all been in vain. Everything. It was too late.

"Dear God," he whispered. "Forgive me. Forgive me. Forgive me."

He saw Klara's face in front of him. Saw Kirsten's broken cheekbone and nose. Why hadn't he acted sooner? From the corner of his eye he saw Josh get up and move toward him. The gun against his shoulder. Josh wouldn't make the same mistake as Kirsten.

"So you escaped the house?" said Josh. "Unbelievable. I didn't think you had it in you. What did you do with Kirsten?"

George said nothing. He barely even heard Josh's voice. Nothing mattered anymore. Nothing.

"Never mind," said Josh. "We don't have time for this right now. Bye, bye, George."

The sound of the shot. Strangely muffled by the storm. Torn by the wind. There was a flash in front of George's eyes. He waited for the pain. Waited for the light, the calm. For the world to cease to exist.

But the only thing he heard was the storm. All he felt was the snow against one cheek and the wet cliff against the other. Confused, he opened his eyes and turned his head toward Josh. But Josh wasn't there.

Instead, a body lay on the cliff. Something dark seemed to be leaking out of its head onto the wet snow. Blood. The second black-clad person had thrown himself into the cover of the precipice, where they must have been hiding when George climbed over the cliff. The man was holding his hand to one ear and screaming something. Maybe he was making radio contact with Reiper.

What had happened? Someone else had fired the shot. George blinked his eyes, got up on all fours, rolled to the side. The world came to life around him.

The other man stood with his back to George, looking up toward the island, over the edge of the cliff. George fumbled around in the pocket of his oilskin coat. Finally he got hold of the gun. His hand was so cold he could barely move his fingers, and he had to force them around the silencer on Kirsten's gun. It got stuck in the lining and George pulled so hard that part of it tore and came out with the gun. He fumbled with the gun, dropped it on the cliff, but grabbed hold of it again before it slid down into the waves. It felt big and clumsy in his hands. Surreal. Everything felt surreal.

In the darkness, George only sensed where the other man was, although he couldn't be more than thirty feet away. Who was it? Chuck? Sean? Those weren't their real names. The man seemed to turn his head, as unsure as George was about what had happened. The pistol was heavy in George's hands. He was lying on his stomach and his fingers were frozen as they held up the pistol, aiming it at the dark silhouette. He forced away all thoughts of guilt, or consequences. Focused on survival. Only that. And then he pulled the trigger.

One, two, three barking shots. Barely audible in the storm. The man screamed, slumped behind the stone, behind the low bush.

Shaking with cold and shock, George crept up the hill. He made a wide arc around the stone the man lay behind. Up toward the little cabin.

I N THE END IT COMES down to chance. The banality of battle. I sit on my haunches. Raise my night-vision binoculars toward the rocks. See the body in the snow. See the man from the sea lying on the cliff, fire a gun, get up on his knees. He's armed. Friend or foe. Chance. I get up, but keep my back arched, make myself small. I can't let him make it to the cottage. Can't take the risk. I take a few quick steps. Worry makes me careless.

I know before I feel the pain. Like I always know. Like I have always known. That bonds are deadly. That it's not the lies, but the truth that threatens our existence. Then suddenly the pain. Somewhere in the stomach region. Somewhere in the back. Intense and completely deadly. And I slip in the snow on the rocks. Spin and fall. Then pain again. In my shoulder, in my hand. Time ceases.

This is how it ends.

———

I lie on my back. The snow falls on my face. I open my eyes and see his shadow, crouching beside me. The pale scar on his cheek glows in the dark. The rifle rests on his lap. He doesn't even look surprised.

"I thought they gave you a desk job?" he says.

I don't say anything. Feel the blood filling my mouth. Spit it out to the side. I knew it was him. Even though Susan didn't want to say his name, one of his names. We look at each other. We are still in Kurdistan, Afghanistan. This is how it ends.

"Susan sent you?" he asks.

I don't say anything.

"You shot one of my men," he says.

Nothing left to lose. Nothing to gain. I nod. Spit blood, but my mouth refills. I let it run over my lips.

"It didn't need to be this way," I say.

My voice is muffled, wheezy, so full of blood and death that I can hardly understand myself. But he's used to listening to dying confessions. He leans closer.

"What way?" he says.

My body is so heavy. So heavy that it falls through the snow, through the cliff. At the same time it's so light. So light that when I close my eyes, I swirl upward, becoming part of the snow, the storm. Disappearing. Lighter than the flakes, lighter than the wind. A body of helium. A body of lead. Above the clouds, the sky is pale blue. At every crossroads, I chose to run. And now it's too late. There's nothing left that can save my soul.

When I open my eyes, he's starting to stand up. He is enormous in the darkness. I'm insignificant now. Not part of his mission. A coincidence. Something unpredictable that he's handled and then left behind. I cough. Forcing the words through the blood.

"She doesn't have to die."

It takes superhuman effort. I'm drowning in my own blood. Somewhere far away, I hear his voice.

"You haven't changed," he says. "That was always your problem. Your bleeding heart."

I force my head to the side to be able to see him. It's so incredibly difficult to open my eyes. At the same moment, I hear a crack. Dull and distinct like a controlled explosion. In a strange, cold light, I see him lift off the ground. Watch him fly, momentarily weightlessly, through the storm. I see him land in the snow. Spread out, still.

Put these rain clothes on," said Klara.

From a worn wooden crate standing just inside the door, she pulled a bundle of old turpentine-scented, yellow rubber and threw it to Gabriella. Klara had already put on some boots and a pair of rubber pants so big they made her look like a child. Gabriella unwrapped the bundle and started pulling on a pair of worn pants.

"It's definitely a boat," said Klara's grandfather.

Despite the American's advice, he was standing on his knees, peering out the window, into the night. The sound of the approaching boat grew louder.

"Well I'll be damned, what sorta lunatic would come in with the wind at his aft."

Grandpa turned and scrutinized Klara, who was buttoning up her raincoat, the hood already pulled down far over her forehead.

"What do you have in mind, Klara?" he said. "You're not gonna run after our American friend, are you?"

Klara adjusted the sleeves of her coat. When she was satisfied, she bent down and opened the cardboard box of shotgun shells. She took out a handful and stuffed them into her pockets.

"I don't know," she said. "But it's good to be prepared. We need to be ready to get out of here on short notice."

She cracked open the shotgun and checked to see that it was still loaded. Then she turned to her grandfather and hesitated for a second.

"Grandpa," she said at last. "You said you were absolutely certain that this man knew my mother."

Klara's grandfather turned to her. He looked tired. Outside, the sound of the engine was growing louder and louder.

"What was it that made you so sure?"

Before her grandpa could reply they heard a crashing, grinding sound below the house. Her grandfather turned back toward the window.

"What was that?" whispered Gabriella.

"The boat's gone aground on those rocks," said Klara's grandfather.

Reflexively, Gabriella moved toward the window, crouching. She could just make out the snow falling, the contours of the nearest bushes. A cliff. There—a movement down by the waterline. But maybe it was her imagination. The subsiding wind was still howling. You could hear the sound of the boat crashing against the cliff. And maybe, in the distance, a voice. Before Gabriella could say anything, a muffled bang cut through the storm.

"What was that?" she said.

Somewhere a voice screamed and fell silent. Gabriella turned to Klara. But all she saw was the front door slamming shut.

December 23, 2013

Sankt Anna's Outer Archipelago, Sweden

T HE WIND HAD DROPPED SLIGHTLY. And the snowfall had
increased. Klara stood with her back against the cabin wall.
The shotgun, cold in her hands. Thoughts racing as fast as her
heart. What was happening? She gently lifted the small flashlight
she had found in the kitchen.

That was when she heard it. Dampened by wind and snow:
rapid footsteps. Then a scraping and a thud. As if someone ran
and then stumbled and fell on the rock. She sank down on one
knee. The shotgun against her shoulder. Both the flashlight and
barrel in her left hand. Someone was coughing, wheezing, spit-
ting. Something that sounded like a voice. Perhaps ten yards
away. Not farther. On the other side of the house. Then another
voice. Labored, whispering. Klara exhaled. Inhaled. It was all or
nothing.

She turned on the flashlight and spun around the corner of the
cabin. Still squatting, with her left knee on the snow, on the cliff.
The butt of the rifle against her shoulder. The barrel and the beam
from the flashlight pointing straight toward the place where the
sounds were coming from. Time stood still.

The light caught three people. Two men dressed in black. One was squatting and one was standing up. On the ground lay the American. Dark blood on white snow.

Someone said something. All sounds seemed delayed, drawn out, impossible to connect or make sense of. The standing man held up a hand, blinded by the light from the flashlight. Everything moved slowly, as if under water. She focused on the man who was squatting beside the American. His face. The scar. The gray hair hidden under a black cap. Eyes that glittered in the light.

It took an eternity for the man with the scar to point the muzzle of his small machine gun at her. An eternity for the other man to raise his weapon. Klara squeezed the trigger and felt the recoil push her backward.

Then the world returned to normal speed. The bang from the gun was deafening. The man with the scar was thrown backward onto the snow-spotted rock and landed awkwardly at the foot of a barren and lone little juniper.

Behind her Klara heard a mechanical coughing. Three times, four, five. Then a clicking sound. When she turned to point the flashlight in that direction, she saw the man who had just been standing up lying on his back in the snow. Klara heard ragged breathing somewhere behind her. A faint moaning. Feet staggering over snow and rock. She turned cautiously in the direction of the sound, back toward the cabin. She ran the flashlight along the side of the cabin until the light finally landed on a strange apparition. The man was tall and slim. His face was full of wounds and peeling tape. His lips were blue with cold. In his hand he held a dark gray gun with a long cylinder attached to it. The man dropped the gun in the snow and slumped against the wall. Closed his eyes.

Klara fumbled with the shotgun, unsure where she should point it. "Who are you?" she said.

She turned the shotgun on the man, took aim, hesitated. She leaned forward. There was something familiar about that broken face.

She took a step toward him. The man held up his hands in defense.

"George," he said. "George Lööw."

Klara stopped, shaking her head. Her ears were ringing from the shot. The wind whipped the snow into her face. George Lööw? Was that really what he'd said?

"Where the hell did you come from?" she said.

George just shrugged and stared dumbly in front of him. Klara hesitated and turned to the American lying in the snow.

"Are you okay?" she said to George while moving toward the American.

"I'm okay. I think."

George's voice was hollow.

Klara leaned over the American, let the light from her flashlight move across his body. There was blood everywhere, too much blood. His eyes were closed but his lips were moving, barely. Blood was running out of the corner of his mouth. Klara put her ear to his mouth, smelled the scent of blood, the stench of death.

"I couldn't protect you."

The man's voice was so weak, so thick.

"Don't give them what they want."

He fell silent. Closed his eyes and opened them again. Klara was quiet. Stroking him gently, hesitantly on his forehead.

"Don't give them what they want. You can't trust them."

Klara struggled to stay upright, fought to remain in control of her body. She felt her hands shaking and shivering, tears welling up in her eyes.

"It'll be okay."

It was all she could say. It meant nothing. Nothing was going to be okay.

Suddenly the American opened his eyes wider. Klara felt him struggling to get up, to lean in closer. His eager voice was so thick with blood and death that Klara couldn't make out what he was trying to say.

"Ssh," she said. "Easy, easy . . ."

She leaned over him and placed his head back in the snow. She positioned her ear over his mouth, feeling the dryness of his lips against her earlobe.

"There is more," he mumbled.

"More of what?" Klara whispered.

Blood was bubbling over the American's lips. He tried to spit and then to swallow.

"Not only . . ."

He lay back on the cliff and, grappling for strength, closed his eyes.

"Not only torture," he mumbled finally. "Too much . . . All this . . . It's too much. Killings. Look for something more. Something that . . . they can't explain away. Something undeniable."

Klara didn't know what to say. She just held his head, just stroked his cheek. And then he opened his eyes again. Saw right into her, right through her.

"Your mother," whispered the American. "She loved you. More than anything."

Then, only silence. Only the wind. Only snow. Klara took his hand in hers. His knotted fist. Frozen. His mouth opened. His eyes glassy, empty. Klara forced open the fist to hold his hand. Something fell out of his hand into the snow. She fumbled for it. The silver was unexpectedly warm. With frozen fingers she pried open the little locket.

December 23, 2013

Sankt Anna's Outer Archipelago, Sweden

G EORGE SAT ON THE FOREDECK of the small open boat and looked around. The night was still pitch-black. The storm had died down, but the boat heaved and jumped in the swells. He had only partial memories of how he got here. Impressions, a dream. After his boat crashed against the rocks, he had only scattered, fragmentary recollections of fear and cold. He noted that he had dry clothes on. Two huge blankets over his shoulders and legs. He was still shivering, but not in the uncontrollable way he had before.

"So, you're still alive."

George turned his head. Klara was sitting next to him on the deck, leaning against the steering console. In the dark, it looked like she was wearing the same yellow rain gear he vaguely remembered from what seemed like several days ago. George nodded.

"Where are we?"

George shouted to be heard over the wind and the boat's engine. The snow swirled around them, mingling with the images flashing in front of his eyes. Muzzles. Kirsten's battered face. The coldness of the cliff. The gun jerking in his hands. The hacking sound of the shots he fired. He pushed away any thought of the consequences of his actions. The falling bodies. He shook his head, as if to clear it.

"My grandfather's boat," replied Klara.

She leaned closer to him to avoid shouting.

"You were really knocked out. Grandpa had an extra set of clothes for you. Then you fell asleep for a while here on the deck. You don't remember?"

He shook his head.

"What happens now?" he said.

Klara shrugged.

"I don't know," she said. "You've got quite a bit of explaining to do."

George turned toward her, the unreality of the past week hitting him with full force. He buried his face in his hands.

"I'm sorry," he said. "I'm so sorry."

"Sorry?" said Klara. "I think you saved my life. All of our lives. If you hadn't shown up in the boat out there, we would've been executed, I guess. "

George shook his head. He pulled the blanket tighter around him and turned to Klara. He could barely make out her face in the darkness.

"But there's so much more than that," he said. "If it weren't for me, you never would have ended up in the middle of all this. I was working for them, for the Americans. I was the one who installed the bug in your offices, it was me—"

"Who sent me the text message in Paris, right?" interrupted Klara.

George nodded. "Well, sure. But you have no idea what I exposed you to. What I exposed myself to."

Klara spat over the rail.

"It doesn't matter now," she said. "What's done is done. We still have to find a way to get ourselves out of this."

A silhouette broke away from the darkness in the boat's stern and came crouching over to them. Another girl in an oversize yellow raincoat. George turned around and saw an older man sitting at the steering console just behind him. The man raised his hand in greeting. In the dark, it looked like he was smiling.

"So you're awake?" the girl said to George.

"Guess so," he muttered.

She kept one hand on the railing and sat down on the deck in front of him.

"My name is Gabriella," she said. "I'm Klara's friend and for the moment also her lawyer. Before we continue, I'd like to suggest that you allow me to represent you as well."

In spite of everything, George felt his lips curling into an approximation of a smile.

"You lawyers. Fucking vultures," he said. "You never miss an opportunity to sell your wares."

In the darkness, he couldn't be sure, but it looked like Gabriella was smiling.

"My rates are very affordable. Pro bono in fact," she said. "But you and Klara need someone to speak for you. If I'm your lawyer no one can force me to reveal where you are, and so on. Our plan now is to have Klara's grandfather take you to another hideout. I have a contact at Säpo that I'll try to sort this out with. Does that work for you?"

George nodded.

"What choice do I have?" he said.

"Good," said Gabriella. "We'll take care of the formalities later. I know it's late and that what you've been through is insane, but I have to ask you to tell me everything you know about the people who've been hunting Klara. It's likely that she, and maybe you too, will be prosecuted for a lot of things. They can threaten to extradite you to the U.S. Right now it feels like what you and Klara know is our only chance of getting you out of all this."

George cleared his throat and turned to Klara again.

"How much do you know, Klara?" he said. "What is this all about?"

Gabriella put her hand on Klara's shoulder before she could start telling him.

"Believe me, George," said Gabriella. "Right now it's better that you don't know all the details. But if I'm going to fix this in some way I need to know everything."

George nodded. He slipped a hand out of the blanket and wiped the melting snow off of his face before turning to Gabriella.

"Okay," he said in a voice loud enough to drown out the engine and the sea. "So here's the deal."

And then he told them. About Reiper. About Merchant & Taylor and the dinner at Comme chez Soi. About the house on Avenue Molière and the night Reiper forced him to cooperate. He told them about his time at Gottlieb and the confidential agreements Reiper had shown him. He told them about breaking into Klara's office and about Kirsten and Josh. About the private plane and Arkösund. About his emergency call. About how he'd almost been executed, but instead overpowered Kirsten. About his whole terrible night, which seemed so distant but wasn't even over yet.

Gabriella interrupted him periodically, asking him for specific details and to repeat things, names, the exact time of his call to 112. Like a legitimate, hard-ass lawyer.

When they'd finished, he felt strangely calm. For the first time since this all started, he wasn't alone. They sat in silence for a moment, listening to the engine and the sea. The snow beating against their cheeks.

George swallowed hard, hesitating.

"What happened on the island," he began. "Reiper and Josh and the whole gang. Are they dead?"

"We didn't stop to check," said Klara. "But I sincerely hope so."

———

After a few minutes, the old man slowed the boat down and leaned over the steering console.

"Klara," he shouted. "Almost there. Are you ready?"

Klara nodded and turned to George.

"Gabriella is changing boats here," she said. "You'll stay with me, okay?"

George nodded.

"Sure," he said. "It's not like I have any other plans. Where are we going?"

Klara glanced toward Gabriella, who shook her head.

"Wait until I leave," she said. "It's better if I don't know where you're going."

The old man steered the boat into the protection of a pair of dark islands. The sea was strangely quiet here, in drastic contrast to earlier in the evening. Somewhere farther in, a lonely, bright light blinked suddenly. He felt his mouth go dry.

"There!" he hissed and knelt down to point. The blanket fell from his shoulders without his noticing it.

"There's someone there. A light!"

Klara took him by the hand and pulled him down on the floor again.

"It's okay," she said. "That's our signal."

She lifted up a square and battered signal lamp and sent a couple of blinks in response. The old man had already put them on course toward the flashing light.

When Klara had finished her exchange, she crawled aft and dug out the bow line. After another minute they were side by side with an old workboat that had undoubtedly seen better days. A huge man with terrible hair, dressed in full rain gear, stood on the foredeck.

"Klara!" he shouted. "What the devil! How're you doin'?"

"We're okay," replied Klara. "But right now it's probably best if we don't talk about it. Gabriella is coming over to you, okay?"

"'A course," said the giant. "But where're you headed?"

He spoke a dialect that was so thick, George had trouble understanding him. The dialect of Östergötland. George had never heard anyone speaking it with such dedication before.

"Bosse, it's better if we talk about all that later. Gabriella needs to get to Stockholm as quickly and as under the radar as possible. Can you take care of that?"

The giant chuckled, leaned over the railing, and grabbed Gabriella around the waist. With a quick lift, he swung her over onto his own boat.

"Under the radar?" he said. "That's my style, and you know it, Klara. Hello there, Gabriella, by the way."

"Hello," said Gabriella.

Klara picked up a small computer bag from the floor and handed it over to Gabriella.

"Well then," said Gabriella. "I'll get a hold of you as soon as I can."

She began to push off from their boat.

"Not so fast," said the giant. "I got somebody to hand over to ya here. She's as stubborn as sin."

An elderly woman with long, almost white hair in a ponytail stepped out of the aft cabin. She patted Gabriella on the cheek.

"How are you, Gabriella?" she said.

Gabriella nodded and hugged the woman.

"Okay," she said. "Everything's going to be okay."

"That's good," said the older woman. "Just be careful now, honey."

The woman was holding a basket, which she handed over to Klara before climbing into their boat with surprising agility.

"Klara, my little darling," she said. "You didn't think I'd let you celebrate Christmas without me? I've brought Christmas dinner with me. A little herring salad, ham, and rye bread. And Grandpa's Christmas schnapps, of course."

"Thank goodness you didn't forget that!" said the old man.

George watched as Klara gently put down the basket on the deck before falling into the older woman's arms.

"Grandma," she sobbed. "Dearest, dearest grandma."

K LARA PULLED THE SOFT WOOL blanket up to her chin and
rested her head in her grandmother's lap. The white couch was
so soft she wondered how it held her up at all. Her cheeks were
glowing from the heat of the fire.

Grandma's dry hands stroked her forehead and hair. George had
stumbled into one of the three small bedrooms and fallen asleep as
soon as they arrived at the boathouse on the eastern shore of Norra
Rimnö. Grandma had covered him with another one of those new
blankets and gently closed the door behind him.

The large boathouse actually belonged to a family from Stockholm who'd bought it a couple of years ago and worked very hard,
obviously spending a lot of money, to turn the upper floor into an
apartment in tacky, faux "New England" style. White walls, navy
blue pillows, and blankets from the Swedish brand Lexington. A
pair of crossed oars hung on one wall. The only thing missing was
a framed photo of the Kennedy family.

If Klara hadn't been in a state of low-intensity shock, it would
have made her laugh.

Some friend of her grandpa's had been given the keys to the
boathouse to keep an eye on it during the fifty weeks in the year

that the family wasn't in the archipelago. Now it was, despite its décor, a perfect hideaway until . . . Yes, until what? Klara didn't have the energy to think. No energy to look back on what had happened or to imagine how it would end. She just wanted to keep lying here on this wonderful couch, in this wonderful warmth, with Grandma's hands gently caressing her forehead. If life consisted of nothing more than this moment, she'd be more than content.

Still she couldn't fall asleep, couldn't relax, couldn't stop worrying and questioning things for even a moment. The past week had been too much. Everything had changed forever. The secrets so extensive she couldn't comprehend them. Mahmoud was dead. She hadn't allowed that fact to sink in. And the American. Her heart started racing again. It was too much.

Cautiously she opened her eyes and pulled away from her grandmother's embrace. The blanket slid down on the floor as she sat up on the couch.

"Grandma?" she said.

Her grandmother turned toward her. The room was dim, but the glow from the fire made her fair skin look like it was lit from within.

"Yes, Klara?" she said.

"The American?" said Klara. "How could Grandpa be so sure he knew my mother? Was it because he had the locket? I mean anyone could have got hold of that."

Grandmother didn't answer, just rose as silently as a cat and walked across the white, painted floorboards to the little basket of Christmas food she'd brought with her. She bent down and pulled out what appeared to be an old, yellowed envelope.

She returned to the couch, sat down next to Klara again, and took one of her hands in her own. Carefully she put the envelope in Klara's other hand.

"Klara," she said. "My sweet Klara."

Her grandmother took a deep breath. Those eyes, thought Klara, they hide nothing at all.

Slowly she released her grandmother's hand and opened the envelope. Inside was a single color photograph. It was stiff and shiny, as if it had just been developed or had been developed a long time ago and stored in a vacuum. Klara swallowed.

The image was overexposed, bathed in light. A man was sitting in the shade on a large balcony. In his arms he held a tiny baby wrapped in a light blue knitted blanket. He squinted into what might have been blinding sunlight and seemed about to put his hand up to cover his face. But the photographer had been too quick.

Dark, thick hair. Olive-colored skin. A curved upper lip and high, well-defined cheekbones that made him look both sensitive and authoritative. On the table in front of him stood a half-full ashtray and a red packet of cigarettes with Russian letters on it. In the background there were blocks of gray, sand-colored apartment buildings, almost translucent in the intense sun.

There was no doubt that the person in the picture was a younger version of the man whose hand Klara held as he died on the island. Klara looked up at her grandmother.

"Turn over the picture," said her grandmother.

Klara hesitated, suddenly unsure if she wanted to know more, if her heart could handle any more. Finally, she flipped the picture over. One sentence, written in clear, precise handwriting: "Klara and her dad, Damascus, June 25, 1980."

GABRIELLA GOT OFF THE SUBWAY at Östermalmstorg. Bosse had found her a ride to Stockholm with some friends of his.

"Under the radar," he said.

Somewhere a church bell was ringing. Advent candles burned in every window. It was like another world, with garlands and Christmas decorations and a thin layer of snow. A world where everything was quiet, tranquil, tastefully lit, and completely free from conflict and death. The streets were empty except for a lone taxi.

"Merry Christmas," said the taxi driver as she jumped into the back.

My God, it actually was Christmas eve. Gabriella just nodded and gave him the address.

———

It didn't even take the taxi ten minutes to get to Djursholm. They passed seven cars and an occasional bus on their way. Was this the most deserted time of the year? Just before seven on the morning of Christmas eve.

Gabriella paid the driver, muttering "Merry Christmas," because it seemed as though he wouldn't let her out of the car if she didn't at least give him that. The streets weren't plowed, and the taxi left solitary tracks across the newly fallen snow as it rolled away almost silently along Strandvägen.

If Wiman's house had seemed spooky the first time she visited, now it looked almost comically cozy. A thick layer of fluffy, inviting new snow covered the manicured hedges, the lawn, and the path leading up to the door. As she carefully opened the gate, snow spilled from its top onto her hands. It was light and as pure as air. Exterior lights were lit, but the windows were dark except for the symmetrically placed Advent candelabra in the window.

Gabriella felt calm. Focused. She registered her surroundings but was absorbed by her task. This was a do-or-die moment. There was no turning back now. No alternatives. This was it.

Light shone warmly from the windows on the shorter side of the house. The kitchen and one of the living rooms, Gabriella suspected. The snow crunched under her feet as she ascended the few steps and rang the doorbell. It took just a few seconds for it to be thrown wide open. A little girl of about five, with long blond hair and wearing a pink nightgown, stood in the softly lit hallway.

"Who are you?" said the girl.

"My name is Gabriella," said Gabriella. "Is your . . . grandfather here?"

"Grandpa isn't dressed yet," said the girl.

She made no move to either call for an adult or let Gabriella in.

"Do you know it's Christmas?" she continued.

"Well," said Gabriella. "I know. But I really need to talk to your grandfather."

"I've been up since five o'clock. You know how I know that? Because I got a watch in my stocking. Wanna see it?"

She held out her wrist, where a small red plastic watch was fastened.

"Maria?" said a familiar voice from inside the warm, cozy house. "Maria? Did you ring the doorbell?"

"A girl with red hair is here," replied Maria.

In the hall behind the girl Gabriella saw an older man approaching. Though he had to be Wiman, he was almost unrecognizable. His hair was not slicked back tightly, but messy and unexpectedly gray. Instead of his rigid, steel-rimmed glasses he wore a tortoiseshell pair that was thicker and rounder. And instead of being dressed in one of his customary Zegna suits, he was wearing a fraying, dark red robe with a *W* embroidered in gold on the breast pocket. His bare, pale legs protruded awkwardly from the bottom of the bathrobe.

"Gabriella?" said Wiman.

He brought his hands through his unkempt hair in a vain attempt to give it some kind of order.

"It's Christmas, for goodness sake. What are you doing here?"

His intonation was as restrained as ever. Just as authoritarian and accustomed to being obeyed. But his eyes avoided Gabriella's, and his hands seemed to have a life of their own, alternating between flattening his hair and pulling on the knot that held the robe together.

"We have to talk," she said. "Now."

———

When Wiman entered the library, he was carrying a small tray of steaming coffee cups and saffron buns. The sky had brightened almost imperceptibly above the water beyond the windows. Gabriella sat in one of the chairs by the fire, immobile in the warm glow. From another part of the house she heard the faint sound of a children's show on television.

"So, Gabriella," said Wiman. "If I were to be completely honest, I'd say visiting me at home on Christmas eve isn't the best way for an associate to show me she's partner material."

The same voice. The same paternalistic irony. But it had no effect on Gabriella now. She could no longer remember how it had felt to simultaneously fear him and long for his respect. It was as if her whole world had shifted. As if a spell had been broken.

"Why did you do it?" she said. "Or I don't give a fuck why. I honestly can't understand how you could do it. You of all people."

Wiman calmly set down the tray on the small table in front of the blazing fire. The same table they had sat at just a few days ago, in what seemed like another time, another world.

"Do what?" Wiman said, sitting down opposite Gabriella in the same chair he had sat in last time.

He studied her with quiet interest.

"What heinous crime have I committed this time?"

Gabriella balked. That gaze. It wasn't the look of a Judas.

"You were the only one who knew Klara was coming back to Sweden," she said. "Just you and me. You were the only one who knew she wanted to return to the islands."

Wiman raised his eyebrows and made a gesture, offering Gabriella some saffron buns. He himself took a small sip of the hot coffee.

"What's happened?" he said.

He leaned forward and looked into her eyes. There was a different expression in them than Gabriella had ever seen before. A note of warmth, something that looked like genuine sympathy. Gabriella had been so sure. It had seemed so obvious that Wiman had somehow betrayed her. Now she felt that certainty slowly dissipate.

"Klara came back yesterday," she began quietly. "We went to Arkösund and then farther out in the archipelago."

It was as if she couldn't stop herself. As if she had to tell him, to put what had just happened into words. Matter-of-factly and as accurately as possible, she let the last twenty-four hours flow out of her.

"I wish you had called me," said Wiman when she finally fell silent.

He leaned forward and refilled Gabriella's coffee cup.

"Would that have changed anything?" she said.

Wiman shrugged.

"Probably not," he said. "I don't know much more about this than you. All I know is that the Cardigans at Säpo don't think your friend is a terrorist. After you were here, I did a little research. I contacted a few of my friends in intelligence but also in—how shall I put this?—more influential circles."

"What do you mean?" said Gabriella.

"The political leadership. The government. It doesn't matter. Your friend has landed herself in a real mess. Not her fault, not at all. There's some data that your friend apparently got hold of and that some Americans want to get back, if I've understood correctly?"

Gabriella slurped the hot coffee and nodded gently in response.

"And your friend has this information?" continued Wiman.

Gabriella took a deep breath and leaned back.

"You might say that," she said.

"And do you have some kind of plan? For what you're going to do? There are extremely powerful interests involved here, as I'm sure I don't need to tell you."

"We have a plan," said Gabriella. "But a pretty flimsy one."

———

Gabriella woke up from the sound of the library door being opened.

She sat up in her chair and instinctively ran her hands through her hair. Oh God, had she fallen asleep? In the middle of all this? The fire had almost burned out. How long had she been asleep?

In the doorway stood Wiman's granddaughter, Maria.

"Are you going to celebrate Christmas with us?" she said. "You can if you want to. My cousins are coming. They have a horse. One time I got to—"

"Maria."

It was Wiman's voice.

"I told you to let Gabriella sleep."

"But she was awake!" Maria said.

The girl crossed her arms and pursed her lips. Wiman bent down and whispered something in her ear that made her shout in delight and run out of the room. It occurred to Gabriella there was something docile about this domestic version of Wiman that was entirely incompatible with the stone cold lawyer image he cultivated at the office.

He stepped into the library and sat down in the chair next to her.

"You fell asleep," he said. "After the night you had, it didn't seem right to wake you. Besides, you're going to need your rest."

"What do you mean?"

When Gabriella had told him about Klara's plan, Wiman had seemed skeptical at first. But he offered to do everything he could, using all his contacts to try to make it work. It was the last thing Gabriella had expected. That Wiman would prove to be loyal.

"While you were sleeping, I did some work. Called in a few favors and racked up some debts, to be honest. But you're going to get your chance, it seems. A plane is on its way across the Atlantic. Someone with decision-making power is on board. Someone from the CIA. They'll be here . . ."

Wiman paused and turned his wrist to consult his watch.

"In seven hours."

F INALLY KLARA LAID THE PHOTO in her lap and looked up. Inside the boathouse, the darkness had started to give way to a slow, gray dawn. Klara's grandmother squatted in front of the stove, carefully laying one more log on the dying embers. The bark crackled before the wood started to blaze.

"So he brought the photo too?" said Klara.

Grandma got up slowly and brushed the imaginary dust from her worn corduroy pants before turning to Klara.

"No," she said.

She looked sad. Guilty. Completely lost.

"I don't understand," said Klara. "Where did you get this picture?"

Grandma sat down on the very edge of the sofa where Klara was still reclining. As far away from her as possible. She looked searchingly at her granddaughter. As if trying to register every slight movement of her face.

"Your grandpa and I have had the picture all these years," she said at last. "It's been in that envelope in my underwear drawer, since it was sent to us by the Ministry for Foreign Affairs along with all of your mother's other belongings a few months after she passed away."

Klara was doing her best to follow along but couldn't make sense of it. Maybe the past week had simply been too much for her. It was as if she couldn't make the pieces fit together.

"You mean you've had this picture all this time?" she said. "That it's just been lying in a drawer? A picture of my father? All this time?"

Klara's grandmother nodded without looking away.

"I'm afraid so," she said.

"And you never thought to show it to me? Didn't you think I'd be interested? You've seen me sitting with the pictures in the attic. Didn't you think I'd want to know?"

She felt the words stick in her throat. She couldn't take any more of this.

"I'm sorry," said her grandmother. "I didn't know what was right. You were so small, so very, very alone. And we, your grandpa and I, have never thought of you as anything other than ours. As our child."

A lone tear made its way down her cheek. She made no move to wipe it away. Klara looked up at her. She'd never seen her cry.

"I just didn't know when to show the picture to you. When you were five? Ten? Fifteen? Twenty? First, you were too little, and then I was so afraid you'd be confused, that you'd feel let down. By him. By us for not trying to find him."

"So it was easier to lie?"

Klara regretted her tone before the words had even left her mouth. Her grandmother didn't look away. Her eyes sparkled blue in the gray morning light.

"Yes," she said. "It was easier to lie. I didn't know where the truth would lead."

N THE LOBBY OF THE Radisson Blu Waterfront the holiday atmosphere was restrained. On the light wood benches there was a scattering of expectant families, from different countries but from the same world: the Ralph Lauren–wearing upper middle class. An enormous Christmas tree decorated with ornaments in discreet shades of gray blended in with the businesslike slate color scheme. In the background, someone sang "Baby, It's Cold Outside" at a perfectly calibrated volume.

Gabriella hadn't even made it halfway to the reception desk when, from the corner of her eye, she saw Anton Bronzelius rising from a chair and approaching her. He was unshaven but otherwise looked exactly as he had a couple of days ago.

He met Gabriella's gaze and nodded almost imperceptibly, first left, then right, as if to indicate that he wasn't alone in the lobby. Gabriella looked cautiously around the room, and it dawned on her that some of the affluent middle-class guests were in fact Bronzelius's colleagues. She swallowed. Oh my God, she thought, we have almost nothing to bargain with.

"Merry Christmas," he said.

He leaned forward and gave Gabriella a hug as he whispered in her ear.

"Give me the phone in the elevator."

"Merry Christmas," replied Gabriella and pulled away so the hug wouldn't seem unnaturally long.

The adrenaline rushed through her, almost blindingly. She barely noticed Bronzelius leading her toward the elevators. He wanted her phone, just as Wiman had said. That might mean that the first part of the plan had gone off without a hitch. Or that Wiman had deceived her. She couldn't think about that now. They had no choice.

She realized Bronzelius was speaking again. Using another, clearer, more formal voice. A voice meant for microphones.

"We're going up to the seventh floor. You'll be meeting my American colleagues there. The floor is cordoned off, and you'll be frisked before you're allowed into the suite."

They stepped into the elevator. As soon as the doors closed, Bronzelius indicated to Gabriella that she should give him the phone. She did as he told her. Do or die.

When the elevator stopped on the seventh floor, Bronzelius mumbled something into his headset and the elevator doors opened silently. The thick carpet muffled the sound of their footsteps, and the lack of windows was disorienting. It was like stepping into another dimension.

Outside a door at the end of the hall stood two large men, both with short hair and wearing dark suits. It took no more than a quick glance for Gabriella to see they were Americans.

"Give me your purse and turn toward the wall," said one of the guards in English as Gabriella and Bronzelius approached.

Gabriella glanced at Bronzelius, who shrugged and nodded. The man gave her bag to his colleague and frisked Gabriella meticulously.

"You're okay," he said, and withdrew.

His colleague pulled the MacBook out of the bag and gave it to her.

"I'll keep the rest until you're done," he said.

Then he muttered something into his headset, took out a white card, and swiped it through the lock on the door. With a metallic beep it unlocked and the man pushed down the handle to let Gabriella in.

Inside the suite's well-proportioned living room a woman was sitting in a modern, red swivel chair. Behind her a stunning view of a winter Stockholm stretched out through the panes of a spectacular glass wall. Gabriella felt as if she could reach out and touch city hall, where it lay under a layer of powdery snow just outside the window.

The woman looked to be in her sixties, perhaps slightly older. She was small and thin, wearing a somber, navy-blue jacket, matching blue pants, and a white top. Her makeup was subtle, and her dyed blond hair was cut in a short and unmemorable style. There was something forgettable about her in general. She was a civil servant, an agency director. Someone you ride the subway with every day for ten years and never notice.

As Gabriella walked slowly toward the small sofa, the woman examined her closely. Her gray eyes were inquisitive and surprisingly youthful. A glimmer of curiosity could be discerned in her pupils. Gabriella heard the mechanical click of the hotel door locking behind her.

———

The woman stood up gracefully in a slow, fluid motion. She went to the window and stood with her back to Gabriella.

"Stockholm is beautiful," she said. "I can't believe I've never been here before."

"Are you Susan?" said Gabriella.

Gabriella shifted her weight and held the computer tightly in her hands. Everything was happening so fast, and this meeting had been arranged so quickly and was so crucial.

"Yes," said the woman. "I'm the director of the Department for Middle Eastern Affairs at the CIA. I'm responsible for what you and your client have been through. I'm very sorry. It's truly unfortunate that you've landed in the middle of all this."

Gabriella said nothing, just sat down gently on one of the sofas. Susan turned her back on the view of city hall and inspected Gabriella again.

"I guess that's the computer all this is about?" she said.

Gabriella leaned forward toward the glass coffee table and reached for one of the bottles standing there. Her mouth was suddenly incredibly dry. She opened a Fanta and took a deep swig directly from the bottle.

December 24, 2013

Norra Rimnö, Sweden

S O MUCH GRAY. THE NEVER-ENDING winter dawn and winter dusk of the archipelago. Waves still crashed against the rocks beside the boathouse's new, sturdy dock, but the storm had passed, heading farther east, leaving Klara with only its aftermath. The consequences. Large snowflakes continued to fall on her as she sat hunched over, with her back against the newly painted house. Nothing remained of what she'd once believed was true. Nothing left of who she'd believed she was. She didn't hear George until he was standing right beside her.

"Merry Christmas, I guess," he said.

Klara turned toward him. His face still looked terrible. Swollen, covered with cuts that were starting to scab over.

"Merry Christmas," she whispered.

He held a blanket out to her. One of the newly purchased, colorful Klippan blankets with which the boathouse seemed to be fully stocked. She took it and wrapped it around her shoulders.

"Won't you come in now?" he said. "Your grandmother seems pretty inconsolable in there."

She buried her face in the soft wool of the blanket.

"I just can't take any more," she murmured.

"It's been a long night," he said. "A long week. A really fucking long week. But you'll freeze to death out here. I don't know what happened between you and your grandmother. And I don't know how much time we have, but wouldn't a ham sandwich be pretty damn good right about now?"

"I'm not hungry," she said.

"Fair enough," he muttered and made himself comfortable on the dock next to her.

She felt George's arm gently snake around her shoulders with increasing confidence, finally grabbing hold and pulling her against his warm body. She let herself be held. Let her head fall against his neck. The sound of the waves. The snowflakes. She didn't even try to stop the tears.

———

When Klara finally broke away, they were both almost completely covered by a thin layer of fresh snow. She brushed it from her hair and stood up. George followed her example. She saw that his teeth were chattering from the cold.

"What happens now?" he said.

Klara shook her head.

"Who knows?" she said. "Gabriella is going to meet her contact at Säpo. She'll call Bosse when she knows something. Then he'll call us."

The door that led to the dock opened, and Klara's grandfather came out with two steaming mugs in his hands.

"Klara," he said. "Sweet girl, come in so you don't catch your death of cold."

He took a few steps onto the snow-covered dock and held the

mugs out to her and George. The sweet scent of mulled wine filled the air. George gratefully accepted his mug, and Grandpa stretched out his hand toward Klara and stroked her wet cheek.

"No matter what your intentions, it'll turn out wrong somehow in the end," he said. "That's the only thing life teaches you."

Klara took the mug and pressed her cheek into his dry hand, felt its warmth against her frozen, wet skin. She shook her head.

"It wasn't wrong," she said. "You weren't wrong. There was no right or wrong. You did what you thought was best. You've always done everything for me."

Grandpa pulled her to him. He smelled faintly of mulled wine, coffee, and alcohol. Somewhere beside them George coughed.

"Oh my God!" he said. "What's in this mulled wine?"

Grandpa turned to him with a sly smile on his lips.

"Half mulled wine and half Archipelago Special," he said. "Bosse's not the only one with access to first-class liquor out here."

December 24, 2013

Stockholm, Sweden

THE SODA DIDN'T HELP. GABRIELLA'S throat felt like sandpaper. She cleared it. Took another sip.

"Yes," she said at last. "That is the computer."

She leaned forward and slid it across the glass table, toward Susan. As she did so, a door opened, and a man exited from the suite's interior. He was dark-haired, serious, wore a dark, wrinkled suit, and seemed to be about the same age as Gabriella. He wore a white shirt, but no tie.

"This is my colleague. He'll verify that this is indeed the right computer," said Susan.

Gabriella's throat constricted even farther.

"All right," she said. "It's encoded. We don't even know what's on it."

She ran her hand through her hair nervously. Thinking she had to take control of this situation, of herself. They'd start to suspect something if she didn't calm down.

"Maybe so," said Susan. "That's likely the case. But I'm afraid we have quite a bit more to discuss with you and your client. You've been subjected to things you shouldn't have been subjected to. And even though it's not your fault, it's still a problem."

The way Susan said it made it sound like a threat. Her eyes were glassy and coldly calculating. It was just like the American on the island had said. If you have nothing to bargain with, you'll have nothing to protect you.

The man in the wrinkled suit threw a quick glance at Gabriella before opening the screen and pressing the power button. Gabriella closed her eyes. The stress was too intense. She heard the clacking of the man's fingers flying over the keyboard. She leaned back in the couch. How could they have imagined this plan would work? When Gabriella opened her eyes cautiously, just a slit, as if she didn't quite dare to see what was happening, the man's forehead was furrowed. His eyes darted across the screen as if he couldn't quite believe what he was seeing. After a few seconds he turned the screen in Susan's direction and looked up at Gabriella.

"Is this some kind of fucking joke?" he said.

Gabriella sat up on the couch. She glanced toward the door she'd come through just a few minutes ago. Come on now!

"How is it possible," Gabriella heard Susan say, "that after everything you've been through, you still don't understand the seriousness of this situation? What in the hell do you hope to accomplish by this?"

Susan did not seem like the kind of woman who usually swore. She turned the screen so that Gabriella could see it too. Against a white background in thick, red letters, FUCK YOU FASCIST PIGS! was emblazoned across the screen. If the situation hadn't been so horribly stressful, Gabriella would have laughed. Blitzie seemed to be exactly as Klara described her. Before Gabriella could say anything she heard the sound of a key card being swiped through the lock on the hotel door. The door was opened partway, and a guard stuck his head into the suite.

"One of our Swedish contacts says he has a phone call for your guest."

The man nodded in Gabriella's direction. She couldn't breathe. It was as if she'd forgotten how. Somehow she managed to open her mouth and squeeze out a few words.

"If you want an explanation," she croaked, "it's probably best that you let me take this call."

She pointed awkwardly toward the door. She had hoped she'd be tougher in this situation. But she was overwhelmed; she had no choice but to let the current carry her.

Susan looked at her in confusion. It seemed as though her polished surface had been scratched.

"A phone call?" she said. "Are you kidding me?"

"No," said Gabriella. "I'm not kidding. If you want that damn information, then you'll have to let me take this call."

Susan shook her head and gestured for the man in the wrinkled suit to leave. He got up and slunk through the door, back to the room he'd come from. She inspected Gabriella carefully, as if to signal that she was still in charge of this situation.

"Okay," she said finally.

Gabriella stood up and walked toward the guard, who held her cell phone in his hand. With a quick glance over her shoulder at Susan she opened the door and stepped out into the windowless corridor.

———

Gabriella ignored the remaining guard at the suite door and started walking down the corridor toward the elevators. She fumbled nervously with the phone and finally pressed it against her ear. This was it.

"Yes," she said. "This is Gabriella."

There was silence on the other end.

"Hello?" she tried again.

It took another second, before a thin metallic voice appeared in her ear.

"It's absolutely disgusting," said someone who could only be Blitzie, her voice channeled through some distortion device. "It's fucking disgusting, what's on this computer. Corpses and torture or whatever you wanna call it. Video and pictures. I haven't had time to look through much of it yet, obviously. But it's absolutely full of this shit, that's for sure."

"So you got the password?" said Gabriella.

It felt like she was floating away from herself. As if she could see everything from above, from outside. The suite with Susan in it and herself only a few yards away, holding the phone in the middle of this suffocating hotel corridor. It was surreal.

"Yeah, yeah," said Blitzie. "Of course. When the correct password was entered into your computer it was automatically sent to me. I just typed it in here. Piece of cake. What do you want me to do now?"

"How much stuff is there?" said Gabriella.

"I don't know," Blitzie replied. "One, two, three . . . at least five of these films where they, you know, torture people, I guess. Maybe fifty photos. Corpses and disgusting things. There are a couple of Word documents as well but I guess—"

Suddenly Gabriella remembered what Mahmoud had said about Lindman, what Klara had said about the dying American: that there was something else, something more. Something impossible to deny. "Open the Word documents," she said.

"Okay," Blitzie said. "Hold on."

There was a moment of silence. Gabriella glanced over toward the guards by the door. They were immobile, their eyes firmly locked on her.

"So," Blitzie said. "I don't know. It's just a list of Arabic names and birthdates."

"Maybe the prisoners," Gabriella mumbled. "Open the other one."

"Same thing," Blitzie said. "Just names and numbers."

There had to be something else. Something that they couldn't wash their hands of. Or had both the American and Lindman been wrong?

"Is that it?" Gabriella said. "You're sure?"

"Well, it's all I can see here. Wait . . . There is a PDF document as well."

She went quiet for a moment.

"Fuck," Blitzie said finally. "You need to see this. I'll send it to your phone, okay? This shit is crazy."

A wave of excitement and relief ran through Gabriella.

"Okay," she said. "Don't do anything with the information yet, okay?"

"I'm not suicidal," replied Blitzie, and hung up.

———

When Gabriella returned to the suite it had gone almost completely dark outside the enormous window. It looked like it was snowing lightly. A beautiful Christmas eve was under way out there. The suite was dark too, the only lighting two dim lamps on a side table.

Susan was in the chair by the window, checking her phone. She looked up when Gabriella opened the door.

"So," she started. "Would you like to tell me what is going on here?"

Gabriella sat down on the sofa and leaned back. The atmosphere in the room had changed considerably. She wondered if Susan understood just how fundamentally. Soon enough she would.

"When your man punched in the password on the computer that I had with me, it was automatically sent to a friend of mine," Gabriella started. "The computer I gave to you was just a shell. The hard drive had been exchanged for the one on my friend's computer. So all the data you've been chasing was in fact not on this computer anymore. Do you understand?"

"All right . . ." Susan said tentatively. "Go on."

"So when my friend received the password, we received access to all the information that is stored on the laptop."

If Susan was shocked or the slightest bit upset she didn't let on. She nodded calmly.

"And what was it that was stored on the laptop?" she said.

"You don't know?" Gabriella said, incredulous. "You sent a gang of murderous thugs after us just as some sort of precaution?"

Susan shook her head calmly and leaned forward slightly in her chair.

"Of course I know the general theme of what was on the computer," she said slowly, as if to a child. "But I don't know the extent. I have understood that there were enhanced interrogations, that the company to which we had outsourced the managing of one of our facilities went rogue."

Gabriella didn't say anything. *Enhanced interrogation*. There was something in that bureaucratic euphemism that sounded even worse than *torture*.

"It's terrible," Susan continued. "It's truly terrible. You must un-

402

derstand that this operation was never sanctioned. We hired this company to manage some of the prisoners and to carry out interrogations in accordance with our internal procedures. Unfortunately they took matters into their own hands. When we discovered it, we immediately took measures to shut them down. Then when we learned that some pictures of this horrible practice had leaked we made the mistake of letting the company convince us that they could put things back in their place. This put you and your friends at danger, for which I am truly sorry. In hindsight, maybe we should have just come clean right away? I mean, what happened was out of our hands. We do what we can to curtail this kind of operation, but unfortunately we can't control every aspect of the intelligence machine, however much we would like to."

Even now, in the face of what Susan certainly must recognize as defeat, she kept up the act. It was eerily impressive.

"My friend died," Gabriella said, her voice cold and empty. "Your fucking decisions led to him being shot down in a fucking grocery store."

"And for that I am so, so sorry," Susan said.

A warmth at the core of her voice shone through the steeliness of her professionalism and made it sound as if she actually meant it.

"Maybe you actually are sorry for that," Gabriella said. "But you are lying about everything else."

Susan pulled back slightly, as if Gabriella had made a halfhearted attempt at slapping her in the face.

"Now why would you say that?" she said.

"Because you are," Gabriella said. "Enhanced interrogation? Really? You really want to call it that? We have pictures and videos of prisoners being burned with cigarettes, butchered, electrocuted, tortured in every conceivable, medieval way you can dream up.

And you still want to stick with this enhanced interrogation routine?"

"But you must understand," Susan began, her voice all steel again. "This was never what we wanted, never what we had instructed or intended it to be. Things got out of hand."

Gabriella just looked at her. Then she quietly slid her phone across the table to her. Susan did not move to take it but just let it lie there, its screen gleaming in the half-light.

"What's that?" she said, nodding at the phone.

"That's a PDF document that we found on the hard drive together with the pictures and films," Gabriella said. "It contains two letters. One is from you to what I believe is the director of the CIA. It's dated about a year ago. You might remember it? In the letter you outline the high success rates of an operation in Afghanistan managed by a company called Digital Solutions. You warn the director that their methods might go beyond the manuals. I think you might even use the word 'brutal'?"

Susan had turned away from Gabriella and was looking out at the steady snowfall.

"The second document," Gabriella continued, "is signed by the director of the CIA. It says that after having consulted with the White House, his decision is to continue the operation managed by Digital Solutions and to do everything to assist them, while keeping them gray. Whatever that means?"

Susan turned back toward Gabriella. There was sadness in her eyes now.

"Gray," she said. "It refers to shadows, I guess. That's what we call it when we maintain deniability. When we remove someone from our databases and accounting systems, erase them from our records, make it seem as if they never existed. And that's what we did."

She sighed and nodded at the phone.

"Not even that letter is recorded anywhere. As you can see, it has no document number. Only a date. But Digital Solutions insisted on knowing that what they were doing was sanctioned."

She shook her head slowly.

"You understand the kind of chaos this will lead to?" she began again. "For Afghanistan, of course. For us. For the entire Arab world. If those pictures are as terrible as your friend seems to think and with the letter making it seem like it was all done as part of an official strategy—how can they not hate us when they see all of that?"

She paused for a moment and seemed to think.

"And it'll cause chaos for you too. For you, but especially for Klara Walldéen and your friend there on the phone. I know it's not your fault, that you're just playing the game you were forced into. And maybe this was the best outcome you could hope for. You made it a little further. But when all of this comes out, there will be no one who can protect you. The interests involved are too powerful. We can't tolerate this type of material being leaked without consequences. Do you understand that? You will be Assange or Snowden at best. Holed up in some embassy or godforsaken country that might accept you. You will be outlaws as soon as this material is out. You're already outlaws."

The American's words on the island. As soon as you have nothing to trade, you have no rights. Don't give them what they want.

"If it comes out," said Gabriella quietly.

Susan leaned forward in her chair and looked her straight in the eye.

"Excuse me?" she said. "What did you say?"

"I said, what you describe—the chaos, the consequences— would happen only if the material were to be made public, right?"

Susan nodded and looked at Gabriella, clearly puzzled.

"Yes?"

"But we're not going to make it public," said Gabriella. "Not now. We're going to protect this information. Make sure that it's copied far and wide so you'll never be able to track it down. But if we find out that you're coming after us, we'll press the button and that information will go directly to the public. I won't even look at the files. Nor will Klara. We don't want to know. And we don't want the chaos on our conscience. We want to survive. We want to leave this behind us."

Gabriella swallowed hard, but the awful taste in her mouth remained. They had gone over it so many times with Klara already in the car down from Stockholm and again in the boat after the horrors on the island. It seemed like an incredible price: not to be able to avenge Mahmoud or to reveal those responsible for all of this. To just let them get away literally with murder. But as they saw it there was no alternative. It was probably true what Susan had said; if the information came out they would be lawless. And even worse, it would ignite Afghanistan and Iraq and who knows what else. There had been enough suffering, that was for sure. It was a staggering thought that a sixteen-year-old girl in Amsterdam was to be the guardian of information that could make half the world explode in uproar, and worse. Gabriella looked at Susan's weary face and thought about all the thousands of secrets she must have to keep. Would she allow herself to relinquish control over this one?

"Can you trust your friend?" said Susan.

Gabriella shrugged.

"I truly hope so."

Susan nodded.

"I don't see that I have any choice," she said. "We don't want this information to get out. Especially not now."

She paused, seemed to be considering something.

"What can I say?" she said at last. "I guess we'll have to hope your friend can be trusted. I think you're aware of what would happen if you can't trust her?"

She was silent. The shadow of a smile passed over her face.

"The balance of terror," she said. "The threat of mutually assured destruction. I never expected to describe the relationship between the U.S. and a couple of young Swedish lawyers in quite those words. But it seems times have changed."

Susan stood up and extended her hand toward Gabriella, who hesitantly took it.

"It really is a new era," said Susan.

"We have one more condition," said Gabriella. "The American who came to the island yesterday. You have to tell Klara everything she wants to know about him."

Susan gave her a defeated look. She suddenly looked human.

"There's always so much at stake," she said. "So much that we lose sight of the people. So much that they cease to have meaning."

She took out a pen from her pocket and wrote something on a piece of paper, which she handed to Gabriella.

"Tell her to contact me when she's up to it. I'll tell her. It's the least I can do for her. It's the least I can do for him."

GEORGE STOOD IN THE DARK stairwell outside his father's door on Rådmansgatan, hesitating. His reflection in the elevator's mirror looked slightly less like a character in a horror movie but still far from his usual, polished self.

On the phone his old man had gone from annoyance to unexpectedly anxious concern when George called late on Christmas eve to tell him about the car accident that had prevented him from making it home for Christmas. To his surprise, George even had to convince him not to get on the next plane to Brussels to visit George in the hospital where he claimed to be recovering.

In reality, he'd been sitting in an apartment in Vasastan, barely a fifteen-minute walk from his family's home. That's where they'd taken them, first by helicopter from the archipelago and then under police escort, after Gabriella's assurance that she'd managed to negotiate some kind of bizarre deal.

He'd realized he was never going to find out what all of this was really about. Klara and Gabriella had been careful about what they said. It involved a computer. Films. The U.S. government. That was all he managed to piece together. Truth be told, he didn't want to know. Some guy from Säpo had even apologized to him for what happened. A terrible mistake. Never tell anyone about what you've been through. He didn't say what would happen if he actually did tell someone. A vague, unspoken threat.

But it didn't matter. There was no risk that he'd tell anyone about it. All he wanted was to forget. Something that insomnia and his few hours of nightmarish sleep hadn't really allowed him to do yet. Everywhere he looked he saw Kirsten's battered face. Any sudden noise sounded like a gunshot.

He pressed the doorbell. Within a few seconds the door was thrown open. His old man stood there with outstretched arms.

"George!" he said. "The prodigal son!"

He embraced George in a way he never had before, or at least as far as George could remember. At last the old man pushed him away to inspect him closely.

"Oh my God!" he said. "You look absolutely terrible! Come in and I'll get you a tall Armagnac. Are you allowed to drink? They didn't put you on any pills that don't mix well, did they? Anyway, forget that, you need a drink. Ellen! Pour a stiff one for George here! I've never seen anyone more in need of a drink!"

———

His old man led him into the living room where the whole family sat gathered in clusters on the sofas—as usual during the holidays. The storybook tree, with its burning candles, was in the corner where it always stood. The overladen dessert table groaned, and a fire was burning with an intensity that George worried might be too much for the fireplace.

Big brothers and brothers-in-law gathered around him to inspect his wounds, pretending to punch him in the stomach, teasing him for being useless at driving, asking about what had happened to the Audi. Ellen pressed a plate of Boxing Day turkey on him with all the trimmings.

———

Finally he sank down into a sofa with a plate of cheese and a glass of port beside him. His extended family had left or retreated to the other rooms. He felt full and warm, drowsy for the first time since the terrible night of the twenty-third. It had been barely three days since he'd assaulted Kirsten and fled to the island by boat. Three days since he shot two men.

And this Christmas stuff. All this comfort and familiarity. Everything he used to loathe. Suddenly, he was defenseless against it. Suddenly it felt like sinking into a warm bath after being so very, very cold. He sat back and allowed himself to enjoy the feeling of peace and security.

———

"Are you asleep?"

George looked up and saw his father's wife Ellen standing in the doorway in her bathrobe. The fire had died down but was still burning faintly, enveloping the room in a soft, warm glow.

"Nah," said George.

His tongue, sweet from the port, was sticking against the dry roof of his mouth. He scrambled up into a sitting position. He had actually fallen asleep.

"We told you we're waiting until tomorrow to give you your presents, so you can recover a little," said Ellen. "But a package arrived for you by courier yesterday. I thought you might want to see what it was."

She held a square package from DHL toward him. She radiated curiosity. George reached out and took the large padded pouch. He ripped off the packaging. Inside it was a box, slightly smaller than a shoe box and completely square. His heart pounded, and he suddenly felt dizzy with fear.

"Thank you, Ellen," he said. "I'll take a look at this later."

"Sure," she said. "You do as you like."

She retreated from the living room, clearly disappointed.

George put the package in front of him on the coffee table and stared at it. It had arrived yesterday. After everything was over. Wild fantasies flashed through his exhausted brain. It was a bomb. They were all going to be blown to bits so they couldn't ever disclose what they knew.

But the package wasn't particularly heavy. If it were a bomb, it couldn't be very powerful. Didn't they have better ways to kill people than with mail bombs, anyway?

Eventually curiosity won over fear. With one decisive movement he lifted the package and ripped open the protective plastic.

Inside there was a cherrywood box. A silver label on the front. George felt his pulse increasing, not with fear but with anticipation. OFFICINE PANERAI was written on the label. He opened the box reverentially.

A Panerai 360 M Luminor lay on a deep blue velvet cushion inside. The jet-black watch face. The soft yellow, luminous numbers. The simple, minimalist design. The pale leather strap with its rough seams. George had to blink to make sure he wasn't imagining it. What could the watch have cost? $50,000? More? If you could even find one anymore. It had been produced in a limited edition of three hundred.

When George was able to breathe normally again, he noticed an envelope on the velvet beside the watch. He opened it up and pulled out a folded piece of paper. The handwritten note was in English:

George,

    Just a token of our appreciation. All's well that ends well. We expect to see you in the office no later than January 3.

The letter was signed by Appleby. George closed the lid of the box with a snap and leaned back on the couch with his eyes closed. Merchant & Taylor. Appleby. Everything he'd been through. Everything they'd allowed him to go through. It was inconceivable that he would go back to the office on the Square de Meeûs. Out of the question.

Slowly, he sat up on the couch again. He leaned over and cracked open the lid of the box. Through the small gap he could see that it was all there. The certificate of authenticity. The extra wristbands. Tiny tools in a small bag. He opened the lid cautiously and reached out to touch the almost invisible glass of the face.

He slowly extricated the watch from the velvet and held it up in the faint glow of the dying fire. He turned and twisted it around. Studying the screws and the inscription on the back.

He had to try it on, just as a test. The soft leather and the cold, pitch-black steel of the casing against his skin. The perfectly balanced weight. It fit around his wrist as if it were made for him, only him.

He couldn't help the smile that spread over his lips. The heat radiating through his body. The pride. Wasn't he worth this kind of life, now more than ever?

KLARA LEANED HER HEAD AGAINST the dirty window of the taxi. Arvo Pärt played through her earbuds. "Spiegel im Spiegel." For a while after Christmas, she'd spent most of her time in her bed at her grandparents', listening to this play on repeat twenty, thirty, forty times a day. Staring up at the ceiling, leaving her room only to poke at her food or go to the bathroom. She'd taken the SIM card out of her phone to avoid calls from Gabriella or any of her casual friends from Brussels. Officially burnt-out and on sick leave.

———

She'd lost track of how many days she lay like that. Maybe a couple of days. Maybe a week. Just the music and Grandma's and Grandpa's worried faces.

In the end, it hadn't been possible to keep Gabriella away, of course. One day she was just sitting on the edge of Klara's bed. A little more anxious than usual. A little older. Ignoring both Klara's protests and her anemic fury, Gabriella managed to get her out of bed.

After forcing her into warm clothes, she had guided her down the stairs, out through the door, and down to the boat where Grandpa, Grandma, and Bosse were already waiting. And then they returned to Smugglers Rock. To take back the archipelago, as Grandpa put it. To expunge the horror. To reclaim their own memories.

They'd only stayed for the afternoon. There were no reminders left of that terrible night. No blood. No bodies. No bullet holes. Nothing. It was just a small, snowy, rocky islet in the middle of the sea. Bosse got the gas stove going and boiled them some coffee. They hardly spoke.

But after that, things became a little easier. Mostly thanks to Gabriella, who took care of all the practical details. Contacting Eva-Karin Boman, presenting herself as Klara's lawyer, and handing over Klara's resignation after she made sure Eva-Karin gave Klara a year of severance pay. Gabriella was tough. Much tougher than Klara. Gabriella had been back at work before New Year's Eve. As a new partner. The youngest one in the firm. Perhaps the youngest in Sweden.

After Klara left her bed, she did her best to stay on her feet. At first she did little things around the house. Cooking with Grandma. Going out on the boat with Grandpa.

After a week, she put on some city clothes and hitched a ride into town with Bosse. She'd started with Söderköping, so as not to be completely overwhelmed by civilization. Bought some paperbacks and ate a pizza on Skönbergagatan. Walked around in the winter landscape, letting the complete normality of it present itself. In the evening, she took the bus to the movies in Norrköping by herself. A worthless comedy. But it made her feel alive again, almost.

And after a few more weeks, she'd gone up to Stockholm for a weekend to visit Gabriella. They'd gone shopping at NK and Nitty Gritty. Eaten oysters at a new bistro. Afterward there were drinks, and Klara made out with a copywriter on a couch at Riche for a while. Laughing. A little drunk. Stumbling home along the frozen water with a 7-Eleven hot dog in her hand. Slowly starting to get used to this quite ordinary, quite wonderful life.

———

But when she got back to the archipelago everything that had happened washed over her again. It was as if she couldn't escape the betrayal. Her father's betrayal, Cyril's betrayal, and most of all her own.

No matter what she did, she couldn't rid herself of the idea that she was responsible for Mahmoud's murder. That she was responsible for her father's murder.

But she couldn't go on like that, lying there in her childhood room dwelling, dwelling, dwelling on it. The only way to avoid it was to stay active.

In mid-March, she contacted her old teacher and Mahmoud's supervisor, Lysander, and they'd met for lunch at the Saluhall in Uppsala.

He was the same. Steel gray hair and a rigid posture. A soft heart that he masked well behind a facade of filterless Gitanes. He knew of course that there had to be something else behind Mahmoud's death than the story in the papers, spread by Bronzelius and his colleagues. You couldn't dupe Lysander into thinking Mahmoud had come into contact with a terrorist network through his research, and then tried to infiltrate it. That this led to his heroic death. But still Lysander didn't try to fish for information from Klara, for which she was grateful. And he agreed without hesitation to let her finish Mahmoud's dissertation.

So she went to Brussels and arranged for the move. Found a

small studio in the Luthagen area in Uppsala and took over Mah-moud's office. Maybe it was unhealthy. Maybe it wasn't a normal grieving process. But it was what she had to do.

And so, finally, when the ice over the Fyris river had disap-peared almost entirely outside her office window, when Uppsala started buzzing about Walpurgis celebrations and the spring ball, Klara opened the drawer where she had kept the note with the e-mail address of the woman who called herself Susan.

━━━

She asked the taxi driver to stop at the Smithsonian Metro station. The early summer warmth hit her as she opened the back door. The Mall was green and full of joggers and people eating lunch. It was her first time in the States. How was it possible that she hadn't been here before? Everything felt so familiar. She removed her earbuds, letting this new world wash over her without a filter.

It took her half an hour to get to Capitol Hill. A quick look at her phone's map application. She took a right turn onto Independence Avenue around the congressional building and then left onto First Street. The smell of summer, hot dogs and onions wafted from the vendors on street corners. Men and women in suits hurried by her on the street, heading to their next important, meaningless meet-ing. It was confusing. Just six months ago, that had been her. But that was another time. Another life.

━━━

And there it was at last, right in front of her. The U.S. Supreme Court building, as white and proud as a Roman temple.

Klara saw her immediately. To the left, halfway up the stairs. Alone, small, and pale. Forgettable. Not someone you'd notice. Just as she'd described herself in her e-mail. Klara looked up at the angled roof of the building. EQUAL JUSTICE UNDER LAW. Was Susan being ironic when she chose this meeting place?

Klara climbed the stairs and sat down diagonally one step behind the woman.

"Welcome to Washington," said Susan, without turning around.

Her eyes seemed to be fastened to the back of the Capitol Building. Klara said nothing.

"Summer came early this year," said Susan.

Klara nodded.

"It would seem so."

Susan took a deep breath.

"So," she said. "What is it you want to know?"

They were surrounded by the sound of the city, the traffic, sirens. Klara leaned forward and filled her lungs with the early summer air. It was time.

"Who was he?" she said.

Susan didn't seem to have heard her at first. Then she turned slowly toward Klara. Her eyes were gray like the rocks of the archipelago, like ashes, like razor blades.

"He liked to swim," she said.

Acknowledgments

THANKS TO MY AGENTS, ASTRI von Arbin Ahlander and Christine Edhäll, for the magic.

To Elizabeth Clark Wessel for the seamless translation.

To my American and Canadian editors, Jennifer Barth and Lorissa Sengara, and the whole team at HarperCollins, for believing in *The Swimmer* and providing invaluable input.

To my UK editor, Laura Palmer, and the team at Head of Zeus for all the support.

To my Swedish editor, Helene Atterling, and Head of Publishing Åsa Selling at Wahlström & Widstrand for giving me the chance.

To all my friends, in particular Pelle Hilmersson and Johan Jarnvik, for reading and laughing.

To my little brother, Daniel, for, well, being my brother.

To my parents, who, on top of everything else parents do, somehow managed to make me believe that I could write.

And to my wife, Liisa, who is not only beautiful but also the smartest person I have ever met.

About the Author

BORN IN STOCKHOLM, SWEDEN, JOAKIM Zander has lived in Syria and Israel and graduated from high school in the United States. He earned a PhD in law from Maastricht University in the Netherlands and has worked as a lawyer for the European Union in Brussels and Helsinki. *The Swimmer* is his first novel; rights have been sold in twenty-eight territories. Zander currently lives in southern Sweden with his wife and two children.